SACRAMENT

CLIVE BARKER

SACRAMENT

HarperCollinsPublishers

HarperCollins books may be purchased for educational, business, or sales promotional use. For information please write: Special Markets Department, HarperCollins Publishers, Inc., 10 East 53rd Street, New York, NY 10022.

FIRST EDITION

Designed by Alma Hochhauser Orenstein

ISBN 0-06-017949-X

96 97 98 99 00 ❖/HC 10 9 8 7 6 5 4 3 2 1

For Malcolm

I am a man, and men are animals who tell stories.
This is a gift from God, who spoke our species into being,
but left the end of our story untold.
That mystery is troubling to us. How could it be otherwise?
Without the final part, we think, how are we to make sense
of all that went before: which is to say, our lives?

So we make stories of our own,
in fevered and envious imitation of our Maker,
hoping that we'll tell, by chance, what God left untold.
And finishing our tale,
come to understand why we were born.

CONTENTS

PART ONE

He Stands Before An Unopened Door

I

To every hour, its mystery.

At dawn, the riddles of life and light. At noon, the conundrums of solidity. At three, in the hum and heat of the day, a phantom moon, already high. At dusk, memory. And at midnight? Oh, then the enigma of time itself; of a day that will never come again passing into history while we sleep.

It had been Saturday when Will Rabjohns arrived at the weather-bullied wooden shack on the outskirts of Balthazar. Now it was Sunday morning, two-seventeen by the scored face of Will's watch. He had emptied his brandy flask an hour before, raising it to toast the Borealis, which shimmered and billowed far beyond Hudson Bay, upon the shores of which Balthazar stood. He had knocked on the door of the shack countless times, calling out for Guthrie to give him just a few minutes of his time. On two or three occasions it seemed the man was going to do so; Will heard him grumbling something incoherent on the other side of the door, and once the handle had been turned. But Guthrie had not appeared.

Will was neither deterred nor particularly surprised. The old man had been universally described as crazy: This by men and women who had chosen as their place of residence one of the bleaker corners of the planet. If anyone knew crazy, Will thought, they did. What besides a certain lunacy inspired people to build a community—even one as small as Balthazar (population: thirty-one)—on a treeless, wind-battered stretch of tidal flats that was buried half the year beneath ice and snow, and was for two of the remaining months besieged by the polar bears who came through the region in late autumn waiting for the bay to freeze? That these people would characterize Guthrie as insane was a testament to how crazy he really was.

But Will knew how to wait. He'd spent much of his professional life waiting, sitting in hides and dugouts and wadis and trees, his cameras loaded, his ears pricked, watching for the object of his pursuit to appear. How many of those animals had been, like Guthrie, crazed and despairing? Most, of course. Creatures who'd attempted to outrun the creeping tide of humankind, and failed; whose lives and habitats were in extremis. His patience was not always rewarded. Sometimes, having sweat or shivered for hours and days he would have to give up and move on, the species he was seeking, for all its hopelessness, preserving its despair from his lens.

But Guthrie was a human animal. Though he had holed himself up behind his walls of weather-beaten boards, and had made it his business to see his neighbors (if such they could be called, the nearest house was half a mile away) as seldom as possible, he was surely curious about the man on his doorstep, who had been waiting for five hours in the bitter cold. This was Will's hope, at least; that the longer he could stay awake and upright the likelier it became that the lunatic would surrender to curiosity and open the door.

He glanced at his watch again. It was almost three. Though he had told his assistant, Adrianna, not to stay up for him, he knew her too well to think she would not by now be a little concerned. There were bears out there in the dark: eight hundred, nine hundred pounds some of them, with indiscriminate appetites and unpredictable behavior patterns. In a fortnight, they'd be out on the ice floes hunting seal and whale. But right now they were in scavenging mode, come to befoul themselves in the stinking garbage heaps of Churchill and Balthazar, and—as had occasionally happened—to take a human life. There was every likelihood that they were wandering within sniffing distance of him right now, beyond the throw of Guthrie's jaundiced porch light, studying Will, perhaps, as he waited on the doorstep. The notion didn't alarm him. Quite the reverse, in fact. It faintly excited him that some visitor from the wilderness might at this very moment be assessing his palatability. For most of his adult life he'd made photographs of the untamed world, reporting to the human tribe the tragedies that occurred in contested territories. They were seldom human tragedies. It was the populace of the other world that withered and perished daily. And as he witnessed the steady erosion of the wilderness, the hunger in him grew to leap the fences and be part of it, before it was gone.

He tugged off one of his fur-lined gloves and plucked his cigarettes out of his anorak pocket. There was only one left. He put it to his numbed lips and lit up, the emptiness of the pack a greater goad than either the temperature or the bears.

"Hey, Guthrie," he said, rapping on the blizzard-beaten door, "how about letting me in, huh? I only want a couple of minutes with you. Give me a break."

He waited, drawing deep on the cigarette and glancing back out into the darkness. There was a group of rocks twenty or thirty yards beyond his Jeep; an ideal place, he knew, for bears to be lurking. Did something move among them? He suspected so. Canny bastards, he thought. They were biding their time, waiting for him to head back to the vehicle.

"Fuck this!" he growled to himself. He'd waited long enough. He was going to give up on Guthrie, at least for tonight. He was going to head back to the warmth of the rented house on Balthazar's Main (and only) Street, brew himself some coffee, cook himself an early breakfast, then catch a few hours' sleep. Resisting the temptation to knock on the door one final time, he left the doorstep, digging for the keys as he strode back over the squeaking snow to the Jeep.

At the very back of his mind, he'd wondered if Guthrie was the kind of perverse old bastard who'd wait for his visitor to give up before opening the door. He was. Will had no sooner vacated the comfort of the porch light when he heard the door grinding across the frosted steps behind him. He slowed his departure but didn't turn, suspecting that if he did so Guthrie would simply slam the door again. There was a long silence. Time enough for Will to wonder what the bears might be making of this peculiar ritual. Then, in a worn voice, Guthrie said, "I know who you are and I know what you want."

"Do you?" Will said, chancing a backward glance.

"I don't let anybody take pictures of me or my place," Guthrie said, as though there was an unceasing parade of photographers at his door.

Will turned now, slowly. Guthrie was standing back from the step, and the porch light threw very little illumination upon him. All Will could make out was a very tall man silhouetted against the murky interior of the shack. "I don't blame you," Will said, "not wanting to be photographed. You've got a perfect right to your privacy."

"Well then, what the fuck do you want?"

"Like I said: I just want to talk."

Guthrie had apparently seen enough of his visitor to satisfy his curiosity, because he now stepped back a pace and started to pull the door closed. Will knew better than to rush the step. He stayed put and played the only card he had. Two names, spoken very softly. "I want to talk about Jacob Steep and Rosa McGee."

The silhouette flinched, and for a moment it seemed certain the man would simply slam the door, and that would be an end to it. But no. Instead, Guthrie stepped back out onto the step. "Do you know them?" he said.

"I met them once," Will replied, "a very long time ago. You knew them too, didn't you?"

"Him, a little. Even that was too much. What's your name again?"

"Will—William—Rabjohns."

"Well . . . you'd better come inside, before you freeze your balls off."

II

Unlike the comfortable, well-appointed houses in the rest of the tiny township, Guthrie's dwelling was so primitive it barely seemed habitable, given how bitter the winters up here could be. There was a vintage electric fire heating its single room (a small sink and stove served as a kitchen, the great outdoors was presumably his bathroom), while the furniture seemed to have been culled from the dump. Its inhabitant was scarcely in better condition. Dressed in several layers of grimy clothes, Guthrie was plainly in need of nourishment and medication. Though Will had heard that he was no more than sixty, he looked a good decade older, his skin red-raw in patches and sallow in others, his hair, what little he had, white where it was cleanest. He smelled of sickness and fish.

"How did you find me?" he asked Will as he closed and triple-bolted the door.

"A woman in Mauritius spoke to me about you."

"You want something to warm you up a bit?"

"No, I'm fine."

"What woman's this?"

"I don't know if you'll remember her. Sister Ruth Buchanan?"

"Ruth? Christ. You met Ruth. Well, well. That woman had a

mouth on her . . . " He poured a shot of whiskey into a well-beaten enamel mug, and downed it in one. "Nuns talk too much. Ever noticed that?"

"I think that's why there are vows of silence."

The reply pleased Guthrie. He loosed a short, barking laugh, which he followed with another shot of whiskey. "So what did she say about me?" he asked, peering at the whiskey bottle as if to calculate how much solace it had left to offer.

"Just that you'd talked about extinction. About how you'd seen the last of some animals."

"I never said anything to her about Rosa and Jacob."

"No. I just assumed if you'd seen one you *might* have seen the other."

"Huh." Guthrie's face knitted up as he thought this through. Rather than be seen to be studying him—this was not a man who took kindly to scrutiny—Will crossed to the table to look at the books that were piled upon it. His approach brought a warning growl from under the table. "Shut up, Lucy!" Guthrie snapped. The dog hushed its growl, and came out of hiding to ingratiate herself. She was a sizable mongrel, with strains of German shepherd and Chow in her bloodline, better fed and groomed than her master. She'd brought her bone out with her, and dutifully carried it to her master's feet.

"Are you English?" Guthrie said, still not looking at Will.

"Born in Manchester. But I was brought up in the Yorkshire Dales."

"England's always been a little too cozy for me."

"I wouldn't call the moors cozy," Will said. "I mean, it's not wild like this, but when the mists come down and you're out on the hills—"

"That's where you met them then."

"Yes. That's where I met them."

"English bastard," Guthrie said. Then, finally looking at Will, "Not you. Steep. Chilly, English bastard." He spoke the three words as if cursing the man, wherever he was. "You know what he called himself?" Will knew. But it would serve him better, he suspected, if he let his host have the moment. "The Killer of Last Things," Guthrie said. "He was proud of it. I swear. Proud of it." He emptied the remnants of the whiskey into his mug but didn't drink. "So you met Ruth in Mauritius, huh? What were you doing there?"

"Taking pictures. There's a kestrel there looks like it's going to be extinct some time soon."

"I'm sure it was grateful for your attention," Guthrie said dryly. "So what do you want from me? I can't tell you anything about Steep or McGee. I don't know anything, and if I ever did I put it out of my head. I'm an old man and I don't want the pain." He looked at Will. "How old are you? Forty?"

"Good guess. Forty-one."

"Married?"

"No."

"Don't. It's a rattrap."

"It's not likely, believe me."

"Are you queer then?" Guthrie said, with a little tilt of his head.

"As it happens, yes."

"A queer Englishman. Surprise, surprise. No wonder you got on so well with Sister Ruth. She Who Must Not Be Touched. And you came all this way to see me?"

"Yes and no. I'm here to photograph the bears."

"Of course, the fucking bears." What little trace of warmth or humor his voice had contained had suddenly vanished. "Most people just go to Churchill, don't they? Aren't there tours now, so you can watch them performing?" He shook his head. "Degrading themselves."

"They just go where they can find a free meal," Will said.

Guthrie looked down at the dog, who had not moved from his side since her reprimand. Her bone was still in her mouth. "That's what *you* do, isn't it?" The dog, happy she was being addressed, whatever the subject, thumped her tail on the bare floor. "Little brown-noser." Guthrie reached down as if to take the bone. The dog's ragged black lips curled back in warning. "She's too bright to bite me and too stupid not to growl. Give it to me, you mutt." Guthrie tugged the bone from her jaws. She let him take it. He scratched her behind her ear and tossed the bone back on the floor in front of her. "I expect dogs to be sycophants," he said, "we made 'em that way. But bears— Jesus, bears shouldn't be fucking nosing around in our garbage. They should stay out there," he vaguely waved in the direction of the bay, "where they can be whatever God intended them to be."

"Is that why you're here?"

"What, to admire the animal life? Christ no. I'm here because being with people makes me vomit. I don't like 'em. I never did."

"Not even Steep?" Will said.

Guthrie shot him a poisonous look. "What in Christ's name kind of question is that?"

"Just asking."

"Fucking stupid question," Guthrie muttered. Then, softening somewhat, he said, "They were something to look at, both of them, and that's the truth. I mean, Christ, Rosa was beautiful. I only put up with talking to Steep to get to her. But he said once I was too old for her."

"How old were you?" Will asked him, thinking as he did so that Guthrie's story was changing slightly. He'd claimed to know only Steep, but apparently he'd known them both.

"I was thirty. Way too old for Rosa. She liked 'em real young. And of course she liked Steep. I mean the two of them, they were like husband and wife and brother and sister and fuck knows what else all rolled into one. I didn't stand a chance with her." He let the subject trail away, and picked up another. "You want to do some good for these bears?" he said. "Get out there on the dump and poison 'em. Teach 'em not to come back. Maybe it'll take five seasons, and that'll be a lot of dead bears, but they'll get the message sooner or later." Finally he downed the contents of his glass, and while the liquor still burned his throat said, "I try not to think about them, but I do—" He wasn't talking about the bears now, Will knew. "I can see both of them, like it was yesterday." He shook his head. "Both of them so beautiful. So . . . *pure*." His lip curled at the word, as though he meant its antithesis. "It must be terrible for them."

"What must be terrible?"

"Living in this filthy world." He looked up at Will. "That's the worst part for me," he said. "That the older I get, the more I understand 'em." Were those tears in his eyes, Will wondered, or simply rheum? "And I hate myself for it so fucking much." He put down his empty glass and with sudden determination announced, "That's all you're getting from me." He crossed to the door and unbolted it. "So you may as well just get the hell out of here."

"Well, thank you for your time," Will said, stepping past the old man and into the freezing air.

Guthrie waved the courtesy away. "If you see Sister Ruth again—"

"I won't," Will said. "She died last February."

"What of?"

"Ovarian cancer."

"Huh. That's what you get for not using what God gave you," Guthrie said.

The dog had joined them at the threshold now and was growling loudly. Not at Will this time, but at whatever lay out there in the night. Guthrie didn't hush her, but stared out at the darkness. "She smells bears. You'd better not hang around."

"I won't," Will said, offering his hand to Guthrie. The man looked down at it in puzzlement for a moment, as though he'd forgotten this simple ritual. Then he took it.

"You should think about what I told you," he said. "About poisoning the bears. You'd be doing them a favor."

"I'd be doing Jacob's work for him," Will replied. "That's not what I was put on the planet to do."

"We're all doing his work just being alive," Guthrie replied. "Adding to the trash heap."

"Well at least I won't be adding to the population," Will said, and started from the threshold toward his Jeep.

"You and Sister Ruth both," Guthrie hollered after him. There was a sudden eruption of fresh barking from his dog, a shrillness in its din that Will knew all too well. He'd heard camp dogs raise a similar row at the approach of lions. There was warning in it, and Will took heed. Scanning the darkness to the left and right of him he was at the Jeep in a half dozen quickened heartbeats.

On the step behind him, Guthrie was yelling something—whether he was summoning his guest back inside or urging him to pick up his pace Will couldn't make out; the dog was too loud. Will blocked out the sound of both voices, man and animal, and concentrated on making his fingers perform the simple function of slipping the key into the lock. They played the fool. He fumbled, and the key slipped out of his hand. He went down on his haunches, the dog's barking shriller by the moment, to pluck it out of the snow. Something moved at the limit of his vision. He looked around, his fingers digging blindly for the key. He could see only the rocks, but that was little comfort. The animal could be in hiding now and on him in five seconds. He'd seen them attack, and they were fast when they needed to be, moving like locomotives to take their quarry. He knew the drill if a bear elected to charge him: drop to his knees, arms over his head, face to ground. Present as small a target as possible, and on no account make eye contact with the animal. Don't speak. Don't move. The less alive you were, the better chance you had of living. There was probably a lesson in that somewhere, though it was a bitter one. Live like a stone and death might pass you by.

His fingers had found the dropped key. He stood up, chancing a backward glance as he did so. Guthrie was still in the doorway; his dog, her hackles raised, was now silent at his side. Will hadn't heard Guthrie hush her; she'd simply given up on this damn fool man who wouldn't come out of the snow when he was told.

On the third try, the key went into the lock. Will hauled open the door. As he did so he heard the bear's roar for the first time. And there it was, barreling out between the rocks. There was no doubting its intention. It had him in its sights. He flung himself into the driver's seat, horribly aware of how vulnerable his legs were, and reached back to slam the door behind him.

The roar came again, very close. He locked the door, put the key into the ignition, and turned it. The headlights came on instantly, flooding the icy ground as far as the rocks, which looked as flat as stage scenery in their glare. Of the bear there was no sign. He glanced back toward Guthrie's shack. Man and dog had retreated behind the locked door. Will put the Jeep in gear and started to swing it around. As he did so he heard the roar again, followed by a thump. The bear had charged the vehicle in its frustration, and was rising up on its hind legs to strike it a second time. Will caught only a glimpse of its shaggy white bulk from the corner of his eye. It was a huge animal, no doubt of that: nine hundred pounds and counting. If it damaged the Jeep badly enough to halt his escape, he'd be in trouble. The bear wanted him, and it had the means to get him if he didn't outpace it. Claws and teeth enough to pry the vehicle open like a can of human meat.

He put his foot on the accelerator, and swung the vehicle around to head it back down the street. As he did so the bear changed tactics and direction, dropping back onto all fours to overtake the Jeep, then cutting in front of it.

For an instant the animal was there in the sear of the headlights, its wedge-snouted head pointing directly at the vehicle. It was not one of the pitiful clan Guthrie had described, their ferality dimmed by their addiction to human refuse. It was a piece of the wilderness still, defying the blaze and speed of the vehicle in whose path it had put itself. In the instant before it was struck, it was gone, disappearing with such speed that its departure seemed almost miraculous, as though it had been a vision conjured by the cold, then snatched away.

As Will drove back to the house, he felt for the first time the poverty of his craft. He had taken tens of thousands of photographs in his professional lifetime, in some of the wildest regions of the planet: the Torres de Paine, the plateaus of Tibet, the Gunung

Leuser in Indonesia. There he had photographed species that were in their last desperate days, rogues and maneaters. But he had never come close to capturing what he had seen in the Jeep's headlights minutes before: the power and the glory of the bear, risking death to defy him. Perhaps it was beyond his talents to do so; in which case it was probably beyond anybody's talents. He was, by general consensus, the best of the best. But the wild was better. Just as it was his genius to wait upon his subject until it revealed itself, so it was the genius of the wild to make that revelation less than complete. The rogues and maneaters were dying out, one by one, but the mystery continued, undisclosed. And would continue, Will suspected, until the end of rogues and mysteries and the men who were fools for them both.

III

Cornelius Botham sat at the table with a hand-rolled cigarette lolling from beneath his blond feather mustache, his third beer of the morning set at his elbow, and surveyed the disemboweled Pentax laid out before him.

"What's wrong with it?" Will wanted to know.

"It's broken," Cornelius deadpanned. "I say we hack a hole in the ice, wrap it in a pair of Adrianna's underpants, and bury it for future generations to discover."

"You can't fix it?"

"Yes, I can fix it," Cornelius said. "That is why I'm here. I can fix everything. But I would prefer to hack a hole in the ice, wrap it in a pair of Adrianna's underpants—"

"It's given good service, that camera."

"So have we all. But sooner or later, if we're lucky, we'll be wrapped in a pair of Adrianna's underpants—"

Will was at the stove, making himself a ragged omelet. "You're obsessing."

"I am not."

Will slid his breakfast onto a plate, tossed two slices of stale bread on top of it, and came to sit at the table opposite Cornelius.

"You know what's wrong with this town?" Cornelius asked.

"Give me an A, B, or C."

This was a popular guessing game among the trio, the trick being to dream up alternatives more believable than the truth.

"No problem," Cornelius said. He sipped a mouthful of beer and then said: "Okay. A, right? There aren't any good-looking women in two hundred miles, besides Adrianna, and that'd be like fucking my sister. Okay? So, B. You can't get any decent acid. And C—"

"It's B."

"Wait, I haven't finished."

"You don't have to."

"Fuck, man. I got a great C."

"It's the acid," Will said. He leaned toward Cornelius. "Right?"

"Yeah." He peered at Will's plate. "What the hell's that?"

"Omelet."

"What did you make it with? Penguin eggs?"

Will laughed, and was still laughing when Adrianna came in out of the cold. "Hey, we got more bears at the dump," she said, her Southern drawl perfectly mismatched with every other detail of her appearance and manner, from her badly trimmed bangs to her heavy-booted stomp. "At least four of 'em. Two adolescents, a female, and a huge male." She looked first at Will, then at Cornelius, then back at Will. "A little enthusiasm, please?"

"Just give me a few minutes," Will said, "I need a couple of cups of coffee first."

"You've got to see this male. I mean," she was struggling for the words, "this is the biggest damn bear I ever saw."

"Maybe the one I saw last night," Will said. "Actually we saw each other. Outside Guthrie's place."

Adrianna unzipped her parka and sat down on the beat-up sofa, flinging aside a pillow and blanket to do so. "He kept you talking for quite a while," she said. "What was the old fuck like?"

"No more crazy than anybody'd be, living in a shack in the middle of nowhere."

"On his own?"

"He had a dog. Lucy."

"Hey," Cornelius cooed. "Does that sound like a man with a supply or what?" He grinned, his eyes popping. "Only a guy with a habit would name his dog Lucy."

"Christ!" Adrianna shouted. "I am so thoroughly sick of hearing you talk about getting high."

Cornelius shrugged. "Whatever," he said.

"We came here to do a job of work."

"And we've done it," Cornelius said. "Every damn undignified, pitiful thing a polar bear can do we've got on film. Bears playing around the broken sewage pipes. Bears trying fucky-fucky in the middle of the dump."

"Okay, okay," Adrianna said, "we did good." She turned to Will. "I still want you to see my bear," she said.

"*Your* bear now, is it?" Cornelius said.

She ignored him. "Just one last shoot," she implored Will. "You won't be disappointed."

"Jeez," Cornelius remarked, putting his legs up on the table. "Leave the man alone. He doesn't want to see the fucking bear. Haven't you got the message?"

"Keep out of this," Adrianna snapped.

"You're so fucking pushy," Cornelius replied. "It's just a bear."

Adrianna was up from the couch and over to Cornelius in two strides. "I told you: keep out of this," she said, and shoved Cornelius's shoulder just hard enough to tip him over. Down he went, clearing half of the doomed Pentax from the table with his boot heel as he went.

"*Come on,*" Will said, setting down his omelet in case there was an escalation in hostilities. If there was, it wouldn't be the first time. Nine days out of every ten Cornelius and Adrianna worked side by side like brother and sister. And on the tenth they fought like brother and sister. Today, however, Cornelius wasn't in the mood for insults or fisticuffs. He got to his feet, brushing his hippie-length hair back out of his eyes, and stumbled to the door, picking up his anorak on his way. "See you later," he said to Will. "I'm going to go look at the water."

"Sorry about that," Adrianna said when he'd gone. "It was my fault. I'll make peace when he gets back."

"Whatever."

Adrianna went to the stove and poured herself a cup of coffee. "So what did Guthrie have to say?"

"Not a lot."

"Why did you even go see him?"

Will shrugged. "Just . . . some stuff from my childhood . . . " he said.

"Big secret?"

Will offered her a slow smile. "Huge."

"So you're not going to tell me?"

"It's nothing to do with us being here. Well, it is and it isn't. I knew Guthrie lived on the bay, so I kind of killed two birds . . ." the words grew soft, "with one stone."

"Are you going to photograph him?" she said, crossing to the window. The Tegelstrom children, who lived across the street, were out playing in the snow, their laughter loud. She peered out at them.

"No," Will said. "I already invaded his privacy."

"Like I'm invading yours?"

"I didn't mean that."

"That's right though, isn't it?" she said gently. "I never get to hear what life was like for little Willy Rabjohns."

"That's because—"

"You don't want to tell me." She was warming to her thesis now. "You know . . . this is how you used to be with Patrick."

"Unfair."

"You used to drive him crazy. He'd call me up sometimes and vent these streams of abuse—"

"He is a melodramatic queen," Will said, fondly.

"He said you were cryptic. You are. He said you were secretive. You're that too."

"Isn't that the same thing?"

"Don't get intellectual. It pisses me off."

"Have you spoken to him recently?"

"Now you're changing the subject."

"I am not. You were talking about Patrick and now *I'm* talking about Patrick."

"I was talking about you."

"I'm bored with me. Have you talked to Patrick recently?"

"Sure."

"And how is he?"

"Up and down. He tried to sell the apartment but he couldn't get the price he wanted so he's staying put. He says it depresses him, living in the middle of the Castro. So many widowers, he says. But I think it's better he's there. Especially if he gets sicker. He's got a strong support group of friends."

"Is whatsisname still around? The kid with the dyed eyelashes?"

"You know his name, Will," Adrianna said, turning and narrowing her eyes.

"Carlos," Will said.

"Rafael."

"Close enough."

"Yes, he's still around. And he doesn't dye his eyelashes. He's got beautiful eyes. In fact he's a wonderful kid. I surely wasn't as giving or as loving as he is at nineteen. And I'm damn sure you weren't."

"I don't remember nineteen," Will said. "Or twenty, come to that. I have a *very vague* recollection of twenty-one—" He laughed. "But you get to a place when you're so high you're not high any-more."

"And that was twenty-one?"

"It was a very fine year for acid tabs."

"Do you regret it?"

"*Je ne regrette rien,*" Will slurred, sloe-eyed. "No, that's a lie. I wasted a lot of time in bars being picked up by men I didn't like. And who probably wouldn't have liked me if they'd taken the time to ask."

"What wasn't to like?"

"I was too needy. I wanted to be loved. No, I *deserved* to be loved. That's what I thought, I deserved to be loved. And I wasn't. So I drank. It hurt less when I drank." He mused for a moment, staring into middle distance. "You're right about Rafael. He's better for Patrick than I ever was."

"Pat likes having a partner who's there all the time," Adrianna said. "But he still calls you the love of his life."

Will squirmed. "I hate that."

"Well you're stuck with it," Adrianna replied. "Be grateful. Most people never have that in their lives."

"Speaking of love and adoration, how's Glenn?"

"Glenn doesn't count. He's in it for the kids. I've got wide hips and big tits and he thinks I'll be fertile."

"So when do you start?"

"I'm not going to do it. The planet's fucked enough without me turning out more hungry mouths."

"You really feel like that?"

"No, but I *think* it," Adrianna said. "I *feel* very broody, especially when I'm with him. So I keep away when there's a chance, you know, I might give in."

"He must love that."

"It drives him crazy. He'll leave me eventually. He'll find some Earth Mother who just wants to make babies."

"Couldn't you adopt? Make you both happy?"

"We talked about it, but Glenn's determined to continue the family line. He says it's his animal instincts."

"Ah, the natural man."

"This from a guy who plays in a string quartet for a living."

"So what are you going to do?"

"Let him go. Get myself a man who doesn't care if he's the last of his line, and still wants to fuck like a tiger on Saturday night."

"You know what?"

"I should have been queer. I know. We would have made a lovely couple. Now, are you going to move your butt? This damn bear's not going to wait forever."

IV

i

As the afternoon light began to fail, the wind veered and came out of the northeast across Hudson Bay, rattling the door and windows of Guthrie's shack like something lonely and invisible, wanting comfort at the table. The old man sat in his old leather armchair and savored the gale's din like a connoisseur. He had long ago given up on the charms of the human voice. It was more often than not a courier of lies and confusions, or so he had come to believe; if he never heard another syllable uttered in his life he would not think himself the poorer. All he needed by way of communication was the sound he was listening to now. The wind's mourn and whine was wiser than any psalm, prayer, or profession of love he'd ever heard.

But tonight the sound failed to soothe him as it usually did. He knew why. The responsibility lay with the visitor who'd come knocking on his door the night before. He'd disturbed Guthrie's equilibrium, raising the phantoms of faces he'd tried so hard to put from his mind. Jacob Steep, with his soot-and-gold eyes and black beard and pale poet's hands; and Rosa, glorious Rosa, who had the gold of Steep's eyes in her hair and the black of his beard in her gaze, but who was as fleshy and passionate as he was sweatless and unmoved. Guthrie had known them for such a short time, and many years ago, but he had them in his mind's eye so clearly he might have met them that morning.

He had Rabjohns there too: with his green milk eyes, too gentle by half, and his hair in unruly abundance, curling at his nape, and the wide ease of his face, nicked with scars on cheek and brow. He hadn't been scarred half enough, Guthrie thought; there was still some measure of hope in him. Why else had he come asking questions, except in the belief that they could be answered? He'd learn, if he lived long enough. There were no answers. None that made sense anyhow.

The wind gusted hard against the window, and loosened one of the boards Guthrie had taped over a cracked pane. He raised himself out of the pit of his chair and, picking up the roll of tape he'd used to secure the board, crossed to the window to fix it. Before he stuck it back in place, blocking out the world, he stared through the grimy glass. The day was close to departure, the thickening waters of the bay the color of slate, the rocks black. He kept staring, distracted from his task not by the sight but by the memories that came to him still, unbidden, unwanted, but impossible to put from his head.

Words first. No more than a murmur. But that was all he needed.

These will not come again—

Steep was speaking, his voice majestic.

Nor this. Nor this—

And as he spoke, the pages appeared in front of Guthrie's grieving eyes; the pages of Steep's terrible book. There, a perfect rendering of a bird's wing, exquisitely colored—

Nor this—

And here, on the following page, a beetle, copied in death; every part documented for posterity: mandible, wing-case, and segmented limb.

Nor this—

"Jesus," he sobbed, the roll of tape dropping from his trembling fingers. Why couldn't Rabjohns have left him alone? Was there no corner of the world where a man might listen in the wail of the wind, without being discovered and reminded of his crimes?

The answer, it seemed, was no, at least for a soul as unredeemed as his. He could never hope to forget, not until God struck life and memory from him, which prospect seemed at this moment far less dreadful than living on, day and night, in fear of another Rabjohns coming to his door and naming names.

"*Nor this . . .*"

Shut up, he murmured to memories. But the page kept flipping in his head. Picture after picture, like some morbid bestiary. What fish was that, that would never again silver the sea? What bird, that would never tune its song to the sky?

On and on the pages flew, while he watched, knowing that at last Steep's fingers would come to a page where he himself had made a mark. Not with a brush or a pen, but with a bright little knife.

And then the tears would begin to come in torrents, and it wouldn't matter how hard the northeasterly blew, it could not carry the past away.

ii

The bears did not make a liar of Adrianna. When she and Will got to the dump, the remnants of the day still with them, they found the animals cavorting in all their defiled glory, the adolescents—one of them the best proportioned female they'd yet spotted; a perfect specimen of her clan—scavenging in the dirt, the older female investigating the rusted carcass of a truck, while the male Adrianna had been so eager for Will to see surveyed his fetid kingdom from atop one of the dump's dozen hillocks.

Will got out of the Jeep and approached. Adrianna, always armed with a rifle under these kind of conditions, followed two or three strides behind. She knew Will's methodology by now: He wouldn't waste film on long shots; he'd get as close as he could without disturbing the animals and then he'd wait. And wait, and wait. Even among his peers—wildlife photographers who thought nothing of waiting a week for a picture—his patience was legendary. In this, as in so many other things, he was a paradox. Adrianna had seen him at publishing parties grinding his teeth with boredom after five minutes of an admirer's chit chat, but here, watching four polar bears on a piece of wasteland, he would sit happily mesmerized until he found the moment he wanted to seize.

It was clear that he was not interested in either the adolescents or the female. It was the old male he wanted to photograph. He glanced over at Adrianna and silently indicated the path he was going to take between the other animals, so as to get as close to his subject as possible. She'd no sooner nodded her comprehension than Will was off, surefooted even on the ice-slickened dirt. The adolescents took no notice of him. But the female, who was certainly large enough to kill either Will or Adrianna with a swipe if she took a mind

to do so, ceased her investigations of the truck and sniffed the air.
Will froze; Adrianna did the same, rifle at the ready if the bear made
an aggressive move. But perhaps because she'd smelled so many people in the vicinity of the dump, the bear wasn't interested in this particular scent. She returned to gutting the truck seats, and Will was
off again, toward the male. By now Adrianna had grasped the shot
Will was after: a low angle, looking up the slope of the hillock so as to
frame the bear against the sky, a fool-king perched on a throne of
shit. It was the kind of image Will had built his reputation upon.
The whole paradoxical story, captured in a picture so indelible and so
inevitable that it seemed evidence of collusion with God. More often
than not such happy accidents were the fruit of obsessive observation. But once in a while, as now, they presented themselves as gifts.
All he had to do was snatch them.

Typically, of course (how she cursed his *machismo* sometimes),
he was going to position himself so close to the base of the hillock
that if the animal decided to come after him he'd be in trouble.
Creeping close to the ground he found his spot. The animal was
either unaware of, or indifferent to, his proximity; it was half turned
from him, casually licking dirt off its paws. But Adrianna knew from
experience that such appearances could be dangerously deceptive.
The wild did not always like to be scrutinized, however discreetly. Far
less adventurous photographers than Will had lost their limbs or
their lives by taking an animal's insouciance for granted. And of all
the creatures Will had photographed, there was none with a more
terrible reputation than the polar bear. If the male chose to come
after Will, Adrianna would have to bring the beast down in one shot,
or it would all be over.

Will had by now found a niche at the very base of the hillock
that suited him perfectly. The bear was still licking its paws, its face
now almost entirely turned away from the camera. Adrianna glanced
back at the other animals. All three were happily engrossed in their
sports, but that was of little comfort. The geography of the dump
allowed for there to be any number of other animals scavenging close
by yet out of sight. Not for the first time she wished she'd been born
with the eyes of a chameleon: side-rigged and independently maneu-
vered.

She looked back at Will. He had crept up the slope just a little
and had his camera poised. The bear, meanwhile, had given up cleaning its paws and was lazily surveying its wretched domain. Adrianna

willed it to move its rump, turn twenty degrees clockwise, and give Will his picture. But it simply raised its scarred snout into the air and yawned, its black velvet lips curling back as it did so. Its teeth, like its hide, were a record of the battles it had fought. Many of them were splintered and several others missing; its gums were abscessed and raw. No doubt it was in constant pain, which probably did nothing for the sweetness of its mood.

The animal's yawn afforded Will a chance to move three or four yards to his left, until the bear was facing him. It was clear by the caution of his advance that he was perfectly aware of his jeopardy. If the animal took this moment to study the ground rather than the sky then Will would have a couple of seconds at best to get out of its way.

But luck was with him. Overhead, a flock of noisy geese were homing, and the bear idly turned its gaze their way, allowing Will to reach his chosen spot and settle there before it dropped its head and once again sullenly surveyed the dump.

At last, Adrianna heard the barely audible click of the shutter and the whir of the film's advance. A dozen shots in quick succession, then a pause. The bear lowered its head. Had it sensed Will? The shutter clicked again, four, five, six times. The bear let out a sharp hiss. It was an unmistakable warning. Adrianna leveled the rifle. Will clicked on. The bear did not move. Will caught two more shots, and then, very slowly, began to rise. The bear took a step toward him, but the garbage beneath its bulk was slick, and instead of following through the animal faltered.

Will glanced back toward Adrianna. Seeing the leveled rifle he motioned it down and stealthily stepped away. Only when he'd halved the distance between the hillock and Adrianna did he murmur, "He's blind."

She looked again at the animal. It was still poised at the top of the hillock, its scarred head roving back and forth, but she didn't doubt what Will had said was true. The animal had little or no sight left, hence its tentativeness, its reluctance to give chase when it was not certain of the solidity of the ground beneath its paws.

Will was at her side now. "You want pictures of any of the others?" she asked him. The adolescents had gone to romp elsewhere, but the female was still sniffing around the truck. He told her no; he'd got what he needed. Then, turning back to look at the bear, he said, "He reminds me of somebody, I just can't think who."

"Whoever it is, don't tell them."

"Why not?" Will said, still staring at the animal. "I think I'd be flattered."

V

When they got back to Main Street, Peter Tegelstrom was out at the foot of his house, perched on a crate nailing a string of Halloween lights along the low-hanging eaves. His children, a five-year-old girl and a son a year her senior, ran around excitedly, clapping and yelling as the row of pumpkins and skulls was unraveled. Will headed over to chat to Tegelstrom; Adrianna followed. She'd made friends with the kids in the last week and a half and had suggested to Will that he photograph the family. Tegelstrom's wife was pure Inuit, her beauty evident in her children's faces. A picture of this healthy and contented human family living within two hundred yards of the dump would make, Adrianna argued, a powerful counterpoint to Will's pictures of the bears. The wife, however, was too shy even to talk to the visitors, unlike Tegelstrom himself, who seemed to Will to be starved for conversation.

"Are you finished with your pictures now?" he wanted to know.

"Near enough."

"You should have gone down to Churchill. They've got a lot more bears there—"

"And a lot of tourists taking pictures of them."

"You could take pictures of the tourists taking pictures of the bears," Tegelstrom said.

"Only if one of them was being eaten."

Peter was much amused by this. His arranging of the lights finished, he climbed down the ladder and switched them on. The children clapped. "There isn't much here to keep them occupied," he said. "I feel bad for them sometimes. We're going to move down to Prince Albert in the spring." He nodded into the house. "My wife doesn't want to, but the babies need a better life than this."

The babies, as he called them, had been playing with Adrianna and at her bidding had gone inside to put on their Halloween masks. Now they reappeared, jabbering and whooping to inspire some fear. The masks were, Will guessed, the shy wife's handiwork: Not gleeful vampires or ghouls, but more troubled spirits, constructed from scraps of sealskin and bits of fur and cardboard, all roughly daubed with red and blue paint. Set on such diminutive bodies they were strangely unsettling.

"Come and stand here for me, will you?" Will said, calling them over to pose in front of the doorway.

"Do I get to be in this?" Tegelstrom asked.

"No," Will said bluntly.

Affably enough, Tegelstrom stepped out of the picture, and Will went down on his haunches in front of the children, who had ceased their hollering and were standing at the doorstep, hand in hand. There was a sudden gravity in the moment. This wasn't the happy family portrait Adrianna had been trying to arrange. It was a snapshot of two mournful spirits, posed in the twilight beneath a loop of plastic lights. Will was happier with the shot than any of the pictures he'd made at the dump.

Cornelius was not yet home, which was no great surprise.

"He's probably smoking pot with the Brothers Grimm," Will said, referring to the two Germans with whom Cornelius had struck up a dope-and-beer-driven friendship. They lived in what was indisputably the most luxurious home in the community, complete with a sizable television. Besides the dope, Cornelius had confided, they had a collection of all-girl wrestling films so extensive it was worthy of academic study.

"So we're done here?" Adrianna said, as she set about making the vodka martinis they always drank around this time. It was a ritual that had begun as a joke in a mud hole in Botswana, passing a flask of vodka back and forth pretending they were sipping very dry martinis at the Savoy.

"We're done," Will said.

"You're disappointed."

"I'm always disappointed. It's never what I want it to be."

"Maybe you want too much."

"We've had this conversation."

"I'm having it again."

"Well I'm not," Will said, with a monotony in his tone Adrianna knew of old. She let the subject drop and moved on to another.

"Is it okay if I take a couple of weeks off? I want to go down to Tallahassee to see my mother."

"No problem. I'm going back to San Francisco to spend some time with the pictures, start to make the connections."

This was a favorite phase of his, describing a process Adrianna had never completely comprehended. She'd watched him doing it: laying out maybe two or three hundred images on the floor and wandering among them for several days, arranging and rearranging them, laying unlikely combinations together to see if sparks flew; growling at himself when they didn't; getting a little high and sitting up through the night to meditate on the work. When the connections were made, and the pictures put in what he considered to be the right order, there was undeniably an energy in them that had not been there before. But the pain of the process had always seemed to Adrianna out of all proportion to the improvement. It was a kind of masochism, she'd decided; his last, despairing attempt to make sense of the senseless before the images left his hands.

"Your cocktail, sir," Adrianna said, setting the martini at Will's elbow. He thanked her, picked it up, and they clinked glasses.

"It's not like Cornelius to miss vodka," Adrianna observed.

"You just want an excuse to check out the Brothers Grimm," Will said.

Adrianna didn't contest the point. "Gert looks like he'd be fun in bed."

"Is he the one with the beer belly?"

"Yep."

"He's all yours. Anyway, I think they're a package deal. You can't have one without the other."

Will picked up his cigarettes and wandered over to the front door, taking his martini with him. He turned on the porch light, opened the door, leaned against the doorjamb, and lit a cigarette. The Tegelstrom kids had gone inside, and were probably tucked up in bed by now, but the lights Peter had put up to entertain them were still bright: a halo of orange pumpkins and white skulls around the house, rocking gently in the gusting wind.

"I've got something to tell you," Will said. "I was going to wait for Cornelius but . . . I don't think there's going to be another book after this."

"I knew you were fretting about something. I thought maybe it was me—"

"Oh God no," Will said. "You're the best, Adie. Without you and Cornelius I'd have given up on all this shit a long time ago."

"So why now?"

"I'm out of love with the whole thing," he said. "None of it makes any difference. We'll show the pictures of the bears and all it'll do is make more people come and watch them getting their noses stuck in mayonnaise jars. It's a waste of bloody time."

"What will you do instead?"

"I don't know. It's a good question. It feels like . . . I don't know—"

"What does it feel like?"

"That everything's winding down. I'm forty-one and it feels like I've seen too much and been too many places and it's all blurred together. There's no magic left. I've done my drugs. I've had my infatuations. I've outgrown Wagner. This is as good as it's going to get. And it's not that great."

Adrianna came to join him at the door, putting her chin on his shoulder. "Oh my poor Will," she said, in her best cocktail clip. "So famous, so celebrated, and so very, very bored."

"Are you mocking my ennui?"

"Yes."

"I thought so."

"You're tired. You should take a year off. Go sit in the sun with a beautiful boy. That's Dr. Adrianna's advice."

"Will you find me the boy?"

"Oh Lord. Are you *that* exhausted?"

"I couldn't cruise a bar if my life depended upon it."

"So don't. Have another martini."

"No, I've got a better idea," Will said. "You make the drinks, I'll go fetch Cornelius. Then we can all get maudlin together."

VI

Cornelius had spent the dregs of the afternoon with the Lauterbach brothers, and had a fine time of it, watching wrestling flicks and smoking their weed. He'd left as darkness fell, intending to head back to the house for a couple of shots of vodka, but halfway along Main Street the prospect of dealing with Adrianna had loomed. He wasn't in the mood for apologies and justifications; they'd only bring him down. So instead of heading back he fished out the fat roach he'd connived from Gert and wandered down toward the water to smoke it.

As he walked, weaving between the houses, the wind carried flecks of snow across the bay, grazing his face. He stopped beneath one of the lamps that illuminated the ground between the backs of the houses and the water's edge and turned his face up to the light so as to watch the flakes spilling down. "Pretty . . ." he said to himself. So much prettier than bears. When he got back, he'd tell Will he should give up with animals and start photographing snowflakes instead. They were a lot more endangered, his gently befuddled wits decided. As soon as the sun came out they were gone, weren't they? All their perfection, melted away. It was tragic.

Will didn't get as far as the Lauterbach house. He'd trudged maybe a hundred yards down Main Street—the wind getting stronger with every gust, the snow it carried thickening—when he caught sight of Cornelius, reeling around, face to the sky. He was obviously high, which was no great surprise. It had always been Cornelius's way of dealing with life, and Will had far too many quirks of his own to be judgmental about it. But there was a time and a place for such excesses, and the Main Street of Balthazar in bear season was not one of them.

"Cornelius!" Will yelled. "Cornelius? Can you hear me?"

The answer was apparently no. Cornelius just kept up his dervish dance under the lamp. Will started down the street in the man's direction, cursing him ripely as he went. He didn't waste his breath shouting, the wind was too strong, but part of the way down the street he regretted not doing so because without warning Cornelius gave up his spinning and slipped out of sight between the houses. Will picked up his pace, though he was tempted to head back to the house and arm himself before pursuing Cornelius any further. If he did so, however, he risked losing the man altogether, and to judge by his stumbling step Cornelius was in no fit state to be wandering alone in the dark. It wasn't so much the bears Will was concerned about, it was the bay. Cornelius was headed toward the shore. One slip on the icy rocks and he'd be in water so cold it would stop his heart.

He'd reached the spot where Cornelius had been dancing and followed his tracks away from the comfort of the streetlight into the murky no-man's-land between the houses and the tidal flats. There he was pleased to discover Cornelius's phantom figure standing maybe fifty yards from him. He'd given up his spinning and his sky watching, and he was standing stone still, staring out toward the darkness of the shore.

"Hey, buddy!" Will called to him. "You're going to get pneumonia."

Cornelius didn't turn. In fact he didn't move so much as a muscle. What kind of pills had he been popping? Will wondered.

"*Con!*" he yelled again. He was no more than twenty yards from Cornelius's back. "It's Will! Are you okay? Talk to me, man."

Finally, Cornelius spoke. One slurred word that stopped Will in his friend's tracks.

"*Bear.*"

There was a cloud of breath at Will's lips. He waited, as still as Cornelius, while the cloud cleared, then scanned the scene to the limit of his vision. First to the left. The shore was empty as far as he could see. Then to the right; the same.

He dared a one-word question: "Where?"

"Ahead. Of. Me." Cornelius replied.

Will took a very slow sideways step. Cornelius's drug-induced senses were not deceiving him. There was indeed a bear maybe sixteen or seventeen yards in front of him, its form barely visible to Will through the snow-flecked murk.

"Are you still there, Will?" Cornelius said.

"I'm here."

"What the fuck do I do?"

"Back off. But, Con, *very, very slowly.*"

Cornelius glanced back over his shoulder, his stricken face suddenly sober.

"Don't look at me," Will said. "Keep your eyes on the animal."

Cornelius looked back toward the bear, which had begun its implacable approach. This wasn't one of the playful adolescents from the dump, nor was it the blind old warrior Will had photographed. This was a fully grown female, a good six hundred pounds.

"Fuck . . . " Cornelius muttered.

"Just keep coming," Will coaxed him. "You're going to be okay. Just don't let her think you're anything worth chasing."

Cornelius managed three tentative backward steps, but his equilibrium was poor after the dervish act, and on the fourth step his heel slid on the slick ground. He flailed for a moment, then recovered his balance, but the harm was done. Hissing her intentions, the bear gave up her plod and came bounding at him. Cornelius turned and ran, the bear roaring in pursuit, her body a blur. Weaponless, all Will could do was dodge out of Cornelius's path and yell himself hoarse in the hope of distracting the animal. But it was Cornelius she wanted. In two bounds she'd halved the distance between them, jaws wide in readiness—

"*Get down!*"

Will threw a glance back in the direction of the voice and there, God save her, was Adrianna, rifle raised.

"*Con!*" she yelled. "*Get your fucking head down!*"

He got the message, and flung himself to the frozen dirt, with the bear a body's length from his heels. Adrianna fired, and hit the animal's shoulder, checking her before she could catch up with her quarry. The animal rose up with an agonized roar, blood staining her fur. Cornelius was still within swatting distance, however, if she chose to take him out. Ducking to make himself as small a target as possible, Will scrambled toward him, and, grabbing his trembling torso, hauled him out of the bear's path. There was a sharp stink of shit off him.

He looked back at the bear. She wasn't done, nowhere near. Roaring so loudly that the ground shook, she started toward Adrianna, who leveled her rifle and fired a second time, at no more than ten yards' range. The animal's roar ceased on the instant, and again she rose up, white and red and vast, teetering for a moment. Then she reeled back like a breaking wave and limped away into the darkness.

The entire encounter—from the moment Cornelius had named his nemesis—had perhaps lasted a minute, but it was long enough for a kind of delirium to have taken hold of Will. He got to his feet, the snowflakes spiraling around him like giddy stars and went to the place where the bear's blood had splashed on the ice.

"Are you all right?" Adrianna asked him.

"Yes," he said.

It was only half the truth. He wasn't hurt, but he wasn't whole either. He felt as though some part of him had been torn out by what he'd just witnessed and had fled into the darkness in pursuit of the bear. He had to go after it.

"*Wait!*" Adrianna yelled.

He looked back at her, trying his best to block out Cornelius's sobbing apologies, and the shouts of people on Main Street as they came sniffing after the bloodshed. Adrianna was staring straight at him, and he knew she was reading the thoughts on his face.

"Don't be a fuck-wit, Will," she said.

"No choice."

"Then at least take the rifle."

He looked at it as though it had just pumped its bullets into him. "I don't need it," he said.

"*Will—*"

He turned his back on her, on the lights, on the people and their asinine questions. Then he loped off toward the shoreline, following the red trail the bear left behind her.

VII

Oh, all the years he'd waited. Waited and watched with his dispassionate eye while something died nearby, recording its passing like the truthful witness he was. Keeping his distance, keeping his calm. Enough of that. The bear was dying, and he would die too if he let her go now, let her perish in the dark alone. Something had snapped in him. He didn't know why. Perhaps because of the conversation with Guthrie, which had stirred up so much pain; perhaps the encounter with the blind bear at the dump; perhaps simply because the time had come. He'd hung on this branch long enough, ripening there. It was time to fall and rot into something new.

He followed the bear's trail along the shoreline parallel to the street with a kind of exulting despair in him. He had no idea what he would do when he caught up with the animal; he only knew he had to be with it in its agonies, given that he was to some degree their author. He was the one who'd brought Cornelius and his habits here, after all. The bear had simply been doing what she would do in the wild when confronted by something threatening. She'd been shot for being true to her nature. No thinking queer could be happy with his complicity in that.

Will's empathy with the animal hadn't totally unseated his urge to self-preservation. Though he followed the trail closely most of the way, he gave the rocks a little distance when he came upon them, in case there were more animals lurking there. But what little light the lamps of Main Street had supplied was now too far behind him to be of much use. It was harder and harder to make out the bloodstains. He had to stop and study the ground to find them, for which pause he was grateful. The icy air was raw in his throat and chest; his teeth ached as though they were all being drilled at the same time; his legs were trembling.

If he was feeling weak, he thought, the bear was surely a damn sight weaker. She'd shed copious amounts of blood now and must be close to collapse.

Somewhere nearby a dog was barking, her alarm familiar.

"Lucy . . ." Will said to himself, and looking up through the flickering snow saw that his pursuit had brought him within twenty yards of the back of Guthrie's shack. He heard the old man shouting now, telling the dog to shut up, and then the sound of the back door being opened.

Light spilled from it, out across the snow. A meager light by comparison with the streetlights half a mile back, but bright enough to show Will his quarry.

The animal was closer to the shore than to the shack, and closer to Will than either: standing on all fours, swaying, the ground around her dark with her free-flowing blood.

"What the fuck's going on out here?" Guthrie demanded.

Will didn't look at him; he kept his eyes fixed on the bear—as hers were fixed on him—while he yelled for Guthrie to go back inside.

"Rabjohns? Is that you?"

"There's a wounded bear out here—" Will yelled at him.

"I see her," Guthrie replied. "Did you shoot her?"

"No!" From the corner of his eye Will could see that Guthrie had emerged from his shack. "Go back inside will you?"

"Are you hurt?" Guthrie hollered.

Before Will could reply the bear was up and, turning her bulk toward Guthrie, she charged. There was time as she roared upon the old man for Will to wonder why she'd chosen to take Guthrie instead of him, whether in the seconds they'd stared at one another she'd seen that he was no threat to her: just another wounded thing, trapped between street and sea. Then she was up and swiping at Guthrie, the blow throwing him maybe five yards. He landed hard, but thanks to some grotesque gift of adrenaline he was on his feet a heartbeat later, yelling incoherently back at his wounder. Only then did his body seem to realize the grievous harm it had been done. His hands went up to his chest, his blood running out between his fingers. His yells ceased and he looked back up at the bear, so that for a moment they stood staring at one another, both bloodied, both teetering. Then Guthrie spoiled the symmetry and fell face down in the snow.

Still standing at the doorstep, Lucy began a round of despairing yelps, but however traumatized she was she plainly had no intention of approaching her master. Guthrie was still alive; he was attempting to turn himself over, it seemed, his right hand sliding on the ice as he tried to lift himself up.

Will looked back the way he'd come, hoping that somebody would be in sight who could help. There was no sign of anyone on the shoreline; perhaps people were making their way along the street. He couldn't afford to wait for them, however. Guthrie needed help now. The bear had sunk down onto all fours again, and by the degree of her sway, she looked ready to keel over entirely. Keeping his eyes on her he cautiously approached the place where Guthrie was lying. The delirium that had seized him earlier had guttered out. There was only a bitter sickness in his belly.

By the time he reached Guthrie's side the man had managed to turn himself over, and it was clear that he was wounded beyond hope of healing: his chest a wet pit, his gaze the same. But he seemed to see Will, or at least to sense his proximity. He reached out as Will bent to him, and caught hold of his jacket.

"Where's Lucy?" he said.

Will looked up. The dog was still at the doorway. She was no longer barking.

"She's okay."

Guthrie didn't hear him reply, it seemed, because he drew Will closer, his hold remarkably strong.

"She's safe," Will told him, more loudly, but even as he spoke he heard the warning hiss of the bear. He glanced back in her direction. Her whole bulk was full of shudders, as though her system, like Guthrie's, was close to capitulation. But she wasn't ready to die where she stood. She took a tentative step toward Will, her teeth bared.

Guthrie's other arm had caught hold of Will's shoulder. He was speaking again. Nothing that made much sense to Will, at least not at this moment.

"*This will . . . not come . . . again, . . .*" he said.

The bear took a second step, her body rocking back and forth. Very slowly Will worked to pull Guthrie's hands off him, but the man's hold was too fierce.

"The bear, . . . " Will said.

"*Nor this, . . .*" Guthrie muttered, "*nor this . . .*" There was a tiny smile on his bloody lips. Did he know, even in his dying agonies, what he was doing: holding down the man who had come with such sour memories, holding him where the bear could claim him?

Will had no choice: If he was going to get out of the bear's way he was going to have to lug Guthrie with him. He started to haul himself to his feet, lifting the old man's sizable frame with him. The motion brought a howl of anguish from Guthrie and his grip on Will's shoulder slipped a little. Will stepped sideways in the direction of the shack, half carrying Guthrie with him like a partner in some morbid dance. The bear had halted and was watching this grotesquerie with black-sequin eyes. Will took a second step, and Guthrie let out another cry, much weaker than the first, and all at once gave up his hold on Will, who didn't have the power left in his arms to support him. Guthrie slipped to the ground as though every bone in his body had gone to water, and in that instant the bear made her move. Will didn't have time to dodge, much less run. The animal was on him in a bound, striking him like a speeding car, his bones breaking on impact, the world becoming a smear of pain and snow, both blazing white.

Then his head struck the icy ground. Consciousness fled for a few seconds. When it returned he raised his hand; he saw that the snow beneath him was red. Where was the bear? He swiveled his gaze left and right looking for her. There was no sign. One of his arms was tucked beneath him, and useless, but there was enough strength in the other to raise him up. The motion made him sick with pain, and he was fearful he was going to lose consciousness again, but by degrees he bullied and coaxed his body up into a kneeling position.

Off to his left, a sniffing sound. He looked in its direction, his gaze flickering. The bear had her nose in Guthrie's corpse, inhaling its perfumes. She raised her vast head, her snout bloody.

This is death, Will thought. *For all of us, this is death*. This is what you've photographed so many times. The dolphin drowning in the net, pitifully quiescent; the monkey twitching among its dead fellows, looking at him with a gaze Will could not stand to meet, except through his camera. They were all the same in this moment, he and the monkey, he and the bear. All ephemeral things, running out of time.

And then the bear was on him again, her claws opening his shoulder and back, her jaws coming for his neck. Somewhere far off, in a place he no longer belonged, he heard a woman calling his name, and his lazy brain thought: *Adrianna's here, sweet Adrianna*—

He heard a shot, then another. Felt the weight of the bear against him, carrying him down to the ground, her blood raining on his face.

Was he saved? he vaguely wondered. But even as he was shaping the thought another part of him, that had neither eyes to see nor ears to hear, nor cared to have either, was slipping away from this place; and senses he had never known he owned were piercing the blizzard clouds and studying the stars. It seemed to him he could feel their warmth, that the distance between their blazing hearts and his spirit was just a thought, and he could be there, in them, knowing them, if he turned his mind to it.

Something checked his ascent, however. A voice in his head that he knew was familiar to him, yet he could not put a name to.

"Where d'you think you're going?" the voice said. There was a sly humor in it. He tried to put a face to the sound, but he saw only fragments. Silky red hair, a sharp nose, a comical mustache. *"You can't go yet,"* the interloper said.

But I want to, he said. It hurts so much, staying here. Not the dying part, the living.

His companion heard his complaints and would take no truck with them. *"Hush yourself,"* he said. *"You think you're the first man on the planet who lost his faith? That's all part of it. We're going to have a serious conversation, you and me. Face-to-face. Man-to—"*

Man-to *what?*

"We'll get to that," the voice replied. It was starting to fade.

Where are you going? Will wanted to know.

"Nowhere you can't find me when the time comes," the stranger replied. *"And it will come, my faithless friend. As sure as God put tits on trees."*

And with this absurdity, he was gone.

There was a moment of blissful silence, when it crossed Will's mind that maybe he'd died after all, and was floating away into oblivion. Then he heard Lucy—poor, orphaned Lucy—howling out her heart somewhere close to him. And coming on the heels of her din, human voices, telling him to be still, be still, he was going to be all right.

"Can you hear me, Will?" Adrianna was asking him.

He could feel the snowflakes dropping on his face, like cold feathers. On his brown, on his lashes, on his lips, on his teeth. And then—far less welcome than the pricking snow—a swelling agony in his torso and head.

"*Will,*" Adrianna said. "*Speak to me.*"

"Ye . . . s," he said.

The pain was becoming unendurable, rising and rising.

"You're going to be all right," Adrianna said. "We've got help coming, and you're going to be all right."

"Christ, what a mess," somebody said. He knew the inflections. One of the Lauterbach brothers, surely; Gert, the doctor, struck off the register for improper distribution of pharmaceuticals. He was giving orders like a field sergeant: Blankets, bandages, here, now, on the double!

"Will?" A third voice, this one close to his ear. It was Cornelius, weeping as he spoke. "I fucked up man. Oh Christ, I'm sorry—"

Will wanted to hush the man's self-recrimination—it was of no use to anybody now—but his tongue would not work to make the words. His eyes, however, opened a fraction, dislodging the dusting of snow in his sockets. He couldn't see Cornelius, nor Adrianna, nor Gert Lauterbach. Only the snow, spiraling down.

"He's still with us," Adrianna said.

"Oh man, oh man," Cornelius was sobbing. "Thank fucking God."

"You hold on," Adrianna said to Will. "We've got you. You hear me? You're not going to die, Will. I'm not going to let you, okay?"

He let his eyes close again. But the snow kept coming down inside his head, laying its hush upon him, like a tender blanket put over his hurt. And by degrees the pain retreated, and the voices retreated, and he slept under the snow, and dreamed of another time.

PART TWO

He Dreams
He Is Loved

I

For a few precious months following the death of his older brother, Will had been the happiest boy in Manchester. Not publicly so, of course. He had quickly learned how to put on a glum face, even to look teary sometimes, if a concerned relative asked him how he felt. But it was all a sham. Nathaniel was dead, and he was glad. The golden boy would reign over him no longer. Now there was only one person in his life who condescended to him the way Papa did, and that was Papa himself.

Papa had reason: He was a great man. A philosopher, no less. Other thirteen-year-olds had plumbers for fathers, or bus drivers, but Will's father, Hugo Rabjohns, had six books to his name, books that a plumber or a bus driver would be unlikely to understand. The world, Hugo had once told Nathaniel in Will's presence, was made by many men, but shaped by few. The important thing was to be one of those few, to find a place in which you could change the repetitive patterns of the many through political influence and intellectual discourse and, failing either of these, through benign coercion.

Will adored hearing his father talk this way, even though much of what Papa said was beyond him. And his father loved to talk about his ideas, though Will had heard him once fly into a fury when Eleanor, Will's mother, had called her husband a teacher.

"I am not, never have been, nor ever will be a *teacher!*" Hugo had roared, his always ruddy face turning a still deeper red. "Why do you always seek to *reduce* me?"

What had his mother said by way of reply? Something vague. She was always vague. Looking past him to something outside the window, probably, or staring critically at the flowers she'd just arranged.

"Philosophy can't be taught," Hugo had said. "It can only be inspired."

Perhaps the exchange had gone on a little longer, but Will doubted it. A short explosion, then peace: That was the ritual. And sometimes a fond exchange, but that too quickly withering. And always on his mother's face the same distracted look whether the subject was philosophy or affection.

But then Nathaniel had died, and even those exchanges had ceased.

He was killed on a Thursday afternoon, crossing the street: run down by a taxicab, the driver racing to carry his passenger to Manchester Piccadilly Station in time for a noon train. Struck square on, he was thrown through the window of a shoe store, sustaining multiple lacerations and appalling internal injuries. He did not die instantly. He held on to life for two-and-a-half days in intensive care at the Royal Infirmary, never regaining consciousness. In the early hours of the third night his body gave up the fight and he died.

In Will's mythologized version of the event, his brother had made the decision, somewhere in the depths of his coma, not to come back into the world. Though he was only fifteen when he died, he had already tasted more of the world's approbation than most men who lived out their biblical spans. Loved to devotion by those who'd made him, blessed with a face nobody could lay eyes upon without wanting to love, Nathaniel had decided to let go of the world while it still idolized him. He had been adored enough, fêted enough. He was already bored with it. Best to be gone, without a backward glance.

After the funeral Eleanor did not stir from the house. She'd always liked to walk and window-shop; she no longer did so. She'd had a circle of women friends with whom she lunched at least twice a week; she would no longer come to the phone to speak to them. Her face lost all its glamor. Her distraction turned to vacuity, her obsessions grew stronger by the day. She would not have the curtains in the living room open, for fear of seeing a taxicab. She could not eat, except off white plates. She would not sleep until every door and window in the house had been treble-locked. She took to praying, usually very quietly, in French, which was her native tongue. Nathaniel's spirit, Will heard her telling Papa one night, was with her all the time: Did Hugo not see him in her face? They had the same bones, didn't they? The same French bones.

Even at the age of thirteen, Will had an unsentimental grasp of the world; he didn't lie to himself about what was happening to his mother. She was going crazy. That was the simple, pitiful truth of it. For several weeks in May she could not bear to be left alone in the house, and Will was obliged to skip school (no great hardship there) and stay at home with her—banned from her presence (she had no wish to see a face that resembled a poor copy of Nathaniel's perfection), but called back with sobs and promises if he was heard opening the front door. Finally, in the middle of August, Hugo sat Will down and told him that life in Manchester had plainly become intolerable for all three of them, and he had decided they would move. "Your mother needs some open skies," he explained, the toll of the months since the accident gouged into his face. He had, in his own words, a pugilist's face; its monolithic rawness an unlikely rock from which to hear fine distinctions of thought and vocabulary spring. But spring they did. Even the simple business of describing the family's departure from Manchester became a linguistic adventure.

"I realize these last few months have been troubling to you," Papa told Will. "The manifestations of grief can be confounding to us all, and I can't pretend to fully understand why your mother's distress has taken such idiosyncratic forms. But you mustn't judge her. We can't feel what she feels. Nobody can *ever* feel what somebody else feels. We can *guess* at it. We can *hypothesize*. But that's it. What happens up here," he tapped his temple, "is hers and only hers."

"Maybe if she talked about it—" Will tentatively suggested.

"Words aren't absolutes. I've told you that before, haven't I? What your mother says and what you hear aren't the same thing. You understand that, don't you?" Will nodded, though he only grasped the crudest version of what he was being told. "So we're moving," Hugo replied, apparently satisfied that he'd communicated the theoretical underpinning of this.

"Where are we going?"

"A village in Yorkshire, called Burnt Yarley. You'll have to change schools but that's not going to be much of a problem for you, is it?" Will murmured no, it wasn't; he hated St. Margaret's. "And it won't hurt for you to be out in the open air a little more. You look so pale all the time."

"When will we go?"

"In about three weeks."

II

i

The move didn't happen quite as planned. Two days after Hugo's conversation with Will, quite without warning, Eleanor broke her own rules and left the house in the middle of the morning and went wandering. She was escorted home in the late evening, having been found weeping in the street where Nathaniel had been struck down. The move was postponed, and for the next fortnight she was watched over by nurses and tended to by a psychiatrist. His medications did some good. Her mood brightened after a few days—she became uncharacteristically jolly, in fact, and dived into the business of packing up the house with gusto. On the second weekend of September, the delayed move took place.

The journey from Manchester took little more than an hour but it might as well have delivered the two-vehicle convoy into another country. With the charmless streets of Oldham and Rochdale behind them they wound their way into open countryside, sweeping moorland steadily giving way to the steeper fells, whose lush green flanks were here and there stripped to pavements of grim, gray limestone. The wind blew hard on the hilltops, buffeting the high-sided van in which Will had asked to be a passenger. With map in hand he followed their route as best he could, his eyes straying from the road they were taking to venture where the names were strangest: Kirkby Malzeard, Gammersgill, Horton-in-Ribblesdale, Yockenthwaite and Garthwaite and Rottenstone Hill. There was a world of promise in such names.

Their destination, the village of Burnt Yarley, was to Will's eyes indistinguishable from a dozen other villages they'd passed through on their way: a scattering of plain, square houses and cottages built of the local limestone and roofed with slate; less than a half-dozen shops (a grocer, a butcher, a newsagent, a post office, a pub), a church with a small churchyard surrounding it, and a steeply humped bridge rising over a river no wider than a traffic lane. There were, however, three or four more substantial residences on the outskirts of the village. One of them would be their new house, he knew: It was the largest house in Burnt Yarley, so beautiful that according to Will's father Eleanor had cried with happiness at the thought of their living in it. We're going to be very happy there, Hugo had said, offering this not as a cherished hope, but as an instruction.

ii

The first sign of that happiness was waiting for them at the front gate: a plumpish, smiling woman in early middle-age who introduced herself to Will as Adele Bottrall and welcomed them all with what seemed to be genuine pleasure. She instantly took charge of the unloading of the car and the moving van, supervising her husband, Donald, and her son, Craig, who was the kind of sullen, thick-necked sixteen-year-old Will would have feared an arbitrary beating from in the yard of St. Margaret's. Here, however, he was a workhorse, eyes downcast most of the time, as he lugged boxes and furniture into the house. Will was given a glass of lemonade by Mrs. Bottrall and wandered around the house to survey it, coming back to the front now and then to watch Craig at his labors. The afternoon was clammy— thunder later, Adele promised, it'll clear the air—and Craig stripped down to a threadbare vest, the sweat trickling down his neck and face from his low hairline, his neck and arms peeling where he'd caught too much sun. Will was envious of his muscularity, of the curling hair at his armpits, and the wispy sideburns he was cultivating. Pretending a concern for the care Craig was exercising with the tables and lamps, he idly followed the youth from room to room, watching him work. Occasionally, Craig would do something that made Will feel as though he shouldn't be watching, though they weren't particularly odd things for anyone to do: passing his tongue over his frizzy mustache, stretching his arms above his head, splashing water on his face at the kitchen sink. Once or twice Craig looked his way, a little bemused at the attention he was getting. When he did Will made sure he was wearing a facsimile of that indifference he'd seen on his mother's face so often.

The unloading went on until the early evening, the house— which had not been lived in for two years—subtly resisting its reoccupation. Interior doors proved too narrow for several of the tea chests, and rooms too small gracefully to accommodate pieces of furniture from the house in the city. As the hours went on, tempers grew tattered. Knuckles were skinned and bloodied, shins scraped, and toes stubbed. Eleanor maintained an imperious calm throughout, seating herself in the bay window, which offered a magnificent panorama of the valley, and sipping herbal tea, while her husband made decisions as to the arrangement of rooms she would never have trusted to him in the old days. Once, trapping his fingers between a box and the wall, Craig let loose a fair stream of foul language, silenced by a hard slap on the back of the head from Adele. Will chanced to witness the blow and saw how Craig's eyes teared up from the sting. He was, Will realized, just a boy, for all his sweat and muscle, and his interest in watching Craig's labors instantly evaporated.

iii

That was Saturday. The night did not bring thunder, as Adele had predicted it would, and the next day the air was already sticky before St. Luke's solitary bell had summoned the faithful to worship. Adele was among the congregation, but her husband and son were not. By the time their task mistress finally reappeared, they had already put in almost two hours of graceless work, unloading the tea chests in such a hamfisted fashion that several pieces of cookery and a Chinese vase had been forfeited.

Alert to the general malaise Will decided to keep out of the way. While the Bottrall clan stomped around below he remained upstairs in the room with the sloped, beamed ceiling that he'd been given. It was at the back of the house, which suited him fine. From the deep-silled window he had a view up the unspoiled slope of the fell, with not a house nor hut in sight, just a few wind-stunted trees and a scattering of hardy sheep.

He was pinning a map of the world up on the wall when he heard the wasp, its last days upon it, come weaving around his head. He snatched up a book and swatted it away, but back it came, its buzz escalating. Again, he struck out at it, but somehow it avoided his blow and winding its way around him, stung him below his left ear. He yelped and retreated to the door as the insect flew a victory circuit around his head. He didn't attempt to swat it a third time, but opened the door, and stumbled downstairs, wailing.

He got no sympathy. His father was in the midst of a heated altercation with Donald Bottrall and shot him such a glance when he approached that he swallowed his complaints. Gulping back tears he went to find his mother. She was once again sitting at the bay window, with a bottle of pills on the arm of her chair. She had a second bottle open, the contents in her palm, and was counting them.

"Mum?" he said.

She raised her eyes from the pills, a look of genteel despair upon her face. "What's wrong?" she said. He told her. "You *are* careless," she replied. "Wasps always get nasty in the autumn. You shouldn't annoy them."

He began to protest that he hadn't annoyed it at all, he'd been the innocent party, but he could see by the expression on her face that she'd already tuned him out. A moment later, she returned to counting the pills. Feeling frustrated and utterly ineffectual, he withdrew.

The sting was really throbbing now, the discomfort fueling his rage. He went back up to the bathroom, found some ointment for insect bites in the medicine cabinet, and gingerly applied it to the sting. Then he washed his face, removing any evidence of tears. He was done with crying, he told his reflection; it was stupid. It didn't make anybody listen.

Feeling not in the least happier, he headed back downstairs. Little had changed. Craig was lounging in the kitchen, his mouth stuffed with something Adele had cooked up; Eleanor was sitting with her pills; and Hugo had taken his argument with Donald—who looked bull-headed enough to give as good as he got—out into the front garden, where they were talking at each other in a red rage. Nobody noticed Will stomp off toward the village, or if they did, nobody cared sufficiently to stop him.

III

The streets of Burnt Yarley were virtually deserted, the shops all closed. Even the little sweetshop, where Will had hoped he might soothe his frustration and his dry throat with an ice cream, was locked up. He peered in through the window, cupping his hands around his face. The interior was as small as the facade suggested, but packed to the rafters with goods, some clearly targeted at the ramblers and hikers who passed through the town: postcards, maps, even knapsacks. Curiosity satisfied, Will wandered on to the bridge. It wasn't large—a span of maybe twelve feet—and built of the same gray stone as the tiny cottages in its immediate vicinity. He sat on the low wall and peered down into the river. The summer had been dry, and there was presently little more than a stream creeping between the rocks below, but the banks were fringed with marsh marigolds and clumps of balsam. There were bees around the balsam in their dozens. Will watched them warily, ready to retreat if one winged its way toward him.

"It's all *stupid*," he muttered.

"What is?" said somebody at his back.

He turned round, and found not one but two pairs of eyes upon him. The speaker, a fair-haired, fair-skinned, and presently heavily freckled girl a little older than himself, was standing at the rise of the bridge, while her companion squatted against the wall opposite Will and picked his nose. The boy was plainly her brother; they had in common broad, plain features and grave, gray eyes. But while she still looked to be in her Sunday best, her sibling was a mess, his clothes wrinkled and grimy, his mouth stained with berry juice. He stared at Will with a scowl.

"What's stupid?" the girl said again.

"This place."

"'Tisn't," said the boy. "*You're* stupid."

"Hush up, Sherwood," the girl said.

"*Sherwood?*" said Will.

"Yeah, Sherwood," came the boy's defiant reply. He scrambled to his feet as if ready for a fight, his legs scabby with old scrapes. His belligerence lasted ten seconds. Then he said, "I want to go play somewhere else." His interest in the stranger had plainly already waned. "*Come on*, Frannie."

"That's not my real name," the girl put in, before Will could remark upon it. "It's Frances."

"Sherwood's a daft name," Will said.

"Oh yeah?" said Sherwood.

"Yeah."

"So who are you?" Frannie wanted to know.

"He's the Rabjohns kid," scabby-kneed Sherwood said.

"How'd you know that?" Will demanded.

Sherwood shrugged. "I heard," he said with a mischievous little smile, "'cause I *listen*."

Frannie laughed. "The things you hear," she said.

Sherwood giggled, pleased to be appreciated. "The things I hear," he said, his voice sing song as he repeated the phrase. "The things I hear, the things I hear."

"Knowing somebody's name isn't so clever," Will replied.

"I know more than that."

"Like?"

"Like you came from Manchester, and you had a brother only he's *dead*." He spoke the D-word with relish. "And your dad's a teacher." He glanced at his sister. "Frannie says she hates teachers."

"Well he's not a teacher," Will shot back.

"What is he then?" Frannie wanted to know.

"He's . . . he's a doctor of philosophy."

It sounded like a fine boast and for a moment it silenced his audience. Then Frannie said, "Is he really a doctor?"

She had unerringly gone to the part of his father's nomenclature Will had never really understood. He put a brave face on his incomprehension. "Sort of," he said. "He makes people better by . . . by writing books."

"That's *stupid*," Sherwood said, crowing the word that had begun their whole exchange. He started to laugh at how ridiculous this was.

"I don't care what you think," Will said, putting on his best sneer. "Anybody who lives in this dump has got to be the biggest stupid person I ever saw. That's what you are—"

Sherwood had turned his back on Will and was spitting over the bridge. Will gave up on him and marched off back toward the house.

"Wait—" he heard Frannie say.

"*Frannie*," Sherwood whined, "leave him alone."

But Frannie was already at Will's side. "Sometimes Sherwood gets silly," she said, almost primly. "But he's my brother, so I have to watch out for him."

"Somebody's going to bash him one of these days. Bash him hard. And it might be me."

"He gets bashed all the time," Frannie said, "'cause people think he's not quite," she halted, drew a breath, then went on, "not quite right in the head."

"*Fraaaannnnie* . . . " Sherwood was yelling.

"You'd better go back to him, in case he falls off the bridge."

Frannie gave her brother a fretful glance. "He's okay. You know, it's not so bad here," she said.

"I don't care," Will replied. "I'm going to be running away."

"Are you?"

"I just said, didn't I?"

"Where to?"

"I haven't made up my mind."

The conversation faltered here, and Will hoped Frannie would go back to her brattish brother, but she was determined to keep the exchange going, walking beside him. "Is it true what Sherwood said?" she asked, her voice softening. "About your brother?"

"Yeah. He was knocked down by a taxicab."

"That must be horrible for you," Frannie said.

"I didn't like him very much."

"Still . . . if something like that ever happened to Sherwood . . . "

They had come to a divide in the road. To the left lay the route back to the house, to the right, a less well-made track that rapidly wound out of sight behind the hedgerows. Will hesitated a moment, weighing up the options.

"I should go back," Frannie said.

"I'm not stopping you," Will replied.

Frannie didn't move. He glanced round at her and saw such hurt in her eyes he had to look away. Seeking some other point of interest, his gaze found the one visible building close to the right-hand track, and more to mellow his cruelty than out of genuine curiosity, he asked Frannie what it was.

"Everybody calls it the Courthouse," she said. "But it isn't really. It was built by this man who wanted to protect horses or something. I don't know the proper story."

"Who lives there?" Will said. As far as he could tell at this distance, it was an impressive looking structure; it almost looked like a temple in one of his history books, except that it was built of dark stone.

"Nobody lives there," Frannie said. "It's horrible inside."

"You went in?"

"Sherwood hid there once. He knows more about it than I do. You should ask him."

Will wrinkled up his nose. "Nah," he said, feeling as though he'd made his attempt at conciliation and he could now depart without guilt.

"*Fraaannnie!*" Sherwood was yelling again. He had clambered up onto the wall of the bridge and was imitating a trapeze artist as he walked along it.

"Get down off there!" Frannie hollered at him, and saying goodbye to Will over her shoulder, hurried back to the bridge to enforce her edict.

Relieved to have the girl gone, Will again considered the routes before him. If he went back to the house now he could slake his thirst and fill the growing hole in his belly. But he'd also have to endure the atmosphere of ill-humor that hung about the place. Better to go walking, he thought, find out what was around the bend and beyond the hedgerows.

He glanced back at the bridge to see that Frannie had coaxed Sherwood down off the wall and that he was now sitting on the ground again, hugging his knees, while his sister stood gazing in Will's direction. He gave her a half-hearted wave and then struck out along the unexplored road, thinking as he went that perhaps the route would be so tantalizing that he'd make good on his boast to the girl, and keep walking till Burnt Yarley was just a memory.

IV

The Courthouse was further than he'd thought. He walked and walked, and every turn in the road showed him another turn and every hedgerow he peered over another hedgerow, until it dawned on him that he'd completely miscalculated the size of the building. It was not near and small; it was far and enormous. By the time he came abreast of it, and surveyed the hedge looking for a way into the field in which it stood, fully one half an hour had passed. The day had grown more uncomfortable than ever, and there were heavy clouds looming over the fells to the northeast. Adele Bottrall's cleansing storm, at last, its billowing thunderheads casting shadows on the heights. Perhaps it would be better to leave this adventuring for another day, he thought. The sting on his neck had begun to pain him afresh and had passed its throb to the bones of his head. It was time to go home, whatever he'd boasted.

But to have come so far and not have anything to tell was surely a waste. Five more minutes he'd be through the hedge and across the field, into the mystery building. Another five and he'd have seen its dank interior, and he could be away, taking a short cut across the fields, content that his trudge had not been in vain.

So thinking he scouted for a gap in the woven hawthorn and, finding a place where the branches looked less tightly meshed, pushed through. He didn't emerge entirely unscathed, but the spectacle on the other side was worth the scratches. The grass in the meadow surrounding the Courthouse was almost up to his chest, and there was life in it everywhere. Peewits erupted from underfoot, hares he could hear but not see raced away at his approach. He instantly forgot his aching head, and strode through the hay and cow parsley like a man lost on safari, his stomach suddenly churning with excitement. Perhaps, after all, this wouldn't be such a bad place to live: away from the dirty streets and the taxicabs, in a place where he could be somebody else, somebody new.

He was just a few yards from the Courthouse now, and any doubts he'd entertained about the wisdom of venturing inside had fled. He climbed the overgrown steps, passed between the pillars (which had the girth of Donald Bottrall), and, pushing open the half-rotted door, stepped inside.

It was colder than he had expected it to be, and darker. Though there had been so little rain that the river had been reduced to a trickle, there was nevertheless a dankness everywhere, as though somehow the building was drawing moisture up from the earth below, and with it came the smell of rot and worms.

The room he'd entered was most peculiar: a kind of semicircular vestibule, with a number of alcoves carved into it that looked as though they might have been intended for statues. On the floor was an elaborate mosaic, depicting a curious collection of objects, some of which Will recognized, others which he did not. There were grapes and lemons, flowers and cloves of garlic; there was what might have been a piece of meat, except that it had maggots crawling out of it and he thought that must be his mistake, because nobody in their right mind would go to the trouble of building a magnificent place like this and then put a picture of a rotted steak on the floor. He didn't linger to puzzle over it for long. A call of distant thunder so deep it reverberated in the walls reminded him of the coming storm. He needed to be out of here in a couple of minutes if he was to have a hope of outrunning the rain. He headed on, into the belly of the building, down a wide, high-ceilinged corridor (it was almost as though the doors and passageways had been designed to let giants pass) and through another door, this less vaulted than the first, into the central chamber.

As he entered there was a clattering in the shadows ahead of him, so loud his heart jumped in his chest. He threw himself back toward the door and would have been away through it—his adventurous spirit quenched—had he not moments later heard the pitiful bleat of a sheep. He studied the chamber. It had a round skylight in the middle of its domed roof, and a beam came down to strike the filthy ground, like a single bright pillar designed to hold the whole magnificence in place. There was a wash of light on the tiers of stone seats that ran round the entire chamber, bright enough to touch the walls themselves. Here, he saw, there were carvings, depicting who knew what? Sporting events, perhaps; he saw horses in one of them, and dogs in another, straining on long leashes.

The bleating came again and, following the sound, Will set eyes on a pitiable sight. A fully grown sheep—its body pitifully thinned by malnutrition, its fleece hanging off it in filthy rags—was cowering in a niche between two tiers of seats where it had retreated upon Will's entrance.

"You're a mess," he said to the animal. Then, more softly: "It's okay . . . I'm not going to hurt you." He started to approach. The sheep regarded him balefully with its bulbous eyes, but it didn't move. "You got stuck in here, didn't you?" he said. "You big dafty. You found your way in and now you can't get out again."

The closer he got to the creature, the more pathetic its condition appeared. Its legs and head and flanks were covered in scrapes, where it had presumably attempted to push its way out. There was one particularly befouled wound along the side of its jaw where flies were busy.

Will had no intention of actually touching the animal. But if he could just scare it in the right direction, he thought, he might get it out into the light where at least it had a chance of finding its way home. The theory had merit. When he climbed up onto one of the tiers of seats, the poor creature, frightened out of its simple wits, fled its bolt-hold in an instant, its hooves clattering on the stone floor. He pursued it to the door, and overtook it. Terrified, the animal reeled around, bleating pitifully. Will put his shoulder against the door and pushed it open. The sheep had retreated to the pool of light in the center of the chamber and stood watching Will with its flanks heaving. Will glanced down the passage to the front door, which was still as he had left it, open wide. Surely the animal could see that far? The sun was still shining out there; the grass swayed in a rising wind, as pliant and seductive as this place was severe.

"Go on!" Will said. "Look! Food!"

The sheep just stared at him, bug-eyed. Will glanced back along the passage and saw that here and there the wall had crumbled and blocks of stone slipped from their place. He let the door go, found a block that he had the strength to move, and rolling it ahead of him, used it to wedge the door open. Then he went back into the chamber and scooting around behind the sheep, shoved it toward the open door. Finally its undernourished brain got the message. It was off down the passage and out through the front door to freedom.

Will was pleased with himself. It wasn't quite the adventure he'd expected to have in this bizarre place, but it had satisfied some instinct in him. "Perhaps I'll be a farmer," he said to himself. Then he headed out, into whatever was left of the day.

V

The episode with the sheep had delayed him in the Courthouse longer than he'd intended, even as he stepped outside the clouds covered the sun, and a gust of wind, strong enough to bow the grass low as it passed, brought a spatter of rain. He would not now be able to outrun a soaking, he knew, but he was determined not to go back the way he'd come. Instead he'd take a shortcut across the fields to the house. He walked to the corner of the Courthouse and tried to spot his destination, but it was out of sight. He knew its general direction, however; he would simply follow his nose.

The rain was getting heavier by the moment, but he didn't mind. The air carried the metallic tang of lightning, sweetened by the scent of wet grass; the heat was already noticeably mellowed. On the fells ahead of him, a few last spears of sunlight were shining through the big-bellied clouds and stabbing the heights.

Just as the storm was filling the valley, so it seemed his senses were filled: with the rain, the grass, the tang, the sunlight and thunder. He could not remember ever feeling as he felt now: that he and the world around him were in every particular connected. It made him want to yell with happiness, he felt so full, so found. It was as though, for the first time in his life, something in the world that was not human knew he was there.

His blessedness made him fleet. Whooping and hollering he ran through the lashing grass like a crazy, while the clouds sealed off the last of the sun and threw lightning down on the hills.

He did his best to hold to the direction he'd set himself, but the rain quickly escalated from a bracing shower to a downpour, and he could soon no longer see slopes that minutes before had been crystalline, so obscured were they by veils of water and cloud. Nor was this his only problem. The first hedgerow he encountered was too thick to be breached and too tall to be clambered over, so he was obliged to go looking for a gate. His trek along the edge of the field disoriented him and it was some time before he found a means of egress: not a gate but a stile, which he hoisted himself over, glancing back at the Courthouse only to find that it too had disappeared from sight.

He didn't panic. There were farmhouses scattered all along the valley, and if he did find himself lost then he'd just strike out for the nearest residence and get directions. Meanwhile he made an instinctive guess at his route, and plowed on first through a meadow of rape and then across a field occupied by a herd of cows, several of which had taken refuge under an enormous sycamore. He was almost tempted to join them, but he'd read once that trees were bad spots to shelter during thunderstorms so on he went, through a gate, onto a track that was turning into a little brook, and over a second stile into a muddy, deserted field. The rainfall had not slowed a jot, and by now he was soaked to the skin. It was time, he decided, to seek some help. The next track he came to he'd follow till it led him somewhere inhabited; maybe he'd persuade a sympathetic soul to drive him home.

But he walked on for another ten or fifteen minutes without encountering a track, however rudimentary, and now the ground began to slope upward, so that he was soon having to climb hard. He stopped. This was definitely not the right way. Half-blinded by the freezing downpour he turned three hundred sixty degrees looking for some clue to his whereabouts, but there were walls of gray rain enclosing him on every side, so he turned his back to the slope and retraced his steps. At least that was what he thought he'd done. Somehow he'd managed to turn himself around, without realizing he'd done so, because after fifty yards the ground again steepened beneath his feet—cascades of water surging over boulders a little way up the slope. The cold and disorientation were bad enough, but what now began to trouble him more was a subtle darkening of the sky. It was not the thunderclouds that were blotting out the light, it was dusk. In a few minutes it would be dark, far darker than it ever got on the streets of Manchester.

He was shivering violently, and his teeth had begun to chatter. His legs were aching, and his rain-pummeled face was numb. He tried yelling for help, but rapidly gave up in the attempt. Between the din of the storm and the frailty of his voice, he knew after a few yells it was a lost cause. He had to preserve his energies, such as they were. Wait until the storm cleared, when he could work out where he was. It wouldn't be difficult, once the lights of the village started to reappear, as they surely would, sooner or later.

And then, a shout, somewhere in the storm, and something broke cover, racing in front of him—

"*Catch it!*" he heard a raw voice say, and instinctively threw himself down to catch hold of whatever was escaping. His quarry was even more exhausted and disoriented than he, apparently, because his hands caught hold of something lean and furry, which squealed and struggled in his grip.

"Hold it, m'lad! Hold it!"

The speaker now appeared from higher up the slope. It was a woman, dressed entirely in black, carrying a flickering lamp, which burned with a fat yellow-white flame. By its light he saw a face that was more beautiful than any he had seen in his life, its pale perfection framed by a mass of dark red hair.

"You *are* a treasure," she said to Will, setting down the lamp. Her accent was not local, but tinged with a little cockney. "You just hold that damn hare a minute longer, while I get my bag."

She set down the lamp, rummaged in the folds of her sleek coat, and pulled out a small sack. Then she approached Will and with lightning speed clawed the squealing hare from his arms. It was in the bag and the bag sealed up in moments. "You're as good as gold, you are," she said. "We would have gone hungry, Mr. Steep and me, if you hadn't been so quick." She set down the bag. "Oh my Lord, look at the state of you," she said, bending to examine Will more closely. "What's your name?"

"William."

"I had a William once," the woman remarked. "It's a lovely name." Her face was close to Will's, and there was a welcome heat in her breath. "In fact I think I had two. Sweet children, both of 'em." She reached out and touched Will's cheek. "Oh but you are *cold.*"

"I got lost."

"That's terrible. Terrible," she said, stroking his face. "How could any self-respecting mother let you stray out of sight? She should be ashamed, she should. *Ashamed.*" Will would have concurred, but the warmth seeping from the woman's fingers into his face was curiously soporific.

"*Rosa?*" somebody said.

"Yes?" the woman replied, her voice suddenly flirty. "I'm down here, Jacob."

"Who've you found now?"

"I was just thanking this lad," Rosa said, removing her hand from Will's face. He was suddenly freezing again. "He caught us our dinner."

"Did he indeed?" said Jacob. "Why don't you step aside, Mrs. McGee, and give me sight of the boy?"

"Sight you want, sight you'll have," Rosa replied, and getting to her feet she picked up the sack and moved a short way down the slope.

In the two or three minutes since Will had caught hold of the hare, the sky had darkened considerably, and when Will looked in the direction of Jacob Steep it was hard to see the man clearly. He was tall, that much was clear, and was wearing a long coat with shiny buttons. His face was bearded, and his hair longer than Mrs. McGee's. But his features were a blur to Will's weary eyes.

"You should be at home," he said. Will shuddered, but this time the cause was not the cold but the warmth of Steep's voice. "A boy like you, out here alone, could come to some harm or other."

"He's lost," Mrs. McGee chimed in.

"On a night like this, we're all a little lost," Mr. Steep said. "There's no blame there."

"Maybe he should come home with us," Rosa suggested. "You could light one of your fires for him."

"Hush yourself," Jacob snapped. "I will not have talk of fires when this boy is so bitter cold. Where are your wits?"

"As you like," the woman replied. "It's no matter to me either way. But you should have seen him take the hare. He was on it like a tiger, he was."

"I was lucky," Will said, "that's all."

Mr. Steep drew a deep breath, and to Will's great delight descended the slope a yard or two more. "Can you get up?" he asked Will.

"Of course I can," Will replied, and did so.

Though Mr. Steep had halved the distance between them, the darkness had deepened a little further, and his features were just as hard to fathom. "I wonder, looking at you, if we weren't meant to meet on this hill," he said softly. "I wonder if that's the luck of this night, for us all." Will was still trying hard to get a better sense of what Steep looked like, to put a face to the voice that moved him so deeply, but his eyes weren't equal to the challenge. "The hare, Mrs. McGee."

"What about it?"

"We should set it free."

"After the chase it led me?" Rosa replied. "You're out of your mind."

"We owe it that much, for leading us to Will."

"I'll thank it as I *skin* it, Jacob, and that's my final word on the thing. My God, you're impractical. Throwing away good food. I'll not have it." Before Steep could protest further she snatched up the sack and was away down the slope.

Only now, watching her descend, did Will realize that the worst of the storm had blown over. The rainfall had mellowed to a drizzle, the murk was melting away; he could even see lights glimmering in the valley. He was relieved, certainly, but not as much as he thought he'd be. There was comfort in the prospect of returning home, but that meant leaving the company of the dark man at his back, who even now lay a heavy, leather-gloved hand upon his shoulder.

"Can you see your house from here?" he asked Will.

"No . . . not yet."

"But it will come clear, by and by?"

"Yes," Will said, only now getting a sense of how the land lay. He had managed somehow to come halfway around the valley during his blind trek and was looking down on the village from a wholly unexpected angle. There was a dirt road not more than thirty yards down the ridge from where he stood; it would lead him, he suspected, back to the route he'd followed to get to the Courthouse. A left at that intersection would bring him back into Burnt Yarley, and then it was just a weary trudge home.

"You should go, my boy," Jacob said. "Doubtless a fellow as fine as you has loving guardians." The gloved hand squeezed his shoulder. "I envy you that, having no parents that I can remember."

"I'm . . . sorry," Will said, hesitating because he was by no means sure a man as fine as Jacob Steep was ever in need of sympathy. He received it, however, in good part.

"Thank you, Will. It's important that a man be compassionate. It's a quality that our sex so often neglects, I think." Will heard the soft cadence of Steep's breathing and tried to fall in rhythm with it. "You should go," Jacob said. "Your parents will be concerned for you."

"No they won't," Will replied.

"Surely—"

"*They won't.* They don't care."

"I can't believe that."

"It's true."

"Then you must be a loving son in spite of them," Steep said. "Be grateful that you have their faces in your mind's eye. And their voices to answer when you call. Better that than emptiness, believe me. Better than silence."

He lifted his hand from Will's shoulder and now touched the middle of his back, gently pushing him away. "Go on," he said softly. "You'll be dead of cold if you don't go soon. Then how would we get to meet again?"

Will's spirits rose at this. "We might do that?"

"Oh certainly, if you're hardy enough to come and find me. But Will, understand me, I'm not looking for a dog to perch on my lap. I need a *wolf.*"

"I could be a wolf," Will said. He wanted to look back over his shoulder at Steep, but that was not, he thought, the most appropriate thing for an aspirant wolf to do.

"Then as I say: Come find me," Steep said. "I won't be far away." And with that he gave Will a final nudge, setting him off on his way down the slope.

Will did not look back until he reached the track, and when he did he saw nothing. At least nothing alive. The hill he saw, black against the clearing sky. And the stars, appearing between the clouds. But their splendor was nothing compared to the face of Jacob Steep; a face he had not yet really seen, but which his mind had already conjured a hundred different ways by the time he reached home, each finer than the one before. Steep the nobleman, fine-boned and fancy; Steep the soldier, scarred from a dozen wars; Steep the magician, his gaze bearing power: Perhaps he was all of these. Perhaps none. Will didn't care. What mattered was to be beside him again, soon, and know him better.

Meanwhile, there was a warm light from the window of his home and a fire in the hearth. Even a wolf might seek the comfort of the hearth now and then, Will reasoned and, knocking on the front door, was let back in.

VI

i

He did not go up the hill the following day to look for Jacob, nor indeed the day following that. He came home to such a firestorm of accusations—his mother in wracking tears, certain he was dead; his father, white with fury, just as certain he wasn't—that he dared not step over the threshold. Hugo wasn't a violent man. He prided himself on his reasonableness. But he made an exception in this case, and beat his son so hard—with a book, of all things—that he reduced them both to tears: Will's of pain, his father's of anguish that he'd lost so much control.

He wasn't interested in Will's explanations. He simply told his son that while he, Hugo, didn't care if Will went wandering for the rest of his damn life, Eleanor did, and hadn't she suffered enough for one lifetime?

So Will stayed at home and nursed his bruises and his rage. After forty-eight hours his mother tried to make some kind of peace, telling him how frightened she'd been that some harm had befallen him.

"Why?" he said to her sullenly.

"Whatever do you mean?"

"I mean why should you worry if something happens to me? You never cared before—"

"Oh, *William*, . . . " she said softly. There was only a trace of accusation in her voice. It was mostly sorrow.

"You don't," he said flatly. "You know you don't. All you ever think about is him." He didn't need to name the missing member of this equation. "I'm not important to you. You said so." This was not strictly the case. She'd never used those precise words. But the lie sounded true enough.

"I'm sure I didn't mean it," she said. "It's just been so hard for me since Nathaniel died—" Her fingers went to his face as she spoke, and gently stroked his cheek. "He was so . . . so. . . "

He was barely listening to her. He was thinking of Rosa McGee, and how she had touched his face and spoken to him softly. Only she'd not been talking about how fine some other boy was while she did so. She'd been telling him what a treasure he was, how nimble, how useful. This woman who had barely known his name had found in him qualities his own mother could not see. It made him sad and angry at the same time.

"Why do you keep talking about him?" Will said. "He's *dead.*"

Eleanor's fingers fell from Will's face, and she looked at him with tear-filled eyes. "No," she said, "he'll never be dead. Not to me. I don't expect you to understand. How could you? But your brother was very special to me. Very precious. So he'll never be dead as far as I'm concerned."

Something happened in Will at that moment. A scrap of hope that had stayed green in the months since the accident withered and went to dust. He didn't say anything. He just got up and left her to her tears.

ii

After two days of homebound penance he went to school. It was a smaller place than St. Margaret's, which he liked, its buildings older, its playground lined with trees instead of railings. He kept to himself for the first week, barely speaking to anyone. At the beginning of the second week, however, minding his own business at lunchtime, a familiar face appeared in front of him. It was Frannie.

"Here you are," she said, as though she'd been looking for him.

"Hello," he said, glancing around to see if Sherwood the Brat was also in evidence. He wasn't.

"I thought you'd be gone on your trip by now."

"I will," he said. "I'll go."

"I know," Frannie said, quite sincerely. "After we met I kept thinking maybe I'd go too. Not with you," she hastened to add, "but one day I'd just leave."

"Go as far away as possible," Will said.

"As far away as possible," Frannie replied, her echoing of his words a kind of pact. "There's not much worth seeing around here," she went on, "unless you go into . . . you know—"

"You can talk about Manchester," Will said. "Just 'cause my brother was killed there . . . it's no big deal to me. I mean, he wasn't really my brother." Will felt a delicious lie being born. "I'm adopted, you see."

"You *are?*"

"Nobody knows who my real mom and dad are."

"Oh wow. Is this a secret?" Will nodded. "So I can't even tell Sherwood."

"Better not," Will replied, with a fine show of seriousness. "He might spread it around."

The bell was ringing, calling them back to their classes. The fierce Miss Hartley, a big-bosomed woman whose merest whisper intimidated her charges, was eyeing Will and Frannie.

"Frances Cunningham!" she boomed, "will you get a move on?" Frannie pulled a face and ran, leaving Miss Hartley to focus her attention on Will. "You are—?"

"William Rabjohns."

"Oh yes," she said darkly, as though she'd heard news of him and it wasn't good.

He stood his ground, feeling quite calm. This was strange for him. At St. Margaret's he had been intimidated by several of the staff, feeling remotely that they were part of his father's clan. But this woman seemed to him absurd, with her sickly sweet perfume and her fat neck. There was nothing to be afraid of here.

Perhaps she saw how unmoved he was, because she stared at him with a well-practiced curl in her lip.

"What are you smiling at?" she said.

He wasn't aware that he was, until she remarked upon it. He felt his stomach churn with a strange exhilaration; then he said, "You."

"What?"

He made the smile a grin. "You," he said again. "I'm smiling at you."

She frowned at him. He kept grinning, thinking as he did so that he was baring his teeth to her, like a wolf.

"Where are you . . . supposed to be?" she said to him.

"In the gym," he replied. He kept looking straight at her; kept grinning. And at last it was she who looked away.

"You'd better . . . get along then, hadn't you?" she said to him.

"If we've finished talking," he said, hoping to goad her into further response.

But no. "We've finished," she said.

He was reluctant to take his eyes off her. If he kept staring, he thought, he could surely bore a hole in her, the way a magnifying glass held to the sunlight burned a hole in a piece of paper.

"I won't have insolence from anyone," she said. "Least of all a new boy. Now get to your class."

He had little choice. Off he went. But as he walked past her he said: "Thank you, Miss Hartley," in a soft voice, and he was sure he saw her shudder.

VII

Something was happening to him. There were little signs of it every day. He would look up at the sky and feel a strange surge of exhilaration, as though some part of him were taking flight, rising up out of his own head. He would wake long after midnight and even though it was bitterly cold, open the window and listen to the world going on in darkness, imagining how it was on the heights. Twice he ventured out in the middle of the night, up the slope behind the house, hoping he might meet Jacob up there somewhere, star watching; or Mrs. McGee, chasing hares. But he saw no sign of them, and though he listened intently to every gossipy conversation when he was in the village—picking up pork chops for Adele Bottrall to cook with apples for Papa or a sheaf of magazines for his mother to flick through—he never heard anybody mention Jacob or Rosa. They lived in some secret place, he concluded, where they could not be troubled by the workaday world. Other than himself, he doubted anybody in the valley even knew they existed.

He didn't pine for them. He would find them again, or they him, when the time was right. He was certain of that. Meanwhile, the strange epiphanies continued. Everywhere around him, the world was making miraculous signs for him to read: in the curlicues of frost on his window when he rose; in the patterns that the sheep made, straggling the hill; in the din of the river, swelled to its full measure by a fall that brought more than its share of rain.

At last, he had to share these mysteries with somebody. He chose Frannie, not because he was certain she'd understand, but because she was the only one he trusted enough.

They were sitting in the living room of the Cunningham house, which was adjacent to the junkyard owned by Frannie's father. The house was small, but cozy, as ordered and neat as the yard outside was chaotic: a framed needlepoint prayer above the mantlepiece, blessing the hearth and all who gathered there, a teak china cabinet with an heirloom elegant tea service but not boastfully displayed, a plain brass clock on the table, and beside it a cut-glass bowl heaped with pears and oranges. Here, in this womb of certainties, Will told Frannie of the feelings that had risen in him of late, and how they had begun the day the two of them met. He didn't mention Jacob and Rosa at first—they were the secret he was most loath to share, and he was by no means certain he would do so—but he did talk about venturing into the Courthouse.

"Oh, I asked my mom about that," Frannie said. "And she told me the story."

"What is it?" Will said.

"There was this man called Bartholomeus," she said. "He lived in the valley, when there were still lead mines everywhere."

"I didn't know there were mines."

"Well there were. And he made a lot of money from them. But he wasn't quite right in the head, that's what mom said, because he had this idea that people didn't treat animals properly, and the only way to stop people being cruel was to have a court, which would only be for animals."

"Who was the judge?"

"He was. And the jury probably." She shrugged. "I don't know the whole story, just those bits—"

"So he built the Courthouse."

"He built it, but he didn't finish it."

"Did he run out of money?"

"My mom says he was probably put in a loony bin, because of what he was doing. I mean, nobody wanted him bringing animals into his Courthouse and making laws about how people had to treat them better."

"That was what he was doing?" Will said, with a little smile.

"Something like that. I don't know if anybody's really sure. He's been dead for a hundred and fifty years."

"It's a sad story," said Will, thinking of the strange magnificence of Bartholomeus's folly.

"He was better put away. Safer for everybody."

"Safer?"

"I mean if he was going to try and accuse people of doing things to animals. We all do things to animals. It's natural."

She sounded like her mother when she spoke like this. Genial enough, but unmovable. This was her stated opinion and nothing would sway her from it. Listening to her, his enthusiasm for sharing what he'd seen began to wane. Perhaps after all she was not the person to understand his feelings. Perhaps she'd think he was like Mr. Bartholomeus, and better put away.

But now, her story of the Courthouse finished, she said, "What were you telling me about?"

"I wasn't," Will replied.

"No, you were in the middle of saying something—"

"Well it probably wasn't important," Will said, "or I'd remember what it was." He got up from his seat. "I'd better be off," he said.

Frannie looked more than a little puzzled, but he pretended not to notice the expression on her face.

"I'll see you tomorrow," he said.

"Sometimes you're really odd," she said to him. "Did you know that?"

"No."

"You know you are," she said, with a faint tone of accusation. "And I think you like it."

Will couldn't keep a smile from his lips. "Maybe I do," he said.

At which juncture, the door was flung open and Sherwood marched in. He had feathers woven into his hair.

"You know what I am?"

"A chicken," Will said.

"No, I'm *not* a *chicken*," Sherwood said, deeply offended.

"That's what you look like."

"I'm Geronimo."

"Geronimo the chicken." Will laughed.

"I hate you," said Sherwood, "and so does everybody at school."

"Sherwood, be quiet," Frannie said.

"They do," Sherwood went on. "They all think you're daft and they talk behind your back and they call you William Dafty." Now it was Sherwood who laughed. "Dafty William! William Dafty!" Frannie kept trying to hush him, but it was a lost cause. He was going to crow till he was done.

"I don't care!" Will yelled above the clamor. "You're a cretin, and I don't care!"

So saying, he picked up his coat and pushing past Sherwood— who had begun a little dance in rhythm with his chant—headed for the door. Frannie was still trying to shush her brother, but in vain. He was in a self-perpetuating frenzy, yelling and jumping.

In truth, Will was glad of the interruption. It gave him the perfect excuse to make his exit, which he did in double-quick time, before Frannie had a chance to silence her brother. He needn't have worried. When he was out of the house, past the junkyard, and at the end of the Samson Road he could still hear Sherwood's rantings emerging from the house.

VIII

i

We moved out here because you wanted to move, Eleanor. Please remember that. We came here because of you."

"I know, Hugo."

"So what are you saying? That we should move again?" Will couldn't hear his mother's despair. Her quiet words were buried in sobs. But he heard his father's response. "Lord, Eleanor, you've got to stop crying. We can't have an intelligent conversation if you just start crying whenever we talk about Manchester. If you don't want to go back there, that's fine by me, but I need some answers from you. We can't go on like this, with you taking so many pills you can't keep count. It's not a life, Eleanor." Did she say, *I know?* Will thought she did, though it was hard to hear her through the door. "I want what's best for you. What's best for us all."

Now Will did hear her. "I can't stay here," she said.

"Well, once and for all: Do you want to go back to Manchester?"

Her reply was simply repetition. "I know I can't stay here."

"Fine," Hugo replied. "We'll move back. Nevermind that we sold the house. Nevermind that we've spent thousands of pounds moving. We'll just go back." His voice was rising in volume; so was the sound of Eleanor's sobs. Will had heard enough. He retreated from the door and scurried upstairs, disappearing from sight just as the living room door opened and his father stormed out.

ii

The conversation threw Will into a state of panic. They couldn't leave, not now. Not when for the first time in his life he felt things coming clear. If he went back to Manchester it would be like a prison sentence. He'd wither away and die.

What was the alternative? There was only one. He'd run away, as he'd boasted he would to Frannie, the first day they'd met. He'd plan it carefully, so that nothing was left to chance: be sure he had money and clothes and, of course, a destination. Of these three the third was the most problematical. Money he could steal (he knew where his mother kept her spare cash) and clothes he could pack, but where was he to go?

He consulted the map of the world on his bedroom wall, matching to those pastel-colored shapes impressions he'd gleaned from television or magazines. Scandinavia? Too cold and dark. Italy? Maybe. But he spoke no Italian and he wasn't a quick learner. French he knew a little, and he had French blood in him, but France wasn't far enough. If he was going to go traveling, then he wanted it to be more than a ferry trip away. America, perhaps? Ah, now there was a thought. He ran his finger over the country from state to state, luxuriating in the names: Mississippi, Wyoming, New Mexico, California. His mood lifted at the prospect. All he needed was some advice about how to get out of the country, and he knew exactly where to get that: from Jacob Steep.

He went out looking for Steep and Rosa McGee the very next day. It was by now the middle of November, and the hours of daylight were short, but he made the most of them, skipping school for three consecutive days to climb the fells and look for some sign of the pair's presence. They were chilly journeys: though there was not yet snow on the hills the frost was so thick it dusted the slopes like a flurry, and the sun never emerged long enough to melt it.

The sheep had already descended to the lower pastures to graze, but he was not entirely alone on the heights. Hares and foxes, even the occasional deer, had left their tracks in the frozen grass. But this was the only sign of life he encountered. Of Jacob and Rosa he saw not so much as a boot print.

Then, on the evening of the third day, Frannie came to the house.

"You don't look like you've got flu," she said to Will. (He'd forged a note to that effect, explaining his absence.)

"Is that why you came?" he said. "To check up on me?"

"Don't be daft," she said. "I came 'cause I've got something to tell you. Something strange."

"What?"

"Remember we talked about the Courthouse?"

"Of course."

"Well, I went to look at it. And you know what?"

"What?"

"There's somebody living there."

"In the Courthouse?"

She nodded. By the look on her face it was apparent whatever she'd seen had unnerved her.

"Did you go in?" he asked her.

She shook her head. "I just saw this woman at the door."

"What did she look like?" Will asked, scarcely daring to hope.

"She was dressed in black—"

It's her, he thought. *It's Mrs. McGee*. And wherever Rosa was, could Jacob be far away?

Frannie had caught the look of excitement on his face. "What is it?" she said.

"It's *who*," he said, "not what."

"Who then? Is it somebody you know?"

"A little," he replied. "Her name's Rosa."

"I've never seen her before," Frannie said. "And I've lived here all my life."

"They keep themselves to themselves," Will replied.

"There's somebody else?"

He was so covetous of the knowledge, he almost didn't tell her. But then she'd brought him this wonderful news, hadn't she? He owed her something by way of recompense. "There's two of them," Will said. "The woman's name is Rosa McGee. The man's called Jacob Steep."

"I've never heard of either of them. Are they Gypsies or homeless people?"

"If they're homeless it's because they want to be," Will said.

"But it must be so cold in that place. You said it was bare inside."

"It is."

"So they're just hiding in an empty place like that?" She shook her head. "Weird," she said. "How do you know them, anyhow?"

"I met them while I was out walking," he replied, which was close enough to the truth. "Thanks for telling me. I'd better . . . I've got a whole lot of things to do."

"You're going to see them, aren't you?" Frannie said. "I want to come with you."

"No!"

"Why not?"

"Because they're not your friends."

"They're not yours either," Frannie said. "They're just people you met once. That's what you said."

"I don't want you there," Will said.

Frannie's mouth got tight. "You know, you don't have to be so horrible about it," she said to Will. He said nothing. She stared hard at him, as if willing him to change his mind. Still he said nothing, did nothing. After a few moments she gave up and, without another word, marched to the front door.

"Are you leaving already?" Adele said.

Frannie had the door open. Her bicycle was propped up against the gate. Without even answering Adele, she got on her bike and was away.

"Was she upset about something?" Adele wanted to know.

"Nothing important," Will replied.

It was almost dark, and cold. He knew from bitter experience to go out prepared for the worst, but it was hard to think coherently about boots and gloves and a sweater when the sound of his heart was so loud in his head, and all he could think was: I've found them, I've found them.

His father was not yet back from Manchester, and his mother was in Halifax today, seeing her doctor, so the only person he had to alert to his departure was Adele. She was cooking and didn't bother to ask him where he was going. Only as he slammed the door did she yell that he should be back by seven. He didn't bother to reply, just set off down the darkening road toward the Courthouse, certain Jacob already knew he was coming.

IX

The soul who had taken the name of Jacob Steep stood on the threshold of the Courthouse and clung to the frame of the door. Dusk was always a time of weakness for both himself and Mrs.

McGee. This dusk was no exception. His innards convulsed, his limbs trembled, his temples throbbed. The very sight of the dimming sky, though it was tonight most picturesque, made an infant of him.

It was the same story at dawn. They were both overtaken at these hours with such fatigue it was all they could do to stand upright. Indeed tonight it had proved impossible for Rosa. She had retreated into the Courthouse and was lying down, moaning, calling for him once in a while. He did not go to her. He stayed at the door and waited for a sign.

That was the paradox of this hour: When he was most unmanned was when he was most likely to hear a call to duty, his assassin's heart roused, his assassin's blood surging. And tonight, he was eager for news. They had languished here long enough. It was time to move on. But first he needed a destination, a dispatch, and that meant facing the sickening spectacle of twilight.

He did not know why this hour was so distressing to their systems, but it was one more proof—if he needed it—that they were not of ordinary stock. In the depths of the night, when the human world was asleep and dreaming its narrow dreams, he was bright and blithe as a child, his body tireless. He could do his worst at that hour, quicker than the quickest executioner with his knife, or better still with his hands, taking lives away. And by day, in countries where the noon heat was crucifying, he was just as tireless. Death's perfect agent, sudden and swift. Day, in truth, suited him better than night, because by day he had the proper light by which to make his drawings, and both as a maker of pictures and a maker of corpses he liked to pay close attention to the details. The sweep of a feather, the slope of a snout, the timbre of a sob, the tang of a puke. It was all worthy of his study.

But whether light or dark had hold of the world, he had the energy of a man a tenth his age. It was only in the gray time that the weakness consumed him, and he found himself clinging to something solid to keep himself standing. He hated the sensation, but he refused to moan. Such complaints were for women and children, not for soldiers. That was not to say he hadn't heard soldiers moan in his time; he had. He'd lived long enough to have known many wars, large and small, and though he had never sought out a battlefield, his work had by chance brought him to a place of combat more than once. He had seen how men responded to their agonies when they were beset. How they wept, how they called for mercy and their mothers.

Jacob had no interest in mercy; neither in its dispensing nor its receiving. He was set against the sentimental world as any pure force must be, entertaining neither kindness nor cruelty in his dealings. He scorned the comfort of prayer and the distractions of fancy; he mocked grief, he mocked hope. He mocked despair also. The only quality he revered was patience, bought with the knowledge that all things pass. The sun would drop out of sight soon enough, and the weakness in his limbs would melt into strength. All he had to do was wait.

From inside, the sound of motion. And then, Rosa's sighing voice, "I've been remembering," she said.

"You have not," he told her. Sometimes the pains of this hour made her delirious.

"I have. I swear," she said. "An island comes to mind. Do you remember an island? With wide, white shores? No trees. I've looked for trees and there are none. *Oh*, . . . " Her words became groans again, and the groans turned into sobs. "Oh, I would die now, gladly."

"No, you wouldn't."

"Come and comfort me."

"I have no wish—"

"You must, Jacob. Oh . . . oh, Lord in heaven . . . why do we suffer so?"

Much as he wanted to stay away, her sobs were too poignant to be ignored. He turned his back on the dying day and strode down the corridor to the Courtroom itself. Mrs. McGee was lying on the ground in the midst of her veils. She had lit a host of candles around her, as though their light might ameliorate the cruelty of the hour.

"Lie with me," she said, looking up at him.

"It will do us no good."

"We may get a child."

"And that will do us no good, either," he replied, "as well you know."

"Then lie with me for the comfort of it," she said, her gaze fond. "It is such agony to be separated from you, Jacob."

"I'm here," he said, curbing his former harshness.

"Not close enough," she said with a tiny smile.

He walked toward her. Stood at her feet.

"Still . . . not close enough," she said to him. "I feel so weak, Jacob."

"It will pass. You know it will."

"At times like this I know *nothing*," she said, "except how much I need you." She reached down and plucked at her skirt, watching his face all the while. "With me," she murmured. "*In me*."

He made no reply. "Are you too weak, Jacob?" she said, still pulling up her skirt. "Is the mystery too much for you?"

"It's no mystery," he replied. "Not after all these years."

Now she smiled, and tugged the skirt to the middle of her thighs. She had fine legs, solid, meaty legs, her skin pearly in the candlelight. Sighing, she slipped her hand beneath her dress and fingered herself, her hips rising to meet her touch.

"It's deep, love," she said. "And dark. And all wet for you." She pulled her skirt up to her waist. "Look," she said. She had spread herself, to give him a look at her. "Don't tell me that isn't a pretty thing. A perfect little cunny, that." Her gaze went from his face to his groin. "And you like the look of it, and don't you pretend you don't."

She was right, of course. As soon as she'd started to raise her skirt his dunder-headed member had started to swell, demanding its due. As if his limbs weren't weak enough, without having to lose blood to its ambition.

"I'm tight, Mr. Steep."

"I'm sure you are."

"Like a virgin on her wedding night I am. Look, I can barely fit my littlest finger in there. You'll have to do me some violence, I suspect."

She knew what effect this kind of talk had upon him. A little shudder of anticipation passed through him, and he proceeded to take off his coat.

"Unbutton yourself," Mrs. McGee said, her voice bruised. "Let me see what you have there."

He cast his coat away and fumbled with the buttons of his mud-spattered pants. She watched him, smiling, as he brought his member out.

"Oh, now look at that," she said, not unappreciatively. "I think it wants a dip in my cunny."

"It wants more than a dip."

"Does it indeed?"

He knelt between her legs, and, reaching out, removed her hand from her sex, to give himself better sight of it. Then he stared.

"What are you thinking?" she said.

He fingered her for a moment, then ran his moistened digit down to her ass. "I'm thinking," he said, "that I'd rather have *this* today."

"Oh would you?"

He pressed his finger in a little way. She squirmed. "Let me put it here," he said. "Just the head."

"There are no children to be had that way," she said.

"I don't care," he replied. "It's what I want."

"Well, I don't," she replied.

He smiled at her. "Rosa," he said softly, "you could not deny me."

He slipped his hands beneath her knees and hoisted them up. "We should give up all hope of children," he said, staring at the dark bud between her buttocks. "They have always come to nothing." She made no reply. "Are you listening, love?" He glanced up at her face. She wore a sorrowful expression.

"No more children?" she said.

He spat in his hand and slickened his prick. Spat again, more copiously, and slickened her ass.

"No more children," he said, drawing her closer to him. "It's a waste of your affections, smothering love on a thing that hasn't even got the wit to love you back."

This was the truth of the matter: that though they had together made children numbering in the many dozens, he had for her sake taken them from her in the moment of their delivery and put them out of their misery, if the cretins ever knew misery. He would dutifully come back when he'd disassembled them and disposed of the pieces, always with the same grim news. That though they were fine to look at, their skulls contained only bloody fluid. Not even a rough sketch of a brain, nothing.

He pushed his prick into her. "It's better this way," he said.

She let out a little sob. He couldn't tell whether it was out of sorrow or pleasure, and at that moment didn't really care. He pressed against the warmth of her muscle, his prick utterly enveloped. Oh, it was good.

"No . . . children . . . then," Mrs. McGee gasped.

"No children."

"Not ever?"

"Not ever."

She reached up and took hold of his shirt, pulling him down toward her.

"Kiss," she said.

"Be careful what you ask for—"

"*Kiss*," she said again, raising her face toward his.

He didn't deny her. He pressed his lips against hers, and let her tongue, which was nimble, dart between his aching teeth. His mouth was always drier than hers. His parched gums and throat drank deep and, murmuring his gratitude against her lips, he pressed hard into her, their hold on one another suddenly frantic. Her hands went to his throat, then to his face, then to his backside, pushing him deeper, while his fingers pulled at her buttons to gain access to her breasts.

"Who are you?" she said to him.

"Anyone," he gasped.

"Who?"

"Pieter, Martin, Laurent, Paolo—"

"Laurent. I liked Laurent."

"He's here."

"Who else?"

"I forget all the names," Jacob confessed.

Rosa brought her hands back up to his face and caught tight hold of it. "Remember for me," she said to him.

"There was a carpenter called Bernard—"

"Oh yes. He was very rough with me."

"And Darlington—"

"The draper. Very tender." She laughed. "Didn't one of them wrap me up in silk?"

"Did he?"

"And poured cream in my lap. You could be him. Whoever he was."

"We have no cream."

"And no silk. Think of something else."

"I could be Jacob," he said.

"You *could*, I suppose," she said, "but it's not as much fun. Think of someone else."

"There was Josiah. And Michael. And Stewart. And Roberto—" She moved her body to the rhythm of his litany. So many men, whose names and professions he'd borrowed to excite her, wrapping himself in their reputations for an hour or a day, seldom longer. "I used to like this game," he said.

"But not any more?"

"If we knew what we were—"

"Hush now."

"Maybe it wouldn't hurt so much."

"It doesn't matter," she said. "Not as long as we're together. As long as you're inside me."

They were knitted now, so tightly wound around each other, limbs and kisses intertwined, they would never be separated.

She started to sob again, the breath pushed out of her with every thrust. Names were still coming to her lips, but they were fragments only, pieces of pieces—

"Sil . . . Be . . . Han . . . "

She was lost to sensation, lost to his prick, to his lips. For his part, he had given up words entirely. Just his breath, expelled into her mouth as though he were resurrecting her. His eyes were open, but he no longer saw her face, nor the candles that shook around them. There were instead vague forms, particles of light and dark, pulsing before him, dark above, light below.

The sight brought a moan from him. "What is it?" Rosa said.

"I . . . don't . . . know," he replied. It pained him to have this sight before him and not understand what he was seeing, like a fragment of music to which he could put no name, though the notes went round and round his head. But for all the anguish it caused him, he would not have had it taken away. There was something in the sight that quickened a secret place, a place he never spoke of, not even to Rosa. It was too tender, that place, too frail.

"Jacob?"

"Yes?"

He looked down at her, and the phantom evaporated.

"Are we done so soon?"

Her hand went between her legs and took hold of his prick. Half its length was still inside her, but it was rapidly softening. He tried to push it back in, but it simply concertinaed against the tightness of her ass, and after a couple of dispiriting attempts he withdrew. She stared at him rancorously.

"Is that it?" she said.

He put his prick away and got to his feet. "For now," he said.

"Oh am I to be fucked in *installments* then?" she said, pulling her skirts down over her pudenda and sitting up. "I give you my ass against my better judgment and you don't even have the decency to finish."

"I was distracted," he said, picking up his coat and putting it on.

"By *what?*"

"I don't know exactly," Jacob snapped. "Lord, woman, it was just a fuck. There'll be others."

"I don't think so," she replied sniffily.

"Oh?"

"I think it's high time we let one another alone. If we're not out to make children, then what's the use of it?"

He stared hard at her. "You mean this?"

"*Yes, I do.* Most certainly. I mean it."

"You realize what you're saying?"

"Indeed I do."

"You'll regret it."

"I don't think so."

"You'll be weeping for want of a fuck."

"You think I'm that desperate for your ministrations?" she said. "Lord, how you deceive yourself. I play along with you, Jacob. I pretend to be aroused, but I have no desire for you."

"That's not so," he said.

She heard the hurt in his voice and was astonished. It was rare and, like all rarities, valuable. Pretending not to notice, she went to her battered leather satchel and pulled out her mirror and, squatting beside the candles for better light, studied her reflection. "It *is* so," she said, after a little time. "Whatever was between us is dying, Jacob. If I loved you once, I forgot how. And frankly I don't much care to be reminded."

"Very well," he said. She caught his image in the glass, saw the look of distress that crossed his face. Rarer than rare, that look.

"As you say," she murmured.

"I think—"

"Yes?"

"I . . . I would like to be alone for a while."

"Here?"

"If you don't mind."

He flicked his fingers together and a feather of flame leaped from them, extinguishing itself above his head. She did not care to watch him exercise this peculiar gift of his. She had her own skills, picked up, as Steep's had been picked up, like jokes or rashes, somewhere along the way. Let him have the room to brood, she thought.

"Will you be hungry later?" she asked him, sounding (much to her perverse delight) like a parody of a wife.

"I doubt it."

"I have a meat pie, if you want something."

"Yes?" he said.

"We can still be civil, can't we?" she said.

He let another flame go from his fingertips. "I don't know," he said. "Maybe."

With that, she left him to his musings.

X

Halfway along the track that led from the crossroads to the Courthouse, Will heard the squeaking of ill-oiled wheels behind him. He glanced over his shoulder to see not one but two bicycle headlights a little distance behind him. Breathing an invective little curse, he stood and waited until Frannie and Sherwood caught up with him.

"Go home," were his first words to them.

"No," said Frannie breathlessly. "We decided to come with you."

"I don't want you to come," Will said.

"It's a free country," Sherwood replied. "We can go wherever we want. Can't we, Frannie?"

"Shut up," Frannie said. Then to Will, "I only wanted to make sure you were okay."

"So why'd you bring him?" Will said.

"Because . . . he asked me," Frannie said. "He won't be a bother."

Will shook his head. "I don't want you coming inside," he said.

"It's a free—" Sherwood began again, but Frannie shushed him.

"All right, we won't," she said. "We'll just wait."

Knowing this was the best deal he was going to be able to make, Will headed into the Courthouse, with Frannie and Sherwood trailing behind. He made no further acknowledgment of their presence, until he got to the hedgerow adjacent to the Courthouse. Only then did he turn and tell them in a whisper that if they made a sound they'd spoil everything and he would never ever speak to them again. With the warning given, he dug through the hawthorn and started up the gently sloping meadow toward the building. It loomed larger by night than it had by day, like a vast mausoleum, but he could see a light flickering within; there was nothing but exhilaration in his heart as he made his way down the passage toward it.

Jacob was sitting in the judge's chair, with a small fire burning on the table in front of him. He looked up when he heard the door creak, and by the flames' light Will had sight of the face he had conjured so many ways. In every detail, he had fallen short of its power.

He had not made a brow wide or clear enough, nor eyes deep enough, nor imagined that Steep's hair, which he had seen in silhouette falling in curly abundance, would be cropped back to a shadow on the top of his skull. He had not imagined the gloss of his beard and mustache, or the delicacy of his lips, which he licked, and licked again, before saying, "Welcome, Will. You come at a strange time."

"Does that mean you want me to go?"

"No. Far from it." He added a few pieces of tinder to the fire before him. It crackled and spat. "It is, I know, the custom to paint a smile over sorrow; to pretend there is joy in you when there is not. But I hate wiles and pretences. The truth is I'm melancholy tonight."

"What's . . . melancholy?" Will said.

"There's honest," Jacob replied appreciatively. "Melancholy is sad, but more than sad. It's what we feel when we think about the world and how little we understand; when we think of what we must come to."

"You mean dying and stuff?"

"Dying will do," Jacob said. "Though that's not what concerns me tonight." He beckoned to Will. "Come closer," he said, "it's warmer by the fire."

The few flames on the table offered, Will thought, little prospect of heat, but he gladly approached. "So why are you sad?" Will said.

Jacob sat back in the ancient chair and contemplated the fire. "It's business between a man and a woman," he replied. "You need not concern yourself with it for a little time yet and you should be grateful. Hold it off as long as you can." As he spoke he reached into his pocket and pulled out more fuel for his tiny bonfire. This time, Will was close enough to see that this tinder was moving. Fascinated, and faintly sickened, Will approached the table, and saw that Steep's captive was a moth, the wings of which he had caught between thumb and forefinger. Its legs and antennae flailed as it was dropped into the flames, and for an instant it seemed the draft of heat would waft it to safety, but before it could gain sufficient height its wings ignited and down it went. "Living and dying we feed the fire," Steep said softly. "That is the melancholy truth of things."

"Except that you just did the feeding," Will said, surprised by his own eloquence.

"So we must," Jacob replied. "Or there'd be darkness in here. And how would we see each other then? I daresay you'd be more comfortable with fuel that didn't squirm as you fed it to the flame."

"Yes . . . " Will said, "I would."

"Do you eat sausages, Will?"

"Yes."

"You like them, I'm sure. A nicely browned pork sausage? Or a good steak and kidney pie?"

"Yes. I like steak and kidney pie."

"But do you think of the beast, shitting itself in terror as it is shunted to its execution? Hanging by one leg, still kicking, while the blood spurts from its neck? Do you?"

Will had heard his father debate often enough to know that there was a trap here. "It's not the same," he protested.

"Oh, but it is."

"No, it's not. I need food to stay alive."

"So eat turnips."

"But I like sausages."

"You like light too, Will."

"There are candles," Will said, "right there."

"And the living earth gave up wax and wick in their making," Steep said. "Everything is consumed, Will, sooner or later. Living and dying we feed the fire." He smiled, just a little. "Sit," he said softly. "Go on. We're equals here. Both a little melancholy."

Will sat. "I'm not melancholy," he said, liking the gift of the word. "I'm happy."

"Are you really? Well that's good to hear. And why are you so happy?"

Will was embarrassed to admit the truth, but Jacob had been honest, he thought; so should he be. "Because I found you here," he said.

"That pleases you?"

"Yes."

"But in an hour you'll be bored with me—"

"No, I won't."

"And the sadness will still be there, waiting for you." As he spoke, the fire began to dwindle. "Do you want to feed the fire, Will?" Steep said.

His words carried an uncanny power. It was as though this dwindling meant more than the extinguishing of a few flames. This fire was suddenly the only light in a cold, sunless world, and if somebody didn't feed it soon the consequences would be grim.

"Well, Will?" Jacob said, digging in his pocket and taking out another moth. "Here," he said, proffering it.

Will hesitated. He could hear the soft flapping of the moth's panic. He looked past the creature to its captor. Jacob's face was utterly without expression.

"Well?" Jacob said.

The fire had almost gone out. Another few seconds and it would be too late. The room would be given over to darkness, and the face in front of Will, its symmetry and its scrutiny, would be gone.

That thought was suddenly too much to bear. Will looked back at the moth, at its wheeling legs and its flapping antennae. Then, in a kind of wonderful terror, he took it from Jacob's fingers.

XI

I'm cold," Sherwood moaned for the tenth time.

"So go home," Frannie said.

"On my own? In the dark? Don't make me do that."

"Maybe I should go in and look for Will," Frannie said. "Perhaps he's slipped, or—"

"Why don't we just leave him?"

"Because he's our friend."

"He's not *my* friend."

"Then you can wait out here," Frannie said, looking for the breaking-place in the hedge. A moment later she felt Sherwood's hand slip into hers.

"I don't want to stay out here," he said softly.

In truth, she wasn't unhappy that he wanted to come with her. She was a little afraid, and therefore glad of his company. Together they pushed through the mesh of the hedge, and hand in hand climbed the slope toward the Courthouse. Once only did she feel a little shudder of apprehension pass through her brother and, glancing toward him in the murk, seeing his fearful eyes looking to her for reassurance, she realized how much she loved him.

The moth was large, and though Will held its wings tight-closed, its fat, grublike body wriggled wildly, its legs pedaling the air. It repulsed him, which made what he was about to do easier.

"You're not squeamish, are you?" Jacob said.

"No . . . " Will replied, his voice far from him, like somebody else's voice.

"You've killed insects before."

Of course he had. He'd fried ants under a magnifying glass; he'd cracked beetles and popped spiders; he'd salted slugs and sprayed flies. This was just a moth and a flame. They belonged together.

And with that thought, he did the deed. There was an instant of regret as the flame withered the moth's legs, then he dropped the insect into the heat, and regret became fascination as he watched the creature consumed.

"What did I tell you?" Jacob said.

"Living and dying," Will murmured, "we feed the fire."

At the courtroom door, Frannie could not quite make out what was going on. She could see Will bending over the table, studying something bright, and by the same brightness glimpsed the face of the man sitting opposite him. But that was all.

She let go of Sherwood's hand and put her finger to her lips to keep him quiet. He nodded, his expression surprisingly less tearful than it had been in the darkness outside. Then she turned her gaze back in Will's direction. As she did so she heard the man on the opposite side of the table say, "Do you want another?"

Will didn't even look up at Steep. He was still watching the fire devour the body of the moth.

"Is it always like this?" he murmured.

"Like what?"

"First the cold and the darkness, then the fire pushing it all away, then more darkness and cold—"

"Why do you ask?" Jacob replied.

"Because I want to understand," Will said.

And you're the only one with the answers, he might have added. That was the truth, after all. He was certain his father didn't have answers to questions like that, nor did his mother, nor any schoolteacher, nor anybody he'd heard pontificate on television. This was secret knowledge, and he felt privileged to be in the company of somebody who possessed it, even if they chose not to share it with him.

"Do you want another or not?" Jacob said.

Will nodded and took the moth from Steep's fingers. "One day won't we just run out of things to burn?" he wondered.

"Oh my Lord," Mrs. McGee said, appearing from the shadows. "Listen to him."

Will didn't look at her. He was too busy studying the cremation of the second moth.

"Yes, we will," Jacob said softly. "And when everything's gone a darkness will come upon the world such as we can none of us imagine. It won't be the darkness of death, because death is not utter."

"A game with bones," the woman said.

"Exactly," said Jacob. "Death is a game with bones."

"We know about death, Mr. Steep and me."

"Oh indeed."

"The children I have carried and lost." She moved behind Will as she spoke, reaching out to finger his hair lightly. "I look at you, Will, and I swear I would give every tooth in my head to call you mine. So wise—"

"It's getting dark," Steep said.

"Give me another moth then," Will demanded.

"So eager," Mrs. McGee remarked.

"*Quickly*," Will said, "before the flame goes out!"

Jacob reached into his pocket, and pulled out another moth. Will snatched it from his fingers, but in his haste he missed catching hold of its wings, and it rose above the table.

"*Damn!*" said Will and, pushing back his chair, along with Mrs. McGee, he stood up and reached for the tinder. Twice he snatched at the air, twice he came away empty-handed. Enraged now, he wheeled around, still grabbing for the moth.

Behind him he heard Jacob say, "Let it go. I'll give you another."

"No!" Will said, jumping to snatch the creature out of the air. "I want this one."

His efforts were rewarded. On his third jump his hand closed around the moth.

"Got it!" he hollered, and was about to deliver it to the flame when he heard Frannie say, "What are you doing, Will?"

He looked up at her. She was standing at the courtroom door, her shape murky and remote.

"Go away," he said.

"Who's this?" Jacob said.

"Just go," Will said, suddenly feeling a little jittery. He didn't want these two parts of his life talking to him at the same time; it made him dizzy. "*Please*," he said, hoping she'd respond to civility. "I don't want you here."

The light was guttering out behind him. If he wasn't quick about it, the fire would die completely. He had to feed it again before it went out. But he didn't want Frannie watching. Jacob would never share what he knew—that knowledge that only the wisest of the wise understood—while she was in the room.

"*Go on!*" he shouted. His yelling didn't move her, but it intimidated the hell out of Sherwood. He fled from Frannie's side, off down one of the passages that led from the courtroom.

Frannie was furious. "Sherwood was right!" she said to him. "You're not our friend. We followed you in case something had happened to you—"

"Rosa . . ." Will heard Jacob whisper behind him, "the other boy. . ." and glanced out the corner of his eye to see Mrs. McGee retreat into the shadows, in pursuit of Sherwood.

Will's head was spinning now. Frannie shouting, Sherwood sobbing, Jacob whispering, and worst of all, the flame dying and the light going with it—

That had to be his priority, he decided, and turning his back on Frannie, reached out to put the moth to the flame. But Jacob was there before him. He had put his entire hand—which he had made into a cage of fingers—into the dying fire. Inside the cage was not one but several moths, which caught alight instantly, their panicked wings fanning one another's flames. An uncanny brightness spilled through Jacob's fingers, and it occurred to Will that he was not seeing anything natural here: that this was some kind of magic. The light washed up over Jacob's face and flattered it into something beyond beauty. He didn't look like a movie star or a man on a magazine cover: He wasn't all gloss and teeth and dimples. He was burning brighter than the moths, as though he could be a fire unto himself if he wanted to be. For an instant (this was all it took) Will saw himself at Jacob's side, walking in a city street, and Jacob was shining out of every pore, and people were weeping with gratitude that he came to light their darkness. Then it was all too much for him. His legs gave out beneath him, and down he went, as though he'd been struck a blow.

XII

Sherwood had intended to retreat to the vestibule, away from the courtroom and the smell of burning there, which turned his stomach. But in the guttering darkness he took the wrong route, and instead of being delivered to the front of the building, he found himself lost in a labyrinth. He tried to double back, but he was too frightened to think clearly. All he could do was stumble on, tears stinging his eyes, as it got darker and darker.

Then, a glimmer of light. It wasn't starlight—it was too warm—but he made for it anyway, and found himself delivered into a small chamber in which somebody had been working. There was a chair and a small desk, and on the desk a hurricane lamp, which shed its light on a selection of items. Wiping away his tears, Sherwood went to look. There were bottles of ink, maybe a dozen of them, and some pens and brushes, and open in the midst of this equipment a book, about the size of one of his schoolbooks but much thicker. The binding was stained and the spine cracked, as though it had been carried around for years. Sherwood reached to flip it open, but before he could do so, a soft voice said, "What's your name?"

He looked up and there, emerging from the doorway on the other side of the chamber, was the woman from the courtroom. Sherwood felt a little shudder of pleasure pass through him at the sight of her. Her blouse was unbuttoned and her skin fairly shone.

"My name's Rosa," she said.

"I'm Sherwood."

"You're a big boy. How old are you?"

"Almost eleven."

"You want to come here, so I can see you better?"

Sherwood wasn't sure. There was definitely something exciting about the way she was looking at him, smiling at him, and maybe if he got a little closer he'd see that unbuttoned place better, which was certainly a temptation. He knew all the dirty words from school, of course, and he'd glimpsed a few well-thumbed pictures that had been passed around. But his schoolmates kept him out of the really smutty conversations, because he was a little daft. What would they say, he thought, if he could tell them he'd set eyes on a pair of naked bosoms, in the flesh?

"My, but you *stare*," Rosa said. Sherwood flushed. "Oh it's quite all right," she said. "Boys should see as much as they want to see. As long as they know how to appreciate it." So saying, she reached up and unbuttoned herself a little further. Sherwood tried to swallow, but he couldn't. He could see the swell of her breasts very easily now. If he stepped a little closer he'd see her nipples and, by the look of welcome on her face, she would not censure him for doing so.

He stepped toward her. "I wonder what you could get up to," she said, "if I let you loose?" He didn't entirely understand what she was talking about, but he had a pretty good idea. "Would you lick my titties for me?" she said.

His head was throbbing now, and there was a pressure in his pants so intense he was afraid he was going to wet himself. And as if her words weren't exciting enough, she was opening her blouse a little further, and there were her nipples, large and pink, and she was rubbing them a little, smiling at him all the time.

"Let's see that tongue of yours," she said.

He stuck out his tongue.

"You're going to have to work hard," she said. "It's a little tongue and I've got big titties. Haven't I?"

He nodded. He was three steps from her, and he could smell her body. It was a strong smell, like nothing he'd quite breathed before, but she could have smelled like manure and it couldn't have kept him from her now. He reached out and laid his fingers upon her breasts. She sighed. Then he put his face to her flesh and began to lick.

"Will . . ."

"He's fine," said the man in the dusty black coat. "He's just overcome with excitement. Why don't you just leave him be and run off home?"

"I won't go without Will," Frannie said, sounding a good deal more confident than she felt.

"He doesn't need your help," the man replied, his tone scoured of threat. "He's perfectly happy here." He looked down at Will. "He's simply a little *overwhelmed*."

Keeping her eye on the man, Frannie went down on her haunches beside Will and, reaching for him, shook him violently. He made a moan, and she chanced a quick look down at him. "Get up," she said. He looked very befuddled. "*Up*," she said.

The man in black had meanwhile settled back in his seat and was shaking the contents of his hand out onto the table. Bright, burning fragments fluttered down. Will was already turning back in the man's direction, though he was not yet standing upright.

"Come back here," the man said to Will.

"*Don't . . .* " Frannie said. The flames on the table were dying down, the room giving away to darkness. She was afraid as she was only afraid in dreams. "*Sherwood!*" she yelled.

"*Sherwood!*"

"Don't listen," the woman said, pressing Sherwood to her breast.

"*Sherwood!*"

He couldn't ignore his sister's summons, not when it had such a measure of panic in it. He pulled away from Rosa's hot skin, the sweat running down his face.

"That's Frannie," he said, pulling himself free of the woman. She was wearing, he saw, a strange expression—her panting mouth open, her eyes quivering. It unnerved him.

"I have to go—" he started to say, but she was plucking at her dress, as if to show him more.

"I know what you want to see," she said.

He retreated from her, his hand thrown out behind him for support.

"You want what's under here," she said, pulling up her hem.

"No," he said.

She smiled at him and kept raising her skirt. Panicked, and confused by the stew of feelings that were bubbling up in him, he stumbled backward, and his weight struck the table. It tipped. The books, the inks, the pens, and, worst of all, the lamp went to the floor. There was a moment when it seemed the flame went out, but then it bloomed with fresh gusto, and the trash around the desk caught on fire.

Mrs. McGee dropped her skirts. "*Jacob!*" she shrieked. "*Oh Jesus Lord, Jacob!*"

Sherwood had more reason to panic than she did, surrounded as he was by combustible materials. Even in his dazed state, he knew he had to get out quickly or be numbered among them. The easiest route was the door by which he'd entered.

"*Jacob!* Get in here, will you?" Rosa was yelling, and without so much as glancing in Sherwood's direction again, she left the chamber to find her companion.

The blaze was getting bigger by the moment, smoke and heat filling the chamber, driving Sherwood back. But as he turned to leave, his body trembling from the excesses of the last few minutes, he caught sight of the book, lying there on the ground.

He had no idea what it contained, but it felt like proof. He would have it when his schoolmates scoffed, to show them and say, "I was there. I did all I told you and more."

Daring the flames, he ducked and snatched the book off the ground. It was a little singed, no more. Then he was away, back through the labyrinth of passages, toward his sister's voice.

"*Sherwood!*"

She and Will were at the Courtroom door.

"I don't want to go," Will growled, and tried to pull himself free of Frannie. But she was having none of it. She kept a bruising grip on his arm, all the while yelling her brother's name.

Jacob, meanwhile, had risen from his place at the table, alarmed by the sound of conflagration, and now by the sight of Mrs. McGee in a state of disarray, demanding that he come right now, *right now.*

He went with her, glancing back at Will once, and nodding such a tiny nod as if to say: Go with her. This is not the moment. Then he was gone, away with Rosa, to put out the flames.

As soon as he was out of sight, Will felt a curious calm pass over him. There was no need to struggle with Frannie anymore. He could simply go with her, out into the open air, knowing that there would be another time, a better time, when he and Jacob would be together. "I'm all right—" he said to Frannie. "I don't need anyone to hold me up."

"I've got to find Sherwood," she said.

"*Here!*" came a holler from the smoky darkness, and out he came, his face smeared with dirt and sweat.

There were no further words. They pelted down the passage to the front door and out, past the pillars, and down the steps, into the cold grass. Only when they were past the hedge, out onto the track, did they halt for breath.

"Don't tell anybody what we saw in there, okay?" Will gasped.

"Why not?" Frannie wanted to know.

"Because you'll spoil everything," Will replied.

"They're *bad*, Will—"

"You don't know anything about them."

"Neither do you."

"Yes, I do. I've met them before. They want me to go away with them."

"Is that true?" Sherwood piped up.

"Shut up, Sherwood," Frannie said. "We're not going to talk about this any longer. It's stupid. They're bad and I know they're bad." She turned to her brother. "Will can do whatever he likes," she said. "I can't stop him. But you're not coming here again, Sherwood, and neither am I." With that she picked up her bicycle and mounted, telling Sherwood to hurry up and do the same. Meekly, he obeyed.

"So you won't say anything?" Will pleaded.

"I haven't made up my mind yet," Frannie replied in an infuriatingly snotty tone. "I'll have to see." With that she and Sherwood pedaled off down the track.

"If you do I'll never speak to you again," Will shouted after her, only realizing when they were out of sight that this was a hollow threat from a boy who'd just declared that he was leaving forever someday soon.

PART THREE

He Is Lost;
He Is Found

I

Is he dreaming?" Adrianna asked Dr. Koppelman one day in early
spring, when her visit to sit at Will's bedside coincided with the
physician's rounds.

It was almost four months since the events in Balthazar and, in
its own almost miraculous way, Will's mauled and fractured body was
mending itself. But the coma was as profound as ever. No sign of
motion disturbed the glacial surface of his state. The nurses moved
him regularly so as to prevent his developing bedsores; his bodily
needs were taken care of with drips and catheters. But he did not,
would not, wake. And often, when Adrianna had come to visit him
through that dreary Winnipeg winter, and looked down at his placid
face, she found herself wondering: *What are you doing?*

Hence her question. She normally had an allergic response to
doctors, but Koppelman, who insisted on being called Bernie, was an
exception. He was in his early fifties, overweight, and to judge by the
stains on his fingers (and his minted breath) a heavy smoker. He was
also honest when it came to his ignorance, which she liked, even
though it meant he didn't really have any answers for her.

"We're as much in the dark as Will is right now," he went on.
"He may be in a completely closed down state as far as his consciousness is concerned. On the other hand he may be accessing memories
at such a deep level that we can't monitor the brain activity. I just
don't know."

"But he could still come out of it," Adrianna said, looking down
at Will.

"Oh certainly," Koppelman said. "At any time. But I can't offer
you any guarantees. There are processes at work in his skull right now
that, frankly, we don't understand."

"Do you think it makes any difference if I'm here with him?"

"Were you and he very close?"

"You mean lovers? No. We worked together."

Koppelman nibbled at his thumbnail. "I've seen cases where the presence of somebody the patient knew at the bedside did seem to help things. But—"

"You don't think this is one of those."

Koppelman looked concerned. "You want my honest opinion?" he said, lowering his voice.

"Yes."

"People have to get on with their lives. You've done more than a lot of people would, coming here, day in, day out. You don't live in the city, do you?"

"No. I live in San Francisco."

"That's right. There was talk about moving Will back, wasn't there?"

"There are a lot of people dying in San Francisco."

Koppelman looked grim. "What can I tell you?" he said. "You could be sitting here for another six months, another year, and he'd still be in a coma. That's a waste of your life. I know you want to do your best for him but . . . you see what I'm saying?"

"Of course."

"It's painful to hear, I know."

"It makes sense," she replied. "It's just . . . I can't quite face the idea of leaving him here."

"He doesn't know, Adrianna."

"Then why are you whispering?"

Caught in the act, Koppelman grinned sheepishly. "I'm only saying the chances are, that wherever he is he doesn't care about the world out here." He glanced back toward the bed. "And you know what? Maybe he's happy."

ii

Maybe he's happy. The words haunted Adrianna, reminding her of how often she and Will had talked—deeply, passionately—about the subject of happiness, and how much she now missed his conversation.

He was not, he had often said, designed for happiness. It was too much like contentment, and contentment was too much like sleep. He liked discomfort—sought it out, in fact (how often had she been stuck in some grim little hide, too hot or too cold, and looked over at him to see him grinning from ear to ear? Physical adversity had reminded him he was alive, and life, he'd told her oh so many times, was his obsession).

Not everybody had found evidence of that affirmation in his work. The critical response to both the books and exhibitions had often been antagonistic. Few reviewers had questioned Will's skills— he had the temperament, the vision, and the technical grasp to be a great photographer. But why, they complained, did he have to be so relentlessly grim? Why did he have to seek out images that evoked despair and death when there was so much beauty in the natural world?

While we may admire Will Rabjohns's consistency of vision, the *Time* critic had written of "Feeding the Fire," *his accounts of the way humanity brutalizes and destroys natural phenomena become in turn brutal and destructive to those very sensibilities it wishes to arouse to pity or action. The viewer gives up hope in the face of his reports. We watch the extinction with despairing hearts. Well, Mr. Rabjohns, we have dutifully despaired. What now?*

It was the same question Adrianna asked herself when Dr. Koppelman went about his rounds. What now? She'd wept, she'd cursed, she'd even found enough of her much-despised Catholic training intact to pray, but none of it was going to open Will's eyes. And meanwhile, her life was ticking on.

This was not the only issue in play. She'd found a lover here in Winnipeg (an ambulance driver, of all things); a fellow called Neil, who was far from her ideal of manhood, but who was plainly attracted to her. She owed him answers to the questions he asked her nightly: Why couldn't they move in together, just try it out for a couple of months, see if it worked?

She sat down on the bed beside Will, took his hand in hers, and told him what was going through her head.

"I know I'll be pulled into this half-assed relationship with Neil if I hang around here, and he's probably more your type than he is mine. He's a bear, you know. He hasn't got a hairy back—" she added hurriedly, "I know you hate hairy backs, but he's big—and a bit of a lunk in a sexy kind of way, but I can't live with him, Will. I can't. And I can't live here. I mean, I was staying for him and for you, and right now you're not taking any notice of me and he's taking too much notice, so it's a bad deal all around. Life's not a rehearsal, right? Isn't that one of Cornelius's pearls of wisdom? He's gone back to Baltimore, by the way. I don't hear from him, which is probably for the best because he always annoyed the fuck out of me. Anyhow, he had that line about life not being a rehearsal and he's right. If I hang around here I'm going to end up moving in with Neil and we're just going to get cozy when you're going to open your eyes—*and Will, you are going to open your eyes*—and you're going to say we gotta go to Antarctica. And Neil's going to say, No you're not. And I'm going to say, Yes I am. And there'll be tears, and they won't be mine. I can't do that to him. He deserves better.

"So . . . what am I saying? I'm saying I have to take Neil out for a beer and tell him it's not going to work, then I have to haul my ass back to San Francisco, and get my shit together, because, baby, thanks to you I have never been so untogether in my whole damn life."

She dropped her voice to a whisper. "You know why. It's not something we've talked about and if you had your eyes open right now I wouldn't be saying it because what's the use? But Will: I love you. I love you so much and most of the time it's okay, because we get to work together and I figure you love me back, in your way. Okay, it's not the way I'd really like it, if I had the choice, but I don't, so I'll take whatever I can. And that's all you're getting. And if you can hear this, you should know, buddy, when you wake up *I will deny every fucking word*, okay? Every fucking word." She got up from beside the bed, feeling tears close. "Damn you, Will," she said. "All you have to do is open your eyes. It's not that difficult. There's so much to *see*, Will. It's icy fucking cold, but there's this great clean light on everything: You'd like it. *Just. Open. Your. Eyes.*" She watched and waited, as if by force of thought she could stir him. But there was no motion, except the mechanical rising and falling of his chest.

"Okay. I can take a hint. I'd better get going. I'll come visit you again before I go." She leaned over him and lightly kissed him on the forehead. "I tell you Will, wherever the hell you are, it's not as good as it is out here. Come back and see me, see the world, okay? We're missing you."

II

The morning after the incident at the Courthouse Will woke in a wretched state, aching from head to foot. He tried to get out of bed, but his legs replayed their imbecilities of the night before and down he went, with such a shout (more of surprise than pain) that his mother came running, to find him sprawled on the floor, teeth chattering. He was duly diagnosed as having flu, and put back to bed, where he was plied with aspirin and scrambled eggs.

Sleet had come in the night and slapped against the window through most of the day. He wanted to be out in it. His fever would turn the icy downpour to steam, he thought, as soon as it fell on him. He'd walk back to the Courthouse like one of the children from the Bible who'd been burned in a furnace but had come out alive; steaming, he'd walk the muddy track, back to where Jacob and Rosa kept their strange counsel. Naked, he'd go, yes naked, through the hedgerow, scraped and nicked, until he got to the door, where Jacob would be waiting to teach him wisdom, and Rosa would be waiting to tell him what an extraordinary boy he was. Into the Courthouse he'd go, into the heart of their secret world, where everything was love and fire, fire and love.

All this, if he could only get up and out of bed. But his body was cheating him. It was all he could do to get as far as the toilet, and even then he had to hold on to the sink with one hand and his penis—which looked very shriveled and ashamed of itself right now—with the other, to be sure he wouldn't fall over, his head was spinning so much. Just after lunch the doctor came to see him. She was a soft-spoken woman with short white hair, though she didn't look old enough to have white hair and a gentle smile. She told him he'd get well as long as he didn't get out of bed and took the medicine she was going to prescribe, then reassured his mother that he'd be right as rain in a week or so.

A week? Will thought. He couldn't wait a week to be back with Jacob and Rosa. As soon as the doctor and his mother had gone he got up and made his uncertain way to the window. The sleet was thickening into snow, and it was sticking a little on the tops of the hills. He watched his breath come and go on the cold glass and determined that he would make himself strong, damn it, simply by telling himself to do so.

He started right then and there: "I will be strong. I will be strong. I will—"

He stopped in mid-flow, hearing his papa's voice in the hall below, and then the sound of his footstep on the stairs. He started back to his bed and just made the safety of the covers when the door opened and his father came in, his face more forbidding than the sky outside the window.

"All right," he said, without a word of greeting, "I want an explanation from you, my lad, and I don't want any of your lies. I want the truth." Will said nothing. "You know why I'm home early?" his father demanded. "Well?"

"No."

"I got a call from Mr. Cunningham. Damn lunatic, calling me in the middle of the day. He tracked me down, he said, *tracked me down*, because his son's in a terrible state. Can't stop the boy crying, apparently, because of some damn thing you've been up to with him." Hugo approached Will's bed. "Now I want to know what stupid stories you've been putting in this brat's head, and don't shake your head at me like that, young man, you're not talking to your mother now. I want answers and I want the truth, you hear me?"

"Sherwood's . . . not quite right," Will said.

"What the hell's that supposed to mean?" Hugo said, spittle flecking his lips.

"He says things without really knowing what he's saying."

"I don't care what's wrong with the little bugger. I just don't want his father coming to find me and accusing me of raising a complete idiot. That's what he called you. An idiot! Which you may be, by the way. Have you got no sense?"

Will was starting to get tearful. "Sherwood's my friend," he spluttered.

"He's not quite right, you said."

"He isn't."

"So what does that make you? If you're his friend, *what does that make you?* Have you got no sense? What were you up to?"

"We just went looking around, and he . . . he got scared . . . that's all."

"You've got a peculiar idea of fun, putting nonsense into a little kid's head." He shook his head. "Where'd you get it all from?" he said, already giving up on his son. Plainly he didn't want an answer, though Will so much wanted to give him one, so much wanted to say: *I didn't make up anything, you dead-eyed old man. You don't know what I know, you don't see what I see, you don't understand any of it—*

But he didn't dare speak the words, of course. He just cast down his eyes and let his father's contempt fall on his head until it was all used up.

*   *   *

Later, his mother came in with pills for him to take. "I heard your father having a talk with you," she said. "You know he's sometimes harsher than he means to be."

"I know."

"He says things."

"I know what he says and I know what he means," Will replied. "He wishes I was dead and Nathaniel wasn't. So do you." He shrugged, the ease of the words, the ease of the pain he knew he was causing was exhilarating. "It's no big deal," he said. "I'm sorry I'm not as good as Nathaniel, but I can't do anything about it." All the time he was talking, looking at his mother, it was not her he was seeing, it was Jacob, giving him a moth to burn, Jacob smiling at him.

"Stop it," his mother said. "I won't listen to you talking like this. The way you behave. Take your pills." Her manner suddenly became detached, as though she didn't quite recognize the boy lying in the bed. "Are you hungry?"

"Yes."

"I'll have Adele heat up some soup for you. Just make sure you stay under the blankets. And take your pills."

As she exited she threw her son an almost fearful look, the way Miss Hartley had at school. Then she was gone. Will swallowed the pills. His body still ached and his head still spun, but he wasn't going to wait very long, he'd already decided, before he was up and out. He'd drink the soup (he'd need the sustenance for the journey ahead) and then he'd dress and go back to the Courthouse. With his plan made he got out of bed again to test the strength of his legs. They didn't feel as unreliable as they had a little while before. With some encouragement, they'd get him where he needed to go.

III

Though Frannie wasn't sick, she suffered a good deal more than Will had the day after the night in the Courthouse. She had managed to smuggle Sherwood and herself into the house and upstairs to clean up before they were seen by their parents and had entertained the hope that they were not going to be questioned until, out of the blue, Sherwood had begun to sob. He'd been thankfully inarticulate about what was causing him to do so and, though both her mother and her father quizzed her closely, she kept her answers vague. She didn't like lying, mainly because she wasn't very good at it, but she knew that Will would never forgive her if she let any details of what happened slip. Her father simply grew cold and remote when his first fury was spent, but her mother was good at attrition. She would work and work at her suspicions, until she had them satisfied. So for an hour and a half Frannie found herself quizzed as to why Sherwood was in such a state. She said they'd gone out to play with Will, become lost in the dark, and they'd got frightened. Plainly her mother doubted every word, but she and her daughter were alike in their tenaciousness. The more Mrs. Cunningham repeated her questions, the more entrenched in her replies Frannie became. At last, her mother grew exasperated.

"I don't want you seeing that Rabjohns boy again," she said. "I think he's a troublemaker. He doesn't belong here and he's a bad influence. I'm surprised at you, Frances. And disappointed. You're usually more responsible than this. You know how confused your brother can get. And now he's in a terrible state. I've never seen him so bad. Crying and crying. I blame you."

This little speech brought the matter to an end for the evening. But sometime before dawn Frannie woke to hear her brother sobbing pitifully again, and then her mother going into his room, and the sobbing subsiding while quiet words were exchanged, and then the weeping coming again, while her mother tried—and apparently failed—to soothe him. Frannie lay in the darkness of her room, fighting back tears of her own. But she lost the battle. They came, oh they came, salty in her nose, hot beneath her eyelids and on her cheeks. Tears for Sherwood, who she knew was the least equipped to deal with whatever nightmares would come of their encounter at the Courthouse; tears for herself, for the lies she'd told, which had put a distance between herself and her mother, who she loved so much; and tears of a different kind for Will, who had seemed at first the friend she needed in this stale place, but who she had, it seemed, already lost.

At last, the inevitable. She heard the handle of her bedroom door squeak as it was turned and her mother said:

"Frannie? Are you awake?

She didn't pretend otherwise, but sat up in bed. "What's wrong?"

"Sherwood just told me some very strange things."

He had told everything: about going to the Courthouse in pursuit of Will, about the man in black and the woman in veils. And more besides. Something about the woman being naked and a fire. Was any part of this true, Frannie's mother wanted to know? And if so, why hadn't Frannie told her?

Despite Will's edict, she had no choice but to tell the truth now. Yes, there had been two people at the Courthouse, just as Sherwood had said. No, she didn't know who they were; no, she hadn't seen the woman undressing, and no, she couldn't be certain she would recognize them again (that part wasn't entirely true, but it was close enough). It had been dark, she said, and she had been afraid, not just for herself but for all three of them.

"Did they threaten you?" her mother wanted to know.

"Not exactly."

"But you said you were afraid."

"I was. They weren't like anybody I'd ever seen before."

"So what *were* they like?"

Words failed her, and failed her again when her father appeared and asked her the same questions.

"How many times have I told you," he said, "not to go near anybody you don't know?"

"I was following Will. I was afraid he was going to get hurt."

"If he had that'd be his business and not yours. He wouldn't do the same for you. I'm damn certain of that."

"You don't know him. He—"

"Don't answer me back," her father snapped, "I'll speak to his parents tomorrow. I want them to know what a damn fool they've got for a son."

With that he left her to her thoughts.

The events of the night were not over, however. When the house had finally become quiet, Frannie heard a light tapping on her bedroom door, and Sherwood sidled in, clutching something to his chest. His voice was cracked with all the crying he'd been doing.

"I've got something you have to see," he said, and crossing to the window he pulled back the curtains. There was a streetlight outside the front of the house, and it shed its light through the rain-streaked glass onto Sherwood's pale, puffy face.

"I don't know why I did it," he began.

"Did what?"

"It was just there, you know, and when I saw it I wanted it." As he spoke he proffered the object he'd been clutching. "It's just an old book," he said.

"You stole it?" He nodded. "Where from? The Courthouse?" Again, he nodded. He looked so frightened she was afraid he was going to start weeping again. "It's all right," she said. "I'm not cross. I'm just *surprised*. I didn't see you with it."

"I put it in my jacket."

"Where did you find it?

He told her about the desk, and the inks and the pens, and while he told her she took the book from his hands and went to the window with it. There was a strange perfume coming off it. She raised it to her nose—not too close—and inhaled its scent. It smelled like a cold fire, like embers left in the rain, but sharpened by a spice she knew she would never find on a supermarket shelf. The smell made her think twice about opening the book, but how could she not, given where it had come from? She put her thumb against the edge of the cover and lifted it. On the inside page was a single circle, drawn in black or perhaps dark brown ink. No name. No title. Just this ring, perfectly drawn.

"It's *his*, isn't it?" she said to Sherwood.

"I think so."

"Does anyone know you took it?"

"No, I don't think so."

That at least was something to be grateful for. She turned to the next page. It was as complex as the previous page had been simple: row upon row upon row of writing, tiny words pressed so close to one another it was almost a seamless flow. She flipped the page. It was the same again, on left and right. And on the next two sheets, the same, and on the next two and the next two. She peered at the script more closely, to see if she could make any sense of it, but the words weren't in English. Stranger still, the letters weren't from the alphabet. They were pretty, though, tiny elaborate marks that had been set down with obsessive care.

"What does it mean?" Sherwood said, peering over her shoulder.

"I don't know. I've never seen anything like it before."

"Do you think it's a story?"

"I don't think so. It isn't printed, like a proper book." She licked her forefinger and dabbed it on the words. It came away stained. "It was written by him," she said.

"By Jacob?" Sherwood breathed.

"Yes." She flipped over a few more pages and finally came to a picture. It was an insect—a beetle of some kind, she thought—and like the writing on the preceding pages it had been set down exquisitely, every detail of its head and legs and iridescent wings so meticulously painted it looked uncannily lifelike in the watery light, as though it might have risen whirring from the paper had she touched it.

"I know I shouldn't have taken the book," Sherwood said, "but now I don't want to give it back, 'cause I don't want to see him again."

"You won't have to," Frannie reassured him.

"You promise?"

"I promise. There's nothing to be afraid of, Sher. We're safe here, with mom and dad to look after us."

Sherwood had put his arm through hers. She could feel his thin body quivering against her own. "But they won't be here always, will they?" he said, his voice eerily flat, as though this most terrible of possibilities could not be expressed unless stripped of all emphasis.

"No," she said. "They won't."

"What will happen to us then?" he said.

"I'll be here to look after you," Frannie replied.

"You promise?"

"I promise. Now, it's time you were back in bed."

She took her brother by the hand and they both tiptoed out along the landing to his room. There she settled him back in his bed and told him not to think about the book or the Courthouse or what had happened tonight anymore, but to go back to sleep. Her duty done she returned to her own bedroom, closed the door and the curtains, and put the book in the cupboard under her sweaters. There was no lock on the cupboard door, but if there had been she would have certainly turned the key. Then she climbed between the now chilly sheets and put on the bedside light, just in case the beetle in the book came clicking across the floor to find her before dawn, which possibility, after the evening's escapades, she could not entirely consign to the realm of the impossible.

IV

i

Will consumed his soup like a dutiful patient, and then, once
Adele had taken his temperature, collected his tray, and gone
back downstairs, quickly got up and dressed. It was by now the middle of the afternoon and the sleety day was already losing its light,
but he had no intention of putting his journey off until tomorrow.

The television had been turned on in the living room—he could
hear the calm, even tones of a newscaster, and then, as his mother
changed channels, applause and laughter. He was glad of the sound.
It covered the occasional squeak of a stair as he descended to the
hallway. There, as he donned scarf, anorak, gloves, and boots, he
came within a breath of discovery, as his father called out from his
study demanding to know from Adele where his tea had got to. Was
she picking the leaves herself, for Christ's sake? Adele did not reply,
and his father stormed into the kitchen to get an answer. He did not
notice his son in the unlit hallway, however, and while he whittered
on to Adele about how slow she was, Will opened the front door and,
slipping through the narrowest crack he could make so as not to have
a draft alert them to his going, was out on his night journey.

ii

Rosa didn't conceal the satisfaction she felt at the absence of the
book. It had burned up in the fire and that was all there was to say in
the matter. "So you've lost one of your precious journals," she said.
"Perhaps you'll be a little more sympathetic in the future when I get
weepy about the children."

"There's no comparison," Steep said, still searching the ashes in
the antechamber. His desk was little more than seared timbers, his
pens and brushes gone, his box of watercolors barely recognizable, his
inks boiled away. His bag containing the earlier journals had been
beyond the scope of the fire, so all was not lost. But the work-in-
progress, his account of the last eighteen years of his vast labor, had
gone. And Rosa's attempt to equate his loss with what she felt when
one of her brats had to be put out of its misery made him sick to his
stomach. "This is the labor of my life," he pointed out.

"Then it's pitiful," she said. "Making books! It's pitiful." She leaned toward him. "Who'd you think you're making them for? Not me. I'm not interested. I'm not remotely interested."

"You know why I'm making them," Jacob said sullenly. "To be a witness. When God comes and demands we tell Him what we've wrought, chapter and verse, we must have an account. Every detail. Only then will we be . . . Jesus! why do I bother explaining it to you?"

"You can say the word. Go on, say it! Say *forgiven*. That's what you used to say all the time. We'd be forgiven." She approached him now. "But you don't really believe that anymore do you?" She gently reached up and put her hands to his face. "Be honest, my love," she said, suddenly soft.

"I still . . . I still believe there's purpose in our lives," Jacob replied. "I have to believe that."

"Well I don't," Rosa said plainly. "I realized after our fumblings this afternoon, I have no healthy desires left in me. None at all. There won't be any more children. There won't be any hearth and home. And there won't be a day of forgiveness, Jacob. That's certain. We're alone, with the power to do whatever we want." She smiled. "That boy—"

"Will?"

"No. The younger one, Sherwood. I had him at my titties, sucking away, and I thought: It's a sickness to take pleasure in this, but Lord, you know that made it all the more pleasurable? And I began to think, when the child had gone, what else would give me pleasure? What's the *worst* I could do?"

"And?"

"My mind fairly began to spin at the possibilities," she said with a smile. "It really did. If we're not going to be forgiven, why try to be something I'm not?" She was staring hard into his face. "Why should I waste my breath hoping for something we'll never have?"

Jacob pulled his face from her hands. "You won't tempt me," he said. "So stop wasting your time. I have my plans laid—"

"The book's burned," Rosa snapped.

"I'll make another."

"And if that burns?"

"Another! And another! I'll be the stronger for this loss."

"Oh, so will I," Rosa said, her features draining of warmth, so that her beauty seemed, for all its perfection, almost cadaverous. "I will be a different woman from now on. I will have pleasure whenever I can take it, by whatever means amuse me. And if someone or something gets a child upon me I'll fetch it out of m'self with a sharpened stick." This notion pleased her. Laughing raucously, she turned her back on Jacob, and spat into the ashes. "There's for your book," she said. She spat again. "And there's for forgiveness." Again she spat. "And there's for God. He'll have nothing more from me."

She said no more. Without looking to see what effect she'd had upon her companion (she would have been disappointed; he was stony-faced), she strode out. Only when she'd gone did Jacob let himself weep. Manly tears, the tears of a commander before a broken army or a father at his son's grave. He didn't simply grieve for the book—though that added to the sum—but for himself. After this, he would be alone. Rosa—his once beloved Rosa, with whom he'd shared his most cherished ambitions—would go her hedonistic way, and he would take his own road, with his knife and his pen and a new journal full of empty pages. Oh, that would be hard after so many years together and the work before him still so monumental and the sky so wide.

Then an unbidden thought: Why not kill her? There would be satisfaction in that right now, no question about it. A quick slice across her pulsing throat and down she'd go, like a felled cow. He'd comfort her in her final moments; tell her how much he had loved her, in his way; how he would dedicate his labors to her until they were finished. Every nest he rifled, every burrow he purified, he would say: *This is for you, my Rosa, and this and this*, until his hands, bloodied and yolked, were done with their weary work.

He pulled his knife from his belt, already imagining the sound of its swoop across her neck, the hiss of her breath from her throat, the fizz of her blood. Then he went after her, back toward the courtroom.

She was waiting for him, turned to face him with her pet ropes—what she liked to call her rosaries—cavorting around her arms like vipers. One leaped as he approached her, finding his wrist with the speed of her will and catching it so tight he gasped at the sensation.

"How *dare* you?" she said. A second rope leaped from her hand and, wrapping itself around his neck, caught hold of his knife hand from behind him. She flicked her eye and it pulled tight, wrenching the blade back toward his face. "You would have murdered me."

"I would have tried."

"I'm no use to you as a womb, so I may as well be crow bait, is that it?"

"No. I just . . . I wanted to simplify things."

"That's a fresh excuse," she said, almost admiringly. "Which eye is it to be?"

"What?"

"I'm going to puncture one of your eyes, Jacob. With this little knife of yours—" She willed the ropes to tighten. They creaked a little. "Which is it to be?"

"If you harm me, it'll be war between us."

"And war's for men, so I would lose? Is that the inference?"

"You know you would."

"I don't know a thing about myself, Jacob, any more than you do. I learned it all watching women do as women do. Perhaps I'd be a very fine soldier. Perhaps we'd have such a war, you and me, that it would be like love, only bloodier." She cocked her head.

"Which eye is it to be?"

"Neither," Jacob said, a tremor in his voice now. "I need both my eyes, Rosa, to do my work. Put one of them out and you may as well take my life with it."

"I want *recompense!*" she said, through her perfect teeth. "I want you to suffer for what you just tried to do."

"Anything but an eye."

"Anything?"

"Yes."

"Unbutton yourself."

"What?"

"You heard me. *Unbutton yourself.*"

"No, Rosa."

"I want one of your balls, Jacob. It's that or an eye. Make up your mind."

"Stop this," he said softly.

"Am I supposed to melt now?" she replied. "Get weak with compassion?" She shook her head. "Unbutton yourself," she said.

His free hand went to his groin.

"You can do it yourself, if that'll make you feel any better. Well? Would it?"

He nodded. She let the ropes about his wrist relax a little.

"I won't even watch," she said. "How's that? Then if you lose your courage for a bit nobody's going to know but you."

The ropes loosed his hand completely now. They returned to Rosa and looped themselves around her neck.

"Go to it."

"Rosa . . . ?"

"Jacob?"

"If I do this—?"

"Yes."

"You'll never talk about it to anybody?"

"Talk about what?"

"That I'm not . . . complete."

Rosa shrugged. "Who'd care?" she said.

"Just agree."

"I agree." She turned her back to him. "Make it the left," she said. "It hangs a little lower, so it's probably the riper of the two."

He stood in the passage when she'd gone and felt the heft of the knife in his hand. He had commissioned it in Damascus, a year after the death of Thomas Simeon, and had used it innumerable times since. Though there had been nothing supernatural about its maker, some authority had been conferred upon it over the years, for it grew sharper, he thought, with every life it took. He would be able to scoop out what the bitch demanded without much trouble, and after all, what did he care? He had no use for what he now cupped in his palm. Two eggs in a nest of skin; that's all they were. He put the tip of the blade to his flesh and drew a deep breath. In the courtroom, down the passage, Rosa was singing one of her wretched lullabies. He waited for a high note, then cut.

V

Will didn't attempt a shortcut back to the Courthouse, but took the road down to the village. At the intersection there was a telephone box, and he thought: I should say good-bye to Frannie. It wasn't so much for friendship's sake as for the pleasure of the boast. To be able to say: I'm going, just as I said I would. I'm going away forever.

He stepped into the box, fumbled for some change, then fumbled again (his fingers chilled, even through his gloves) to find the Cunninghams's number in the out-of-date directory. It was there. He dialed and prepared to disguise his voice if Frannie's father came on the line. Her mother answered, however, and with a hint of frostiness brought her daughter to the phone. Will got straight to the point: He swore Frannie to secrecy then told her he was leaving.

"With *them?*" she said, her voice barely more than a whisper.

He told her it was none of her business. He was simply going away.

"Well I've got something that belongs to Steep," she said.

"What?"

"It's none of *your* business," she countered.

"All right," Will said. "Yes, I'm going with them." There was no doubt in his feverish head that this was so. "Now . . . what have you got?"

"You mustn't say anything. I don't want them to come looking."

"They won't."

She paused a moment. Then she said, "Sherwood found a book. I think it belongs to Steep."

"Is that *all?*" he said. A book? Who cared about a book? But he supposed she needed some memento of this adventure, however petty.

"It's not just any book," she insisted. "It's—"

But Will was already done with the conversation. "I have to go," he said.

"Wait, Will—"

"I haven't got time. 'Bye, Frannie. Say 'bye to Sherwood, will you?"

He put the receiver down, feeling thoroughly pleased with himself. Then he left the relative comfort of the telephone box, and set out on the track to Bartholomeus's Courthouse.

The fallen snow had frozen and formed a glittering skin on the road ahead, upon which a new layer of snow was being deposited as the storm intensified. Its beauty was his to appreciate, and his alone. The people of Burnt Yarley were at home tonight, beside their fires, their cattle gathered into sheds and byres, their chickens fed and locked up in their coops for the night.

The mounting blizzard soon turned the scene ahead of him into a white blur, but he had sufficient wits about him to watch for the place in the hedge where he'd previously gained access to the field and, spotting it, dug his way through. The Courthouse was not visible, of course, but he knew that if he trudged directly across the meadow he'd reach its steps in due course. It was harder going than the road, and his body, for all his determination, was showing signs of surrender. His limbs felt jittery, and the urge to sink down in the

snow for a while and rest grew stronger with every step. But he saw
the Courthouse now, coming out of the blizzard. Jubilant, he wiped
the snow from his numbed face, so that the blaze in him—in his
eyes, in his skin—would be readily seen. Then he started up the step.
Only when he reached the top did he realize that Jacob was in the
doorway, silhouetted against a fire burning in the vestibule. This was
not a piffling blaze like the one Will had fed: It was a bonfire. And he
did not doubt for a moment it had living fuel. He could not see
what, exactly, nor did he much care. It was his idol he wanted to see,
and be seen by—more than seen, embraced. But Jacob did not move,
and a terror came upon Will that he'd misunderstood everything,
that he was no more wanted here than at the house he'd left. He
stopped one step shy of the top and waited for judgment. It did not
come. He was not even certain Jacob had even seen him.

And then, out of the shadowed face, a soft, raw voice.

"I came out here without even knowing why. Now I see."

Will dared a syllable. "Me?"

Jacob nodded. "I was looking for you," he said, and opened his
arms.

Will would have gone into them happily, but his body was too
weak to get him there. As he climbed the final step he stumbled, his
outstretched hands moving too slowly to protect his head from striking the cold stone. He heard Jacob let out a little shout as he fell,
then the sound of the man's boots crunching on the frost as he came
to help.

"Are you all right?" he asked.

Will thought he answered, but he wasn't certain. He felt Steep's
arms beneath him, however, lifting him up, and the warmth of the
man's breath on his frozen face. I'm home, he thought, and passed out.

VI

i

Thursday's evening meal in the Cunningham house was in winter
a hearty lamb stew, mashed potatoes, and buttered carrots, preceded always by the prayer that the family recited before every meal:

"For what we are about to receive may the Lord make us truly thankful." There was very little talk around the table tonight, but that was not unusual: George Cunningham was a great believer in things having their proper time and place. The dinner table was for dining, not for talking. There was only one exchange of any length, which took place when George, observing Frannie toying with her food, told her sharply to eat up.

"I'm not really hungry," Frannie replied.

"Are you sickening for something?" he said. "I wouldn't be surprised after yesterday."

"George," his wife said, casting a fretful glance at Sherwood, who was also not showing much of an appetite.

"Well look at the pair of you," George said, his tone warming. "You look like a pair of drowned pups, you do." He patted his daughter's hand. "A mistake's a mistake, and you made one, but that's the end of it as far as your mom and I are concerned. As long as you learned your lesson. Now you eat up. And give your dad a smile." Frannie tried. "Is that the best you can do?" Her father chuckled. "Well, you'll brighten up after a good night's sleep. Have you got a lot of homework?"

"A bit."

"You go up and do it, then. Your mom and Sherwood'll take care of the dishes."

Grateful to be away from the table, Frannie took herself upstairs, fully intending to prepare for the history test that was looming, but the book before her was as incomprehensible as Jacob's journal, and a good deal less intriguing. At last she gave up on the life of Anne Boleyn, and guiltily pulled the journal out of its hiding place to puzzle over it afresh. She had scarcely opened it, however, when she heard the telephone ring and her mother, having talked for a few moments, called her to the landing. She slid the journal out of sight beneath her study books and went to the top of the stairs.

"It's Will's father on the phone," her mother said.

"What does he want?" Frannie said, knowing full well.

"Will's disappeared," her mother said. "Do you know where he might have gone?"

Frannie gave herself a few moments to think it over. While she did so she heard the gale bringing snow against the landing window, and thought of Will out there somewhere, in the freezing cold. She knew exactly where he'd go, of course, but she'd made a promise to him, and she intended to keep it.

"I don't know," she said.

"He didn't say where he was when he telephoned?" her mother asked.

"No," she said, without hesitation.

This news was duly communicated to Will's father, and Frannie took herself back to her bedroom. But she could no longer concentrate on study, legitimate or no. Her thoughts returned over and over to Will, who had made her a coconspirator in his escape plans. If any harm came to him she would be in some measure responsible, or at least she'd feel that way, which would amount to the same thing. The temptation to confess what little she knew, and be relieved of its weight, was almost overwhelming. But a promise was a promise. Will had made his decision: He wanted to be out in the world somewhere, far from here, and wasn't there a part of her that envied him the ease of his going? She would never have that ease, she knew, as long as Sherwood was alive. When her parents were old or dead, he would need someone to watch over him, and—just as she had promised him—that someone would have to be her.

She went to the window and cleared a place on the fogged glass with the heel of her hand. Snow blazed through the glow from the streetlight, like flakes of white fire, driven by the wind that whined in the telephone wires and rattled around the eaves. She'd heard her father say fully a month before that the farmers at the Plow were warning that the winter would be cruel. Tonight was the first proof of their prophecies. Not the cleverest time to run away, she thought, but the deed was done. Will was out there in the blizzard somewhere. He'd made his choice. She only hoped the consequences weren't fatal.

ii

In his narrow bed in the narrow room beside Frannie's, Sherwood lay wide awake. It wasn't the storm that kept sleep from coming. It was pictures of Rosa McGee: Bright flickering pictures that made everything he'd ever seen in his head before look like black and white. Several times tonight it felt as if she was right there in the room with him, the memory of her was so overpowering. He could see her clearly, her titties shiny-wet with his spit. And though she'd scared him at the end, raising her skirts that way, it was that moment he replayed more often than any other, hoping each time to extend her motion by a few seconds, so that this time the dress would rise up to her belly button and he would get to see what she'd been wanting to show him. He had several impressions of what it was: a kind of lop-sided mouth, a patch of hair (perhaps greenish, like a little bush), a simple round hole. Whatever form it took, however, it was wet; of that he was certain, and sometimes he thought he saw drops of that wetness running down the insides of her thighs.

He could never tell anybody about these memories, of course. He wouldn't be able to boast about what had happened with Rosa once he was back among his schoolmates, and he certainly wouldn't talk about it in adult company. People already treated him as strange. When he went out shopping with his mom, they'd peer at him, pre-tending they weren't, and talk about him in lowered voices. But he heard. They said he was odd; they said he was a little wrong in the head; they said he was a cross to bear and it was good his mom was a Christian woman. He heard it all. So these rememberings had to stay hidden away, where people couldn't see them, or else there'd be more whispers, more shaken heads.

He didn't mind. In fact he liked the idea of keeping Rosa locked up in his brain, where only he could go and look at her. Perhaps he would find a way to talk to her, as time went by, persuade her to lift her skirts a little higher, a little higher, until he could see her secret place.

In the meantime he worked his belly and hips against the weight of the sheet and blankets, pressing his hand hard against his mouth as though his palms were her breasts and he was back licking them; and though he had cried himself dry in the last little while, all his tears were forgotten in the thrill of the memory, and the strange hot-ness in his groin.

Rosa, he murmured against his hand; *Rosa, Rosa, Rosa* . . .

VII

By the time Will opened his eyes the fire, which had been in its heyday when he arrived, was not in its embery dotage. But Jacob had laid his guest close to it, and there was still sufficient heat in its dwindling flame to drive the last of the chill from Will's bones. He sat up, and realized he was wrapped in Jacob's military coat and naked beneath.

"That was brave," somebody on the other side of the fire said.

Will squinted to see the speaker better. It was Jacob, of course. He was lounging against the wall, staring through the flames at Will. He looked a little sick himself, Will thought, as though in sympathy with his own condition; but whereas Will's illness had left him worn and weak, Steep glittered in his hurt: pale, gleaming skin, shiny curls pasted to the thick muscle of his neck. His coarse gray shirt was unbuttoned to his navel, his chest arrayed with a fan of dark hair that ran over the ridges of his belly to his belt. When he smiled, as he did now, his eyes and teeth glistened, as though made of the same implacable stuff.

"You're sick, and yet you found your way though this blizzard. That shows courage."

"I'm not sick," Will insisted. "I mean . . . I *was* a little, but I feel fine now—"

"You look fine."

"I am. I'm ready to go any time you want to."

"Go where?"

"Wherever you want," Will said. "I don't care. I'm not afraid of the cold."

"Oh this isn't cold," Jacob said. "Not like some winters we've endured, the bitch and me." He glanced back toward the courtroom, and through the smoke Will thought he saw a contemptuous look cross Jacob's face. A heartbeat later, his gaze came Will's way once more, and there was a new intensity in it. "I think maybe you were sent to me, Will, by some kind god or other, to be my companion. You see, I won't be traveling with Mrs. McGee after tonight. We've decided to part company."

"Have you . . . traveled with her for long?"

Jacob leaned forward from his squatting position and picking up a stick, poked at the fire. There was still fuel concealed in the embers, and it caught as he raked them over. "More than I care to remember," he said.

"So why are you stopping now?"

By the light of the spluttering flames (whatever had been cremated here, it had been fatty) Will saw Jacob grimace. "Because I hate her," he replied. "And she hates me. I would have killed her tonight, if I'd been quicker. And then we'd have had us a fire, wouldn't we? We could have warmed half of Yorkshire."

"Would you really have killed her?"

Jacob raised his left hand into the light. It was gummy with something that looked like blood, but mixed with flakes of silvery paint. "This is mine," he said. "Shed because I failed to shed hers." His voice dropped to a murmur. "Yes. I would have killed her. But I would have regretted it, I think. She and I are intertwined in some fashion I've never understood. If I'd done harm to her—"

"You'd have hurt yourself?" Will ventured.

"You understand this?" he said, almost puzzled. Then, more quietly: "Lord, what have I found?"

"I had a brother," Will replied, by way of explanation. "When he died I was happy about it. Well, not happy. That sounds horrible—"

"If you were happy, say so," Jacob replied.

"Well I was," Will said. "I was glad he was dead. But since he died I'm different. It's the same with you and Mrs. McGee in a way, isn't it? If she'd died you'd be different. And maybe you wouldn't be the way you wanted to be."

"I don't know either," Jacob replied softly. "How old was your brother?"

"Fifteen and a half."

"And you didn't love him?" Will shook his head. "Well that's plain enough," Jacob said.

"Do you have any brothers?" Will asked him. Now it was Jacob who shook his head. "What about sisters?"

"None," he said. "Or if I did, I don't remember them, which is possible."

"Having brothers and sisters and not remembering?"

"Having a childhood. Having parents. Being born."

"I don't remember being born," Will said.

"Oh you do," Jacob said. "Deep, deep inside," he tapped his breastbone, "—there's memory in there somewhere, if you knew how to find it."

"Maybe it's in you too," Will said.

"I've looked," Jacob said. "Looked as deep as I dare. Sometimes I think I get a taste of it. A moment of epiphany, then it's gone."

"What's an epiphany?" Will asked.

Jacob smiled, happy to be a teacher. "A little piece of bliss," he said. "A moment when for no reason you seem to understand everything or know that it's there for the understanding."

"I don't think I've ever had one of those."

"You wouldn't necessarily remember if you had. They're hard to hold on to. When you do, it's sometimes worse than forgetting them completely."

"Why?"

"Because they taunt you. They remind you there's something worth listening for, watching for."

"So tell me one," Will said. "Tell me an epiphany."

Jacob grinned. "There's an order."

"I didn't mean—"

"Don't tell me you didn't mean it if you did," Jacob said.

"I did," Will said, beginning to see a pattern in what Jacob asked of him. "I want you to tell me an epiphany."

Jacob poked the fire one last time, and then leaned back against the wall.

"Remember how I said I'd endured colder winters than this?"

Will nodded.

"There was one worse than any other. The winter of seventeen thirty-nine. Mrs. McGee and I were in Russia—"

"Seventeen thirty-nine?"

"No questions," Jacob said. "Or you'll have nothing more. It was the bitterest cold I've ever known. Birds froze in flight and fell out of the air like stones. People perished in their millions and lay in stacks unburied because the earth was too hard to be dug. You can't imagine . . . well, perhaps you can." He gave Will a curious little smile. "Can you see it in your mind's eye?"

Will nodded. "So far," he said.

"Good. Well now. I was in St. Petersburg, with Mrs. McGee in tow. She had not wanted to come, as I recall, but there was a learned doctor there by the name of Khrouslov who had theorized that this lethal cold was the beginning of an age of ice, that acre by acre, soul by soul, species by species, it would grasp the earth." Jacob closed his stained hand into a fist as he spoke, until the knuckles blazed white. "Until there was nothing left alive." Now he opened his hand, and lightly blew the silvery dust of dried blood off his palm into the dying fire. "Plainly, I needed to hear what the man had to say. Unfortunately by the time I arrived he was dead."

"Of the cold?"

"Of the cold," Jacob replied, indulging the question despite his edict. "I would have left the city there and then," he went on, "but Mrs. McGee wanted to stay. The Empress Anna, having recently executed a number of well-loved men, had commanded an ice palace to be built as a distraction for her disgruntled subjects. Now if there's one thing Mrs. McGee loves it's artifice. Silk flowers, wax fruit, china cats. And this palace was to be the greatest piece of fakery ice and man could create. The architect was a fellow called Eropkin. I got to know him briefly. The empress had him executed as a traitor the following summer—it wasn't the last winter of the world, you see, except for him. But for the months his palace stood, there on the river bank between the Admiralty and the Winter Palace, he was the most admired, the most lionized, the most adored man in St. Petersburg."

"Why?" Will said.

"Because he'd made a masterpiece, Will. I don't suppose you've ever seen an ice palace? No. But you understand the principle. Blocks of ice were cut from the river, which was solid enough to march an army over, then carved, and assembled, just the way you'd build an ordinary palace.

"Except . . . Eropkin had genius in him that winter. It was as though his whole career had been leading up to this triumph. He'd only let the masons use the finest, clearest ice, blue and white. He had ice trees carved for the gardens around the palaces, with ice birds in their branches and ice wolves lurking between. There were ice dolphins, flanking the front doors, that seemed to be leaping from spumy waves, and dogs playing on the step. There were a bitch, I remember, lying casually at threshold, suckling her pups. And inside—"

"You could go inside?" Will said, astonished.

"Oh certainly. There was a ballroom, with chandeliers. There was a receiving room with a vast fireplace and an ice fire burning in the grate. There was a bedroom, with a stupendous four-poster bed. And of course people came in their tens of thousands to see the place. It was better by night than by day I think, because at night they lit thousands of lanterns and bonfires around it, and the walls were translucent, so it was possible to see layer upon layer of the place—"

"Like you had X-ray eyes."

"Exactly so."

"Is that when you had your moment of . . . of—"

"Epiphany? No. That comes later."

"So what happened to the palace?"

"What do you think?"

"It just melted."

Jacob nodded. "I went back to St. Petersburg in the late spring, because I'd heard the papers of the learned Dr. Khrouslov had been discovered. They had, but his wife had burned them, mistaking them for love letters to his mistress. Anyway, it was by then early May and every trace of the palace had gone.

"And I went down to the Neva—to smoke a cigarette or take a piss, something inconsequential—and while I was looking down into the river something seized hold of my—I want to say my soul, if I have one—and I thought of all those wonders, the wolves and dolphins and spires and chandeliers and birds and trees, there, somehow *waiting* in the water. *Being* in the water already, if I just knew how to see them—" He wasn't looking at Will any longer, but staring into what remained of the fire, his eyes huge. "Ready to spring into life. And I thought, if I throw myself in, and drown in the river, and dissolve in the river, then next year when the river freezes and the Empress Anna commands another palace to be built I'll be in every part of it. Jacob in the bird. Jacob in the tree. Jacob in the wolf."

"But none of it'd be alive."

Jacob smiled. "That was the *glory* of it, Will. Not to be alive. That was the perfection. I stood there on the riverbank and the *joy* in me, oh, Will, the sheer . . . sheer . . . brimming bliss of it. I mean God could not have been happier at that moment. And that, to answer your question, was my Russian epiphany." His voice trailed away, in deference to the memory, leaving only the soft popping of the dying fire. Will was content with the hush; he needed time to mull over all he'd just been told. Jacob's story had put so many images into his head. Of carved ice birds sitting on carved ice perches, more alive than the frozen flocks that had dropped out of the sky. Of the people—Empress Anna's complaining subjects—so astonished by the spires and the lights that they forgot the deaths of great men. And of the river the following spring, with Jacob sitting on its banks, staring into the rushing waters and seeing bliss.

If somebody had asked him what all this meant, he wouldn't have had any answers. But he would not have cared. Jacob had filled up some empty place in him with these pictures and he was grateful for the gift.

At last, Jacob roused himself from his reverie and, giving the fire one last, desultory poke, said, "There's something I need you to do for me."

"Whatever you want."

"How strong are you feeling?"

"I'm fine."

"Can you stand?"

"Of course." Will proceeded to do so, lifting the coat up with him. It was heavier and more cumbersome than he's imagined, however, and as he rose it slipped off him. He didn't bother to pick it up. There was scarcely any light for Jacob to see him naked by. And even if he did, hadn't he taken Will's clothes off, hours before, and laid him down beside the fire? They had no secrets, he and Jacob.

"I feel fine," Will pronounced, as he shook the numbness from his legs.

"Here," Jacob said. He pointed to Will's clothes which had been laid out to dry on the far side of the fire. "Get dressed. We have a hard climb ahead of us."

"What about Mrs. McGee?"

"She has no business with us tonight," Jacob replied. "Or indeed, after our deeds on the hill, any night."

"Why not?" said Will.

"Because I won't need her for company, will I? I'll have you."

VIII

i

Burnt Yarley was too small to merit a policeman of its own; on the few occasions police assistance was needed in the valley, a car was dispatched from Skipton. Tonight the call went out at a little before eight—a thirteen-year-old boy missing from his home—and the car, containing Constables Maynard and Hemp, was at the Rabjohns residence by half past. There was very little by way of information. The lad had disappeared from his bedroom sometime between six and seven, approximately. Neither his temperature nor his medication were likely to have induced a delirium, and there was nothing to indicate an abduction, so it had to be assumed he'd left of his own volition, with his wits about him. As to his whereabouts, the parents had no clue. He had few friends, and those he had knew nothing. The father, whose condescending manner did nothing to endear him to the officers, was of the opinion that the boy had made for Manchester.

"Why the hell would he do that?" Doug Maynard, who had taken an instant dislike to Rabjohns, wanted to know.

"He hadn't been very happy recently," Hugo replied. "We'd had some hard words, he and I."

"*How* hard?"

"What are you implying?" Hugo sniffed.

"I'm not implying anything; I'm asking you a question. Let me put it more plainly. Did you give the lad a beating?"

"Good God, no. And may I say I resent—"

"Let's put your resentments over to one side for now, shall we?" Maynard said. "You can resent me all you like when we've found your kid. If he *is* wandering around out there then we haven't got a lot of time. The temperature's still dropping—"

"Would you kindly keep your voice down!" Hugo hissed, glancing toward the open door. "My wife's in a bad enough state as it is."

Maynard gave his partner a nod. "Have a word with her will you, Phil?"

"There's nothing she knows that I don't," Hugo replied.

"Oh you'd be surprised what a child will tell one parent and won't tell the other," Maynard replied. "Phil'll be gentle, won't you, Phil?"

"Kid gloves." He slipped away.

"So you didn't hit him," Maynard said to Hugo. "But you've had some words—"

"He'd been behaving like a damn fool."

"Doing what?"

"Nothing of any significance," Hugo said, waving the question away. "He went off one afternoon—"

"So he's run away before?"

"He was not running away."

"Maybe that's what he told *you*."

"He doesn't lie to me," Hugo snapped.

"How would you know?"

"Because I can see right through the boy," Hugo replied, giving Maynard the weary gaze he usually reserved for particularly slow students.

"So when he went off for the afternoon, do you know where he went?"

Hugo shrugged. "Nowhere, as usual."

"If you were as communicative with your son as you're being with me it's no wonder he's a runaway," Maynard said. "*Where did he go?*"

"I don't need a lecture on parenting from the likes of you," Hugo replied. "The boy's thirteen. If he wants to go traipsing the hills that's up to him. I didn't ask for details. I was only angry because Eleanor was so upset."

"You think he went onto the fells?"

"That was the impression I got."

"So tonight he could be doing the same thing?"

"Well he'd have to be completely out of his mind to go up there on a night like this, wouldn't he?"

"It depends how desperate he is, doesn't it?" Maynard replied. "Frankly if I had you for a father I'd be suicidal."

Hugo began an outraged retort, but Maynard was already on his way out of the room. He found Phil in the kitchen, pouring tea. "We've got a hill search on our hands, Phil. You'd better see what help we can get locally." He peered out of the window. "It's getting worse out there. What state's the mother in?"

Phil made a face. "Out of it," he said. "She's got enough pills in there to sedate the whole bloody village. She must have been quite a looker too."

"So that's why you're making her tea," Doug replied, nudging him in the ribs. "You wait 'till I tell your Kathy."

"Makes you wonder, eh?"

"What?"

"Rabjohns and her and the kid." He stirred a spoonful of sugar into the tea. "Not a lot of happiness."

"What's your point?"

"Nothing," Phil said, tossing the spoon into the sink. "Just not a lot of happiness, that's all."

ii

It wasn't the first time a search party had been organized in the valley. At least once or twice a year, usually in the early spring or late autumn, a fell-walker would be late returning to a rendezvous and, if the situation was deemed sufficiently serious, a team of volunteers would be drummed up to help with the search. The fells could be treacherous at such times—sudden mists swept in to obscure the way, scree and boulders could prove unreliable perches. Usually these incidents ended happily. But not always. Sometimes a body came down from the hills on a stretcher. Sometimes—rarely, but sometimes—no trace was ever found, the victim gone into a crevice or a pothole and never retrieved.

*   *   *

At a little after ten Frannie heard cars in the street and got up out
of bed to see what was going on. It wasn't hard to guess. There was
a knot of perhaps twelve men—all bundled up against the blizzard—conferring in the middle of the street. Though they were
some distance away and the snow was thick, she could name a few
of them. Mr. Donnelly, who had the butcher's shop, was recognizable (there wasn't a bigger belly in the village, and his son Neville,
with whom Frannie went to school, was shaping up the same way).
She also recognized Mr. Sutton, who ran the pub, his big red beard
as distinct as Mr. Donnelly's stomach. She looked for her father,
but she couldn't see him. He'd broken his ankle playing football the
previous August, and it was still giving him trouble, so Frannie
assumed he'd decided (or been persuaded by her mom) not to join
the search party.

The men were dividing up now; four groups of three and one
group of two. She watched while they all trudged back to their cars
and, with much shouting back and forth, got in. There was a small
traffic jam in the middle of the street while some of the vehicles
turned around and others came alongside one another so that drivers
could exchange last minute instructions, but the street finally emptied, the sound of the car engines receding into silence as the
searchers went their separate ways.

Frannie stood by the window watching the snow erase the criss-
crossed tire marks in the street and felt faintly sick. Suppose something were to happen to one of the men, how would she feel then,
when she'd watched them set off into the storm all the time knowing
where Will had gone? "You're a creep, Will Rabjohns," she said, her
lips touching the icy glass. "If I ever see you again, you're going to be
so sorry." It was an empty threat, of course, but it comforted her a little to rage against him for putting her in this impossible situation.
And for leaving her—that was even worse, in its way. She could bear
the responsibility of silence, but the thought that he'd run off into the
world and left her here when she'd gone to all the trouble, and the
indignity, of making friends with him was unforgivable.

As she got back into bed, she heard her father's voice downstairs. He hadn't gone. That at least was some comfort to her. She
couldn't catch what he was saying, but she was reassured by the slow,
familiar rhythms of his voice and, soothed by them as surely as by a
lullaby, she let her unhappiness go and fell asleep.

IX

i

The climb was not arduous for Will, not with Jacob at his side. All the man had to do when the way became too steep or slippery was to lay his bare hand lightly on the back of Will's neck, and a portion of Jacob's strength would pass from fingers to nape, enabling Will to match him stride for stride. Sometimes, after a touch like this, it seemed to Will he was not climbing at all, but gliding over the snow and rock, effortlessly.

The wind was too strong for words to be exchanged, but more than once he felt Jacob's mind moving close to his. When it did, his thoughts went where they were directed: Up the slope, where their destination could be glimpsed on occasion; and down, into the valley they'd escaped, its petty perfection visible when the gusts dropped. Will was not shocked by this intimacy, mind with mind. Steep was unlike other people; Will had realized that from the very beginning. *Living and dying, we feed the fire*—that was not a lesson that just anybody could teach. He'd joined forces with a remarkable man, whose secrets would slowly be uncovered as they grew to know each other in the years to come. Nor would there be any limit to their knowing: That thought was clearer in his head than any other, and he was certain Steep had read it there. Whatever this man asked of him, he would supply. That was how it would be between them from now on. It was the least he could do, for someone who had already given him more than any other living soul.

ii

Down in the Courthouse, Rosa sat in the dark and listened. Her hearing had always been acute, sometimes distressingly so. There were times—days, weeks even—when she would deliberately drink herself into a mild state of befuddlement (usually on gin, but scotch would do) in order to muffle the sounds that came at her from every direction. It didn't always work. In fact it had backfired on her several times, and instead of dimming the din of the world it had simply stripped her of her power to control her own wits. Those were terrible times, sickening times. She would rage around, threatening to do herself harm—pricking out her ears or plucking out her eyes—and might have done it too, if Jacob hadn't been there to soothe her with a fuck. That usually did the trick. She'd have to be careful with the drinking in future, she mused, at least until she found someone to couple with her in Steep's place. It was a pity the boy was so young, otherwise she might have toyed with him for a while. She'd have worn him out, of course, all too quickly. When on occasion she'd taken any man besides Steep to her bed, she'd always been disappointed. However virile, however heated they appeared to be, none of them had ever shown a smidgen of Jacob's staying power. Damn it, but she would miss him. He had been more than a husband to her, more than a lover; he'd been a goad to excess, calling forth all manner of behavior she'd never have dared indulge, much less enjoy, in any other company, man or beast.

Beast. Now there was a thought. Maybe she would be wiser looking for a fuck-mate outside her own species. She'd dallied with this before, a stallion called Tallis had been the lucky creature. But she hadn't given the affair full rein, so to speak; it had seemed at the time a cumbersome way to be serviced, not to say unsanitary. With Jacob gone, however, she would certainly need to broaden her palate. Maybe with a little patience she'd find a creature the equal of her ardor, out in the wild.

Meanwhile, she listened: to the snow, falling on the Courthouse roof and on the step, on the grass, on the road, on the houses, on the hills; to a dog, barking; to cattle, lowing in a byre; to the babble of televisions, and the bawling of children, and somebody old and phlegmatic (she couldn't tell whether it was a man or a woman; age eroded the distinctions) talking nonsense in his or her sleep.

Then, somebody closer. Footfalls on the icy road; a breath, snatched from chapped lips. No, it wasn't one breath, it was two, both male. After a moment, one spoke.

"What about the Courthouse?" It was a fat man's voice, she judged.

"I suppose we could take a look," said the other, without much enthusiasm. "If the kid had some sense, he'd get out of the cold."

"If he'd had some sense, the little bugger wouldn't have run away in the first place."

They're coming in here, Mrs. McGee thought, rising from the judge's chair. They're looking for the child—compassionate men, how she *loved* compassionate men!—and they think maybe they'll find him in here.

She brushed the hair back from her brow and pinched some color into her cheeks. It was the least she could do. Then she started to unbutton her dress, so as to hold their attention when they entered. Perhaps after all she would not have to stoop to barnyard couplings; perhaps two would replace the departed one, at least for tonight.

iii

The worst of the storm had cleared to the southwest by the time Will and Jacob came within sight of the summit. Through the thinning snow, Will saw that up ahead there was a stand of trees. Leafless, of course (what the season had not taken the night's wind had surely stripped), but growing so close together, and sufficiently large in number that each had protected the other in their tender years, until they had matured into a dense little wood.

Now, with the gale somewhat diminished, Will asked a question out loud, "Is that where we're going?"

"It is," said Jacob, not looking down at him.

"Why?"

"Because we have work to do."

"What?" Will asked. The clouds were coming unknitted over the heights, and even as he put this question a patch of dark star-pricked sky appeared beyond the trees. It was as though a door were opening on the far side of the wood, the sight so perfect Will almost believed it had been stage managed by Jacob. But perhaps it was more likely—and more marvelous, in its way—that they had arrived at this moment by chance, he and Jacob being blessed travelers.

"There's a bird in those trees, you see," Jacob went on. "Actually there's a pair of birds. And I need you to kill them for me." He said this without any particular emphasis, as though the matter was relatively inconsequential. "I have a knife I'd like you to use for the job." Now he looked Will's way, intently. "Being a city boy you're probably not as experienced with birds as you are with moths and such."

"No, I'm not," Will admitted, hoping he didn't sound doubtful or questioning. "But I'm sure it's easy."

"You eat bird-meat, presumably," Jacob said.

Of course he did. He enjoyed fried chicken and turkey at Christmas. He'd even had a piece of the pigeon pie Adele had made once she'd explained that the pigeon wasn't the filthy kind he knew from Manchester. "I love it," he said, the notion of this deed easier when he thought of a barbecued chicken leg. "How will I know which birds you want me to—"

"You can say it."

"Kill?"

"I'll point them out, don't worry. It's as you say: *easy*." He had said that, hadn't he? Now he had to make good on the boast. "Be careful with this," Jacob said, passing the knife to him. "It's uncommonly sharp."

He received the weapon gingerly. Was there some charge passed through its blade into his marrow? He thought so. It was subtle, to be sure, but when his hand tightened around the hilt he felt as though he knew the knife like a friend, as though he and it had some long-standing knowledge of one another.

"Good," Jacob said, seeing Will fearlessly clasping the weapon. "You look as if you mean business."

Will grinned. He did; no doubt of it. Whatever business this knife was capable of, he meant.

They were at the fringes of the wood now and, with the clouds parted, the starlight polished every snow-laden twig and branch until it glittered. There remained in Will a remote tic of apprehension regarding the deed ahead—or rather, his competency in the doing of it; he entertained no doubts about the killing itself—but he showed no sign of this to Jacob. He strode between the trees a pace ahead of his companion and was all at once enveloped in a silence so profound it made him hold his breath for fear of breaking it.

A little way behind him, Jacob said, "Take it slowly. Enjoy the moment."

Will's knife hand had a strange agitation in it however. It didn't want any delay. It wanted to be at work, *now*.

"Where are they?" Will whispered.

Jacob put his hand on the back of Will's neck. "Just look," he murmured, and though nothing actually changed in the scene before them, at Jacob's words Will saw it with a sudden simplicity, his gaze blazing through the lattice of branches and mesh of brambles, through the glamour of sparkling frost and starlit air, to the heart of this place. Or rather to what seemed to him at that moment its heart: two birds, huddled in a niche at the juncture of branch and trunk. Their eyes were wide and bright (he could see them blinking, even though they were ten yards from him) and their heads were cocked.

"They see me," Will breathed.

"See them back."

"I do."

"Fix them with your eyes."

"I am."

"Then finish it. *Go on.*"

Jacob pushed him lightly, and lightly Will went, like a phantom in fact, over the snow-decorated ground. His eyes were fixed on the birds every step of his way. They were plain creatures. Two bundles of ragged brown feathers, with a silver of sheeny blue in their wings. No more remarkable than the moths he'd killed in the Courthouse, he thought. He didn't hurry toward them. He took his time, despite the impatience in his hand, feeling as though he were gliding down a tunnel toward his target, which was the only thing in focus before him. If they fled now, they still could not escape him, of that he was certain. They were in the tunnel with him, trapped by his hunter's will. They might flutter, they might peck, but he would have their lives whatever they did.

He was perhaps three strides from the tree—raising his arm to slit their throats   when one of the pair took sudden flight. His knife hand astonished him. Up it sped, a blur in front of his face, and before his eyes could even find the bird the knife had already trans-fixed it. Though strictly speaking it had not been his doing, he felt proud of the deed.

Look at me! he thought, knowing Jacob was watching him. *Wasn't that quick? Wasn't that beautiful?*

The second bird was rising now, while the first flapped like a toy on a stick. He hadn't time to free the blade. He just let his left hand do as the right had done, and up it went like five-fingered lightning to strike the bird from the air. Down the creature tumbled, landing belly up at Will's feet. His blow had broken its neck. It feebly flapped its wings a moment, shitting itself. Then it died.

Will looked at its mate. In the time it had taken to kill the sec-ond bird, the first had also perished. Its blood, running down the blade, was hot on his hand.

Easy, he thought, just as he'd said it would be. A moment ago they'd been blinking their eyes and cocking their heads, hearts beat-ing. Now they were dead, both of them, spilled and broken. Easy.

"What you've just done is *irreversible*," said Jacob, laying his hands upon Will's shoulders from behind. "Think of that." His touch was no longer light. "This is not a world of resurrections. They've gone. Forever."

"I know."

"No, you don't," Jacob said. There was as much weight in his words as in his palms. "Not yet, you don't. You see them dead before you, but knowing what that means takes a little time." He lifted his left hand from Will's shoulder and reached around his body. "May I have my knife back? If you're sure you've finished with it, that is."

Will slid the bird off the blade, bloodying the fingers of his other hand in the doing, and tossed the corpse down beside its mate. Then he wiped the knife clean on the arm of his jacket—an impressively casual gesture, he thought—and passed it back into Jacob's care, as cautiously as he'd been lent it.

"Suppose I were to tell you," Jacob said softly, almost mournfully, "that these two things at your feet—which you so efficiently dispatched—were the last of their kind?"

"The last birds?"

"No," Jacob said, indulgently. "Nothing so ambitious. Just the last of *these* birds."

"Are they?"

"*Suppose they were,*" Jacob replied. "How would you feel?"

"I don't know," Will said, quite honestly. "I mean, they're just birds."

"Oh now," Jacob chided, "*think again.*"

Will obeyed. And as had happened several times in Steep's presence, his mind grew strange to itself, filling with thoughts it had never dared before. He looked down at his guilty hands, and the blood seemed to throb on them, as though the memory of the bird's pulse was still in it. And while he looked he turned over what Jacob had just said.

Suppose they were the last, the very last, and the deed he'd just done was irreversible. No resurrections here. Not tonight, not ever. *Suppose they were the last,* blue and brown. The last that would ever hop that way, sing that way, court and mate and make more birds who hopped and sung and courted that way.

"Oh," he murmured, beginning to understand. "I . . . changed the world a little bit, didn't I?" He turned and looked up at Jacob. "That's it, isn't it? That's what I did! I changed the world."

"Maybe . . . " Jacob said. There was a tiny smile of satisfaction on his face, that his pupil was so swift. "If these were the last, perhaps it was more than a little."

"Are they?" Will said. "The last, I mean?"

"Would you like them to be?" Will wanted it too much for

words. All he could do was nod. "Another night, perhaps," Jacob said. "But not tonight. I'm sorry to disappoint you, but these," he looked down at the bodies in the grass, "are as common as moths." Will felt as though he'd just been given a present and found it was just an empty box. "I know how it is, Will. What you're feeling now. Your hands tell you you've done something wonderful, but you look around and nothing much seems to have changed. Am I right?"

"Yes," he said. He suddenly wanted to wipe the worthless blood off his hands. They'd been so quick and so clever; they deserved better. The blood of something rare, something whose passing would be of consequence. He bent down and, plucking up a fistful of sharp grass, began to scrub his palms clean.

"So what do we do now?" he said as he worked. "I don't want to stay here any longer. I want to . . . "

He didn't finish his chatter, however, for at that moment a ripple passed through the air surrounding them, as though the earth itself had expelled a tiny breath. He ceased his scrubbing and slowly rose to his feet, letting the grass drop.

"What was that?" he whispered.

"You did it, not I," Jacob replied. There was a tone in his voice Will had not heard before, and it wasn't comforting.

"What did I do?" Will said, looking all around for some explanation. But there was nothing that hadn't been there all along. Just the trees, and the snow and the stars.

"I don't want this," Jacob was murmuring. "Do you hear me? I don't want this." All the weight had vanished from his voice, so had the certainty.

Will looked around at him. Saw his stricken face. "Don't want *what?*" Will asked him.

Jacob turned his fretful gaze in Will's direction. "You've more power in you than you realize, boy," he said. "A lot more."

"But I didn't *do* anything," Will protested.

"You're a conduit."

"I'm a *what?*"

"Damn it, why didn't I see? Why didn't I *see?*" He backed away from Will, as the air shook again, more violently than before. "*Oh Christ in Heaven. I don't want this.*"

His anguish made Will panic. This wasn't what he wanted to hear from his idol. He'd done all he'd been asked to do. He'd killed the birds, cleaned and returned the knife, even put a brave face on his disappointment. So why was his deliverer retreating from him as though Will were a rabid dog?

"*Please*," he said to Steep, "I didn't mean it, whatever it was I did, I'm sorry . . . "

But Jacob just continued to retreat. "It's not you. It's *us*. I don't want your eyes going where I've been. Not there, at least. Not to him. Not to *Thomas*—"

He was starting to babble again, and Will, certain his savior was about to run, and equally certain that once he was gone it would be over between them, reached and grabbed hold of the man's sleeve. Jacob cried out and tried to shake himself free, but in doing so Will's hand, seeking better purchase, caught hold of his fingers. Their touching had made Will strong before; he'd climbed the hill light-footed because Jacob's flesh had been laid on his. But the business of the knife had wrought some change in him. He was no longer a passive recipient of strength. His bloodied fingers had been granted talents of their own, and he could not control them. He heard Jacob cry out a second time. Or was it his own voice? No, it was *both*. Two sobs, rising as though from a single throat.

Jacob had been right to be afraid. The same rippling breath that had distracted Will from cleaning his hands was here again, increased a hundredfold, and this time it inhaled the very world in which they stood. Earth and sky shuddered and were in an instant reconfigured, leaving them each in their terror: Will sobbing that he did not know what was happening; Jacob, that he did.

i

Later, with the good butcher Donnelly dead, Geoffrey Sauls, who had accompanied him into the Courthouse that night, would offer a bowdlerized version of what happened within. This he did to protect both the memory of the deceased man, who'd been his drinking and darts partner for seventeen years, and Donnelly's widow, whose grief would have been cruelly exacerbated by the truth. Which was: They had climbed the steps of the Courthouse thinking that perhaps they'd be the heroes of the night. There was somebody inside, no doubt of that, and more than likely it was the runaway. Who else was it going to be, they reasoned. Donnelly had been a pace or two ahead of Sauls and had therefore arrived in the courtroom first. Sauls had heard him mutter something awestruck and had come to Donnelly's side to find not the missing boy but a woman, standing in the middle of the chamber. There were two or three fat candles set on the ground close to where she stood, and by their flattering light he saw that she was partially undressed. Her breasts, which had a gloss of sweat upon them, were bared, and she'd hoisted up her skirt high enough that her hand could roam between her legs, a smile spreading across her face as she pleasured herself. Though her body was firm (her breasts rode as high as an eighteen year old's), her features bore the stamp of experience. Not that she was lined or flabby; her skin was perfect. But there was about her lips and eyes a confidence that belied her flawless cheeks and brow. In short, Sauls knew the instant he set eyes upon her that this was a woman who knew her mind. He didn't like that one bit.

Donnelly, on the other hand, did. He'd had a couple of double brandies before setting out, and they'd loosened his tongue. "You're a lovely," he said appreciatively. "Aren't you a bit cold?"

The woman gave him the reply he'd surely been hoping for. "You look like you've got plenty of meat on you," she said, earning a chuckle from the butcher. "Why don't you come over here and warm me up a bit?"

"*Del*," Sauls warned, catching hold of his friend's arm, "We're not here for shenanigans. We're here to find the boy."

"Poor Will," the woman said. "A lost lamb if ever there was one."

"Do you know where he is?" Geoffrey said.

"Maybe I do and maybe I don't," the woman replied. Her eyes were fixed on Donnelly, her hands still playing away.

"Is he here somewhere?" Sauls asked her.

"Maybe he is and maybe he isn't."

The reply made Sauls more uneasy than ever. Did it mean she had the boy a prisoner here? God help him if she did. There was a gleam of lunacy in her eyes and in this whorish display of hers. Though he loved Delbert dearly, no sane woman would be inviting him to touch her the way she was right now: her dress lifted so high her privates were on display, her fingers plunged into them to the second knuckle.

"I'd keep your distance if I were you, Delbert," Sauls advised.

"She just wants a bit o' fun," Del replied, swaying toward the woman.

"The boy's here somewhere," Sauls said.

"So go find him," Donnelly replied dreamily, raising his sausage fingers to fondle the woman's breasts. "I'll keep her distracted."

"I'll take you both on if you like," the woman suggested.

But Delbert wasn't feeling democratic. "*Go on*, Geoffrey," he said, his tone faintly threatening. "I can handle her on my own, thank you very much."

Geoffrey had only brawled with Delbert once in his life (over a contested darts match, naturally), and he'd come off much the worse. The butcher was more bulk than brawn, but Geoffrey was a bantamweight, and within half a minute he'd found himself flat on his back in the gutter. Given that he couldn't hope physically to pry Del from the object of his affection, he had little choice but to do as the man said, and go look for the child. He did so quickly, so as not to be gone from the courtroom itself for very long. With his torch-beam lighting the way ahead he searched the passages and chambers in a systematic fashion, calling for the boy as though for a lost dog.

"Will? Where are you? Come on. It's okay. Will?"

In one of the rooms he came upon what he assumed to be the whore's belongings: two or three bags, and some scattered articles of clothing, along with a variety of paraphernalia that looked vaguely erotic in purpose. (He didn't have time to study them closely. But many months later, when the trauma of this night had receded, his mind would guiltily revisit this litter, and obsess on it, imagining the purpose to which she had put these barbed rods and silken cords.) In a second chamber he found a still more disturbing sight. Overturned furniture, ashes underfoot, fragments of charred debris. What he didn't find was the boy; all the other rooms, and there were several, were deserted. The layout of the place was tricky to grasp, especially in his present state of anxiety. He might well have got lost in the maze of chambers and passages had he not heard Delbert start to shout, or sob maybe—yes, it was a sob—and followed the din back through the corridors, through the room with the ashes, and that unholy boudoir, to the courtroom.

And now, of course, we come to that part he kept from telling in its entirety, preferring to risk a lie than defame his friend. Delbert was not, as Sauls would later testify, laying inert on the floor, sobbing to be saved. Supine he certainly was, his pants and underwear somewhere around his boots, his head and arms thrown back. But there was no appeal in his cry, except perhaps that the woman straddling him, her hands digging into the mottled fat of his belly, ride him harder, harder.

"*Jesus, Del*," Sauls said, appalled at the sight.

Delbert's little eyes, upside-down in the wet, hot bulk of his head, burned with pleasure.

"Go. Away." he said.

"No, no . . . " the woman panted, beckoning Geoffrey to her and proffering her breast. "I can use him here."

Even in the throes of his delirium, however, Donnelly was feeling proprietorial. "Fuck off, Geoffrey," he said, skewing his head around to get a better fix on the competition. "I saw her first."

"I think it's time you shut up!" the woman snapped, and for the first time Geoffrey saw that there was something wrapped around Del's neck. From what he could see it looked to be no more than a thin piece of rope with a few beads threaded along its length, except that it moved, in serpentine fashion, its tail twitching between Del's pink tits, its body sliding upon itself as it tightened its grip. Del suddenly made a choking sound, and his fingers went up to his throat, scrabbling at the cord. His red face suddenly got redder still.

"Now, *come here*," the woman instructed Geoffrey, sweetly enough. He shook his head. If he'd had any urge to touch the creature, it had been scared out of him. "I'm not going to tell you again," she said to Sauls. Then, glancing down at Delbert, she murmured, "Do you want it tighter?" A pitiful gurgling sound was all that escaped him, but the snake-rope seemed to take that as a yes and duly tightened.

"*Stop!*" Sauls said, "you're killing him!" She stared at him, her face as blank as it was beautiful, so he said it again, in case the bitch in her heat hadn't understood what she was doing. But she understood. He saw that now, saw the look of pleasure cross her face as poor Delbert bucked and thrashed beneath her. He had to stop her, and quickly, or Del would be dead.

"What do you want?" he said, approaching her.

"Kiss me," she said, her eyes become slits in a face that was somehow simpler than it had been moments ago, as though it were being unmade before his eyes by some invisible sculptor. He would have preferred to clamp his mouth to his own mother-in-law's maw than kiss the moist hole in the whore's face, but Del's life was ebbing away by the gasp. A few moments more, and it would be gone. Steel-

ing his courage, he pressed his lips against the unbecoming flesh of
her mouth, only to have her take hold of his hair—what little he
had—and haul back his head. "Not *there!*" she said, the words coming on a breath so balmy and sweetly scented he momentarily forgot
his fear. "Here! Here!"

She pressed his face down toward her bosom, but as he stooped
to service her Delbert's flailing arms caught hold of Geoffrey's right
boot and pulled. He stumbled backward, vaguely aware that this was
more farce than tragedy, his outstretched hand raking the woman's
pristine skin as he tried to prevent himself falling. It was no use.
Down he went, ass first, the breath knocked out of him.

As he raised his head he saw the woman climbing off Delbert,
clutching her breast. "Look what you did," she said to him, showing
him the marks where his fingernails had caught her. He protested
that it had been an accident. "Look!" she said again, advancing on
him. "You *marked* me!"

Behind her, Delbert was gurgling like a monstrous baby, his arms
no longer strong enough to flail or his legs to kick. There was another
of the woman's pet ropes slithering around his groin, Geoffrey saw,
most of its length constricting the base of his prick, so that it stood
up—even now, even as the last of his life went out of him—stout and
stiff.

"He's *dying*," Sauls said to the woman.

She glanced back at the body on the ground. "So he is," she
remarked. Then, looking back at Geoffrey, "But he got what he
wanted, didn't he? So now, the question is: What do *you* want?"

He wasn't going to lie. He wasn't going to tell her he wanted her
body, however finely made she was. He'd only end the same way as
Del. So he told the truth.

"I want to *live*," he said. "I want to go home to my wife and my
kids and pretend this never happened."

"You can never do that," she replied.

"I could!" he insisted. "I swear I could!"

"You wouldn't come after me, for killing your friend?"

"You won't kill him," Geoffrey said, thinking perhaps he was
making some headway with the woman. She'd had her fun, hadn't
she? She'd successfully terrorized them both, reduced him to a quivering mess and Delbert to a human dildo. What more did she need?
"If you let us go, we won't say a word. I promise. Not one word."

"I think it's too late for that," the woman replied. She was standing between Geoffrey's legs now. He felt horribly vulnerable.

"Let me at least help Delbert," he begged. "He's not done any harm to you. He's a good family man and—"

"The world's filled with *family men*," she said contemptuously.

"For pity's sake, he's not done you any harm."

"Oh, Jesus," she said, exasperated. "Help him, then, if you must."

He watched her warily as he scrambled to his feet, anticipating a blow or a kick. But none came. Instead she allowed him to go to Delbert, whose face was by now purplish, his lips flecked with bloody spittle, his eyes rolled up beneath his fluttering lids. There was still breath in him, but precious little; his chest heaved with the effort of drawing air through his constricted windpipe. Fearing the battle was already lost he dug his fingers between cord and flesh and pulled. Del drew a faint, wheezing breath, but it was his last.

"Finally," the woman said.

Geoffrey thought she was referring to Del's passing, but looking down at the man's groin realized his error. In extremis, Del was spurting like a whale.

"Jesus Christ," Geoffrey said, nauseated.

The woman wandered over to admire the spectacle. "You could try the kiss of life," she said. "You might still bring him back."

Geoffrey looked down at Del's face, at his foamy lips and bulging sockets. Maybe there was a remote chance of starting his heart again—and maybe a better friend than he would have attempted it—but nothing on God's earth could have convinced him at that moment to put his lips to the lips of Delbert Donnelly.

"No?" said the woman.

"No," said Geoffrey.

"So you let him die. You couldn't bear to kiss him, and now he's dead." She turned her back on Sauls and wandered away. This was not a pardon, Geoffrey knew, just a stay of execution.

"Oh Mary, mother of God," Geoffrey said softly. "Help me in my hour of need—"

"You don't need a Virgin right now," the woman said, "you need somebody with a little more experience. Somebody who knows what's best for you."

Geoffrey didn't turn to look at her. She'd experienced some mesmeric hold over Del, he was certain of it, and if he met her eyes she'd get into his head the same way. Somehow he had to find a way out of here without looking at her. And then there were those damn ropes to be considered. The one that had garroted Del had already slith-

ered away. He didn't want to look at Del's groin to see what had
become of the other, but he had to assume it was loose somewhere.
He would have one chance at escape, he knew. If he was not quick
enough, or somehow lost his bearings and missed the exit, she would
have him. However offhand she was being right now, she could not
afford to let him escape, not after what he'd witnessed.

"Do you know the story of this place?" she asked him. Happy to
have her distracted by conversation, he told her no, he didn't. "It was
built by a man who felt injustice very deeply."

"Oh?"

"We knew him, Mr. Steep and myself, many, many years ago. In
fact, he and I were intimate, for a short time."

"Lucky man," Geoffrey replied, hoping to flatter. Her talk was all
delusory, of course. Though he knew little about the Courthouse, he
was certain it had been standing a century at least.

"I don't remember him well," she fantasized. "Except for his
nose. He had the largest nose I have seen. Monolithic. And he swore
it was this that made him so sympathetic to the condition of animals—" While she babbled, Geoffrey covertly cast his eyes left and
right, the better to orient himself. Though he couldn't actually see
the door that led to freedom, he guessed it to be just out of sight
near his left shoulder. Meanwhile, the woman chattered on: "They're
so much more sensitive to odors than we are. But Mr. Bartholomeus,
because of his nose, claimed he could smell more like an animal than
a man. Ambrosial, myrrhic, mephitic. He'd divided the smells up, so
he had a name for every one: putrid, musky, balsamic. I forget the
others. In fact, I forget him, except for his nose. It's funny what you
remember about people, isn't it?" She paused. Then: "What's your
name?"

"Geoffrey Sauls." Was that her footfall behind him? He had to
get going, or she'd be upon him. He scanned the ground for her
lethal rosaries.

"No middle name?" she said.

"Oh. Yes." He could see nothing moving, but that didn't mean
they weren't there, in the shadows. "Alexander."

"That's a lot prettier than Geoffrey," she said, her voice closer to
him. He glanced back down at Del's dead face, to give himself that
last jolt of motivation, and then he was up and turning toward the
door. He'd guessed right. There it was, ahead of him now. From the
corner of his eye he glimpsed the whore and felt her eyes burning
into him. He didn't give them the opportunity to work their hex on

him. Loosing a shout he'd learned in the Territorial Army (it was designed to accompany a bayonet charge, while this was a retreat, but what the hell?), he fled for the exit. His senses were more acute than they'd been since boyhood, his adrenaline-flooded system alive to every nuance. He heard the whine of the rosaries as they flew and, glancing over his shoulder, saw them in the air like beaded lightning, flying toward him. He dodged to his right, ducking as he did so, and watched them fly past him, striking the door. There they writhed for a heartbeat, and in that beat he snatched at the handle and threw the door wide. His own strength astonished him. Though the door was heavy it swung fully open, its hinges screeching, and slammed against the wall.

"Alexander," the woman called, her voice silky. "Come back. Do you hear me, Alexander?"

He pelted down the passage, unmoved by her summons, and for a very good reason. Only his mother, whom he had hated with all his heart, had ever called him by that name. The woman could call to him using all the voices of the sirens, and if she hung that dreaded Alexander upon him he would be immune.

Out now, down the steps and into the snow, plowing toward the hedgerow, never looking back. He plunged through the thicket and out onto the road with his lungs burning, his heart drumming, and such a sense of happiness he was almost glad he was alone to enjoy it. Later, when he recounted this, he would talk quietly and mournfully of how he'd lost his friend. For now, he shouted, and laughed, and felt (oh, the perversity of this) all the more glorious because he'd not only outwitted the whore but had Del's death as proof of how terrible his jeopardy had been.

Whooping, then, and stumbling, he returned to his car, which was parked some fifty yards away and undaunted by the icy road (nothing could harm him now; he was inviolate), he drove with foolhardy speed back into the village to sound the alarm.

ii

Back in the Courthouse, Rosa was not a happy woman. She'd been content enough until Alexander and his overweight comrade had arrived, sitting dreaming of finer places and balmier days. But now her dreams had been interrupted, and she had to make some quick decisions.

There'd be a mob at the gates soon enough, she knew: Alexander would make certain of that. They'd be feeling righteous and wrathful, and they'd surely attempt some mischief upon her person if she didn't make herself scarce. It would not be the first time she'd been harried and harassed this way. There'd been an unsavory incident in Morocco only the year before, in which the wife of one of her occasional consorts had led a minor jihad against her, much to Jacob's amusement. The husband, like the fat fellow lying at her feet now, had died *in flagrante delicto*, but—unlike Donnelly—had expired with a broad smile on his face. It was the smile that had truly inflamed his wife: That she'd never seen its like in her life had put her in murderous mood. And then in Milan—oh, how she'd loved Milan—there'd been a worse scene still. She had lingered there for several weeks while Jacob went south and had fallen into the company of the transvestites who plied their hazardous trade about the Parco Sempione. She'd always loved things artificial, and these beauties, who were self-created females to a man (the *viados*, the locals called them, meaning "fawns") had enchanted her. In their company she'd felt a strange sisterhood, and might have elected to stay in that city had one of the pimps, a casual sadist by the name of Henry Campanella, not earned her ire. Hearing that he'd made a particularly savage assault on one of his herd, Rosa had lost her temper. This happened infrequently, but when it did, blood invariably flowed, and copiously. She'd choked the bastard on what had passed for his manhood and left the corpse in the Viale Certosa, on public display. His brother, who was also a pimp, had raised a small army from the criminal fraternity and would have slaughtered her if she hadn't fled to Sicily and the comfort of Steep. Still, she often thought of her sisters in Milan, sitting around chatting about surgeries and silicone, while they plucked and teased and squeezed themselves into a semblance of femininity. And when she thought of them, she sighed.

Enough of memories, she told herself. It was time to vacate the premises, before the dogs came after her, two-legged and four. She carried a candle into her little dressing room and packed up her belongings, keeping her senses sharp every moment. Remotely, she thought she heard raised voices and assumed that Alexander was at the village, telling tales, the way men liked to do.

Finishing her packing hurriedly, she said farewell to the body of Delbert Donnelly and, calling her rosaries to her, made her departure. She had intended to head off northeast along the valley, putting the village and its idiots as far behind her as she could. But once she was out in the snow, her thoughts turned to Jacob. She was of half a mind to leave him in ignorance of what her deeds had unleashed.

But in her heart she knew she owed him the warning, for sentiment's sake. They had spent so many decades together, arguing, suffering, and in their curious way devoting themselves to one another. Though his recent frailties disenchanted her, she could not leave him until she'd performed this last duty.

Turning her face to the hills, which had emerged from the retiring blizzard, she rapidly sought him out. She had no need of senses in this: There was in them both a compass for which the other was north; all she had to do was let the needle swing and settle, and there he would be. Lugging her bags, she started up the slope in his direction, leaving a trail in the snow that she was well aware her pursuers would follow. So be it, she thought. If they come, they come. And if blood has to be spilled, I'm in a fine frame of mind to spill it.

XI

It was a sudden spring. The breath out of the earth came and went, and when it passed, it took winter with it. The trees were miraculously clothed in leaf and blossom, the frosted earth gave way to blades of summer grass, to bluebells and wood anemone and melancholy thistle; sunlight danced everywhere. In the branches birds courted and nested, and from the quickened thicket a red fox appeared, regarding Will with a fearless gaze before trotting off about his business, his whiskers and coat gleaming.

"Jacob?" said a reedy voice off to Will's left. "I thought not to see you again so soon."

Will turned to the speaker and found a man standing a few yards off, leaning against a graceful ash. The tree was better dressed than he, his stained shirt, coarse pants and ill-made sandals far less flattering than the flickering leaves. Otherwise, man and tree had much in common. Both slender in body and limb, yet finely made. The man, however, boasted something the tree could not: eyes of such a flawless blue it seemed the sky had found its way into his head.

"I must tell you, my friend," he said, staring not at Jacob but at Will, "if you still hope to persuade me to go with you, you're wasting your breath."

Will looked around at Jacob in the hope of some explanation, but Jacob had gone.

"I told you the truth yesterday. I have nothing left to give Ruke-nau. And I will not be seduced with tales of the Domus Mundi—"

Stepping away from the tree, the man walked toward Will, and to add to the sum of the mysteries here, Will realized that, though the stranger was several years his senior, and lankily tall, they were looking at one another eye to eye, which meant that he had somehow sprung up a foot and a half in height.

"I don't want to know the world that way, Jacob," the man was saying. "I want to see it through my own eyes."

Jacob? Will thought. He's looking straight at me and he's calling me Jacob. That means I'm in Steep's body. I'm looking out through his eyes! The idea didn't frighten him; quite the reverse. He stretched a little, and it seemed to him he could feel the muscle of the man enveloping him, heavy and strong. He inhaled and smelled his own sweat. He raised his hand and fingered the silken curls of his beard. It was the most extraordinary feeling. Though he was the possessor here, he felt possessed, as though being in Steep had put Steep in his being.

There were appetites in his hips and head he'd never felt before. He wanted to be off, away from this melancholic youth, out under the sky testing this borrowed flesh, running until his lungs were furnaces, stretching until his joints cracked. To go naked in this glorious anatomy, yes! Wouldn't that be fine? To eat in it, piss from it, stroke its long limbs.

But he was not the master here; memory was. He had sufficient freedom to scratch his beard or his groin, but he couldn't leave the business that had brought Steep back to this place. All he could do was sit behind Jacob's gilded eyes and listen to what had been said this sunlit day. He had conjured this encounter against Steep's will, it had seemed—*I don't want this*, Jacob had said, over and over—yet now that it was here, it had a momentum all of its own, and he wasn't about to contest its authority, for fear he lose the simple joy of standing in the man, flesh in flesh.

"Sometimes, Thomas," Jacob was saying, "you look at me as though I were the very Devil."

The other man shook his head, his greasy hair falling across his forehead. He pushed it back with a long-fingered hand, stained red and blue. "If you were the Devil, you wouldn't be Rukenau's creature now, would you?" he said. "You wouldn't let him dispatch you off to bring home runaway painters. And if you came for me, I wouldn't be able to resist you. And I can, Jacob. It's hard, but I can." He lifted his hand up above his head and drew down a blossom-laden branch to sniff. "I had a dream last night, after you'd gone. I dreamed I was up in the heavens, higher than the highest cloud, looking down at the earth, and there was somebody close to me, whispering in my ear. A soft voice, neither a woman nor a man."

"Saying what?"

"That in all the universe, there was only one planet so perfect, one so blue and bright as this. One so prodigious in its creations. And that this glory was God's very being."

"God's delusion, Thom. That's what it is."

"No, listen to me! You've spent too much time with Rukenau. All this around us right now isn't some trick God's playing on us." He let the branch he'd been holding go, and it sprang back into place, dropping petals down on Thomas's head and shoulders. He didn't notice. He was too inflamed by his dream and the telling of it. "God knows the world through us, Jacob. He adores it with our voices. He makes our hands do it service. And at night, He looks out through our eyes, out into the immensity, and names the stars, so that in time we'll sail to them." He dropped his head. "That's what I dreamed."

"You should tell it to Rukenau. He loves to read the meaning in dreams."

"But there's nothing to decipher," Thomas replied, grinning at the ground. "That's the genius of it, don't you see?" He looked up at Will again, the sky in his head pristine. "Poor Rukenau. He's been reciting his liturgies for so long, he's more in love with them than with the true sacrament."

"And what's that, pray tell?"

"*This*," Thomas said, plucking one of the petals off his shoulder. "I have the Holy of Holies here, the Ark of the Covenant, the Sangraal, the Great Mystery itself, right here on the tip of my little finger. Look!" He proffered the petal, balanced on his digit. "If I could paint this perfection," he stared at the petal as he spoke, as though mesmerized by the sight, "put it on a sheet of paper so that it showed its true glory, every painting in every chapel in Rome, every illumination of every Book of Hours, every picture I ever made for every one of Rukenau's damned invocations would be," he paused for the word, "superfluous." He blew the petal from his finger, and it rose up a little way before starting its descent. "But I cannot make such a painting. I labor and I labor, and I make only failures. Jesus. Sometimes, Jacob, I wish I'd been born without fingers."

"Well, if you have so little use for their skills, then lend your fingers to me," Jacob said. "Let me use them to make pictures half as fine as yours, and I will be the happiest man in creation."

Thomas grinned, regarding Jacob quizzically. "You say the strangest things."

"*I* say strange things," Jacob replied. "You should hear yourself, today or any day." He laughed and Thomas laughed along with him, his defeat momentarily forgotten.

"Come back to the island with me," Jacob said, approaching Thomas cautiously, as though afraid of startling him. "I'll make sure Rukenau doesn't make a workhorse out of you."

"That's not the point."

"I know how he always wants things *his* way, how he badgers you. I won't let it happen, Thom, I swear."

"Since when did you have that much authority?"

"Since I told him Rosa and I'd go off and leave him if he didn't let us play a little. *You wouldn't dare leave me,* he said. *I know your nature and you don't. If you desert me, you'll never know what you are or how you came to be.*"

"And what did you say to that?"

"Oh, you'll be proud of me. I said: *It's true, I don't know what made me. Yet was I made and made with love. And that may be knowledge enough to live in bliss.*"

"Oh Lord, I wish I'd been there to see his face."

"He wasn't happy." Jacob chuckled. "But what could he say? It was the truth."

"So prettily put, too. You should be a poet."

"No, I want to paint like you. I want us to work side by side, and you teach me how to see the flow in things, the way you do. The island's so beautiful, and there's just a few fishermen who live there, too cowed to say boo to the likes of us. We can live as though we were in Eden: you, me, and Rosa."

"Let me think about it," Thomas said.

"One more persuasion."

"Leave it alone now."

"No. Hear me out. I know you don't trust Rukenau's gnostics, and a lot of the time, in truth, they confound me too—but the Domus Mundi isn't an illusion. It's glorious, Thomas. You'll be astonished when you move in it and feel it move in you. Rukenau says it's a vision of the world from the inside out—"

"And how much laudanum does he have you imbibe before you see this vision?"

"None. I swear. I wouldn't lie to you, Thom. If I thought this was just another delirium, I'd tell you to stay here and paint petals. But it isn't. It's something divine, something we're allowed to know if our hearts are strong enough. Lord, Thom, just imagine the petals you could paint if you studied them first in the seed. Or in the shoot. Or in the sap that made a bud come from a twig."

"That's what the Domus Mundi shows you?"

"Well, to be honest, I haven't dared go very far inside. But yes, that's what Rukenau says. And if we were together, we could go *deep*, *deep* inside. We could see the seed of the seed, I swear."

Thomas shook his head. "I don't know whether to be excited or afraid," he said. "If what you're telling me's true, then Rukenau has a way to God."

"I think he has," Jacob said softly. He studied Thomas, who could no longer look at him. "I won't press you for an answer now," he said. "But I have to know yea or nay by noon tomorrow. I've already lingered here longer than I intended."

"I'll have made up my mind by tomorrow.'"

"Don't look so melancholy, Thom," Jacob said. "I meant to inspire you."

"Maybe I'm not ready for the revelation."

"You're ready," Jacob said. "More than me, certainly. More than Rukenau, probably. He's brought into being something he doesn't understand, Thom. You could help him, I dare say. Well, we'll say no more about it today. Just promise me you won't get drunk and maudlin thinking about all of this. I fear for you when you get into those villainous moods of yours."

"I won't," Thomas replied. "I'll be merry thinking of you and me and Rosa going naked all day."

"Good," said Jacob, leaning over to touch Thomas's unshaven cheek. "Tomorrow, you'll wake up and wonder why you waited so long."

With that, he turned his back on Thomas and started to stride away. If this was the end of the memory, Will thought, it was hard to see why Jacob had been so troubled at the prospect of reliving it. But the past was not done with its unraveling yet. On the third stride, Will felt the world inhale again, and the sunlight suddenly dimmed.

He looked up through the blossomed branches. In an instant, the perfect sky had been blinded by clouds and the wind brought rain against his face.

"Thomas?" he said, and turning on his heel, looked back toward the place where the painter had been standing. He was nowhere to be seen.

This is tomorrow, Will thought. *He's come for his answer.*

"Thomas?" Jacob called again. "Where are you?" There was dry dread in his voice and a churning in his bowels, as though he already knew something was amiss.

The thicket ahead of him shook, and the red fox walked into view, redder today than he'd been the day before. He licked his chops as he went, his long gray tongue curling up around his snout. Then he slunk away.

Jacob's gaze didn't follow him, but went instead to the clump of wild rose and hazel from which the animal had emerged.

Oh Jesus, a voice murmured. *Look away. You hear me?*

Will heard, but his eyes continued to scrutinize the thicket. There was something on the ground beyond the tangle; he couldn't yet see what.

Look away, damn you! Steep raged. *Are you listening to me, boy?*

He means me, Will thought; the boy he's talking to is me.

Quickly! Steep said. *There's still time!* His rage mellowed into a plea. *There's no need for us to see this,* he said. *Just let it go, boy. Let it go.*

Perhaps the pleading was a distraction intended to conceal an attempt to take control, because the next moment Will's head was filled with a rushing sound, and the scene in front of him gasped, then flickered out.

The next instant, he was back in the winter wood, his teeth chattering, the taste of salt blood in his mouth from a bitten lip. Jacob was still in front of him, his eyes streaming with tears.

"Enough," he said. But the distraction, whether intentional or no, only kept the memory at bay a moment. Then the world shook again, and Will was back in Jacob's trembling body, standing in the rain.

The last of Jacob's resistance seemed to have melted away. Though the man's gaze had flitted from the blossom during their brief departure, all Will had to do was call it back to the rose thicket and it dutifully went. There was one last, exhausted sound from the man that might have been a word of protest. If it was, Will failed to catch it and would not have acted upon the objection anyway. He was the master of this anatomy now: eyes, feet, and all that lay between. He could do what he wished with it, and right now, he didn't want to run or eat or piss: He wanted to see. He commanded Steep's feet to move, and they carried him forward, until he had sight of what the thicket had concealed.

It was Thomas the painter, of course. Who else? He was lying faceup in the wet grass, his sandals and his pants and his stained shirt strewn about him, his corpse become a palette arrayed with colors of its own. Where the painter had exposed his skin to the sun over the years—his face and neck, his arms and feet—he was tanned a ruddy sienna. Where he had been covered, which was to say every other place, he was a sickly white. Here and there, in the bony clefts of his chest and the groove of his abdomen, and at his armpits, he had gingery hair. But there were upon him colors far more shocking than these. A patch of vivid scarlet on his groin where the fox had dined on his penis and testicles. And pooling in the paint pots of his eyes the same bright hue, where birds had taken his tender sight. And along the flank of his body a flap of livid fat exposed by the teeth or beak of a creature wanting to partake of his liver It was a more radiant yellow than a buttercup.

Happy now? Jacob murmured.

Whether this question was meant for his occupant or the corpse before them, Will did not dare inquire. He'd dragged Jacob to revisit this appalling vision against the man's wishes, and now he felt shame at what he'd done. Sickened too. Not at the sight of the body. That didn't bother him particularly; it was no more horrible than the meat hanging up in a butcher's window. What made him want to look away was the thought that this thing before him was probably the way Nathaniel had looked, give or take a wound. Will had always imagined Nathaniel somehow perfected in death; his injuries erased by kindly hands, so that his mother could remember him immaculate. Now he knew differently. Nathaniel had been thrown through a shoe store window. There was no concealing wounds so deep. No wonder Eleanor had wept for months and locked herself away; no wonder she'd taken to eating pills instead of bread and eggs. He hadn't understood how terrible it must have been for her, sitting beside Nathaniel's bed, while he slipped away. But he understood now. And understanding, he blushed with shame at his cruelty.

He'd had enough. It was time to do as Steep had wanted all along, and look away. But now the shoe was on the other foot, and Steep knew it.

Do you want to take a closer look? Will heard him say, and the next moment Steep was going down on his haunches beside Thomas's corpse, scrutinizing it wound by wound. It was Will who flinched now, his curiosity more than sated. But Jacob would not give him release. *Look at him,* Steep murmured, his gaze going to Thomas's mutilated groin. *That fox made a meal of him, eh?* There was a phony jocularity in Steep's tone. He felt this as deeply as Will; perhaps more so. *Serves him right. He should have got some pleasure from his prick while he still had it to wave around. Poor, pathetic Thomas. Rosa tried to seduce him more than once but he could never get it up. I told him: If you don't want Rosa, who has everything a man could want in a woman, then you can't want a woman at all. You're a sodomite, Thom. He said I was too simple.*

Steep leaned over and peered more closely at the wound. The fox's needle teeth had done a neat job. If not for the blood and a few remnants of tissue, the man could have been born unsexed. "Well, you look like the simple one now, Thomas," Steep said, taking his gaze from gelded groin to blinded head.

There was another color here, which Will had not noticed until now. On the inner surfaces of the painter's lips, and on his teeth and tongue, a bluish tinge.

"You poisoned yourself, didn't you?" Steep said. He leaned closer to Thomas's face. "Why did you do a damn fool thing like that? Not because of Rukenau, surely. I would have protected you from him. Didn't I promise?" He reached out and brushed the back of his fingers across the man's cheek, the way he had as they parted the day before. "Didn't I tell you you'd be safe with Rosa and me? Oh Lord, Thom. I would not have seen you suffer." He leaned back from the body and, in a louder voice than he'd used hitherto, as though making a formal declaration, said, "Rukenau's to blame. You gave him your genius; he paid you in lunacy. That makes him a thief, at very least. I won't serve him after this. And I will never forgive him. He can stay in his wretched house forever, but he won't have me for company. Nor Rosa neither." He got to his feet. "Goodbye, Thom," he said, more softly. "You would have liked the island." Then he turned his back on the body, the way he'd turned his back on the living man the day before, and strode away.

As he did so, the scene began to flicker out, the pattering rain, the roses and the body that lay under both, dimming in a heartbeat. But as they went, Will caught a glimpse of the fox, standing at the limit of the trees, gazing back at him. A shaft of sun had pierced the rain clouds and found the animal, stretching its lean flanks and keen head and flickering brush in gold. In the instant before his vision fled, Will met the beast's unblinking stare. There was nothing contrite in its look, no shame that it had fed on pudenda today. I'm a beast, its stare seemed to say, don't you dare judge me.

Then they were both gone—the fox and the sun that blessed it—and Will was back in the dark copse above Burnt Yarley. In front of him stood Jacob, his hand still caught in Will's grip.

"Had enough?" Steep said.

By way of reply, Will simply let go of the man's hand. Yes, it was enough. More than enough. He looked all around him, to be certain nothing of what he'd witnessed had lingered, reassured by what he saw. The trees were once again leafless, the ground frosted, and the only corpses upon it two birds—one broken, one stabbed. In fact, he was by no means certain that this was even the same wood.

"Did it . . . happen here?" he asked, looking back at Jacob.

The man's tear-stained face was slack, his eyes glazed. It took a few moments for him to focus his attention upon the question. "No," he said, finally. "Simeon lived in Oxfordshire that year—"

"Who's Simeon?"

"Thomas Simeon, the man you just met."

Will tried the name for himself, "Thomas Simeon—"

"It was the May of seventeen-thirty. He was twenty-three years old. He poisoned himself with his pigments, which he mixed himself. Arsenic and sky blue."

"If it happened in some other place," Will said, "why did you remember it?"

"Because of you," Jacob replied, softly. "You brought him to mind, in more ways than one." He looked away from Will, out through the trees toward the valley. "I'd known him since he was about your age. He was like my own to me. Too gentle for this world of illusions. It made him mad, trying to find his way through this profligate Creation." He glanced back at Will, his eyes as sharp as his blade. "God's a coward and showoff, Will. You will come to understand this, as the years go by. He hides behind a gaudy show of forms, boasting how fine His workings are. But Thomas had it right. Even in his wretched state, he was wiser than God." Jacob raised his hand palm up in front of his face, his little finger extended. The significance of the gesture was perfectly clear. All that was missing was the petal. "If the world were a simpler place, we would not be lost in it," he said. "We wouldn't be greedy for novelty. We wouldn't always want something new, always something new! We'd live the way Thomas wanted to live, in awe of the mysteries of a petal." Even as he spoke, Steep seemed to hear the yearning in his own voice, and turned it to ice. "You made a mistake, boy," he said, his hand closing into a fist. "You drank where it wasn't wise to drink. My memories are in your head now. So's Thomas. And the fox. And the madness."

Will didn't like the sound of this at all. "What madness?" he said.

"You can't see all that you've seen, you can't know what we now both know, without something souring." He put his thumb to the middle of his skull. "You've supped from here, *wunderkind,* and neither of us can ever be the same. Don't look so frightened. You were brave enough to come with me this far—"

"But only because *you* were with me—"

"What makes you think we can ever be apart after this?"

"You mean we can still go away together?"

"No, that won't be possible. I'll have to keep you at a distance—a *great* distance—for both our sakes."

"But you just said—"

"That we'd never be apart. Nor will we. But that doesn't mean you'll be at my side. There would be too much pain for both of us, and I don't wish that for you any more than you wish it for me."

He was talking the way he would to an adult, Will knew, and it soothed a little of the disappointment. This talk of pain between them, of places where Jacob didn't want to look: This was the vocabulary one man would use talking to another. He would diminish himself in Jacob's eyes if he answered like a petulant child. And what was the use? Plainly, Jacob wasn't going to change his mind.

"So . . . where will you go now?" Will said, attempting to be casual.

"I'll go about my work."

"And what's that?" Will said. Jacob had spoken of his work several times, but he'd never been specific about it.

"You already know more than's best for either of us," Jacob replied.

"I can keep a secret."

"Then keep what you know," Jacob said. "There," he put his fist to his chest . . . "where only you can touch it."

Will made a fist of his numb fingers and echoed Jacob's gesture. It earned him a wan smile.

"Good," he said. "Good. Now . . . go home."

Those were the words Will had hoped so hard not to hear. Hearing them now, he felt tears pricking his eyes. But he told himself he wasn't to cry—not here, not now—and they receded. Perhaps Jacob saw the effort he'd made, because his face, which had been stern, softened.

"Maybe we'll find each other again, somewhere down the road."

"You think so?"

"It's possible," he said. "Now, go off home. Leave me to meditate on what I've lost." He sighed. "First the book. Then Rosa. Now you." He raised his voice a little. "I said go!"

"You lost a book?" Will said. "Sherwood's got it." Will waited, daring to hope the information might give him a reprieve. Another hour in Jacob's company, at least.

"Are you sure?"

"I'm sure!" Will said. "Don't worry, I'll go get it from him. I know where he lives. It'll be easy."

"Now don't be lying to me," Jacob warned.

"I wouldn't do that." Will said, offended at the accusation. "I swear."

Jacob nodded. "I believe you," he said. "You would be of great service to me if you put the book back in my hand."

Will grinned. "That's all I want to do. I want to be of service."

XII

i

There was no magic in the descent: no sense of anticipation, no strengthening hand laid on Will's nape to help him negotiate the snow-slickened rocks. Jacob had done all the touching he intended to do. Will was left to fend for himself, which meant that he fell repeatedly. Twice he slithered several yards on his rump, bruising and scraping himself on buried boulders as he tried to bring his careening to a halt. It was a cold, painful, and humiliating journey. He longed for it to be over quickly.

Halfway down the hill, however, his misery was made complete by the reappearance of Rosa McGee. She appeared out of the murk calling for Jacob, with sufficient alarm in her voice that Jacob told Will to wait while he spoke to her. Rosa was plainly agitated. Though Will could hear nothing of the exchange, he saw Jacob lay a reassuring hand on her, nodding and listening, then replying with his head close to hers. After perhaps a minute, he returned to Will and told him, "Rosa's had a little trouble. We're going to have to be careful."

"Why?"

"Don't ask questions," Jacob replied, "just take my word for it. Now," he pointed down the hill, "we have to hurry."

Will did as he was told and headed on down the slope. He cast one backward glance at Rosa and saw that she'd squatted down on a flat-topped rock, from which she seemed to be staring back toward the Courthouse. Had she been ousted, he wondered? Was that what all her distress was about? He would probably never know. More weary and dispirited by the stride, he continued his descent.

There was, he saw, a good deal of activity in the streets of the village: several cars with their headlights blazing, people gathered in groups here and there. The doors of many of the houses stood open, and people were standing on the steps in their nightclothes, watching events.

"What's going on?" Will wondered aloud.

"Nothing we need concern ourselves with," Jacob replied.

"They're not looking for me, are they?"

"No, they're not," Jacob said.

"It's her, isn't it?" Will said, the mystery of Rosa's distress suddenly solved. "They're after Rosa."

"Yes, I'm afraid they are," Jacob replied. "She's got herself in some trouble. But she's perfectly capable of looking after herself. Why don't we just stop for a moment and examine our options?" Will duly stopped, and Jacob descended the slope a stride or two, until they stood just a couple of yards apart. It was the closest he'd been to Will since the wood. "Can you see where your friends live from here?"

"Yes."

"Point it out to me, will you?"

"You see past where the police car's parked, there's a bend in the road?"

"I see."

"There's a street just round the bend, going left?"

"I see that, too."

"That's Samson Road," Will said. "They live in the house with the junkyard beside it."

Jacob was silent for a few seconds while he studied the lay of the land.

"I can get the book for you," Will reminded him, just in case he was thinking of going on alone.

"I know," Jacob said. "I'm relying on you. But I don't think it'd be very wise for us to just walk through the middle of the village right now."

"We can go around the back," Will said. He pointed out a route that would take them another half-hour to complete but would keep them out of the way of witnesses.

"It seems the wisest option," Jacob said. He teased off his right-hand glove, and reached into his coat to take out his knife. "Don't worry," he said, catching Will's anxious glance, "I won't taint it with human blood unless it's strictly necessary."

Will shuddered. An hour ago, climbing the hill with Jacob, he'd felt happier than he'd felt in his life before; the feel of that blade had made his palm tremble with pleasure, and the little deaths he'd caused filled him with pride. Now all that seemed like another world, another Will. He looked down at his hands. He'd never finished scrubbing them clean, and even in the murk he could see that they were still stained with the bird's blood. He felt a spasm of self-disgust. If he could have fled then and there, he might well have done so. But that would have left Jacob searching for the book on his own, and Will didn't dare risk that—not while he was carrying that knife of his. Will knew from experience how self-possessed it could be, how eager to do harm.

Turning his back on man and knife, he resumed his descent, no longer heading directly into the village but around it, so as to bring them undiscovered to the Cunninghams's doorstep.

ii

When Frannie woke, the clock beside the bed said five-twenty-five. She got up anyway, knowing that her father, who had always been an early riser, would also be up in the next fifteen minutes.

In fact, she found him in the kitchen, already fully dressed, pouring himself a cup of tea and smoking a cigarette. He gave her a grim little smile of welcome. "Something's going on out there," he said, spooning sugar into his tea. "I'm going out to see what's happening."

"Have some toast first," she said. She didn't wait for a reply. She took a loaf out of the bread bin, then went to the drawer for the breadknife, then to the cooker to turn on the grill, and back to slice the bread—and all the time, toing and froing, she was thinking how strange it was to be pretending that there was nothing really different about the world this morning, when she knew in her heart that this wasn't so.

It was her father who finally spoke, his back to her as he gazed out of the kitchen window. "I don't know," he said. "Things going on these days . . . " he shook his head, "used to be safe for folks."

Frannie had slid two slices of the thickly cut bread beneath the grill and, fetching her favorite mug out of the cupboard, poured herself some tea. Like her dad, she sugared it heavily. They were the two sweet tooths in the family.

"It makes me scared for you, sometimes," her father said, turning back to look at Frannie, "the way the world's going."

"I'll be all right, Dad," she said.

"I know you will," he said, though his expression belied his words. "We'll all be fine." He opened his arms to her, and she went to him, hugging him hard. "Only you'll see as you get older," he said, "there's more bad out there than good. That's why you work hard to make a safe place for the people you love. Somewhere you can lock the door." He rocked her in his embrace. "You're my princess, you know that?"

"I know," she said, smiling up at him.

A police car roared past, siren blaring. The happiness faded from George Cunningham's face.

"I'll butter us some toast," Frannie said, patting his chest. "That'll make us feel better." She pulled the slices out from under the grill and flipped them over. "You want some marmalade?"

"No thanks," he said, watching her as she fussed around: to the fridge for some butter, then back to the cooker, where she picked up the hot toast and put it on a plate. Then she slathered on the butter, the way she knew he liked it.

"There," she said, presenting him with the toast. He wolfed it down, murmuring his approval.

All she needed now was milk for her tea. The carton was empty, but the milkman might have arrived by now, so she padded through to the front door to fetch the delivery.

The front door had been bolted top and bottom, which was unusual. Plainly her parents had gone to bed nervous. Frannie reached up and unbolted the top then, stooping to unbolt the bottom, opened the door.

There was still no sign of the day, not a glimmer. It was going to be one of those winter days when light barely seemed to touch the world before it was gone again. The snow had stopped falling, however, and the street looked like a well-made bed in the lamplight—plump white pillows piled against walls and quilts laid on roofs and pavements. She found the sight comforting in its prettiness. It reminded her that Christmas would soon be here, and there'd be reasons for songs and laughter.

The step was empty; the milk was late being delivered today. Oh well, she thought, I'll have to do without.

And then, the sound of feet crunching on snow. She looked up and saw somebody had appeared at the opposite side of the street. Whoever it was stood beyond the lamplight, but only for a few moments. Realizing he'd been seen, he stepped out of the gray gloom and into view. It was Will.

XIII

i

Rosa waited on the rock, listening. They would be upon her soon, her pursuers. She could hear every creak of their snow-caked boots as they followed her trail up the hillside to where she sat. One of them—there were four—was smoking as he climbed (she could see the pinprick of his cigarette, brightening whenever he drew on it); one of them was young, his breathing easier than that of his companions; one took out a flask of brandy every now and then and, when he offered it around, had a distinct slur in his voice. The fourth was quieter than the others, but sometimes, if she listened very carefully, she thought she heard him murmuring something to himself. It was too indistinct for her to understand, but she suspected it was a prayer.

Her exchanges with Jacob had been quite straightforward. She'd freely admitted to what she'd done in the Courthouse and told him he'd better get out of harm's way before the mob was upon them.

He'd told her he would not be leaving the vicinity just yet; he had work to do in the village. When she asked him what manner of work, he told her he wasn't about to share secrets with a woman who'd probably be under interrogation before dawn.

"Is that a dare, Mr. Steep?" she said.

"You might take it that way, I suppose," he'd replied.

"Would you have their deaths on my conscience?" she'd said, to which he'd replied, *What conscience?*

His response had amused her mightily, and for a few moments, standing there on the hillside with Jacob, it had almost seemed like old times.

"Well," she said, "now you've been warned."

"Is that all you're going to do?" Jacob had replied. "Warn me, then walk away?"

"What else do you suggest?" she said with a little smile.

"I want you to make sure they don't come after me."

"So say it," she'd whispered. "Say: *Kill them for me, Rosa.*" She'd leaned closer to him; his heartbeat had quickened. She'd heard it, loud and clear. "If you want them dead, Jacob, then all you have to do is ask." Her lips were so close to his ear, they were almost touching. "Nobody's going to know but us."

He'd said nothing for a few seconds, and then, in that resigned voice of his, he'd murmured the words she'd wanted to hear, "Kill them for me." Then he'd gone on his way with the boy.

Now she waited, feeling altogether happier. Though he'd been willing to kill her just a few hours before, she more and more thought it would be better for them both if they made peace. She'd exacted her revenge for his attempt on her life, so she was willing to put the incident behind her, if things could be permanently healed between them. And they could, she was certain, with a little work, a little patience. Maybe their relationship could never be quite what it had been before—there'd be no further attempts at children, she was resigned to that—but a healthy marriage wasn't carved in stone. It changed, deepened and matured. That was how it could be between Jacob and herself, by and by. They would learn a fresh respect for one another, find fresh ways to express their devotion.

Which brought her back to the purpose of this vigil on the rock. What more perfect way of demonstrating her love than this: to commit murder for him?

She held her breath and listened intently. The man with the

slurred voice was complaining about the climb; he couldn't go any further, he was saying. He'd have to leave them to go on without him.

"*No, no,*" she said to herself softly. She was ready to take four lives, and four lives she would take. No excuses.

While the men debated, she made her own decision: No more waiting. If they were going to procrastinate then she would take control of events and go to them. Drawing a deep breath, she rose from her squatting place, clambered down off the rock and, almost girlish with anticipation, began to retrace her tracks to where her victims stood.

ii

Will looked terrible. Gray face, clothes torn and sodden, his gait a shambling limp. He looked the way Frannie imagined somebody dead would look. Dead, but come back in the middle of the night to say good-bye.

She put that stupidity out of her head. Will needed help: That was all that mattered right now. Though she was barefoot, she stepped off the threshold and started toward him, her legs plunged shin-deep in snow. "Come on into the warm," she said to him.

He shook his head. "There's no time," he said. He sounded as sick as he looked. "I just came to get the book back."

"You told him?"

"Yes . . . I had to," Will said. "It's *his* book, Frannie, and he wants it back."

She stopped advancing, suddenly realizing her naïveté. Will wasn't here unaccompanied. Jacob Steep was with him. Out of sight, somewhere in the darkness beyond the lamplight, but close at hand. Was that why Will looked so ill, she wondered? Had Steep hurt him somehow? Keeping her head directed at Will, she looked for a sign of motion in the shadows behind him. Somehow she had to get Will off the street and back into the safety of the house, without arousing Steep's suspicion.

"The book's upstairs," she said, as casually as she could. "Just come on in while I fetch it for you."

Will shook his head, but there was sufficient hesitation before he did so for her to think he might be tempted to step into the warmth if she pressed a little harder.

"Come on," she said. "It won't take me more than a minute or two. There's tea. And buttered toast—" (they were, she knew, just simple domesticities, set against whatever claim Steep had upon him; pitiful, probably, in the scheme of things. But they were all she had).

"I don't . . . want to come in," he said.

She shrugged. "Okay," she said lightly. "I'll go and get the book." She turned back toward the house, wondering already what she was going to do once she got inside. Did she leave the door open, hoping to coax Will over the threshold, or did she close it, protecting the house and her family from the man watching in the shadows?

She compromised, leaving the door an inch ajar in case Will changed his mind. Then, teeth chattering, she started upstairs. From the kitchen, her father said, "Did you get the milk?"

"I'll be down in a minute, Dad," she called, and hurried to her room. She knew exactly where she'd hidden the book, of course: She had it in her hands in seconds, and was halfway back to the hallway when she heard Sherwood say, "What are you doing?"

She glanced up to the landing, attempting to keep the book out of his bleary sight. But she wasn't quick enough.

"Where are you taking that?" he said, moving to the top of the stairs to pursue her.

"*Stay up there!*" she ordered him, imitating her mother's severest tone. "I mean it, Sherwood."

Her instruction didn't slow him a jot. Worse, it brought her father out of the kitchen, hushing her. "You'll wake your mom, Frannie." His gaze went from the staircase to the door, which the wind had blown wide. "No wonder there's such a draft!" he said, striding to close it.

Panicking now, she raced down the stairs to intercept him. "I'll close it! It's okay!" But she was too late. Her father was there ahead of her, staring out into the snow. He had seen Will.

"What the hell's going on?" he said, glancing back at Frannie, who was by now just a yard behind him. "Did you know he was here?"

"Yes, Dad."

"God Almighty!" he said, raising his voice. "Have you kids no sense? William? Come on in here right now. You hear me!"

Frannie could see Will over her father's shoulder, and remotely hoped he might obey. But instead he retreated a few steps.

"*Come back here!*" George demanded, stepping out of the house to lend weight to his order.

"Dad, *don't*—" Frannie began.

"Shut up!" her father snapped.

"He's not on his own, Dad," Frannie said.

That was enough to slow her father. "What are you talking about?"

Frannie had reached the front doorstep. "Please, leave him alone."

Her father's strained temper broke. "*Go inside!*" he yelled. "You hear me, Frances?" She was certain the whole neighborhood heard him. It would only be a matter of time before everyone was out in the street, asking questions. The best thing for everyone was for her to get the book into Will's hands and let him deliver it to Steep. It was Steep's property, when all was said and done. Everyone would be better off if it was back where it belonged.

But before she could defy her father's edict and step outside, Sherwood grabbed hold of her.

"Who's out there?" he said. His morning breath was foul, his grip clammy.

"It's just Will," she lied.

"You're fibbing, Frannie," he said. "It's them, isn't it?" He was looking past her now, out into the darkness. "Rosa?" he said softly. Then, saying, "I'll take the book!" he tried to snatch it out of Frannie's grip. She refused to relinquish it. Using all her strength, she shoved her brother hard in the middle of the chest, pushing him back down the hallway. Mrs. Cunningham was descending the stairs now, demanding to know what was going on, but Frannie ignored her and stepped back out into the snow, just in time to see her father closing on Will, who seemed to have no strength left to retreat. His ashen face was slack, his body swaying.

"Don't . . . ." Frannie heard him say, as her father reached out for him. Then, as Mr. Cunningham's hand was laid upon him, he collapsed, his eyes rolling up beneath his fluttering lids.

Frannie didn't linger to see what state he was in. She strode on past her father, who was having too much difficulty keeping Will's dead weight from carrying them both to the ground to stop her, and out into the middle of the street. She raised the journal as she did so, high above her head, where Steep could see it.

"This is what you want," she said, almost under her breath. "Come and get it."

She turned three hunded sixty degrees, waiting for him to show himself. There was her mother at the front doorstep, demanding that she come back inside this second. There was their next door neighbor, Mrs. Davies, standing at her front gate with her bratty terrier Benny yapping fit to bust. There was the milkman, Arthur Rathbone, stepping out of his van, with a puzzled look on his face.

And then, as she began her second turn, there was Steep. He was approaching her with a steady stride, his gloved hand already outstretched to claim his prize. She wanted to keep the largest distance possible between the enemy and the front door of her house, so she didn't wait until he came to her but went to meet him on the opposite side of the street. Curiously, she felt only the tiniest twinge of fear. This street was her world—nagging mother, yapping dog, milkman, and all. He had little authority here, even in the dark.

They were within a couple of yards of each other now, and she could see better the look on his face. He was happy, his eyes glued to the book in her hand.

"Good girl," he murmured to her and had it out of her hand before she was even aware that it was gone.

"He didn't mean to take it," she called after him, just in case he bore Sherwood some ill will. "He didn't know it was important." Steep nodded. "It *is* important, isn't it?" she said, hoping against hope he'd leave her with a clue, however vague, as to the nature of the book's contents. But if he understood her intention, he wasn't about to give anything away. Instead, he said, "Tell Will to watch out for Lord Fox, will you?"

"Lord Fox?"

"He'll understand," Steep said. "He's part of the madness now."

With that, he turned his back on her and was gone, off down the street—past her father's yard, past Arthur Rathbone, who wisely stepped out of his way, past the postbox at the corner, and out of sight.

She kept watching the corner for several seconds after he'd gone, deaf to the sobs and yells and yappings. She felt suddenly bereft. A mystery had gone from her hands, and now she'd never solve it. All she had to vex her were her memories of those pages and their tiny hieroglyphics, laid out like a wall built to keep her from understanding what lay on the other side.

"*Frannie?*"

Her mother's voice.

"*Will you come back in here?*"

Even now, though Steep was long gone, it was hard for Frannie to look away.

"Now, Frannie!"

At last, she reluctantly turned her gaze back toward the house. Her father had managed to half-carry, half-haul Will to the doorstep, where her mother stood hugging Sherwood.

There would be hell to pay now, Frannie thought. Questions and more questions, and no chance of concealing anything. Not that it mattered after tonight. Will was back, his adventures over before they'd begun: She didn't need to protect him with lies. All that remained was to tell the truth, however strange that was, and take the consequences. Heavy-hearted and empty-handed, she trudged back toward the threshold, where Sherwood was sobbing against their mother's bosom, sobbing as though he'd never stop.

XIV

Three hours later, with the gloomy day dawned and a second blizzard moving in, Jacob and Rosa found each other on the Skipton road, a few miles north of the valley. They'd not made an explicit arrangement to meet, yet they came to the place (from different directions: Jacob from the valley itself, Rosa from her rock in the hills) within five minutes of each other, as though the rendezvous had been planned.

Rosa was in a bit of a haze as to what she'd actually done to her pursuers, but it had turned into quite a chase, she knew.

"One of them ran and ran," she said. "And I was so mad when I caught up with him, I . . . I . . . " She stopped, frowning. "I knew it was terrible, because he was like a baby, you know? The way they get." She laughed. "Men," she said, "they're all babies. Well, not all. Not you, Jacob."

A gust of snow-flecked wind carried the sound of sirens in their direction.

"We should be on our way," Jacob said, looking up the highway and down. "Which way do you want to go?"

"Whichever *you're* taking," she replied.

"You want to go together?"

"Don't you?"

Jacob wiped his nose, which was running, with the back of his glove. "I suppose so," he said. "Until they've given up looking for us, at least."

"Oh, let them come," Rosa said, with a sour smile. "I'd like to tear out their throats, every one of them."

"You can't kill them all," Jacob said.

Her smile sweetened. "Can't we?" she said, for all the world like a child wheedling for some indulgence. It amused Jacob, despite himself. She always had some little performance to entertain him: Rosa the schoolgirl, Rosa the fishwife, Rosa the poetess. Now Rosa the slaughterer, so busy with her murders she couldn't remember what she'd done to whom. If he wasn't to travel alone, then who better to go with than this woman who knew him so well?

It was not until the next day, reading *The Daily Telegraph* in a café in Aberdeen, that they got some sense of what Rosa had actually done, and even then the newspaper uncharacteristically chose discretion as to the details. Two of the four bodies found on the hill had been dismembered and some portions of one remained unaccounted for. Jacob didn't inquire as to whether she had eaten them, buried them, or scattered them along her route of retreat for the delectation of local wildlife. He simply read the account, then passed it over to Rosa.

"They've got good descriptions of us both," he remarked.

"From the kids," she said.

"Yes."

"I should go back and kill them," Rosa drawled. Then, with a spurt of venom, "In their beds."

"We brought it on ourselves," Jacob said. "It's not the end of the world." He grinned into his Guinness. "Or maybe it is."

"I vote we head south."

"I've no objection."

"Sicily."

"Any particular reason?"

She shrugged. "Widows. Dust. I don't know. It just struck me as a place to lie low, if that's what you want to do."

"It won't be for long," Jacob said, setting down his empty glass.

"You've got a feeling?"

"I've got a feeling."

She laughed. "I love it when you have feelings," she said, lightly cupping his hand in hers. "I know we've said some hard things to one another in the last little while—"

"Rosa—"

"No, no, hear me out. We've said some hard things and we meant them, let's be honest, we meant them. But . . . I do love you."

"I know."

"I wonder if you know how much I love you?" she said, leaning a little closer to him. "Because I don't." He looked puzzled. "What I feel for you is so deep in me—it goes so far down into my soul, Jacob—into the very heart of who I am. There's no seeing the end of it." She was gazing deep in his eyes and he returning her gaze, unblinking. "Do you understand what I'm telling you?"

"It's true for me—"

"Don't say it if it's not."

"I swear it's true," Jacob replied. "I don't understand it any more than you do, but we belong together; I concede it." He leaned a little further and kissed her unpainted lips. She tasted of gin; but beyond the alcohol was that other taste, the like of which no mouth but this, his Rosa's mouth, had in it. If any man had told him at that moment she was less than perfection, he would have killed the bastard on the spot. She was a wonderment, when he saw her like this, with unclouded eyes. And he the luckiest man alive to be walking the earth with her. So what if it took another century to be done with this work? He had Rosa at his side, an ever-present sign of what lay at the end of his endeavor.

He kissed her harder, and she replied with kisses of her own, deep, deep kisses, which inspired him to return them in kind, until they were so wrapped about each other that nobody in the place dared so much as glance their way, for fear of blushing.

Later, they adjourned to a piece of wasteground adjacent to a railroad track. There, with dusk upon the isle, and another snow, they finished the lovemaking they'd left off in the Courthouse. There was no paucity of passion this time: They were so elaborately intertwined that a passenger in one of the many trains that flew by while they coupled, glimpsing them there in the dirt, might have thought they were seeing not two beings but one: a single nameless animal, squatting beside the tracks, waiting to cross to the other side.

XV

i

Will knew he wasn't awake. Though he was lying in his own bed in what appeared to be his own room—though he could hear his own mother's voice from somewhere below—he was dreaming it all. The certain proof? His mother wasn't speaking, she was singing, in French, her voice reedy but sweet. This was absurd. His mother hated the sound of her own singing voice. She'd mouthed the words when they'd sung hymns in church. And there was other evidence, more persuasive still. The light that came in through the cracks between the curtains was a color he'd never seen light before: a gilded mauve that made everything it fell upon vibrate, as though it were singing some song of its own, in the language of light. And where it failed to fall, there was a profound stillness, and shadows that had their own uncanny hue.

"These are the strangest dreams," somebody said.

He sat up in bed. "Who's there?"

"Aren't they, though? Dreams within dreams. They're always the strangest."

Will studied the darkness at the foot of his bed from which this voice was emanating, squinting to get a clearer picture of the speaker. The man was wearing red, Will thought, a fur coat, perhaps? A peaked hat?

"But I suppose it's like those Russian dolls, isn't it?" the man in the coat went on. "You know the ones I mean? They have a doll inside a doll inside—of course you know. A man of the world like you. You've seen so much. Me, I've seen a patch of moorland five miles square." He halted for a moment to chew on something. "Excuse my noise," he said, "But I am so damn hungry . . . What was I saying?"

"Dolls."

"Oh yes. The dolls. You do understand the metaphor? These dreams are like the Russian dolls; they fit inside one another." He paused to chew a little more. "But here's the twist," he said. "It works in either direction—"

"Who are you?" Will said.

"Don't interrupt me. I suppose it's a bit of a stretch, but imagine we're in some parallel universe in which I've rewritten all the laws of physics—"

"I want to see who I'm talking to," Will insisted.

"You're not talking to anyone. You're dreaming. I've rewritten all the laws of physics and every doll fits inside every other doll, doesn't matter what size they are."

"That's stupid."

"Who are you calling stupid?" the stranger replied and, in his anger, stepped out of the shadows.

It wasn't a man in a fur coat and a peaked cap: It was a fox. A dream of a fox, with a burnished coat and needle whiskers and black eyes that glittered like black stars in its elegantly snouted head. It stood easily on its hind legs, the pads of its forepaws slightly elongated, so they resembled stubby fingers.

"So now you see me," the fox said. Will could see only one reminder, in all its poised perfection, of the wild beast it had been: a spatter of blood on the patch of white fur at its chest. "Don't worry," the fox said, glancing down at the marks, "I've already fed. But then you remember Thomas."

Thomas—

Dead in the grass, his genitals eaten off—

"Now don't be judgmental," the fox chided. "We do what we have to do. If there's a meal to be had, you have it. And you start with the tenderest parts. Oh, look at your face. Believe me, you'll be putting a lot of pee-pees in your mouth before you're very much older." Again, the laughter. "That's the glory of the flow, you see? I'm talking to the boy, but the man's listening.

"It makes me wonder if you really and truly dreamed this, all those years ago. Isn't that an interesting conundrum? Did you lie at the age of eleven and dream about me, coming to tell you about the man that you'd grow up to be, a man who'd one day be lying in a coma dreaming about you, lying in your bed, dreaming a fox," he shrugged, "and so on. Following any of this?"

"No."

"It's just rumination. The kind of thing your father'd probably enjoy debating, except that he'd be debating with a fox and I don't think that'd fit his vision of things at all. Well . . . it's his loss."

The fox moved to the side of the bed, finding a spot where the light fell fetchingly on its coat. "I wonder at you," it said, studying Will more closely. "You don't look like a coward."

"I wasn't," Will protested. "I would have taken the book to him myself, but my legs—"

"I'm not talking to the boy you were," the fox said, looking hard at him. "I'm talking to the man you are."

"I'm not . . . a man," Will protested softly. "Not yet."

"Oh now stop this. It's wearisome. You know very well that you're a grown man. You can't hide in the past forever. It may seem comfortable for a while, but it'll smother you sooner or later. It's time you woke up, my dear fellow."

"I don't know what you're talking about."

"Christ, you are *so stubborn!*" the fox snapped, losing his air of civility. "I don't know where you think all this nostalgia's going to get you! It's the future that matters." He leaned close to Will's head, until they were almost eyeball to eyeball. "Do you hear me in there?" he hollered. His breath was rank, and the stench of it reminded Will of what the creature had eaten; how well-pleased it had looked trotting away from Simeon's corpse. Knowing this was all a dream didn't make him feel any the less intimidated; if the fox came sniffing for what little Will had between his legs, he'd put up a fight, but the chances were he'd lose. Bleed to death, in his own bed, while the fox ate him alive—

"Oh Lord," the fox said, "I can see coercion's going to get me nowhere." He retreated from the bed a step or two, sniffed, and said, "May I tell you an anecdote? Well, I'm going to tell you anyway. It happened I met a dog, lying around where I go to hunt. I don't usually consort with domesticated breeds, but we got to chatting, the way you do sometimes, and he said to me, Lord Fox—he called me Lord Fox—he said: Sometimes I think we made a terrible mistake, us dogs, trusting them. Meaning your species, my lad. I said, Why? You don't have to scavenge like me. You don't have to sleep in the rain. He said that's not important in the grand scheme of things. Well, I laughed. I mean, since when did a dog ever think about the grand scheme of things? But give this mutt his due, he was a bit of a thinker.

"We made our choice, he said. We hunted for them, we herded for them, we guarded their brats. God knows, we helped them make a civilization, didn't we? And why? I said I didn't know; it was beyond me. Because, he said, we thought they knew how to take care of things. How to keep the world full of meat and flowers.

"Flowers? I said. (There's only so much pretension I can take from a dog.) Don't be absurd. Meat, yes. Meat, you'd want them taking care of, but since when did a dog care for the smell of cherry blossom?

"Well, he got very sniffy at that. This conversation's over, he said, and ponced off."

The fox was by now back at the bottom of Will's bed.

"Get the message?" he asked Will.

"Sort of."

"This is no time to be sleeping, Will. There's a world out there needs help. Do it for the dogs if you must. But do it. You pass that along to the man in you. You tell him to *wake up.* And if you don't," Lord Fox leaned over the bedboard, and narrowed his glittering eyes, "I'll come back and have your tender parts in the middle of the night. Understand me? I'll come back sure as God put tits on trees." His mouth opened a little wider. Will could smell the flesh on his breath. "*Understand me?*"

"Yes," he said, trying to keep from looking at the beast. "Yes! Yes! Yes!"

"*Will.*"

"Yes! Yes!"

"Will, you're having a nightmare. Wake up. Wake up."

He opened his eyes. He was in his room, lying in his bed, except that Lord Fox had gone, along with that nameless light. In their place, a human presence. Close to the bed, Johnson, who had just shaken him out of sleep. And at the door, wearing a far less compassionate expression, his mother.

"What on earth were you dreaming about?" Dr. Johnson wanted to know. Her palm was pressed against his brow. "Do you remember?" Will shook his head. "Well, you've got quite a fever, my lad. It's no wonder you're having strange dreams. But you'll mend." She pulled a prescription pad from her bag and scrawled on it. "He'll need to stay in bed," she said as she got up to leave. "Three days at least."

ii

This time Will had no trouble obeying: He felt so weak he couldn't have escaped the house even if he'd wanted to, which he didn't. He had no reason to go anywhere now, not with Jacob gone. All he wanted to do was put a pillow over his head and shut out the world. And if he smothered himself in the process, so what? There was nothing left to live for, except pills, recriminations, and dreams of Lord Fox.

                    *   *   *

If things looked grim when he woke, they looked worse a couple of hours later, when two policemen arrived to ask him questions. One was in uniform and sat in the corner of his bedroom, slurping from a mug of tea supplied by Adele. The other—a droopy man who smelled of stale sweat—sat on the edge of Will's bed, introduced himself as Detective Faraday, and then proceeded to ply Will with questions.

"I want you to think very carefully before you answer me, son. I don't want lies and I don't want fabrications. I want the truth, in plain words. This isn't a game, son. Five men are dead."

This was news to Will. "You mean . . . they were killed?"

"I mean they were *murdered*, by the woman who was with this man who abducted you." Will wanted to say: He didn't abduct me; I went because I wanted to go. But he held his tongue, and let Faraday babble on. "I want you to tell me everything he said to you, everything he did, even if he told you to keep it a secret. Even if . . . even if some of the things he said or did are hard to talk about." Faraday lowered his voice here, as though to reassure Will that this would be secret stuff, just between the two of them. Will wasn't convinced for a moment, but he told Faraday he'd answer any questions he was asked.

That's what he did, for the next hour and a quarter, with both Faraday and the constable taking notes on what he was telling them. He knew some of what he recounted sounded strange, to say the least, and some of it, especially the part about burning the moths, made him seem cruel. But he told it all anyway, knowing in his heart nothing he told these dull men would ever allow them to find Jacob and Rosa. He had no information about where Steep and McGee lived or where they were going. All he knew for certain, all he cared about, was that he wasn't with them.

There was another interview two days later, this time from a man who wanted to talk to Will about some of the stories he'd told Faraday, especially the part about seeing Thomas, alive and dead. The interviewer's name was Parsons, but he invited Will to please call him Tim, which Will pointedly refused to do, and he kept circling around the business of how Jacob had touched him. Will was as plain as he could be: He said that when they were climbing the hill and Jacob lay a hand on him, he felt strong. Later, he explained, in the copse, it had been him who'd done the touching.

"And that's when you felt like you were in Jacob's skin, is that right?"

"I knew it wasn't real," Will said. "I was having this dream, only I wasn't asleep."

"A vision . . . " Parsons said, half to himself.

Will liked the sound of it. "Yes," he said, "it was a vision." Parsons jotted something down. "You should go up there and look," Will said to him.

"Do you think I might have a vision, too?"

"No," Will said. "But you'd find the birds, if they haven't been eaten by . . . foxes or whatever . . . "

He caught a fearful look on the man's face. He wouldn't go up the hill to look for the birds, today or any time. For all his understanding looks and his gentle persuasions, he didn't want to see the truth, much less know it. And why? Because he was afraid. Faraday was the same, and the constable. All of them afraid.

The next day, the doctor pronounced that he was well enough to get up and move around the house. Seated in front of the television, he watched an update on the murders at Burnt Yarley, with the reporter standing in the street outside Donnelly's butcher shop. Sightseers had come from all over the country, apparently, despite the inclement weather, to see the site of the atrocities.

"This little hamlet," the reporter said, "has had more visitors in its icy streets the last four days than in half a century of summers."

"And the sooner they go home again," said Adele, emerging from the kitchen with a tray of vegetable soup and cheese and chutney sandwiches for Will, "the sooner we can all go back to normal." She set the tray on Will's lap, warning him that the soup was very hot. "It's so *morbid*," she said, as the reporter interviewed one of the visitors. "Coming to see a thing like this. Have people no decency?" With that, she retreated to her steak-and-kidney-pie making in the kitchen. Will kept watching, hoping there'd be some mention of him, but the live coverage from the village now ceased, and the newscaster returned to report on how the search for Jacob and Rosa had spread to Europe. There was evidence that two people fitting their description had been linked to crimes in Rotterdam and Milan within the last five years, the most recent report from northern France, where Rosa McGee had been involved in the deaths of three people, one of them an adolescent girl.

Will knew it was shameful to feel the pleasure he did, hearing this catalogue of deeds. But he felt it nevertheless, and he'd learned from Jacob to speak his feelings truthfully, though in this case the only person he was telling was himself. And what was the truth? That even if Jacob and Rosa turned out to be the most bloodthirsty pair in history, he couldn't regret having crossed their paths. They were his connection to something bigger than the life he'd been leading, and he would hold on to their memory like a gift.

Of all the people who talk to him during this period of recuperation, it was, surprisingly, his mother who knew most intimately the way he was thinking. He had no verbal proof of this; she kept her exchanges with him brief and functional. But the expression in her eyes, which had been until now a vague fatigue, was now sharpened into wariness. She no longer looked through him as she'd been wont to do. She scrutinized him (several times he caught her doing so when she thought he wasn't watching) with something strange in her eyes. He knew what it was. Faraday and Parsons were afraid of the mysteries he'd talked about. His mother was afraid of him.

"It's brought up all the bad memories, I'm afraid," his father explained to him. "We were doing so well and *now this*." He had called Will into his study to have this little talk. It was, of course, a monologue. "It's all perfectly irrational, of course, but your mother has this very Mediterranean streak in her." He had not looked at Will more than once so far, but gazed out of the window at the sleet, lost in his own ruminations. Like Lord Fox, Will thought, and smiled to himself. "But she feels as though somehow . . . oh, I don't know, somehow death's followed us here." He had been twirling a pencil in his fingers, but now he tossed it down on his well-ordered desk. "It's such nonsense," he snorted, "but she looks at you and—"

"She blames me."

"No, no," said Hugo. "Not blames. Connects. That's it, you see. She makes these . . . *connections*." He shook his head, mouth drawn down in disgruntlement. "She'll snap out of it eventually," he said. "But until then we just have to live with it. God knows." Finally, he swung his leather writing chair around and looked at Will between the piles of papers. "In the meanwhile, please do your best not to get her stirred up."

"I don't do—"

"—anything. I know. And once this whole tragic nonsense is over and done with, she'll be on the mend again. But right now she's very sensitive."

"I'll be careful."

"Yes," said Hugo. He returned his gaze to the gloom beyond the window. Assuming the conversation was over, Will rose. "We should really talk more about what happened to you," Hugo said, his distracted tone suggesting that he felt no urgency to do so. Will waited. "When you're well," Hugo said. "We'll talk then."

iii

The conversation never happened. Will's strength returned, the interviews ceased, the television crews moved on to some other corner of England, and the sightseers went soon after. By Christmas, Burnt Yarley belonged to itself again, and Will's brief moment of notoriety was over. At school, there was the inevitable gauntlet of jokes and petty cruelties to run, but he felt curiously inured against them. And once it was plain that the name-calling and the whispers were not discomforting him, he was left alone.

There was only one real source of pain: that Frannie kept her distance from him. She spoke to him only once in that period before Christmas, and it was a short conversation.

"I've got a message for you," she said. He asked from where, but she refused to name the source. When she told him the message, however, he didn't need the name. Nor, in fact, did he need the information. He'd already had a visit from Lord Fox. He knew he was part of the madness, for as long as he lived.

As for Sherwood, he didn't come back to school at all until the third week of January, and when he did he was in a much subdued state. It was as if something had broken in him, the part that had turned his lack of mental grasp into a strange kind of attribute. He was pale and listless. When Will tried to talk to him, he clammed up, or started to get teary. Will quickly learned his lesson and left Sherwood to heal at his own speed. He was glad that the boy had Frannie to look after him. She protected Sherwood fiercely if anyone tried to pick on him. People soon got the message. They left brother and sister alone, just as they left Will.

This slow aftermath was in its way as strange an experience as the events that had preceded it. Once all the hoopla died down (even the Yorkshire press had given up the story by early February, having nothing to report), life resumed its usual even pace, and it was as if nothing of any consequence had happened. Of course, there were occasional references made to it (mainly in the form of sick jokes passed around at school) and in a host of minor ways the village had changed (it no longer had a butcher, for one; and there were more people at church on Sundays), but the winter months, which were brutally cold that year, gave people time to either bury their sorrow or talk it through, all behind doors that were often blocked by drifts of snow. By the time the blizzards receded, folks were done with their grieving and were ready for a fresh start.

On the twenty-sixth of February, there was a change in the weather so sudden that it had the quality of a sign. A strange balm came upon the air, and for the first night in ninety there was no frost. It wouldn't last, the naysayers at the pub predicted: Any plant fool enough to show its nose would have it nipped off soon enough. But the next day was just as warm, and the day following, and the day following, and the day following that. Steadily, the sky began to clear, so that by the end of the first week of March, it was a gleaming swath of blue above the valley, busy with birds, and the naysayers were silenced.

Spring had arrived, the gymnast season, all muscle and motion. Though Will had lived through eleven springs in the city, they were wan imitations of what he witnessed that month. More than witnessed, felt. His senses were brimming, the way they'd brimmed that first day outside the Courthouse, when he'd felt such union with the world. His spirits, which had been downcast for months, finally looked up from his feet and flew.

All was not lost. He had a head full of memories, and hidden among them were hints of how he had to proceed from here: Things he knew nobody else in the world would have been able to teach him, and that perhaps nobody else in the world would understand.

Living and dying, we feed the fire.

Suppose they were the last.

Jacob in the bird. Jacob in the tree. Jacob in the wolf.

Clues to epiphanies, all of them.

From now on, he would have to look for epiphanies on his own. Find his own moments when the world spun and he stood still, when it would be as though he was seeing through the eyes of God. And until that time, he would be the careful son Hugo had asked him to be. He'd say nothing to stir up his mother, nothing to remind her of how death had followed them. But his compliance would be a pretense. He did not belong to them, not remotely. They would be from this time temporary guardians, from whose side he would slip as soon as he was able to make his way in the world.

iv

On Easter Sunday, he did something he'd been putting off since the
mellowing of the weather. He retraced the journey he'd taken with
Jacob, from the Courthouse to the copse where he'd killed the birds.
The Courthouse itself had the previous year inspired much morbid
interest among sightseers and had as a consequence been fenced off,
the wire hung with signs warning trespassers that they would be
liable to prosecution. Will was tempted to scramble under the fence
and take a look at the place, but the day was too fine to waste
indoors, so he began to climb. There was a warm gusty wind blowing,
herding white clouds, all innocent of rain, down the valley. On the
slopes, the sheep were stupid with spring and watched him
unalarmed, only darting off if he yelled at them. The climb itself was
hard (he missed Jacob's hand at his neck), but every time he paused
to look around, the vista widened, the fells rolling away in every
direction.

He had remembered the wood with uncanny accuracy, as
though—despite his sickness and fatigue—that night his sight had
been preternaturally sharp. The trees were budding now, of course,
every twig an arrow aiming high. And underfoot, blades of brilliant
green where there'd been a frosted carpet.

He went straight to the place where he'd killed the birds. There
was no trace of them. Not so much as a bone. But simply standing on
the same spot, such a wave of yearning and sorrow passed through
him that it made him gasp for breath. He'd been so proud of what
he'd done here. (*Wasn't that quick? Wasn't that beautiful?*) But now
he felt a bit more ambiguous about it. Burning moths to keep the
darkness at bay was one thing, but killing birds just because it felt
good to do so? That didn't feel so brave, not today, when the trees
were budding and the sky was wide. Today it felt like a dirty memory,
and he swore to himself there and then that he'd told the story for
the last time. Once Faraday and Parsons had filed away their notes
and forgotten them, it would be as though it had never happened.

He went down on his haunches, to check one final time for evidence of the victims, but even as he did so he knew he'd invited
trouble. He felt a tiny tremor in the air as a breath was drawn and
looked up to see that the wood itself had not changed in any detail
but one. There was a fox a short distance from him, watching him
intently. He stood on all fours like any other fox, but there was something about the way he stared that made Will suspicious. He'd seen
this defiant gaze before, from the dubious safety of his bed.

"*Go away!*" he shouted. The fox just looked at him, unblinking and unmoved. "*D'you hear me?*" Will yelled at the top of his voice. "*Shoo!*" But what had worked like a charm on sheep didn't work on foxes. Or at least not this fox.

"Look," Will said, "Coming to bother me in dreams is one thing, but you don't *belong* here. This is the real world."

The fox shook its head, preserving the illusion of its artlessness. To any gaze but Will's, it seemed to be dislodging a flea from its ear. But Will knew better: It was contradicting him.

"Are you telling me I'm dreaming *this* as well?" he said.

The animal didn't bother to nod. It simply perused Will, amiably enough, while he worked the problem out for himself. And now, as he puzzled over this curious turn of events, he vaguely recalled something Lord Fox had mentioned in his rambling. What had he said? There'd been some talk of Russian dolls, but that wasn't it. An anecdote about a debate with a dog; no, that wasn't it either. There'd been something else his visitor had mentioned. Some message that had to be passed along. But *what? What?*

The fox was plainly close to giving up on him. It was no longer staring in his direction, but sniffing the air in search of its next meal.

"Wait a moment," Will said. A minute ago, he'd been wanting to drive it away. Now he was afraid it would do as he'd wished and go about its business before he'd solved the puzzle of its presence.

"Don't leave yet," he said to it. "I'll *remember.* Just give me a chance—"

Too late. He'd lost the animal's attention. Off it trotted, its brush flicking back and forth.

"Oh, *come on,*" Will said, rising to follow it. "I'm trying my best."

The trees were close together, and in his pursuit of the fox, their bark gouged him and their branches raked his face. He didn't care. The faster he ran, the harder his heart pumped and the harder his heart pumped the clearer his memory became—

"I'll get it!" he yelled after the fox. "Wait for me, will you?"

The message was there, on the tip of his tongue, but the fox was outpacing him, weaving between the trees with astonishing agility. And all at once, twin revelations. One, that this was *not* Lord Fox he was following, just a passing animal that was fleeing for its fleabitten life. And two, that the message was to wake, wake from dreams of foxes, Lords or no, *into the world—*

He was running so fast now, the trees were a blur around him.

And up ahead, where they thinned out, was not the hill but a growing brightness; not the past, but something more painful. He didn't
want to go there, but it was too late to slow his flight, much less halt
it. The trees were a blur because they were no longer trees, they'd
become the walls of a tunnel, down which he was hurtling, out of
memory, out of childhood.

Somebody was speaking at the far end of the tunnel. He couldn't
catch hold of precisely what was being said, but there were words of
encouragement, he thought, as though he were a runner in a
marathon, being coaxed to the finishing line.

Before he reached it, however—before he was back in that place
of wakefulness—he was determined to take one last look at the past.
Ungluing his eyes from the brightness ahead, he glanced back over
his shoulder, and for a few precious seconds glimpsed the world he
was leaving. There was the wood, sparkling in the spring light—every
bud a promise of green to come. And the fox! Lord, there it was,
darting away about the business of the morning. He pressed his sight
to look harder, knowing he had only moments left, and it went where
he willed, back the way he'd come, to look down the hillside to the
village. One last heroic glance, fixing the sight in all its myriad
details. The river, sparkling; the Courthouse, moldering; the roofs of
the village, rising in slated tiers; the bridge, the post office, the telephone box from which he'd called Frannie that night long ago,
telling her he was running away.

So he was. Running back into his life, where he would never see
this sight again, so finely, so perfectly—

They were calling him again, from the present. "Welcome back,
Will . . . " somebody was saying to him softly.

Wait, he wanted to tell them. Don't welcome me yet. Give me
just another second to dream this dream. The bells are ringing for
the end of the Sunday service. I want to see the people. I want to see
their faces, as they come out into the sun. I want to see—

The voice again, a little more insistent. "Will. *Open your eyes.*"

There was no time left. He'd reached the finishing line. The past
was consumed by brightness. River, bridge, church, houses, hill, trees,
and fox—gone, all gone, and the eyes that had witnessed them,
weaker for the passage of years, but no less hungry, opened to see
what he'd become.

PART FOUR

He Meets The
Stranger In His Skin

I

i

It's going to take time to get you up and moving normally again," Dr. Koppelman explained to Will a few days after the awakening. "But you're still reasonably young, reasonably resilient. And you were fit. All that puts you ahead of the game."

"Is that what it's going to be?" Will said. He was sitting up in bed, drinking sweet tea.

"A game? No, I'm afraid not. It's going to be brutal some of the time."

"And the rest?"

"Merely horrendous."

"Your bedside manner's for shit, you know that?"

Koppelman laughed. "You'll love it."

"Says who?"

"Adrianna. She told me you had a distinctly masochistic streak. *Loved* discomfort, she said. Only happy when you were up to your neck in swamp water."

"Did she tell you anything else?"

Koppelman threw Will a sly smile. "Nothing you wouldn't be proud of," he said. "She's quite a lady."

"Lady?"

"I'm afraid I'm an old-fashioned chauvinist. I haven't called her with the news, by the way. I thought it'd be better coming from you."

"I suppose so," Will said, without much enthusiasm.

"You want to do it today?"

"No, but leave me the number. I'll get round to it."

"When you're feeling a little better," Koppelman looked a little embarrassed, "I wonder if you'd do me a favor? My wife's sister Laura works in a bookstore. She's a big fan of your pictures. When she heard I was looking after you, she practically threatened my life if I didn't get you back to work, happy and healthy. If I brought in a book, would you sign it for her?"

"It'd be my pleasure."

"That's good to see."

"What?"

"That smile. You've got reason to be happy, Mr. Rabjohns. I wasn't betting on you coming out of this. You took your time."

"I was . . . wandering," Will replied.

"Anywhere you remember?"

"A lot of places."

"If you want to talk to one of the therapists about it at some point, I'll set it up."

"I don't trust therapists."

"Any particular reason?"

"I dated one once. He was the most royally fucked up guy I ever met. Besides, aren't they supposed to take the pain away? Why the hell would I want that?"

When Koppelman had gone, Will revisited the conversation, or rather the latter part of it. He hadn't thought about Eliot Cameron, the therapist he'd dated, in a long time. It had been a short affair, conducted at Eliot's insistence behind locked doors in a hotel room booked under an assumed name. At first the furtiveness had tickled Will's sense of play, but the secrecy soon began to wear out its welcome, fueled as it was by Eliot's shame at his orientation. They had argued often, sometimes violently, the fisticuffs invariably followed by a sensational bout of lovemaking. Then had come the publication of Will's first book, *Transgressions*, a collection of photographs whose common theme was animal trespassers and their punishment. The book had appeared without attracting a single review and seemed destined for total obscurity until a commentator in the *Washington Post* took exception to it, using it as an object lesson in how gay artists were tainting public discourse.

It is tasteless enough, the man had written, *that ecological tragedies be appropriated as political metaphor, but doubly so when one considers the nature of the pleading involved. Mr. Rabjohns should be ashamed of himself. He has attempted to turn these documents into an irrational and self-dramatizing metaphor for the homosexual's place in America: and in doing so has demeaned his craft, his sexuality and— most unforgivably—the animals whose dying throes and rotting carcasses he has so obsessively documented.*

The piece sparked controversy, and within forty-eight hours Will found himself in the middle of a fiercely contested debate involving ecologists, gay rights lobbyists, art critics, and politicians in need of the publicity. A strange phenomenon rapidly became evident: Everyone saw what they wanted to see when they looked at him. For some he was a mud-spattered wheel, raging around amongst prissy aesthetes. For others he was simply a bad boy with good cheekbones and a damn strange look in his eyes. For another faction still he was a sexual outsider, his photographs of less consequence than his function as a violator of taboos. Ironically, even though he'd never intended the agenda he'd been accused of promulgating, the controversy had done to him what the *Post* piece had claimed he was doing to his subjects: It had turned him into metaphor.

In desperate need of some simple affection, he'd sought out Eliot. But Eliot had decided the spotlight might spill a little light on him and had taken refuge in Vermont. When Will finally found his way through the maze the man had left to conceal his route, Eliot told him it would be better all around if Will left him alone for a while. After all, he'd explained in his inimitable fashion, it wasn't as if they'd ever really been lovers, was it? Fuck-buddies maybe, but not lovers.

Six months later, while Will was on a shoot on the Ruwenzori massif, an invitation to Eliot's wedding had found its torturous way into his hands. It was accompanied by a scrawled note from the groom-to-be saying that he perfectly understood Will wouldn't be able to make it, but he didn't want him to feel forgotten. Fueled by a heroic perversity, Will had packed up the shoot early and flown back to Boston for the wedding. He'd ended up having a drunken exchange with Eliot's brother-in-law, another therapist, in which he'd loudly and comprehensively trashed the entire profession. They were the proctologists of the soul, he'd said; they took a wholly unhealthy interest in other people's shit. There had been a cryptic telephone message from Eliot a week later, telling Will to keep his distance in future, and that had been the end of Will's experience with therapists. No, not quite true. He'd had a short fling with the brother-in-law, but that was another adventure altogether. He had not spoken to Eliot since, though he'd heard from mutual friends that the marriage was still intact. No children, but several houses.

ii

"How long's this going to take?" Will asked Koppelman next time he came around.

"What, to get you up and about?"

"Up, about, and out of here."

"Depends on you. Depends how hard you work at it."

"Are we talking days, weeks—?"

"At least six weeks," Koppelman replied.

"I'll halve it," Will said. "Three weeks and I'm gone."

"Tell your legs that."

"I already did. We had a great conversation."

"By the way, I got a call from Adrianna."

"Shit. What did you tell her?"

"I had no choice but to tell her the truth. I did say you were still feeling woozy, and you hadn't felt like calling up all your friends, but she wasn't convinced. You'd better make your peace with her."

"First you're my doctor, now you're my conscience?"

"I am indeed," he replied gravely.

"I'll call her today."

She made him squirm.

"Here's me going around in a fucking depression thinking about you lying there in a coma and you're not! You're awake, and you don't have the fucking time to call me up and tell me?"

"I'm sorry."

"No you're not. You've never been sorry for anything in your life."

"I was feeling like shit. I didn't talk to anybody." Silence. "Peace?" Still silence. "Are you still there?"

"Still here."

"Peace?"

"I heard you the first time: You are an egocentric fucking son of a fucking bitch, you know that?"

"Koppelman said you thought I was a genius."

"I never said genius. I may have said talented, but I thought you were going to die so I was feeling generous."

"You cried."

"Not *that* generous."

"Christ, you're a hard woman."

"All right, I cried. A little. But I will not make that mistake again, even if you feed yourself to a fucking *pack* of polar bears."

"Which reminds me. What happened to Guthrie?"

"Dead and buried. There was an obituary in *The Times*, believe it or not."

"For Guthrie?"

"He'd had quite a life. So . . . when are you coming back?"

"Koppelman's pretty vague about that right now. It's going to be a few weeks, he says."

"But you'll come straight home to San Francisco, won't you?"

"I haven't made up my mind."

"There's a lot of people care about you here. Patrick, for one. He's always asking after you. And there's me, and Glenn—"

"You're back with Glenn?"

"Don't change the subject. But yes, I'm back with Glenn. I'll open up your house, get it together for you so you can have a real homecoming."

"Homecomings are for people who have homes," Will said. He'd never much liked the house on Sanchez Street; never much liked any house, in fact.

"So pretend," Adrianna told him. "Give yourself some time to kick back."

"I'll think about it. How is Patrick, by the way?"

"I saw him last week. He's put on some weight since I saw him."

"Will you call him for me?"

"No."

"Adrianna—"

"You call him. He'd like that. A lot. In fact that's how you can make it up to me, by calling Patrick and telling him you're okay."

"That is the most fucked up piece of logic."

"It isn't logic. It's a guilt trip. I learned it from my mother. Have you got Patrick's number?"

"Probably."

"No excuses. Write it down. Have you got a pen?" He rummaged for one on the table beside his bed. She gave him the number and he dutifully jotted it down. "I'm going to speak to him tomorrow, Will," Adrianna said. "And if you haven't called him there'll be trouble."

"I'll call him, I'll call him. Jesus."

"Rafael walked out on him, so don't mention the little fuck's name."

"I thought you liked him."

"Oh he knows how to turn on the charm," Adrianna said, "but he was just another party-boy at heart."

"He's young. He's allowed."

"Whereas we—"

"Are old and wise and full of flatulence."

Adrianna giggled. "I've missed you," she said.

"And quite right too."

"Patrick's got himself a guru, by the way: Bethlynn Reichle. She's teaching him to meditate. It's quite nostalgic really. Now when I see Pat we sit cross-legged on the floor, smoke weed, and make peace signs at one another."

"Whatever he's telling you, Patrick was *never* a flower child. The summer of love didn't reach Minneapolis."

"He comes from Minneapolis?"

"Just outside. His father's a pig farmer."

"*What?*" said Adrianna, in mock outrage. "He said his dad was a landscape artist—"

"Who died of a brain tumor? Yeah, he tells everybody that. It's not true. His dad's alive and kicking and living in pigshit in the middle of Minnesota. And making a mint from the bacon business, I might add."

"Pat's such a lying bastard. Wait till I tell him."

Will chuckled. "Don't expect him to be contrite," he said. "He doesn't do contrite. How are things going with Glenn?"

"We putter on," she said unenthusiastically. "It's better than a lot of folks have got. It's just not inspired. I always wanted one grand romance in my life. One that was reciprocated, I mean. Now I think it's too late." She sighed. "God, listen to me!"

"You need a cocktail, that's all."

"Are you allowed to drink yet?"

"I'll ask Bernie. I don't know. Did he try and put the moves on you, by the way?"

"What, Koppelman? No. Why?"

"I just think he was smitten with you, that's all. The way he talks about you."

"Well why the hell didn't he say something?"

"You probably intimidated him."

"L'il ol' me? Nah. I'm a pussy-cat, you know that. Not that I would have said yes if he'd offered. I mean, I've got some standards. They're low, granted, but I've got 'em and I'm proud of 'em."

"Have you considered becoming a comedienne?" Will said, much amused. "You'd probably have a decent career—"

"Does this mean you meant what you said in Balthazar? About giving it all up?"

"I think it's the other way round," Will said. "Photography's done with me, Adie. And we've both seen enough boneyards for one lifetime."

"So what happens now?"

"I finish the book. I deliver the book. Then I wait. You know how I like waiting. Watching."

"For *what*, Will?"

"I don't know. Something wild."

II

i

The following day, inspired by the conversation with Adrianna, he pushed his physiotherapy harder than his body was ready for and ended up feeling worse than he'd felt since coming out of the coma. Koppelman prescribed pain killers, and they were powerful enough to induce a pleasant light-headedness, in which state he made his promised call to Patrick. It was not Patrick who answered the phone, but Jack Fisher, a black guy who'd been in and out of Patrick's circle for the last half decade. An ex-dancer, if Will's memory served. Lean, long limbed, and fiercely bright. He sounded weary, but welcomed Will's call.

"I know he wants to talk to you, but he's asleep right now."

"That's okay, Jack. I'll call another day. How's he doing?"

"He's getting over a bout of pneumonia," Fisher replied. "But he's doing better. Getting about a bit, you know. I heard you had a bad time."

"I'm mending," Will said. Flying, more like. The pain killers had by now induced a more than mild euphoria. He closed his eyes, picturing the man at the other end of the line. "I'm going to be there in a couple of weeks. Maybe we can have a beer."

"Sure," Jack said, sounding a little perplexed at the invitation. "We can do that."

"Are you looking after Patrick right now?"

"No, I'm just visiting. You know Patrick. He likes having people around. And I give a great foot massage. You know what? I hear

Patrick calling. I'll take the phone through to him. It was good talking to you, bro. Give me the nod when you're back in town. Hey, Patrick? Guess what?" Will heard a muffled exchange. Then Jack was back on the line. "Here he is, bro."

The phone was handed over, and Patrick said, "Will? Is this really you?

"It's really me."

"Jesus. That's so weird. I was sitting by the window, having a siesta, and I swear I was dreaming about you."

"Were we having fun?"

"We weren't doing much of anything. You were just *here* . . . in the room with me. And I liked that."

"Well I'll be there in the flesh soon enough. I was just telling Jack, I'm getting back on my feet."

"I read all the articles about what happened. My mother kept clipping them for me and sending them down. Never trust a polar bear, eh?"

"She couldn't help herself," Will said. "So how are you doing?"

"Hanging in there. I lost a lot of weight, but I'm putting it back on again, bit by bit. It's hard though, you know. Sometimes I get so tired and I think: This is just too much trouble."

"Don't even think about it."

"That's all I can do right now is think. Sleep and think. When are you here?"

"Soon."

"Make it sooner. We'll have a party. Like the old days. See who's still around—"

"*We're* still around, Patrick," Will replied, the sorrow that was barely buried in their exchange turning his pain-killer high into something dreamily elegiac. They were in a world of endings, of early and unexpected good-byes, not so unlike the time from which he'd woken. He felt a tightness in his chest and suddenly feared tears. "I'd better be going," he said, not wanting to upset Patrick. "I'll check in again before I arrive."

Patrick wasn't going to let him off so quickly. "You *are* up for a party?" he said.

"Sure—"

"Good. Then I'll get planning. It's good to have things to look forward to."

"Always," Will said, his throat so full he couldn't put a longer reply together.

"Okay, I'll let you go, buddy," Patrick replied. "Thanks for calling. It must have been that siesta, right?"

"Must have."

There was a silence then, and Will realized that Patrick had sensed the suppressed tears in his voice.

"It's all right," Patrick said softly. "The fact that we're talking makes it all right. See you soon."

Then he was gone, leaving Will listening to the buzz of the empty line. He let the receiver slip from his ear, his body so suddenly and completely overcome by tears he had no control over his limbs. It felt good, in a cleansing way. He sat there for ten, maybe fifteen minutes, sobbing like a child, catching his breath, thinking it was done, only to have another wave of weeping follow. He wasn't just crying for Patrick, or for that remark about seeing who was still around to invite to the party. He was crying for himself, for the boy he'd met again in his coma, the Will who was still inside him somewhere, wandering.

The skies that boy had seen were there too, and the fells and the fox, filed away in his memory. What a conundrum that was: That in this age of extinctions, some of which he'd chosen to document, his memory should have penned a book of his days so perfect that all he had to do was dream and they were conjured as though they'd never slipped by, as though—did he dare believe this?—the passing of things, of days and beasts and men he'd loved, was just a cruel illusion and memory, a clue to its unmasking.

ii

The next day he was, if anything, harder on himself than he'd been the day before. The fox was right. There was work to do out in the world—people to see, mysteries to solve—and the sooner he had bullied his body into shape, the sooner he'd be on his way.

In a short time, his tenacity brought results. Day by day, session by session, his limbs strengthened and his stamina increased; he began to feel restored and rejuvenated. In spite of Koppelman's gentle mockery, he sent out for a selection of homeopathic medicines to supplement his diet and was sure they were in no small part responsible for the speed of his recovery. Koppelman had to admit he hadn't seen anything quite like it. Within ten days Will was making plans for his trip back to San Francisco. A call to Adrianna, asking her to open up the Sanchez Street house and air it out (which she'd in fact already done), a call to his editor in New York, telling her of his imminent change of location, and of course a second call to Patrick. This time the prodigal Rafael answered, returned and apparently forgiven. No, Patrick wasn't at home, he told Will, he was at the hospital, having his blood checked. He'd be back later, but Rafael didn't know when. He'd just take a message and pass it along. Make sure it gets to him, Will said, to which Rafael curtly replied, "I'm not stupid," and slammed the phone down.

"You've made a remarkable recovery, but you're still going to need to be kind to yourself." This was Koppelman's farewell speech. "No trip to the Antarctic in the next few months. No standing up to your neck in swamp water."

"What am I going to do for fun?" Will quipped.

"Contemplate how lucky you are," Koppelman said. "Oh . . . by the way . . . my sister-in-law—"

"Laura."

Koppelman beamed. "You remembered? I brought her book for you to sign." He rummaged in the bag he'd brought with him. Out came a copy of *Boundaries*. "I had a look through it last night," he said. "Grim stuff."

"Oh it's gotten a lot worse since then," Will said, taking the pen from Koppelman's breast pocket, and relieving him of the book. "There's a couple of species in here lost the fight."

"They're extinct?"

"As the dodo." He opened the book to the title page, and scrawled an inscription.

"What the hell does that say?"

"*For Laura. Best wishes.*"

"And that scrawl underneath's your signature?"

"Yep."

"Just so I know what to tell her."

He left two days later. There were no direct flights to San Francisco, so he was obliged to change planes in Chicago. It was at most a minor inconvenience, and he was so happy to be back in the stream of people that the drudgery of getting through O'Hare became positively pleasurable. By late afternoon he was in the plane that would carry him west and, seated by the window, ordered a whiskey in celebration. He hadn't had any alcohol in several months, and it went straight to his head. Pleasantly happy, he let sleep overtake him, as the sky ahead darkened.

By the time he awoke the day had long gone, and the lights of the city by the bay were glittering below.

III

i

San Francisco had not been Will's first port of call when he'd come to America. That honor had fallen to Boston, where he had gone at the age of nineteen, having decided that whatever he was yearning for he'd never find it in England. He didn't find it in Boston either. But during the fourteen months he lived there a new Will emerged, falteringly at first, then with fearless abandon. He had known his sexual preferences long before he left England. He'd even acted upon his desires on a few occasions, though never in a state of complete sobriety. In Boston, however, he learned to be happily queer, reinventing himself after his own idiosyncratic mode. He wasn't a corn-fed American beauty; he wasn't a plaid-shirted macho man; he wasn't a style queen; he wasn't a leather boy: He was his own peculiar creature, desired and pursued for that very reason. Qualities that would have gone unnoticed in a bar in Manchester (some of them obvious, like his accent, some so subtle he couldn't have named them) were here rare and coveted. He learned the nature of his advantage quickly and exploited it shamelessly. Eschewing the uniform of the day (sneakers, tight jeans, white T-shirt) he dressed like the impoverished English lad he was, and it worked like a charm. He seldom went back to an empty bed, unless he wished to do so; and in a few months had gone through three love affairs, two of which he'd concluded. The last had been his first and bitterest taste of unreciprocated love. The object was one Laurence Mueller, a television producer nine years Will's senior. Blond, sleek, and sexually adroit, Larry had drawn Will into a heady romance only to drop him cold after six weeks, a pattern he was notorious for repeating. Heartbroken, Will had mourned over the loss for half a summer, salving the hurt as best he could with behavior that would probably have killed him five years later. In the sex emporia of the Combat Zone and in the darkness of the Fenway, where on weekend nights a sexual bacchanalia was in constant progress, he played out every sexual scenario his libido could conjure, to put Larry's dismissal of him from his mind.

The hurt had faded by September, but not before he'd had a pot-induced revelation. Sitting in a steam room, meditating on his misery, he realized that Larry's desertion had awoken in him some of the same pain he'd felt when Steep had departed. Turning over this realization, he'd sat sweating in the tiled room for an unhealthy time, ignoring the hands and the glances that came his way. What did it mean? That somewhere in his attachment to Jacob there'd been sexual feeling? Or that in his midnight encounters in the Shrubbery there was somewhere buried the hope that he'd find a man who would deliver on Steep's promises and take him out of the world into a place of visions? He'd finally left the steam room to its orgiasts, his head thumping too hard for him to think clearly. But the questions remained with him thereafter, troubling him. He countered them the plainest way he knew how. If a man who approached bore even the slightest resemblance to his memory of Steep—the color of his hair, the shape of his mouth—Will rejected him with talismanic cruelty.

ii

It wasn't the Larry Mueller saga that drove him from Boston, it was an icy December. Coming out of the restaurant where he worked as a waiter into the maw of a Massachusetts blizzard, he decided he'd had enough of being frozen and it was time to head for balmier climes. His first thought was Florida, but that night, talking over the options with the bartender at Buddies, he heard the siren-song of San Francisco.

"I've only been out to California once," the bartender, whose name (Danny) was tattooed on his arm in case he forgot it, told him, "but man, I was so close to staying. It's faggot paradise. It really is."

"As long as it's warm."

"There's places warmer," Danny conceded. "But shit, if you want to be hot then go live in fucking Death Valley, right?" He leaned over to Will, lowering his voice. "If I didn't have my other half," (Danny's long-time lover, Frederico—the other half in question— was sitting five yards along the bar), "I'd be back there, living the life. No question."

It was a pivotal exchange. Within two weeks Will had packed his bags and was gone, leaving Boston on a day of sparkling frost that almost made him regret his decision, the city looked so beautiful. There was another kind of beauty waiting for him at the end of his journey, however, a city that enraptured him far beyond his expectations. He found a job working for one of the community newspapers and, one momentous day, missing a photographer to cover a piece he was writing about his adopted city, he borrowed a camera to do the job himself. It wasn't love at first sight. His initial photographs were so piss-poor he couldn't use them. But he liked the feeling of the camera in his hands, liked being able to circumscribe the world through the lens. And the subject before him was the tribe in whose heartland he lived: the queens, the cowboys, the dykes, the mannequins, the sex-fiends, the drag artists, and the leather devotees whose homes, bars, clubs, grocery stores, and Laundromats spread from the intersection of Castro and Eighteenth, north to Market, south to Collingwood Park.

While he learned his craft, he also learned how to be a wild boy between the sheets, until he had quite a reputation as a lover. He seldom played anonymously now, though there were plenty of places to do so. He wanted deeper experiences and found them in the beds and embraces of a dozen men, none of whom had his heart, but all of whom excited him in their various ways. There was Lorenzo, a forty-year-old Italian who had left a wife and children in Portland to come be what he'd already known he was on his wedding day. There was Drew Dunwoody, a muscle-boy who was for a time almost as devoted to Will as to his own reflection. There was Sanders, who was the closest Will had to a sugar-daddy, an older man (he had been admitting to forty-nine for five years) who lent him the first three months' rent on a one-room apartment near Collingwood Park and later a down payment on a secondhand Harley. There was Lewis the insurance man, who never said a word in company, but who poured out his lyrical soul to Will behind closed doors and who subsequently flowered into a minor poet. There was Gregory, beautiful Gregory, dead of an accidental overdose at twenty-four. And Joel, and Mescaline Mike, and a boy who'd said his name was Derrick, but who was later discovered to be an AWOL marine by the name of Dupont.

In this charmed circle, Will grew up, grew strong. The plague was not yet upon them, and in hindsight this would come to seem a Golden Age of hedonism and excess, which Will, by an act of equilibrium that still astonished him, managed to both observe and indulge. Soon, though he didn't know it, death would come and start to lay its fatal fingers on many of the men he photographed, an arbitrary culling of beauties and intellects and loving souls. But for seven extraordinary years, before the shadow fell, he bathed daily in that queer river supposing it would rush like this forever.

iii

It had been Lewis, the insurance man turned poet, who'd first talked about animals with him. Sitting on the back porch of Lewis's house on Cumberland watching a raccoon raid the trash cans, they'd fallen to talking about what it would be like to inhabit for a time the body and spirit of an animal. Lewis had been writing about seals and was presently so obsessed with the subject, he said, that they entered his dreams nightly.

"Big, sleek, black seals," he said, "just hanging out."

"On a beach?"

"No, on Market Street," Lewis said with a giggle. "I know it sounds stupid, but when I'm dreaming it they look like they belong there. I did ask one of them what they were doing, and he said they were checking out the lay of the land for when the city drops into the ocean."

Will watched the raccoon efficiently sorting through the trash. "I dreamed about this talking fox when I was a kid" he said softly. Maybe it was Lewis's hashish—he never failed to find good ganja— but the memory was crystalline: "Lord Fox," he said.

"*Lord* Fox?"

"Lord Fox," Will replied. "He scared the fuck out of me, but he was comical at the same time."

"Why'd he scare you?" Will had never spoken about him to anyone, and even now—though he liked and trusted Lewis—he felt a twinge of reluctance. Lord Fox was part of a much bigger secret (the great secret of his life), and he was covetous of it. But gentle Lewis was pressing for further explanation. "Tell me," he said.

"He'd eaten somebody," Will replied. "That's what scared me about him. But then I remember he told me this story."

"About what?"

"It wasn't even a story really. It was just a conversation he'd had with a dog."

"Yeah?" Lewis laughed, thoroughly engaged.

Will repeated the substance of Lord Fox's exchange with the dog, amazed at how easily he could recall it, though it was a decade and a half since he'd dreamed the dream.

"We hunted for them, we herded for them, we guarded their brats. And why? Because he thought they knew how to take care of things. How to keep the world full of meat and flowers—"

Lewis liked what he heard. "I could get a poem out of that," he said.

"I wouldn't risk it."

"Why not?"

"He might come after you for a slice of the profits."

"What profits?" Lewis said. "This is poetry."

Will didn't reply. He was watching the raccoon, who had done scavenging and was scampering away with its booty. And while he was watching, he was thinking of Lord Fox, and of Thomas the painter, living and dead.

"You want some more?" Lewis said, handing the nub of the reefer back to Will. "Hey, Will? You listening?"

Will was staring into the darkness, his thoughts as furtive as the raccoon. Lewis was right. There was a kind of poetry in the story Lord Fox had told. But Will wasn't a poet. He couldn't tell the story with words. He had only his eyes, and his camera, of course.

He took the extinguished reefer from Lewis's fingers and reignited it, pulling the pungent smoke deep into his lungs. It was powerful ganja, and he'd already had more than usual. But he was feeling greedy tonight.

"Are you thinking about the fox?" Lewis asked him.

Will turned his blurred gaze in Lewis's direction. "I'm thinking about the rest of my life," he replied.

In his own mythology of himself, the journey that would take him out into the wildernesses of the world, to the places where species were perishing for the simple crime of living where they felt the need to live, began that night on Lewis's porch, with the reefer, the raccoon, and the story of Lord Fox. This was a simplification of course. He'd been bored with chronicling the Castro for a while and was ready for a change long before that night. As for the direction that desire might point in, it did not come clear in the space of a conversation. But over the next few weeks, his idling thoughts returned to this exchange several times, and he started to turn his camera away from the throngs of the Castro, toward the animal life that coexisted with people in the city. His first experiments were unambitious, late juvenilia, at best. He photographed the sea lions that congregated on Pier 39, the squirrels in Dolores Park, and the next-door neighbor's dog, who regularly stopped the traffic by squatting to take a dump in the middle of Sanchez Street. But the journey that would in time take him very far from the Castro and from squirrels, seals, and defecating dogs, had begun.

He had dedicated Transgressions, his first published collection, to Lord Fox. It was the least he could do.

IV

i

Adrianna came to visit, unannounced, the morning after he got back into the city. She brought a pound of French Roast from the Castro Cheesery and Zuccotto and St. Honore's cake from Peverelli's in North Beach, where she'd now moved in with Glenn. They hugged and kissed in the hallway, both a little teary-eyed at the reunion.

"Lord, I've missed you," Will told her, his hands cupping her face. "And you look so fine."

"I dyed my hair. No more gray. I will have this hair color at a hundred and one. Now what about you?"

"I'm better every day," Will said, heading through to the kitchen to brew some coffee. "I still creak a bit when I get up in the morning, and the scars itch like buggery after I've had a shower, but otherwise I'm back in working order."

"I had my doubts. So did Bernie."

"You thought I might just slip away quietly?"

"It crossed my mind. You looked very peaceful. I asked Bernie if you were dreaming. He said he didn't know."

"It wasn't like dreaming, it was like going back in time. Being a boy again."

"Was that fun?"

He shook his head. "I'm very happy to be back."

"You've got a great place to come back to," she said, wandering to the kitchen door and surveying the hallway. She'd always loved the house, more than Will, in truth. The size of the place, along with the intricacy of the layout (not to mention the excesses its stylishly under-furnished rooms had hosted) lent it a certain authority, she thought. Most of the houses in the neighborhood had seen their share of pri-apics, of course, but it wasn't just high times that haunted the boards here. It was a host of other things: Will's rages when he couldn't make the connections, and his howls of revelation when he did; the din of excited conversation around maps which had upon them an exhilarat-ing paucity of roads; evenings of debate on the devolution of certainty and drunken ruminations on fate and death and love.

There were finer houses in the city, to be sure, but none, she'd be willing to bet, more marinated in midnight profundities than this.

"I feel like a burglar," Will said, pouring coffee for them both. "Like I broke into somebody's apartment and I'm living their life for them."

"You'll get back into the groove after a few days," Adrianna said, taking her coffee and wandering through to the large tile room where Will always laid out his pictures. The length of one wall was a notice-board, on which over the years he'd pinned up exposure or printing errors that had caught his eye, pictures too dark or burned out to be useful, but which he nevertheless found intriguing. His consump-tives, he called these unhealthy pictures, and had more than once observed, usually in his cups, that this was what he saw when he imagined how the world would end. Blurred or indecipherable forms in a grainy gloom, all purpose and particularity gone.

She perused them idly while she sipped her coffee. Many of the photographs had been up on the wall for years, their unfixed images decaying further in the light.

"Are you ever going to do anything with these?" she said.

"Like *burn* them, you mean?" he said, coming to stand beside her.

"No, like publishing them."

"They're fuck-ups, Adie."

"That'd be the point."

"A deconstructionist wildlife book?"

"I think it'd attract a lot of attention."

"Fuck the attention," Will said. "I've had all the attention I ever want. I've said *Look what I did, Daddy* to the whole wide world and my ego is now officially at peace." He went to the board and started to pull the pictures down, the pins flying.

"Hey, be careful, you'll tear them!"

"So?" he said, chucking the pictures down. "You know what? This feels *good!*" The floor was rapidly littered with photographs. "That's more like it," he said, stepping back to admire the now empty wall.

"Can I have one for a souvenir?"

"One."

She wandered amongst the scattered pictures, looking for a picture that caught her fancy. Stooping, she picked up an old and much-stained photograph.

"What did you choose?" he said. "Show me."

She turned it to him. It resembled a nineteenth-century spiritualist picture, those pale blurs of ectoplasm in which believers detected the forms of the dead. Will named its origins instantly.

"Begemder Province, Ethiopia. It's a walia ibex."

Adrianna flipped the photograph over to look at it again.

"How the hell do you know that?"

Will smiled. "I never forget a face," he said.

ii

The following day he went to visit Patrick, in his apartment up at the top of Castro. Though the pair had lived together on Sanchez Street for almost four of their six years together, Patrick had never given up the apartment, nor had Will ever pressured him to do so. The house, in its spare, functional way, was an expression of Will's undecorative nature. The apartment, by contrast, was so much a part of who Patrick was—warm, exuberant, enveloping—that to have given it up would have been tantamount to losing a limb. There at the top of the hill he had spent most of the money he earned in the city below (where he had been until recently an investment banker) creating a retreat from the city, where he and a few chosen lotus-eaters could watch the fog come and go. He was a big, broad handsome man, his Greek heritage as evident in his features as the Irish: heavy-lidded and laden eyes, a thug of a nose, a generous mouth beneath a fat black mustache. In a suit, he looked like somebody's bodyguard; in drag at Mardi Gras, like a fundamentalist's nightmare; in leather, sublime.

Today, when Rafael (who had apparently recanted and come home) escorted Will into the living room he found Patrick sitting at the window dressed in a baggy T-shirt and drawstring linen pants. He looked well. His hair was cropped to a graying crewcut,

and he wasn't as beefy as he'd been, but his embrace was as powerful as ever.

"Lord, look at you," he said, standing back from Will to appreciate him. "You're finally starting to look like your photograph." (This
was a back-handed compliment, and an on-going joke, begun when
Will had chosen an unflattering jacket photograph for his second
book on the grounds that it made him look more authoritative.)
"Come and sit down," he said, gesturing to the chair that had been
put opposite his in the window. "Where the hell's Rafael gone? You
want some tea?"

"No, I'm fine. Is he looking after you okay?"

"We're doing better," Patrick said, easing back into his own
chair. Only now, in the tentativeness of this maneuver, did Will get a
sense of his delicacy. "We argue, you know—"

"So I heard."

"From Adrianna?"

"Yeah, she said—"

"I just tell her the juicy bits," Patrick said. "She doesn't get to
hear about what a sweetheart he is most of the time. Anyway, I have
so many angels watching over me it's embarrassing."

Will looked back down the length of the room. "You've got some
new things," he said.

"I inherited some heirlooms from dead queens," he said.
"Though most of it doesn't mean much if you don't know the story
that goes with it, which is kind of sad, because when I'm gone,
nobody will know."

"Rafael isn't interested?"

Patrick shook his head. "It's old men's talk as far as he's concerned. That little table's got the strangest origins. It was made by
Chris Powell. You remember Chris?"

"The fix-it man with the beautiful butt."

"Yeah. He died last year, and when they went in his garage they
found he'd been doing all this carpentry. Making chairs and tables
and rocking horses."

"Commissions?"

"Apparently not. He was just making them in his spare time, for
his own satisfaction."

"And keeping them?"

"Yeah. Designing them, carving them, painting them, and leaving them all locked up in his garage."

"Did he have a lover?"

"A blue-collar honey like that, are ya kidding? He'd had hundreds."
Before Will could protest, Patrick said, "I know what you're asking and,
no, he didn't have anyone permanent. It was his sister found all this
beautiful work when she was cleaning out his house. Anyway, she asked
me around to see if I wanted something to remember him by, and of
course I said yes. I really wanted a rocking horse, but I didn't have the
balls to ask. She was a rather prim little soul, from somewhere in
Idaho. Obviously the last thing she wanted to be doing was going
through her cute fag brother's belongings. God knows what she found
under the bed. Can you imagine?" He gazed out toward the cityscape.
"I've heard it happen so often now. Parents coming to see where their
baby ran away to live, because now he's dying, and of course they find
Queer City, the only surviving phallocracy." He mused a moment.
"What must it be like for those people? I mean we do stuff in broad
daylight here they haven't even invented in Idaho."

"You think so?"

"Well, you think back to Manchester, or, what was the place in
Yorkshire?"

"Burnt Yarley?"

"Wonderful. Yeah. Burnt Yarley. You were the only queer in
Burnt Yarley, right? And you left as soon as you could. We all leave.
We could so we can feel at home."

"Do you feel at home?"

"Right from the very first day. I walked along Folsom and I
thought: This is where I want to be. Then I went into the Slot and
got picked up by Jack Fisher."

"You did not," Will said. "You met Jack Fisher with me, at that
art show in Berkeley."

"Shit! I can't lie to you, can I?"

"No, you can lie," Will said magnanimously, "I just won't believe
you. Which reminds me, Adrianna thought your father—"

"Was dead. Yeah. Yeah. She gave me hell. Thanks very much."
He pursed his lips. "I'm beginning to have second thoughts about
this party," he groused. "If you're going to go around telling the truth
to everyone I'm going to have a shit time, and I know the party's for
you, but if I'm not having fun then *nobody's* going to have fun—"

"Oh we can't have that. How about I promise not to contradict
anything you've said to anybody as long as it's not a personal defama-
tion?"

"Will, I could never defame you," Patrick said, with heavily feigned sincerity, "I might tell everyone you're a no-good egotistic sonofabitch who walked out on me. But defame you, the love of my life? Perish the thought." Performance over, he leaned forward and laid his hands on Will's knees. "We went through this phase, remember? Well at least I did—when we thought we were going to be the first queers in history never to get old? No, that's not true. Maybe we'd get old, but very, very slowly so that by the time we were sixty we could still pass for thirty-two in a good light? It's all in the bones, that's what Jack says. But black guys look good any age so he doesn't count."

"Do you have a point?" Will smiled.

"Yes. Us. Sitting here looking like two guys the world has not used kindly."

"I never—"

"I know what you're going to say: You never think about it. Well you wait till you go out cruising. You're going to find a lot of little muscle-boys wanting to call you Daddy. I speak from experience. I think it must be a gay rite of passage. Straights feel old when they send their kids off to college. Queens feel old when one of those college kids comes up to them in a bar and tells them he wants to be spanked. Speaking of which—"

"Spanking or college boys?"

"Straights."

"Oh."

"Adrianna's going to bring Glenn on Saturday, and you mustn't laugh but he's had his ears pinned back surgically, and it makes him look weird. I never noticed before, but he's got a kind of pointy head. I think the protruding ears were a *distraction*. So, no laughing."

"I won't laugh," Will assured him, perfectly certain Patrick was only telling him for mischief's sake. "Is there anything you want me to do for Saturday?"

"Just turn up and be yourself."

"That I can do," he said. "Okay. I'm on my way." He leaned over and kissed Patrick lightly on the lips.

"You can see yourself out?"

"Blindfolded."

"Will you tell Rafael it's pill time? He'll be in his bedroom on the telephone."

Patrick had it right. Rafael was sprawled on his bed with the telephone glued to his ear, talking in Spanish. Seeing Will at the door he sat upright, blushing.

"Sorry," Will said, "the door was open."

"Yeah, yeah, it was just a friend, you know?" Rafael said.

"Patrick said it's pill time."

"I know," Rafael replied. "I'm coming. I just got to finish with my friend."

"I'll leave you two alone," Will said. Before he'd even closed the door Will heard Rafael picking up the thread of his sex talk while it was still warm. Will went back to the living room to tell Patrick the message had been delivered, but in the minute or so since his departure Patrick had fallen asleep and was snoring softly in his chair. The wash of late afternoon light softened his features, but there was no erasing the toll of years and grief and sickness. If being called Daddy was a rite of passage, Will thought, so's this: looking in on a man I fell in love with in another life and knowing that there was love there still, as plentiful as ever, but changed by time and circumstance into something more elusive.

He would gladly have watched Patrick a while longer, calmed by the familiarity of his face, but he didn't want to be hanging around when Rafael emerged, so he left the sleeper to his slumbers and headed off out of the apartment, down the stairs and into the street.

Why, he wondered, when there'd probably been more literary ink spilled on the subject of love than any other—including freedom, death, and God Almighty—could he not begin to grasp the complexities of what he felt for Patrick? There were many scars there, on both sides, cruel things said and done in anger and frustration. There were petty betrayals and desertions, again, on both sides. There were shared memories of wild sex and domestic high jinks and times of loving lucidity, when a glance or a touch or a certain song had been nirvana. And then there was now, feelings extricated from the past, but being woven into patterns neither of them had anticipated. Oh, they'd known they'd grow old, whatever Patrick remembered. They'd talked, half jokingly, about withering into happy alcoholics in Key West or moving to Tuscany and owning an olive grove. What they'd never talked about, because it had not seemed likely, was that they would be in here, in the middle of their lives, and talking like old men: Remembering their dead peers and watching the clock until it was time for pills.

V

i

"Did you meet the mystical Bethlynn Reichle?" Adrianna wanted to know when Will told her about Patrick. They were brunching at Café Flore on Market Street the following day: spinach frittatas, home fries, and coffee. Will told her no, there'd been neither sight nor mention of the woman.

"According to Jack, he sees her practically every other day. Jack thinks it's all pretty phony. And of course she charges a fortune for an hour of her precious time."

"I can't imagine Pat falling for anything too airy-fairy."

"I don't know. He's got that fey Irish streak in him. Anyway, she's given him these chants he has to repeat four times a day, which Jack swears are Zulu."

"What the fuck does Jack know about Zulu? He was born and bred in Detroit."

"He says it's a race memory." Will made a despairing face. "Glenn's got a great new word, by the way, which is kind of appropriate. Lucidiots. That's what he calls people who talk too fast, seem to be perfectly lucid—"

"And are, in fact, idiots. I like that. Where'd he get it from?"

"It's his. He made it up. Words beget words. That's the *cri du jour.*"

"Lucidiots," Will said again, most entertained. "And she's one of them, huh?"

"Bethlynn? For sure. I haven't met her, but she's gotta be. Oh, now . . . I shouldn't be telling you this, but Pat asked me if it'd be in appalling taste if he ordered a cake for the party shaped like a polar bear."

"To which you said?"

"Yes. It would be in appalling taste."

"To which he said: *Good.*"

"Right."

"Thanks for the warning."

ii

That night, around eleven or so, he decided to forgo a sleeping pill and go out for a drink. It was Friday, so the streets were alive and kicking and, on the five-minute walk up Sanchez to Sixteenth, he met the appreciative eyes of enough guys to be certain he could get lucky tonight if the urge took him. Some of that cockiness was knocked out of him, however, when he stepped into Gestalt, a bar that, according to Jack (whom he'd called for the inside scoop), had opened two months before and was the hot place for the summer. It was filled to near capacity, some of the customers locals here for a casual beer with friends, but many more geared up and wired for the weekend. In the old days there had been certain tribal divisions in the Castro: leather men had their watering holes, drug aficionados, theirs; the preppie boys had gathered in a different spot; the hustlers, and the queens, especially the older guys, would never have been seen in a black bar, or vice versa. Here, however, there were representatives of every one of those clans, and more. Was that a man in a rubber suit, leaning against the bar sipping bourbon? Yes it was. And the guy waiting his turn at the pool table, his nose pierced and his hair carved in concentric circles, was he the lover of the Latino man in the well-cut suit who was making a beeline for him? To judge by their smiles and kisses, yes. There was even a good proportion of women in the throng; a few, Will thought, straight girls come to ogle the queers with their boyfriends (this was a risky business; any boyfriend who agreed to the trip was probably half-hoping to be gang-banged on the pool table), the rest lesbians (again, of every variation, from the kittenish to the mustached). Though he was a little intimidated at the sheer exuberance of the scene, he was too much of a voyeur to leave. He eased his way through the crowd to the bar and found a niche at the far end where he had a wide-angle view of the room. With two beers in him, he started to feel a little more mellow. Excepting a few glances cast his way nobody took much notice of him, which was fine, he told himself, just fine. And then, as he was ordering a third beer (his last for the night, he'd decided) somebody stepped up to the bar beside him and said, "I'll have the same. No I won't. I'll have a tequila straight up. And he's paying."

"I am?" said Will, looking around at a man maybe five years his junior, whose present hapless expression he vaguely knew. Narrowed brown eyes watched him under upturned brows, a smile, with dimples, waited in readiness for when Will said—

"Drew?"

"Shit! I shoulda taken the bet. I was with this guy." He glanced back down the bar at a husky fellow in a leather jacket; the guy waved, obviously chomping at the bit for an invitation to join them. Drew looked back at Will, "He said you wouldn't recognize me after all this time. I said betcha. And you did."

"It took a moment."

"Yeah. Well . . . the hairline's not what it used to be," Drew said. A decade and a half before, when they'd had their fling, Drew had sported a curly clump of golden brown hair that hung over his forehead, its most ambitious curls tickling the bridge of his nose. Now it was gone. "You don't mind?" he said. "The tequila, I mean? I wasn't even sure it was you at first. I mean I heard . . . well, you know what you hear. I don't know half the time what to believe and what not to believe."

"You heard I was dead?"

"Yeah."

"Well," said Will, clinking his beer can against Drew's brimming glass of tequila. "I'm not."

"Good," Drew said, clinking back. "Are you still living in the city?"

"I just returned."

"You bought a house on Sanchez, right?" Their affair had preceded the purchase, and upon its cooling they'd not remained friends. "Still got it?"

"Still got it."

"I dated somebody on Sanchez, and he pointed it out to me. 'That's where the famous photographer lives.'" Drew's eyes widened at the quoted description. "Of course, I didn't know who. Then he told me and I said—"

"Oh, *him*."

"No, I was really proud," Drew said, with sweet sincerity. "I don't keep up with art stuff, you know, so I hadn't really put two and two together. I mean, I knew you took pictures, but I just remembered seals."

Will roared with laughter. "Christ, the seals!"

"You remember? We went to Pier Thirty-nine together? I thought we were going to get buzzed and watch the ocean, but you got obsessed with the seals. I was so pissed off." He emptied half his tequila glass in one draw. "Funny, the things that stick in your head."

"Your buddy's waving at you, by the way," Will said.

"Oh, Lord. It's a sad case. I had one date with him and now every time I come in here he's all over me."

"Do you need to get back to him?"

"Absolutely not. Unless you want to be on your own? I mean, you've got the pick of the crowd here."

"I wish."

"You're still in great shape," Drew said. "I'm kinda running to seed here." He looked down at a belly that was no longer the washboard it had been. "It took me an hour to put these jeans on, and it'll take me twice as long to get 'em off." He glanced up at Will. "Without help, that is," he said. He patted his stomach. "You took some pictures of me, do you remember?"

Will remembered: a sticky afternoon of beefcake and baby oil. Drew had been quite the muscle-boy back then, competition standards, and proud of it. A little too proud perhaps. They'd broken up on Halloween Night, when he'd found Drew stark naked and painted gold from head to foot, standing in the backyard of a house on Hancock like an ithyphallic idol surrounded by devotees.

"Have you still got those pictures?" Drew asked.

"Oh, I'm sure. Somewhere."

"I'd love to see 'em . . . sometime." He shrugged, as though when was of no consequence, though both of them had known two minutes before, when he'd mentioned his jeans, that Will would be helping him out of them tonight.

As they made their way back to the house Will wondered if perhaps he'd made a mistake. Drew kept up a virtually unbroken monologue, none of it particularly enlightening, about his job selling advertising space at the *Chronicle*, about the unwanted attentions of Al, and the adventures of his ineptly neutered cat. A few yards from the door, however, he stopped in mid-flow and said: "I'm running off at the mouth, aren't I? Sorry. I'm just nervous I guess."

"If it's any comfort," Will said, "so am I."

"Really?" Drew sounded doubtful.

"I haven't had sex with anyone in eight or nine months."

"Jeez," Drew said, plainly relieved. "Well we can just take it real slowly."

They were at the front door. "That's good," Will said, letting them in, "slowly's good."

In the old days sex with Drew had been quite a show: a lot of posing and boasting and wrestling around. Tonight it was mellow. Nothing acrobatic, nothing risky. Little in fact, beyond the simple pleasure of lying naked together in Will's big bed with the pallid light from the street washing over their bodies, holding and being held. The greed for sensuality Will would once have felt in this situation, the need to exhaustively explore every sensation, seemed very remote. Yes, it was still there; another night, perhaps, another body—one he didn't remember in its finest hour—and perhaps he'd be just as possessed as he'd been in the past. But for tonight, gentle pleasures and modest satisfactions. There was just one moment, as they were undressing, and Drew first saw the scars on Will's body, when the liaison threatened to become something a little headier.

"Oh my, oh my," Drew said, his voice breathy with admiration. "Can I touch them?"

"If you really want to."

Drew did so, not with his fingers but with his lips, tracing the shiny path the bear's claws had left on Will's chest and belly. He went down on his knees in the process and, pressing his face against Will's lower abdomen, said, "I could stay down here all night." He'd slipped his hands behind his back; plainly he was quite ready to have them tied there if it took Will's fancy. Will ran his fingers through the man's hair, half-tempted to play the game. Bind him up, have him kissing scars and calling him sir. But he decided against it.

"Another night," he said, and pulling Drew up and into his arms, escorted him to bed.

iii

He woke to the sound of rain, pattering on the skylight overhead. It was still dark. He glanced at his watch—it was four-fifteen—then over at Drew, who was lying on his back, snoring slightly. Will wasn't sure what had woken him, but now that he was conscious he decided to get up and empty his bladder. But as he eased out of bed he caught, or thought he caught, a motion in the shadows across the room. He froze. Had somebody broken into the house? Was that what had woken him? He studied the darkness, looking and listening for further signs of an intruder, but now there was nothing. The shadows were empty. He looked back at his bedmate. Drew was wearing a tiny smile in his sleep and was rubbing his bare belly gently, back and forth. Will watched him for a moment, curiously enraptured. Of all the unlikely people to have broken his sexual fast with, he thought, Drew the muscle-boy, softened by time.

The rain got suddenly heavier, beating a tattoo on the roof. It stirred him to get up and go to the bathroom, a route he could have covered in his sleep. Out through the bedroom door, then first left onto the cold tile; three paces forward, turn to the right, and he could piss in certain knowledge his aim was true. He drained his bladder contentedly, then headed back to the bedroom, thinking as he went how good it would feel to slip his arms around Drew.

Then, two paces from the door, he again glimpsed a motion from the corner of his eye. This time he was quick enough to catch sight of the intruder's shadow, as the man made his escape down the stairs.

"*Hey,*" he said, and followed, thinking as he did so that there was something suspiciously playful about what was happening. For some reason he didn't feel in the least threatened by the presence of this trespasser; it was as though he knew already there was no harm here. As he reached the bottom of the stairs and pursued the shadow back down the hall toward the file room he realized why: He was dreaming. And what more certain proof of that than the sight awaiting him when he entered the room? There, casually leaning on the window sill twenty feet from him and silhouetted against the raining glass, was Lord Fox.

"You're naked," the creature remarked.

"So are you," Will observed.

"It's different for animals. We're more comfortable in our skins." He cocked his head. "The scars suit you."

"So I've been told."

"By the fellow in your bed?"

"Yep."

"You can't have him hanging around, you realize that? Not the way things are going. You'll have to get rid of him."

"This is a ridiculous conversation," Will said, turning to go. "I'm heading back to bed." He was already there, of course, and asleep, but even in dream form he didn't want to linger down here chatting with the fox. The animal belonged to another part of his psyche, a part he'd begun to put at a healthier distance tonight, with Drew's compliance.

"Wait a moment," said the fox. "Just take a look at this."

There was a crisp enthusiasm in the animal's words that made Will glance back. There was more light in the room than there'd been moments before, its source not shed from streetlights outside, but from the photographs, his poor consumptives, which were still scattered on the floor where he'd tossed them. Leaving his place at the window Lord Fox stepped between the pictures, coming into the middle of the room. By the strange luminescence the photographs were giving off, Will could see a voluphious smile upon the animal's face.

"These are worth a moment's study, don't you think?" the fox said.

Will looked. The light that emanated from the photographs was uncertain and for good reason. The bright, blurred forms in the pictures were *moving*: fluttering, flickering, as though they were being consumed by a slow fire. And in their throes, Will recognized them. A skinned lion, hanging from a tree. A pitiful tent of elephant hide, hanging in rotted scraps over one of the poles of its bones. A tribe of lunatic baboons beating each other's children to death with rocks. Pictures of the corrupted world, no longer fixed and remote, but thrashing and twitching and blazing out into his room.

"Don't you wish they looked like this when people saw them?" the fox said. "Wouldn't it change the world if they could see the horror this way?"

Will glanced up at the fox. "No," he said, "it wouldn't change a thing."

"Even this," the animal said, staring down at a picture that lay between them. It was darker than the others, and at first he couldn't make out the subject. "What is it?"

"You tell me," the fox said.

Will went down on his haunches and looked at the picture more closely. There was motion in this one too: a deluge of flickering light falling on a form sitting at the center of the picture.

"Patrick?" he murmured.

"Could be," the fox replied. It was Patrick for sure. He was slumped in his chair beside his window, except that somehow the roof had been stripped off his house and the rain was pouring in, running down over his head and body, glistening on his forehead and his nose and his lips, which were drawn back a little, so that his teeth showed. He was dead, Will knew. Dead in the rain. And the more the deluge beat on him the more his flesh bruised and swelled. Will wanted to look away. This wasn't an ape, this wasn't a lion, it was Patrick, his beloved Patrick. But he'd trained his eyes too well. They kept looking, like the good witnesses they were, while Patrick's face smeared, and all trace of who or even what he'd been was steadily erased beneath the assault of the rain.

"Oh God," Will murmured.

"He feels nothing, if that's any comfort," the fox said.

"I don't believe you."

"So look away."

"I can't. It's in my head now." He advanced on the animal, suddenly enraged. "What the fuck have I done to deserve this?"

"That's the mother of all questions, isn't it?" he said, unperturbed by Will's rage.

"And?"

The animal shrugged. "God wants you to see. Don't ask me why. That's between you and God. I'm just the go-between." Flummoxed by this, Will glanced back down at the picture of Patrick. The body had disappeared, dissolved in the rain. "Sometimes it's too much for people," the fox went on, in its matter-of-fact fashion. "God says: *Take a look at this*, and people just lose their sanity. I hope it doesn't happen to you, but there are no guarantees."

"I don't want to lose him," Will murmured.

"I can't help you there," the animal replied. "I'm just the messenger."

"Well you tell God from me—" Will started to say.

"*Will?*"

There was another voice behind him. He glanced over his shoulder, and there was Drew standing in the doorway, with a sheet wrapped around his middle.

"Who are you talking to?" he said.

Will looked back into the room, and for a moment—though he was now awake—he thought he glimpsed the animal's silhouette against the glass. Then the vision was gone, and he was standing naked in the cold, with Drew coming to drape the sheet over his shoulders.

"You're clammy," Drew said.

He was, running with a sickly sweat. Drew put his arms around Will's chest, locking his hands against his breastbone and laying his head against Will's neck. "Do you often go walkabout in your sleep?"

"Once in a while," Will replied, staring at the littered floor, still half-thinking he might catch a glittering light in one of the pictures. But there was nothing.

"Shall we go back to bed then?" Drew said.

"No, actually I'd prefer to stay up for a while," Will said. He'd had enough dreams for one night. "You go back up. I'm going to make myself some tea."

"I can stay with you, if you want."

"I'm okay," Will told him. "I'll be up in a while."

Drew bequeathed the sheet to Will and headed on upstairs,

leaving Will to go brew himself a pot of Earl Grey. He didn't particularly want to revisit the images that had just come to find him, but as he sat sipping his tea he couldn't help but picture the uncanny life his littered photographs had taken on as he dreamed them. It was as though they contained some freight of meaning he'd neglected to see or understand and had chosen to communicate it to him in his sleep. But what? That death was terrible? He knew that better than most. That Patrick was going to die, and there was nothing Will could do about it? He knew that too. He chewed it over and over, but he couldn't make much sense of the experience. Perhaps he was looking for significance where there was none. How much credence should he be giving a dream that showcased a talking fox claiming to be God's messenger? Probably very little.

And yet, hadn't there been a hair's-breadth moment at the end, after Drew had called his name, and he'd woken, when the fox had lingered, as though it were testing the limits of its jurisdiction, ready to trespass where it had no business being?

He returned to bed at last. The rainstorm had passed over the city and the only sound in the room was Drew's peaceful breath. Will slipped between the sheets as delicately as possible so as not to wake him, but somewhere in his slumber, Drew knew his bedmate had come back, because he turned to face Will, his eyes still closed, his breathing even, and found a place against Will's body where they fitted together comfortably. Will was certain he wouldn't sleep, but he did, and deeply. There were no further visits. God and His messenger left him undisturbed for the rest of the night and when he woke it was to sunlight and kisses.

VI

Patrick was as good as his threat: The centerpiece of the buffet table at the party was a large cake in the shape of a rather portly polar bear, complete with a fine set of fangs and a lascivious pink tongue. It inevitably invited questions, and Patrick directed all inquiries to Will, who was then obliged to tell the story of the attack a dozen times, compressing it with every repetition until it was honed to the impressively casual: Sure, I got chewed up by a bear.

"Why didn't you tell me?" Drew said, when the information had found its way around the room to him. "I thought you'd got the scars in a crash. But Jesus, a bear!" He couldn't resist smiling. "That's really something."

Will claimed the slice of chicken and artichoke pizza Drew was devouring and finished it up.

"Are you trying to tell me something?" Drew said. "Like stop eating?"

"No."

"You think I'm too fat, don't you? Admit it."

"I think you're just fine," Will said patiently. "You have my permission to eat every slice of pizza you can get your sticky fingers on."

"You're a god," Drew said, and returned to the buffet table.

"Are you two picking up where you left off?"

Will looked up around and there was Jack Fisher, elegant as ever, with a brooding white boy in tow. There were the usual hugs and how-dos before Jack got round to introducing his friend. "This is Casper. He doesn't believe I know you."

Casper pumped Will's hand, stumbling over some words of admiration. "You were one of my idols when I was a kid," he said. "I mean, shit, your stuff's so *real*, you know? I mean, it's the way things are, isn't it? All fucked up?"

"Casper's a painter," Jack explained. "I bought a little erection of his. He only paints dicks. Don't you, Casper?" The boy looked a little discomfited. "It's a small market," Jack said, "but it's devoted."

"I'd love to . . . maybe show you some of my work sometime," Casper said.

"Why don't you go get us a drink?" Jack said. Casper frowned; he clearly didn't want to play the waiter. "And I'll persuade Will to buy a painting." Reluctantly, Casper departed. "They're pretty good, actually," Jack said. "And he means what he says, about you being an idol of his. Sweet, isn't he? I'm seriously thinking of taking him off to Louisiana and settling down with him."

"You'll never do it," Will said.

"Well, I'm certainly over this fucking town," Jack said wearily. He lowered his voice a little. "The truth is, I'm sick of sick people. I know how that sounds, but you know me, I call it the way I see it. And I've got more scratched-out addresses in my little book that I care to count."

"How old's Casper?" Will said, watching the fellow weave back toward them with two glasses of scotch.

"Twenty. But he knows all he needs to know." Fisher grinned conspiratorially, but Will looked away. He didn't want to leer over this kid who for all Jack's domestic talk would be out on his ass, fucked and forgotten, within a month.

"You must drop in at the studio," Jack said, picking up the hype now that Casper was back within earshot. "He's doing a whole series of sperm pieces next—" He stopped in mid sentence. "Uh-oh," he murmured, his gaze going to the door, where a striking woman in her fifties, dressed in flowing gray, had just made an entrance. She surveyed the thirty or so guests somewhat imperiously, then, spotting Patrick, headed directly over to him. He left off his conversation with Lewis, who was using the event to circulate a very slim volume of his poems, and went to greet her. She lost her regal manner as Patrick hugged her, kissing his cheek and laughing raucously at something he said.

"Is that Bethlynn?" Will said.

"Yep," said Jack. "And I'm not in the mood, so you're on your own. Just don't let her have the ruby slippers." With that, and a sly smile, he made himself scarce, Casper in tow.

Will was fascinated, watching Bethlynn chat with Patrick. He was hanging on her every syllable, no doubt of that, his body language suggesting an uncharacteristic meekness on his part. He nodded now and again, but had his eyes downcast a lot of the time as he listened intently to her wisdom.

"So *that's* her." Adrianna had sidled up to Will, and was casually attempting to scrutinize the pair while she nibbled a piece of polar bear icing. "Our Lady of the Crystals."

"Does anybody like her?" Will said.

"This is the first time any of us have even seen her. I don't think she descends to the mortal plane very often, though Lewis claims to have seen her shoplifting eggplants." She guffawed behind her hand at this unlikely vision. "Of course, Lewis is a poet, so his testimony doesn't really count."

"Where's Glenn?"

"Throwing up."

"Too much cake?"

"No, he gets nervous when he's around a lot of people. He thinks they're all looking at him. It used to be that he thought they were looking at his ears, but since he got his ears fixed he thinks they're trying to work out what's different about him." Will tried to suppress a laugh, but failed. It erupted from him so loudly Patrick looked up and at him. The next moment he was leading Bethlynn across the room. Adrianna pressed a little closer to Will's side, to be sure she was included in the introductions.

"Will," Patrick said, "I'd like to introduce you to Bethlynn." He was beaming like a schoolboy. "This is so great," he said. "The two most important people in my life—"

"I'm Adrianna, by the way."

"I'm sorry," Patrick said. "Bethlynn, this is Adrianna. She works with Will."

Close up, Bethlynn looked a good deal older than she'd first appeared, her high-boned, almost Slavic features etched with fine lines. Her hand, when she took Will's, was cool, and when she spoke her voice was so low and husky Will had to lean closer to hear what she was saying. Even then he only caught ". . . in your honor."

"The party," Patrick prompted.

"Pat's always been a master at throwing shindigs," Will said.

"That's because he's a natural celebrant," Bethlynn replied. "It's a sacred quality."

"Oh, is giving parties sacred these days?" Adrianna chipped in. "I hadn't heard."

Bethlynn ignored her. "Patrick's gifts burn more brightly every day." The woman went on, "I see it. Manifest." She glanced around at him. "How long have we been working together?"

"Five months," Pat replied, still beaming like a blessed acolyte.

"Five months, and every day burning brighter," Bethlynn said.

Out of nowhere, Will heard himself say, *"Living and dying, we feed the fire."*

Bethlynn frowned, narrowed her eyes as though she was listening to the echo of Will's words to be certain she'd heard them right. Then she said, "What fire do you mean?"

Will was of half a mind to withdraw the remark, but if the man who'd coined it had taught him anything, it was the importance of speaking up for your beliefs. The trouble was, he didn't really have an answer. This phrase, which had dogged him for three decades, was not readily explicable, which was perhaps why it had proved so tenacious. Bethlynn, however, wanted a reply. She watched Will with her big gray eyes, while he floundered.

"It's just a phrase," he said. "I don't know. I guess it means . . . fire's fire, isn't it?"

"You tell me," she said.

There was a distinct smugness in her scrutiny, which irritated him. Instead of letting the challenge slide, he said, "No, you're the expert on burning brightly. You've probably got a better theory than me."

"I don't have theories. I don't need them," Bethlynn said. "I have the truth."

"Oh, my mistake," Will replied. "I thought you were just flailing around like the rest of us."

"You're very cynical, aren't you?" she said. "Very disappointed."

"Thanks for the analysis, but—"

"Very hurt. There's no shame in admitting it."

"I'm not admitting to anything," Will replied.

She was getting under his skin, and she knew it. A tide of beatitude had swept over her face. "Why are you so defensive?" she said.

Will threw up his hands. "Anything I say now, you're going to use against me—"

"It's not *against* anyone," she replied. Patrick had finally snapped out of his saccharine fugue and tried to interject, but Bethlynn ignored him. Moving a little closer to Will, as if to lend him the comfort of her proximity, she said, "You're going to do yourself some harm if you don't learn to forgive." She had laid her hand on his arm. "Who are you *so angry* at?"

"I'll tell you," he said. She smiled in expectation of his unburdening. "There's this fox—"

"Fox?" she said.

"He's driving me crazy. I know I should kiss his fleabitten ass and tell him I forgive his trespasses." She gave a darting glance to Patrick, which he took as a signal to engineer her departure. "But it's not easy with foxes." Will went on. "Because I hate the fucking things. I hate 'em." Bethlynn was retreating now. "Hate 'em, hate 'em, hate 'em—" And she was gone, escorted away into the crowd.

"Nice going," Adrianna remarked. "Subtle, understated. Nice."

"I need a drink," Will said.

"I'm going to find Glenn. If he's still sick I'll take him home, so if I don't see you later, enjoy the rest of the party."

"What the hell did you say to her?" Jack wanted to know, when he caught up with Will and the whiskey bottle.

"It's all a blur."

"I just loved that look on her face."

"You were watching?"

"Everybody was watching."

"I should apologize."

"Too late. She just left."

"Not to her, to Patrick."

He found Pat in the room at the back of the apartment they had together dubbed the conservatory, a space occupied by out-of-season decorations, old furniture, and several burgeoning marijuana plants. He was smoking a fat reefer in their midst, staring at the wall.

"That was stupid," Will said. "I fucked up and I'm really sorry."

"No, you're not," Patrick said. "You think she's a big ol' fake and you wanted to show her how you felt." His voice was gravelly. There was no anger in it, not even resentment, only fatigue. "You want some of this?" he said, glancing back at Will briefly as he proffered the joint. His eyes were red.

"Oh Jesus, Pat—" Will said, wanting to weep himself at the sight of Patrick's unhappiness.

"Do you want some or not?" Patrick sniffed. Will took the joint and inhaled a solid lungful. "I need Bethlynn right now," Pat went on. "I can guess what you think about her, and I'd probably be thinking the same thing if I was standing where you are. But I'm not. I'm here. You're there. It's fucking miles, Will." He drew a short, almost panicked breath. "I'm dying. And I don't like it. I'm *not* at peace, I'm *not* reconciled—" He turned to claim the joint back from Will. "I'm not . . . finished with being here. Not. Remotely. Finished." He took another hit off the joint, then handed it back to Will, who burned it to the nub. They looked at each other, both holding lungsful of smoke, effortlessly meeting one another's gaze. Then expelling the smoke as he talked, Patrick said, "I've never been that interested in what goes on outside these four walls. I've been quite happy with a little pot and a great view. You'd come back with your pictures and I'd think, Well, fuck it, I don't want to see the world if it's like that. I don't want to know about fucking extinction. It's depressing. Everybody agrees: Death's depressing. I'll just shut it out. But I couldn't. It was here all the time. Right here. In me. I didn't lock it out, I locked it in."

Will stepped toward him, until their faces were no more than a foot apart.

"I want to apologize to Bethlynn," he said. "Whatever I think about her, I still acted like a prick."

"Agreed."

"Will she see me if I grovel sufficiently?"

"Probably not. But you could maybe call at her house." He smiled. "It would make me very happy."

"That's what's important."

"You mean that?"

"You know I mean it."

"So, while you're in a generous mood, can I ask you to do something else for me? You don't have to do it right now. It's more something for the future."

"Tell me."

Patrick gave him the cock-eyed look that he always got when he was high, and reaching between them, caught hold of Will's fingers. "I want you to be here with me," he said, "when it's time for me to . . . leave. Permanently, I mean. Rafael's wonderful, and so's Jack and so's Adrianna. But they're not you. Nobody's ever come close to you, Will." His eyes shone with sorrow. "Will you promise me?"

"I promise," Will replied, letting his own tears fall.

"I love you, Will."

"I love you, too. That's not going to change. Ever. You know that."

"Yeah. But I like hearing it anyway." He made a valiant attempt to smile. "I think we should go distribute joints among the needy." He picked up the tin cookie jar on the table. "I rolled about twenty. You think that'll be enough?"

"Man, you've got it all planned out," Will said.

"I'm a natural celebrant," Patrick said as he headed out to distribute this bounty. "Hadn't you heard?"

VII

Just about everyone got high, except for Jack, who had become self-righteously sober the year before (after two decades of chemical excess) and Casper, who was forbidden to smoke the weed because Jack couldn't. Drew became democratically flirtatious under the influence, then, realizing where his best hopes of gratification lay, followed Will into the kitchen and offered up a graphic description of what he wanted to do when they got back to Sanchez Street.

As it turned out, by the time the party broke up, Drew was so much the worse for weed and beer he said he needed to go home and sleep it off. Will invited him back to the house, but he declined. He didn't want anyone, especially Will, watching him throw up in the toilet, he said: It was a private ritual. Will drove him home, made sure he got to his apartment safely, and then went home himself. Drew's verbal foreplay had left him feeling horny, however, and he contemplated a late night cruise down to the Penitent to find some action. But the thought of getting geared up for the hunt at such a late hour dissuaded him. He needed sleep more than a stranger's hand. And Drew would be sober tomorrow.

Again, he seemed to wake, disturbed by sirens on Market or a shout from the street. Seemed to wake, and seemed to sit up and study the shadowy room, just as he had two nights before. This time, however, he was wise to the trick his sleeping mind was playing. Resisting the urge to sleepwalk to the bathroom, he stayed in bed, waiting for the illusion of wakefulness to pass.

But after what seemed to be minutes, he grew bored. There was a ritual here, he realized, that his subconscious demanded he enact, and until he played it out he wouldn't be allowed to dream something more restful. Resigned to the game, he got up and wandered out onto the landing. There was no shadow on the wall this time to coax him down the stairs, but he went anyway, following the same route as he had when he'd last come into the company of Lord Fox: along the hallway and into the file room. Tonight, however, there were no lights spilling from the photographs on the ground. Apparently the animal wanted to conduct the dream debate in darkness.

"Can we get this over with as quickly as possible?" Will said, stepping into the murk. "There's got to be a better dream than—"

He stopped. The air around him shifted, displaced by a motion in the room. Something was moving toward him, and it was a lot larger than a fox. He started to retreat, heard a hiss, saw a vast, gray bulk rise up in front of him, the slab of its head gaping, letting on to a darkness that made the murk seem bright—

A bear! Christ in Heaven! Nor was this just any bear. It was his wounder, coming at him with her own wounds gouting, her breath foul and hot on his face.

Instinctively, he did as he would have done in the wild: He dropped to his knees, lowered his head, and presented as small a target as possible. The boards beneath him reverberated with the weight and fury of the animal; his scars were suddenly burning in homage to their maker. It was all he could do not to cry out, even though he knew this was just some idiot dream; all he could do not to beg it to stop and let him alone. But he kept his silence, his palms against the boards, and waited. After a time, the reverberations ceased. Still he didn't move, but counted to ten, and only then dared to move his head an inch or two. There was no sign of the bear. But across the room, leaning against the window as nonchalantly as ever, was Lord Fox.

"There are probably a plethora of lessons here," the creature said, "but two in particular come to mind." Will gingerly got to his feet while the fox shared his wisdom. "That when you're dealing with animal spirits—and that's what you've got on your hands, Willy, whether you like it or not—it's best to remember that we're all one big happy family, and if I'm here then I've probably got company. That's the first lesson."

"And . . . what's the second?"

"*Show me some respect!*" the fox barked. Then, suddenly all reason, "You came in here saying you want to get it over with as quickly as possible. That's insulting, Willy."

"Don't call me Willy."

"Ask me politely."

"Oh, for fuck's sake. *Please* don't call me Willy."

"Better."

"I need something to drink. My throat's completely dry."

"Go get yourself something," the fox said, "I'll come with you."

Will went into the kitchen, and the fox padded after him, instructing him not to turn on the light. "I much prefer the murk," the animal said. "It keeps my senses sharp."

Will opened the fridge and got out a carton of milk. "You want something?"

"I'm not thirsty," the fox said. "But thank you."

"Something to eat?"

"You know what I like to eat," the fox replied, and the image of Thomas Simeon lying dead in the grass entered Will's head with sickening clarity.

"Jesus," Will said, letting the fridge door slam closed.

"Come on," the fox said, "where's your sense of humor?" He

stepped out of the deep shadows into a wash of gray light from the window. He looked, Will thought, more vicious than he had last time they'd met. "You know, I think you should ask yourself," he said, "in all seriousness, if perhaps you're not coming apart at the seams. And if you are, what the consequences are going to be for those around you. Particularly your new lover-boy. I mean, he's not the most *stable* of characters, is he?"

"Are you talking about Drew?"

"Right. Drew. For some reason, I was thinking his name was Brad. I think in all fairness you should let him go, or you'll end up dragging him down with you. He'll go nuts on you, or try to slit his wrists, one of the two. And you'll be responsible. You don't want that on your plate. Not with the rest of the shit you've got to deal with."

"Are you going to be more specific?"

"It's not his war, Will. It's yours and yours alone. You signed on for it the day you let Steep take you up the hill."

Will set down the carton of milk and put his head in his hands. "I wish I knew what the hell you wanted," he said.

"In the long view," the fox said, "I want what every animal wants in its heart—except maybe for the dogs—I want your species gone. To the stars, if you can get there. To rot and ruin, more likely. We don't care. We just want you out of our fur."

"And then what?"

"Then nothing," the fox replied with a shrug. His voice went to a wistful murmur. "The planet keeps going round, and when it's bright it's day and when it's not it's night, and there's no end to the simple bliss of things."

"The simple bliss of things," Will said.

"It's a pretty phrase, isn't it? I think I got it from Steep."

"You'd miss all of that, if we were gone—"

"Words, you mean? I might, for a day or two. But it'd pass. In a week I'd have forgotten what good conversation was and I'd be a happy heart again. The way I was when Steep first clapped eyes on me."

"I know I'm just dreaming this, but while you're here . . . what do you know about Steep?"

"Nothing you don't," the fox said. "There's a good part of him in you, after all. You take a long look at yourself, one of these days." The fox approached the table now, lowering his voice to an insinuating whisper. "Do you really think you'd have wasted most of your natural span taking pictures of tormented wildlife if he hadn't put that knife in your hands? He *shaped* you, Will. He sowed the hopes and the disappointments, he sowed the guilt and the yearning."

"And he sowed you at the same time?"

"For better or worse. You see, I'm nothing important. I'm just the innocent fox who ate Thomas Simeon's private parts. Steep saw me trotting away and he decided I was a villain. Which was very unfair of him, by the way. I was just doing what any fox with an empty belly would do, seeing a free meal. I didn't know I was eating anybody important."

"Was Simeon important?"

"Well, obviously he was to Steep. I mean Jacob really took this dick-eating business to heart. He came *after* me, like he was going to tear off my head. So I *ran*, I ran so far and so fast—" This wasn't Will's memory of the event, as he'd witnessed it through Steep's eyes, but Lord Fox was on a roll, and Will didn't dare interrupt. "And he kept coming after me. There was no escaping him. I was in his memory, you see? In his mind's eye. And let me tell you, he's got a mind like a steel trap. Once he had me there was no tricking my way out. Even death couldn't spring me from his head." A raw sigh escaped the animal. "Let me tell you," he said, "it's not like being in your head. I mean, you've got a messed up psyche, no doubt about it, but it's nothing compared with his. *Nothing.*"

Will knew bait when it was being trailed. But he couldn't help himself, he bit. "Tell me," he said.

"What's he like? Well . . . if *my* head's a hole in the ground and *yours* is a shack—no offense intended—then *his* is a fucking cathedral. I mean, it's all spires and choirs and flying buttresses. *Incredible.*"

"So much for the simple bliss of things."

"You're quick, aren't you?" the fox said appreciatively. "Soon as you see a little weakness in a fellow's argument, you're in."

"So he's got a mind like a cathedral?"

"That makes it sound too sublime. It isn't. It's decaying, year by year, day by day. It's getting darker and colder in there, and Steep doesn't know how to stay warm, except by killing things, and that doesn't work as well as it used to."

Will's fingers remembered the velvet of the moth's wings, and the heat of the fire that would soon consume them. Though he didn't speak the thought, the fox heard it anyway. "You've had experience of his methodologies, of course. I was forgetting that. You've seen his madness at first hand. That should arm you against him, at least a little."

"And what happens if he dies?"

"I escape his head," the fox said. "And I'm free."

"Is that why you're haunting me?"

"I'm not *haunting* you. Haunting's for ghosts and I'm not a ghost. I'm a . . . what am I? I'm a memory Steep made into a little myth. The Animal That Devoured Men. That's who I am. I wasn't really interesting as a common or garden fox. So he gave me a voice. Stood me on my hind legs. Called me *Lord* Fox. He made me just as he made you." The admission was bitter. "We're both his children."

"And if he lets you go?"

"I told you: I'm away free."

"But in the real world you've been dead for centuries."

"So? I had children while I was alive. Three litters to my certain knowledge. And they had children, and their children had children. I'm still out there in some form or other. You should sow a few oats yourself, by the way, even if it does go against the grain. It's not as if you don't have the equipment." He glanced down at Will's groin. "I could feed a family of five on that."

"I think this conversation's at an end, don't you?"

"I certainly feel much better about things," the fox replied, as though they were two belligerent neighbors who'd just had a heart to heart.

Will got to his feet. "Does that mean I can stop dreaming now?" he said.

"You're not dreaming," the fox replied. "You've been wide awake for the last half hour—"

"Not true," Will said, evenly.

"I'm afraid so," the fox replied. "You opened up a little hole in your head that night with Steep, and now the wind can get in. The same wind that blows through his head comes whistling through that shack of yours—"

Will had heard more than enough. "That's it!" he said, starting toward the door. "You're not going to start playing mind games with me."

Raising his paws in mock surrender, Lord Fox stood aside, and Will strode out into the hallway. The fox followed, his claws tap-tapping on the boards.

"Ah, Will," he whined, "we were doing so well—"

"I'm dreaming."

"No, you're not."

"I'm dreaming."

"No!"

At the bottom of the stairs, Will reeled around and yelled back, "Okay, I'm not! I'm crazy! I'm completely fucking ga-ga!"

"Good," the fox said calmly, "we're getting somewhere."

"You want me to go up against Steep in a straitjacket, is that it?"

"No. I just want you to let go of some of your saner suppositions."

"For instance?"

"I want you to accept the notion that you, William Rabjohns, and I, a semimythical fox, can and do coexist."

"If I accepted that I'd be certifiable."

"All right, try it this way: You recall the Russian dolls?"

"Don't start with them—"

"No, it's very simple. Everything fits inside everything else—"

"Oh, Christ . . . " Will murmured to himself. The thought was now creeping upon him that if this was indeed a dream—and it was, it had to be—then maybe all that had gone before, back to his waking, was also a dream; he *never woke*, but was still comatose in a bed in Winnipeg—

His body began to tremble.

"What's wrong?" the fox said.

"Just shut up!" he yelled, and started to stumble up the stairs.

The animal pursued him. "You've gone very pale. Are you sick? Get yourself some peppermint tea. It'll settle your stomach."

Did he tell the beast to shut up again? He wasn't sure. His senses were phasing in and out. One moment he was falling up the stairs, then he was practically crawling across the landing, then he was in the bathroom, puking, while the fox yattered on behind him about how he should take care, because he was in a very delicate frame of mind (as if he didn't know) and all manner of lunacies could creep up on him.

Then he was in the shower, his hand, ridiculously remote from him, struggling to grasp the handle. His fingers were as weak as an infant's, then the handle turned suddenly and he was struck by a deluge of icy water. At least his nerve endings were fully operational, even if his wits weren't. In two heartbeats his body was solid goose flesh, his scalp throbbing with the cold.

Despite his panic, or perhaps because of it, his mind was uncannily agile, leaping instantly to the places where he'd felt such numbing cold before. In Balthazar, of course, as he lay wounded on the ice, and on the hill above Burnt Yarley, lost in the bitter rain. And on the banks of the River Neva, in the winter of the ice palace—

Wait he thought. That isn't my memory.

The birds dropping dead out of the sky—

That's a piece of Steep's life, not mine.

The river like a rock, and Eropkin—poor, doomed Eropkin— building his masterwork out of ice and light—

He shook his head violently to dislodge these trespassers. But they wouldn't go. Frozen into immobility by the icy water, all he could do was stand there while Steep's unwanted memories came flooding into his head.

VIII

He was standing in the crowded street in St. Petersburg, and if the cold had not already snatched his breath, the sight before him would have done so: Eropkin's palace, its walls raised forty feet high and glittering in the light of the torches and bonfires that were blazing on every side. They were warm, those fires, but the palace did not shed a drop of water, for their heat could not compete with the frigid air.

He looked around at the throng who pressed at the barricades, daring the hussars who kept them in check with boots and threats. By Christ, how they stank tonight! Fetid clothes on fetid bodies.

"Rabble . . . " he murmured.

To Steep's left, a beet-faced brat was shrieking on her father's shoulders, snot frozen at her nostrils. To his right a drunkard with a grease-clogged beard reeled about with a woman in an even more incapacitated state clinging to his arm.

"I hate these people," said a voice close to his ear. "Let's come back later when it's quiet."

He looked round at the speaker, and there was Rosa, her exquisite face, pink from the cold, framed by her fur-lined hood. Oh, but she was beautiful tonight, with the lantern flames flickering in her eyes.

"Please, Jacob," she said, tugging on his sleeve in that little-girl-lost fashion that she knew worked so well. "We could make a baby tonight, Jacob. Truly, I believe we could." She was pressing close to him now, and he caught the scent of her breath; a fragrance no Parisian perfumerie could ever hope to capture. Even here, in the heart of an iron winter, she had the smell of spring about her. "Put your hand on my belly, Jacob," she said, taking his hand in hers and placing it there. "Isn't that warm?" It was. "Don't you think we might make a life tonight?"

"Maybe," he said.

"So let's be away from these animals," she said. "Please, Jacob. *Please.*"

Oh, she could be persuasive when she was in this coquettish mood. And truth to tell he liked to play along.

"Animals, you say?"

"No better," she replied, with a growl of contempt in her voice.

"Would you have them dead?" he asked her.

"Every one of them."

"Every one?"

"But you and me. And from our love a new race of perfect people would come, to have the world the way God intended it."

Hearing this, he couldn't refrain from kissing her, though the streets of St. Petersburg were not like those of Paris or London, and any display of affection, especially one as passionate as theirs, would be bound to draw censure. He didn't care. She was his other, his complement, his completion. Without her, he was nothing. Taking her glorious face in his hands, he laid his lips on hers, her breath a fragrant phantom rising between their faces. The words that breath carried still astonished him, though he had heard them innumerable times.

"I love you," she told him. "And I will love you as long as I have life."

He kissed her again, harder, knowing there were envious eyes upon them, but caring not at all. Let the crowd stare and cluck and shake their heads. They would never feel in all their dreary lives what he and Rosa felt now: the supreme conjunction of soul and soul.

And then, in the midst of the kiss, the din of the crowd receded and completely disappeared. He opened his eyes. They were no longer standing on the street side of the barricades, but were at the very threshold of the palace. The thoroughfare behind them was deserted. Half the night had passed in the time it took to draw breath. It was now long after midnight.

"Nobody's going to spy on us?" Rosa was asking him.

"I've paid all the guards to go and drink themselves stupid," he told her. "We've got four hours before the morning crowd starts to come and gawp. We can do what we like in here."

She slipped the hood back off her head and combed her hair out with her fingers so that it lay abundantly about her shoulders. "Is there a bedroom?" she said.

He smiled. "Oh yes, there's a bedroom. And a big four-poster bed, all carved out of ice."

"Take me to it," she said, catching hold of his hand.

Into the palace they ventured, through the receiving room, which was handsomely appointed with mantelpiece and furniture, through the vast ballroom with its glittering stalactite chandelier, through the dressing room, where there was arranged a wardrobe of coats and hats and shoes, all perfectly carved out of ice.

"It's uncanny," Jacob said, glancing back toward the front door, "the way the light refracts." Though they had ventured deep into the heart of the structure, the glow from the torches set all around the palace was still bright, flickering through the translucent walls. To other eyes it would surely have aroused only wonder, but Jacob was discomfited. Something about the place awoke in him a memory he couldn't name.

"I've been somewhere like this before," he said to Rosa.

"Another ice palace?" she said.

"No. A place that's as bright inside as it is out."

She ruminated on this for a moment. "Yes. I've seen such a place," she said. She wandered from his side and ran her palm over the crystalline wall. "But it wasn't made of ice," she said. "I'm sure not—"

"What then?"

She frowned. "I don't know," she said. "Sometimes, when I try to remember things, I lose my way."

"So do I."

"Why is that?"

"Consorting with Rukenau maybe."

She spat on the floor at the sound of his name. "Don't talk about him," she said.

"But there's a connection, sweet," Steep said. "I swear there is."

"I won't hear you talk about him, Jacob," she said, and hurried away, her skirts hissing across the icy floor.

He followed her, telling her he'd say no more about Rukenau if it troubled her so much. She was angry now—her rages were always sudden, and sometimes brutal—but he was determined to placate her, as much for his own equilibrium as for hers. Once he had her on the bed, he'd kiss her rage away, easily; open her warm body to the cold air and lick her flesh till she sobbed. Her flesh could stand to be naked here. She complained of the cold, of course, and demanded he buy her furs to keep her from freezing, but it was all a sham. She'd heard other women demand such things from their husbands and was playing the same petulant game. And just as it seemed to be her wifely duty to pout and stamp and flee him in some invented tantrum, so it was his to pursue and coerce, and end up taking her body—forcibly, if necessary—until she confessed that his only errors were errors of love, and she adored him for them. It was an absurd rigmarole, and they both knew it. But if they were to be husband and wife, then they were to play out the rituals as though they came naturally. And in truth, some portion of them did. This part, for instance, where he caught up to her and held her tight, told her not to be a ninny, or he'd have to fuck her all the harder. She squirmed in his arms, but made no attempt to escape him. Only told him to do his worst, his very worst.

"I'm not afraid of you, Jacob Steep," she said. "Nor your fucks."

"Well, that's good," he said, lifting her up and carrying her through to the bedroom. The bed itself was in every way of perfect replica of the real thing, even to the dent in the pillow, as though some frigid sleeper had a moment past risen from the spot. He gently laid her there, her hair spread upon the snowy linen, and began to unbutton her. She had forgiven his talk of Rukenau already, it seemed. Forgotten it, perhaps, in her hunger to have Steep's flesh in her, a desire as sudden as her rages, and sometimes just as brutal.

He had bared her breasts, and put his mouth to her nipple, sucking it into the heat of his mouth. She shuddered with pleasure and pressed his head to the deed, reaching down to pull at his shirt. He was as hard as the bed on which they lay. Eschewing all tenderness, he hoisted up her skirt, found the place beneath where his prick ached to go, and slid his fingers there, whispering in her ear that she was the finest slut in all of Christendom and deserved to be treated accordingly. She caught his face in her hands and told him to do his worst, at which invitation he removed his fingers and pressed his prick to service, so suddenly her cry of complaint echoed through the glacial halls.

He took his time, as she demanded he did, laying his full weight upon her as he climbed to his discharge. And as he climbed, and her shouts of pleasure came back to him off the ceiling and walls, the feeling that had caught him in the passage came again: that he had been in a place which this palace, for all its glories, could not approach in splendor.

"So bright—" he said, seeing its luminescence in his head.

"What's bright?" Rosa gasped.

"The deeper we go," he said "the brighter it gets—"

"Look at me!" she demanded. "*Jacob! Look at me!*"

He thrust on mechanically, his arousal no longer in service of her pleasure, or even his own, but fueling the vision. The higher he climbed, the brighter it became, as though the spilling of his seed would bring him into the heart of this glory. The woman was writhing under his assault, but he paid her no mind; he just pressed on, and on, as the brightness grew, and with it his hope that he would know this place by and by, name it, comprehend it.

The moment was almost upon him; the blaze of recognition certain. A few more seconds, a few more thrusts into her void, and he'd have his revelation.

Then she was pushing him away from her, pushing his body with all her strength. He held on, determined not to be denied his vision, but she was not going to indulge him. For all her squealing and sobbing, she only ever played at subjugation—the way she played at the lost girl or the needy wife—and now, wanting him away from her, she had only to use her strength. Almost casually, she threw him out and off her, across the gelid bed. Instead of spilling his seed in the midst of revelation, he discharged meekly, in half-finished spurts, too distracted by her violence to catch the vision that had been upon him.

"You were thinking of Rukenau again!" she yelled, sliding off the bed and tucking her breasts from view. "I warned you, didn't I? I warned you I'd have no part of it!"

Jacob sealed his eyes, hoping to catch a glimpse of what had just escaped him. He'd been so close, so very close. But it had gone, like a firework dying in the heavens.

And in the dark, the sound of water, splashing down over him. He opened his eyes—and found that he'd slumped down in the shower, while the icy water continued to berate his skull.

"Christ," he murmured, reaching up feebly and shutting off the flow. Then he lay gasping and shuddering in the draining water.

What the hell was happening to him? First dreams within dreams. Now visions within visions? He was either having the mother of all nervous breakdowns, which was an unpalatable thought to say the least, or else—or else what? That Lord Fox was right? Was that even an option? Was it remotely possible that whatever the animal was— symptom or spirit—it was telling him some kind of metaphysical truth, and all that his skull contained was, like a Russian doll, itself contained? Or rather, that his mind's contents, which included his memories of Steep and a bloody-snouted fox, were paradoxically enveloped by some portion of those contents; Steep indoctrinating him with his own mythology, in which that same bloody-snouted fox had been raised to lordship?

"All right," he said to the animal, too exhausted to argue with it any longer. "Suppose for the sake of some peace and quiet I go along with what you're telling me? Does that mean I don't have to think about fucking Rosa any more? Because I'm sorry, that's just not my idea of a fun night on the town. Are you listening to me?"

There was no reply forthcoming from the fox. He hauled himself to his feet, grabbed a towel to wrap around his trembling body, and staggered, still dripping, out onto the landing. It was deserted. He went downstairs. The file room, the darkroom, the kitchen were all deserted. The fox had gone.

He sat down at the kitchen table, where the carton of milk he'd been drinking from still stood and was suddenly, almost inexplicably, overtaken by a fit of gentle laughter. His situation was absurd: He'd spent the night trading metaphysics with a fox, whose only purpose, it seemed, was to open Will's head up to a notion of its own reality. Well, it had succeeded. Whether he was dreaming or being dreamed, whether Steep was in his head, or he was in Steep's, whether the fox was myth, mischief, or fleabitten proof of his lunacy, it was all part of a journey he had no choice but to take. His recognition of that fact, and his acceptance of it, were curiously comforting. He'd trekked to so many wild places in his life that he'd finally run out of faith with such journeys. But perhaps they had all been taken in order to bring him back home, and set him on a journey he could not have found until he despaired of every other.

He emptied the carton of milk and—still smiling to himself at the absurdity and simplicity of this—went to bed. His sheets were a luxury after the cold bed in Eropkin's palace and, drawing the quilt up around him, he fell into a contented sleep.

IX

From the verandah of what had once been the Portuguese commander's residence in Suhar, in Oman, Jacob had a magnificent view across the Gulf to Jask, and up the coast to the Strait of Hormuz. It was many centuries since the occupiers had vacated the country, and the modest mansion had fallen into grievous decay. Nevertheless, he and Rosa had been very comfortable here for the last twenty-two days. Though the town had dwindled into dusty obscurity since imperialist days, it was notable for one peculiarity: A band of transvestites, locally known as Xanith and claiming to be possessed by the spirits of minor female divinities, wandered its streets. As ever, Rosa was happiest in the presence of men who pretended her sex, and hearing of this extraordinary tribe had demanded Steep accompany her in search of them, given that she'd been at his side on a number of successful killing sprees of late. He had plenty of work to do on his journals, transposing the notes he'd taken at the extinction sites into a final form, so he agreed to go along with her, though he emphasized that when his work resumed he would be stepping up the scale of his endeavours and would expect her full cooperation. Things had gone well for him of late. A dozen near-certain extinctions in the last seven months, eight of them, it was true, minor forms of South American insect life, but all grist to the fatal mill. And now, all guided into legend by his careful hand.

Today, however, those triumphs seemed very remote. Today his ink and pen lay untouched, because his hands trembled too much. Today all he could do was think about Will Rabjohns.

"What on earth are you obsessing on him for?" Rosa wanted to know when she came upon Jacob, sitting mournfully on the verandah.

"It was the other way about," he said. "I hadn't given a thought to him in a very long time. But he's been giving some thoughts to me, apparently."

"I thought you read me something about him being murdered?" she said, picking up a sliver of tangerine from his abandoned plate and chewing on the bitter rind.

"No, not murdered. Attacked. By a bear."

"Oh, that's right," she said. "He takes pictures of dead animals.

You had that book of his." She tossed the nibbled rind aside and selected a fresh one. "That's your influence, I daresay."

"I'm sure," Jacob said. Clearly the thought gave him no pleasure. "The trouble is, influence works both ways."

"Oh, so you're thinking of becoming a photographer?" Rosa said with a chuckle.

The look Jacob gave her made the rind seem sweet. "I don't want him in my thoughts," he said. "And he's there. Believe me."

"I believe you," she said. Then, after a pause, "May I . . . ask how he got there?"

"There are things between him and me I never told you," Steep replied.

"The night on the hill," she said flatly.

"Yes."

"What did you do to him?"

"It's what he did to me—"

"And what was that? Do tell."

"He's a psychic, Rosa. He saw deep into me. Deeper than I care to look myself. He took me to Thomas—"

"Oh Lord," said Rosa wearily.

"Don't roll your fucking eyes at me!"

"All right, all right, calm down. We can deal with the kid very easily—"

"He's not a kid anymore."

"In our scale of things, he's an infant," Rosa said, putting on her best placating tone. She crossed to Jacob's chair, gently parted his knees, and went down on her haunches between them, looking up at him fondly. "Sometimes you let things get out of all proportion," she said. "So he's been rummaging around in your head—"

"St. Petersburg," Jacob said. "He was remembering St. Petersburg. Us in the palace. And it was more than just memory. It was as though he was looking for some *weakness* in me."

"I don't remember your being weak that night," Rosa cooed.

Jacob didn't warm to her flattery. "I don't want him prying anymore," he said.

"So we'll kill him," Rosa replied. "Do you know where he is right now?" Jacob shook his head, his expression almost superstitious. "Well, he shouldn't be hard to find, for God's sake. We should simply go back to England, and start looking where we first found him. What was that little shithole called?"

"Burnt Yarley."

"Oh, of course. That's where Bartholomeus built that ridiculous courthouse of his." She gazed off into middle distance, glassy-eyed. "That hawk of a nose he had. Oh my Lord."

"It *was* grotesque," Jacob said.

"But he was so tender about living things. Like the boy."

"There's nothing tender about Will Rabjohns," Steep muttered.

"Really? What about the pictures in his book?"

"That's not tenderness, it's guilt. And a touch of morbidity. There's a hard heart in that man. And I want it stilled."

"I'll do it myself," Rosa said. "Gladly."

"No. It falls to me."

"Whatever you want, love. Let's just do it and forget him. You can put him in one of your little books when he'd dead and gone." She picked up the most recent journal and flipped through it until she reached a blank page. "Right here," she said. "Will Rabjohns. Extinct."

"Extinct," Steep murmured. "Yes." He smiled. "Extinct, extinct, extinct." It was like a mantra: a void where thought would go, where life would go.

"I'd better make my farewells," Rosa said and, leaving him on the verandah, went back down into the town for a last hour in the company of the Xanith.

She arrived back at the mansion, fully expecting to find Jacob still sitting in his chair, brooding. But not so. In her absence, he had not only packed all their belongings, but had a vehicle waiting at the front gate to carry them down the coast to Masquat on the first leg of their trek back to Burnt Yarley.

X

i

Will didn't stir until a little after nine, but when he did he felt remarkably clearheaded. He got up and contemplated the shower for a few moments, wondering if he wasn't inviting trouble by stepping in. He defiantly ran the water cold and stepped under its barrage. There were no visions forthcoming, and after a minute of this masochism, he turned the heat up a little and scrubbed himself clean.

Dried, dressed, and on his second cup of coffee, he called Adrianna. Glenn picked up, sounding adenoidal. "I got some kind of allergy," he said. "My nose won't stop running. You want to speak to Adrianna?"

"May I?"

"No, 'cause she's not here. She's gone to see about getting a job."

"Where?"

"At the city-planning department. I met this woman at Patrick's party who was looking for someone, so she's gone to check it out."

"I'll call back later then," Will said. "You take care of your allergies."

His next call went to Patrick, whose first question was, "How are you feeling this morning?"

"Pretty good, thank you."

"No regrets, huh? Shit. I was afraid of this. The whole thing was a fiasco."

It took a minute or two for Will to convince him that just because nobody had fallen in love or out of a window didn't mean the party hadn't been memorable. Patrick reluctantly conceded that maybe he was just feeling nostalgic this morning, sitting in the litter, but in the old days a party wasn't even considered to have occurred unless somebody ended up being screwed in the bath while the guests offered a rousing chorus from *Aïda*. "I must have missed that particular night," Will said, to which Patrick replied that no, they'd both been there, but poor Will's memory had been fried standing in the sun taking family portraits of water buffalo.

"Moving on—" Will said.

"You want Bethlynn's whereabouts," Patrick said.

"Yes, please."

"She lives in Berkeley, on Spruce Street." Will jotted down directions, warned once again not to try calling her first, because she'd almost certainly slam the phone down on him. "She doesn't like any air of negativity around her," Patrick explained.

"And I'm Mr. Negativity?"

"Well, face it, honey, nobody looks at your books and thinks, gee, what a lovely planet we live on. In fact—now, Will, I don't want you to get steamed about this—Bethlynn took a glance at one of your books and told me to get it out of the apartment."

"She did *what?*"

"I told you, don't get mad. It's the way she thinks. She sees things in terms of good vibrations and bad vibrations."

"So you had a book burning on Castro."

"No, Will—"

"What else went? *Naked Lunch? King Lear?* Bad vibes in *Lear,* man, better toss it out!"

"Shut up, Will," Patrick replied mildly. "I didn't say I agreed with her, I'm just telling you where her head's at. And if you really and truly want to make peace with her, then you're going to have to work with that."

"Okay," Will said, calming down a little. "I'll make as nice as I can make. Maybe I'll offer to do her a book of sunflowers to make up for all those bad vibes. Big yellow sunflowers on every page, with a quote from the *Bhagavadgita* underneath."

"You could do worse, man o' mine," Patrick pointed out. "People need some light in their lives right now."

Oh, there's light in my pictures, Will thought, remembering how they'd flickered at the fox's feet, the eyes of the hunted and the bones they'd become shining out at him. There was light aplenty. It just wasn't the kind of illumination Bethlynn would want to meditate upon.

ii

Later, as the cab carried him over the bridge, he looked back at the fog and the sun-draped hills and thought for the first time in many years how fine a city San Francisco was to live in, one of the few places left on earth where the human experiment was still conducted in an atmosphere of passionate civility.

"You a visitor?" the driver wanted to know.

"No. Why?"

"You keep looking back like you never saw the place before."

"It feels like that today," Will said, which so confounded the man it silenced him efficiently for the rest of the trip.

However it sounded, it was true. He felt as though his eyes were clearer today than they'd been in years, both literally and figuratively. Not only did the sights around him seem crystalline, but he was taking pleasure where his gaze would never have lingered before. Everywhere he looked there were nuances of tone and color to delight him. In the cedars, in the storefronts, in the cracked leather of the seat in front of him. And on the sidewalk, faces glimpsed that he would never see again, every one of them a burgeoning glory of its own. He didn't know where this newfound clarity was coming from, but it was as if he had been looking through a dirty lens for most of his life and become so familiar with the grime that now, when the glass was miraculously cleansed, it was a revelation. Was this what the fox had meant by the simple bliss of things?

He elected to get out of the cab two blocks shy of Bethlynn's house, in part because he wanted to luxuriate in this feeling a little before he met with her, and in part to prepare a speech of reconciliation. The latter purpose, however, was abandoned the moment he started to walk. The confines of the cab had been a limitation on his hungry sight. Now, alone on the sidewalk, the world rushed away from him in every direction and, in the same moment, came careening back to show him its wonders. There were clouds above his head that the wind had teased into frills and fripperies; the decaying boards of a home across the street paraded glorious patterns of peeling paint. A flock of pigeons, dining on the crumbs of a discarded doughnut, performed an exquisite dance as they fluttered and settled, then rose in a glorious flight and swooped away.

This was not the condition that he'd expected to be in when he went to confront Bethlynn, but as long as she didn't misinterpret the smile he could not remove from his face, perhaps it wasn't an inappropriate state. If she was indeed the sensitive Patrick had claimed her to be, then she'd know his euphoria was genuine. Focusing attention on the simple business of walking two blocks to her door was problematical, however. Everywhere he looked, sights distracted him. A wall, a roof, a reflection in a window: All demanded he take the time to stand and gawp. How many days, weeks, months of his life had he waited in a mud hole or a tree on another continent for a glimpse of something he wanted to put on film—and how often left the field unsatisfied?—while here, all along, on this street ten miles from where he lived were profligate glories, eager to be seen? And if he'd spent that time teaching his camera to see with the eyes he was using right now—taught it even a tiny part of that sight—would he not have converted every soul who saw his pictures to the greater good? Would they not have looked astonished, and said *Is this the world?* and realizing that it was, become its protector?

Oh God, why had the fox not opened his head fifteen years ago, and saved him all that wasted time?

It took him the better part of an hour to walk the two blocks to reach the porch of Bethlynn's unostentatious bungalow, but by the time he did, he had his wits about him again and was ready to take the smile off his face and play the reformed reprobate. She took a little time to respond to his rapping however, during which time the intricacy of the cracks on the step drew his admiration and, when she finally opened the door, he looked up at her with an asinine smirk on his face.

"What do you want?" she said.

He mumbled the barest minimum: "I came to apologize."

"Did you really?" she said, her appraisal of him less than promising.

"I was . . . looking at the cracks on your step," he said, trying to explain his smile away.

She scrutinized him a little harder. "Are you all right?" she said.

"Yes . . . and . . . no," he replied.

She kept staring at him, with a look on her face he couldn't quite interpret. Plainly she was sensing something about him other than how well he'd cleaned his teeth this morning. And whatever it was—his aura, his vibrations—she seemed to trust what she felt, because she said, "We can talk inside," and stepping back from the door, ushered him into the house.

XI

The interior was not what he expected at all. There were no astrological charts, no incense burners, no healing crystals on the table. The large room she brought him into was sparsely but comfortably furnished, the walls a calming beige and bare but for a family photograph. The only other decoration was a vase of camellias set on the sill. The window was open a little way, and the breeze sweetened the room with the scent of the blooms.

"Please sit down," she said. "Do you want something to drink?"

"Some water would be just great. Thank you."

She went to get it, leaving him to settle into the comfort of the sofa. He'd no sooner done so than an enormous tabby cat leaped up onto the armrest—his nimbleness belying his bulk—and, purring in anticipation of Will's touch, vamped toward him. "My God, you're quite a piece of work," Will said.

The cat put his head beneath his hand, and pressed itself against his palm.

"Genghis, stop being pushy," Bethlynn said, returning with the water.

"Genghis? As in Khan?"

Bethlynn nodded. "The terrorizer of Christendom." She set Will's water on the table, and sipped from her own glass. "A pagan to his core."

"The cat or the Khan?"

"Both," Bethlynn said. "Don't be too flattered. He likes every-one."

"Good for him," Will said. "Look, about Pat's party: It was my fault. I was in one of my contrary moods, and I'm sorry."

"One apology's quite sufficient," Bethlynn said, her tone warmer than her vocabulary. "We all make assumptions about people. I made some about you, I'll admit, and they were no more flattering than those you made about me."

"Because of my pictures?"

"And some articles I'd read. Maybe you were misrepresented, but I must say you seemed very much the professional pessimist."

"I wasn't misrepresented. It was just . . . a consequence of what I'd seen." Despite his best efforts, he felt the same idiot smile she'd met on the doorstep creeping back onto his face as he talked. Even in this almost ascetically plain room, his eyes were bringing him revela-tions. The sunlight on the wall, the flowers on the sill, the cat on his lap—all sheen and shift and flutes of color. It was all he could do not to let the threads of his sober exchange with Bethlynn go, and babble like a child about what he was seeing and seeing.

"I know you probably think a lot of what I share with Patrick is sentimental nonsense," Bethlynn was telling him, "but healing isn't a business for me, it's a vocation. I do what I do because I want to help people."

"You think you can *heal* him?"

"Not in the medical sense, no. He has a virus. I can't make it curl up and die. But I *can* put him in touch with the Patrick that isn't sick. The Patrick that can never *be* sick, because he's part of some-thing that's beyond sickness."

"Part of God?"

"If that's the word you want to use," Bethlynn said. "It's a little Old Testament for me."

"But God's what you mean?"

"Yes, God's what I mean."

"Does Patrick know that's what's going on? Or does he think he's going to get better?"

"You don't need to ask me that," Bethlynn said. "You know him at a far deeper level than I do. He's a very intelligent man. Just because he's ill doesn't mean he's lying to himself."

"With respect," Will said, "that's not what I'm asking."

"If you're asking have I been lying to him, the answer's no. I've never promised him he'd get out of this alive. But he can and will get out *whole*."

"What do you mean by that?"

"I mean once he finds himself in the eternal, then he won't be afraid of death. He'll see it for what it is. Part of the process. No more nor less."

"If it's part of the process, why did it matter if he looked at my pictures or not?"

"I wondered when we'd get to that," Bethlynn said, easing back in her chair. "I just . . . didn't feel they were a positive influence on him, that's all. He's very raw at the moment, very responsive to influences good and bad. Your pictures are extremely powerful, Will, there's no question about that. They exercised an almost mesmeric hold on me when I first saw them. I'd go as far as to say they're a form of magic."

"They're just pictures of animals," Will said.

"They're a lot more than that. And—if you'll forgive my saying so, which you may not—a lot less." On another day, in another state of mind, Will would have been rising to the defense of his work by now. Instead he listened with an easy detachment. "You disagree?" Bethlynn said.

"About the magic part, yes."

"When I say magic I'm not talking about something from a fairy tale. I'm talking about working change in the world. That's what your art's intended to do, isn't it? It's an attempt, a misdirected one, I think, but perfectly sincere attempt to *work change*. Now you could say all art's trying to do that, and maybe it is, but you know the forces your work plays with. It's trying for something more potent than a picture of the Golden Gate Bridge. In other words, I think you have the instincts of a shaman. You want to be a go-between, a channel by which some vision that's larger than the human perspective—perhaps it's a divine vision, perhaps it's demoniacal, I'm not sure you'd know the difference—is communicated to the tribe. Does any of that sound plausible to you or are you just sitting there thinking I talk too much?"

"I'm not thinking that at all," Will said.

"Has anybody else ever talked to you about this?"

"One person, yes. When I was a kid. He was—"

"*Don't,*" Bethlynn said, hurriedly raising her hands in front of her as though to ward off this information. "I'd prefer you didn't share that with me."

"Why not?"

She got up to her feet and wandered over to the window, gently pinching a dead leaf from the camellias. "The less I know about what moves you the better for all concerned," she said. Her voice had an artificial equanimity in it. "I've enough shadows of my own without inheriting yours. These things pass along, Will. Like viruses."

Not a pretty analogy. "It's as bad as that?" Will said.

"I think you're in an extraordinary place right now," she said. "When I look at you I see a man who has the capacity to do great good, or . . . " She shrugged. "Perhaps I'm being simplistic," she said. "It may not be a question of good and evil." She looked round at him, her face fixed in a mask of impassivity, as though she didn't want to give him a clue to how she was feeling. "You're a bundle of contradictions, Will. I think a lot of gay men are. They want something other than what they were taught to want, and it—I don't know what the word is—it *muddies* them somehow." She stared at Will, still preserving her mask. "But that's not quite what's going on with you," she said. "The truth is, I don't *know* what I see when I look at you, and that makes me nervous. You could be a saint, Will. But somehow I doubt it. Whatever moves in you . . . Well, to be perfectly honest, whatever moves in you frightens me."

"Maybe we should stop this conversation now," Will said, putting Genghis out of his lap and getting to his feet, "before you start exorcising me."

She laughed lightly at this, but without much conviction. "It's certainly been nice talking with you," she said, her sudden formality a certain sign that she was not going to reveal anything more.

"You *will* keep working with Patrick?"

"Of course," she said, escorting him to the door. "You didn't think I was going to give up on him just because we'd had a few sour words? It's my responsibility to do whatever I can do. Not just for him, for me. I'm on a journey of my own. That's why it's a little confusing when I meet someone like you on the road." They were at the door. "Well, good luck," she said, shaking Will's hand. "Maybe we'll meet again one of these days."

And with that she ushered him onto the step and, without waiting for a reply, closed the door.

XII

i

He walked home. It took him almost five hours, his trek fueled by Hershey bars and doughnuts, washed down with a carton of milk, all consumed as he walked. Either he was steadily becoming more used to the sights his eyes were showing him or else his brain (perhaps for his own protection) had got the trick of dialing down the amount of information he was assimilating. Whatever the reason, he didn't feel the need to linger with the same obsessiveness, but wandered on his way taking mental snapshots of sights that drew his attention, then pressing on. The conversation with Bethlynn had been more enlightening than he'd expected it to be and, as he walked, taking his snapshots, he turned fragments of it over in his head. Whether or not there was indeed a God-part of Patrick, a part that would never sicken or die, she was plainly quite sincere in that belief, and if the possibility comforted Patrick (while putting food in the cat's bowl) then there was no harm in it. Her assessment of Will, however, was another deal completely. She'd made, it seemed, an instinctual judgment about him, based in part on what she'd heard from Patrick, in part on articles that she'd seen, and in part on the work. He was a man with a dark heart, she'd decided, who wanted to taint others with that darkness. So far, so simple. Whether she was right or wrong, there was nothing there that an intelligent individual with a little imagination might not have construed. But there was more to her theory; more, he suspected, than she'd been willing to share with him. He was an unwitting shaman, that, at least, she'd been ready to tell him. Working change, inducing visions. And why? Because somebody in his past (somebody she didn't even want him to *name*) had planted a seed.

That could only be Jacob Steep. Whatever else Jacob had done, good and bad, he'd been the first person in Will's life to give him, if only for a few hours, a sense that he was special. Not a poor second best to a dead brother, the lumpen clod to Nathaniel's perfected angel, but a chosen child. How many times in the three decades since that night on the hilltop had he revisited the winter wood, the weapon buzzing in his hand as he strode toward his victims? And seen their blood flow? And heard Jacob, at his back, whispering to him: *Suppose they were the last. The very last.*

What had his life to date been but an extended footnote to that encounter: an attempt to make some idiot recompense for the little murders he'd committed at Steep's behest, or rather for the unalloyed joy he'd taken in the thought of shaping the world that way?

If there was some buried desire in him to be more than a witness to extinctions—to be, as Bethlynn had said, a worker of change— then it was because Steep had planted that desire. Whether he had done it intentionally or not was another question entirely. Was it possible that the whole initiation had been stage-managed to make him into some semblance of the man he'd become? Or had Jacob been about the work of making a child into a murderer and simply been interrupted in the process, leaving the smeared, unfinished thing Will was to stumble off and puzzle out its purpose for itself? Most likely he would never know. And in that he shared a common history with most of the men who wandered Folsom and Polk and Market this late afternoon. Men whose mothers and fathers—however loving, however liberal—would never understand them the way they understood their straight children, because these gay sons were genetic cul-de-sacs. Men who would be obliged to make their own families: out of friends, out of lovers, out of divas. Men who were self-invented, for better or worse, makers of styles and mythologies that they constantly cast off with the impatience of souls who would never find a description that quite fitted. If there was a sadness in this there was also a kind of unholy glee.

He almost wished Steep were here, so he could show him the sights. Take him into the Gestalt and buy him a beer.

ii

By the time he got home it was almost six o'clock. There were three messages on the answering machine from Drew, one from Adrianna, and one from Patrick, reporting that he'd just had what he characterized as an *intriguing* conversation with Bethlynn.

"I couldn't figure out whether she liked you or not, but you certainly made an impression. And she was very insistent about there not being any kind of rift between her and me. So, good job, buddy. I know how hard that was for you to do. But thanks. It means a lot to me."

Having listened to the messages, he went to sluice off the sweat of his journey and, roughly toweling himself dry, wandered into the bedroom and lay down. Despite his fatigue, he had a sense of simple physical well-being he couldn't remember having had for a long time: months, perhaps years, before the events in Balthazar. There was a gentle tremor in his muscles, and in his head an almost reverent calm.

So calm, in fact, that a perverse notion came trotting in to disturb it.

"Where are you, fox?" he said, very quietly.

The empty house made its cooling and settling sounds, as houses do, but there was nothing amid the ticks and creaks that might have indicated Lord Fox's presence. No tapping of his claws on the boards, no swish of his tail against the wall.

"I know you're there somewhere."

This wasn't a lie. He believed it. The fox had walked the line between dreams and the waking world on two occasions; now Will was ready to join him in that place and see what the view was like. But first the animal had to show itself.

"Stop being coy," Will said. "We're in this together." He sat up. "I want to be *with* you," he said. "That sounds sexual, doesn't it? Maybe that's what it is." He closed his eyes and tried to conjure the animal behind his lids. Its gleaming fur and glittering teeth, its sway and swagger. It was *his* animal, wasn't it? First his tormentor, then his truth teller—the eater of dick-flesh and the dropper of bon mots. "Where the fuck are you?" he wanted to know. Still it didn't come.

Well, he thought, isn't this a perfect little paradox? After rejecting the fox's wisdom for so long, he'd finally come round to understanding its place in his life, and the damn creature wasn't playing.

He got up off the bed and was about to try his luck in another room when the telephone rang. It was Drew. "What happened to you?" he wanted to know. "I've been calling and calling."

"I went over to Berkeley to kowtow to Bethlynn. Then I walked back, which was wonderful, and now I'm talking to you, which is even more wonderful."

"You are up, buddy. Have you been poppin' some pills?"

"Nope. I'm just feeling good."

"Are you in the mood for some fun tonight?"

"Like what?"

"Like I come over, and we lock the doors and make some serious love?"

"I'd like that."

"Have you eaten?"

"Chocolate and doughnuts."

"That's why you're flying. You're on a sugar rush. I'll bring some food with me. We'll have a love feast."

"That sounds decadent."

"It will be. I guarantee. I'll be over in an hour."

"By which you mean two."

"You know me so well," Drew said.

"Oh no. I've got lots to learn," Will breathed.

"Like what?"

"Like what kind of face you pull when I'm fucking the bejeezus out of you."

Adrianna returned his call as he was making himself the ritual martini. He asked her how the job interview had gone. Like shit, she told him; the instant she'd walked into the planning offices she'd known that after a week working there she'd be stir-crazy. "When we were out in the mud somewhere being bitten to death by bugs," she said, "I used to wish I had a nice clean job in a nice clean office with a view of the Bay Bridge. But I realized today: I can't do it. Simple as that. I'll end up doing somebody serious harm with a typewriter. So I don't know. I'll find something that suits me eventually, but you're quite a hard act to follow, Will. What's that clinking sound?"

"I'm making a martini."

"That brings back memories," she sighed. Then, "Remember what you said in *Balthazar*, about how you felt everything was running down? Now I know how you feel."

"It'll pass," he said. "You'll find something else."

"Oh, so the ennui's yesterday's news, is it? What changed your mind? Drew?"

"Not exactly—"

"He makes a cute drunk, by the way, which I always think's a good sign. Oh shit, I'm late for dinner." She hollered to Glenn that she was on her way, then whispered, "We're dining with the other members of his string quartet. I swear, if they break into four-part harmony over the soup, I'm leaving him. See you later, hon."

The conversation over, he carried his drink through to the file room and finally tidied up the photographs he'd cast on the floor, a job he'd been putting off since Lord Fox had ignited their phantom life. It was a simple, almost domestic task, and yet like so much else that he'd seen and done today, it felt charged, as though filled with hidden significance. Not so hidden, perhaps. His initiation into the mysteries of his new existence had begun here, with these pictures. They had been, as it were, a map of the territory he was to explore. Now the map could be put away. The journey had begun.

With all the pictures stowed, he went back upstairs to shave, and there in the mirror had confirmation that what he'd sensed in the room below was true. The face he saw was not one that he remembered ever seeing before. The physiognomy was his, surely enough—the bones, the scars, the creases—but the way he looked at himself (and thus the way he looked back) was in some subtle fashion different and, in the matter of a man's gaze, a subtlety is everything. Here was the rarest creature in his universe; the great beast that had been, until now, too far from him to be seen: behind the next copse, over the next hill. In truth, it had perhaps been easier to find than he'd pretended, but fear had kept him from looking too hard. Now he wondered why. There was nothing so terrible here, nothing unfathomable. Just the child become a man, just the hair going to gray, and the skin a little leathery from too much noonday sun.

He thought of the fox, extolling the virtues of heterosexuality, of his children making children making children. Will would not have the comfort of their progression. There would be no offspring to carry this face into futurity. He was in a race of one.

Suppose this were the last.

Well, it was. And there was something pungent and powerful about that thought, the thought of living and dying and passing away in the heat of his own fine fire.

"So be it," he said, and set to shaving.

XIII

Drew was a mere thirty-five minutes late, which was more certain testament to his enthusiasm for the coming liaison than his flushed cheeks or the tightness of his pants. He had hauled no less than six bags of produce from the market to a cab and from the cab to the front door. Will offered to help, but he said he didn't trust Will not to peek and, kissing him on the cheek with self-enforced discretion, instructed him to go watch television while he got everything ready. Unused to being bossed around, Will was thoroughly charmed and dutifully did as he was instructed.

There was nothing on television that caught his attention for more than thirty seconds. He sat watching with the volume turned low, hoping to interpret the sounds of preparation in the kitchen and the bedroom above, like a child going through Christmas gifts guessing what they were through the paper. At last, Drew came back. He'd showered (his hair still slicked back) and changed into some more provocative clothing: a loose, but well-cut vest that showed off his ample arms and shoulders, and a pair of beige linen drawstring pants that looked designed for easy access.

"Follow me," he said, and led Will up the stairs.

By now, night had fallen and the bedroom was lit with just a few judiciously placed candles. The bed had been stripped back and every cushion or pillow in the house nested upon it, while the floor had been laid with fresh white sheets, on which the cornucopia Drew had lugged from the market had been arrayed.

"There's enough food here to feed the five thousand," Will said. "Without the miracle."

Drew beamed. "It's healthy to be excessive once in a while," he said, slipping his arm around Will's waist. "It's good for the soul. Besides, we deserve it."

"We do?"

"You do anyway. I'm just the slave-boy here. Ownership's yours for the night."

Will put his mouth to Drew's face—cheeks, brows, chin, lips.

"Food first," the slave-boy protested. "I've got pears, peaches, strawberries, blueberries, kiwi-fruit—no grapes, they're a cliché— some cold lobster, some shrimp, Brie, Chardonnay, bread of course, chocolate mousse, carrot cake. Oh, there's some really rare beef if you're in the mood, and hot mustard to go with it. Anything else?" He scanned the food. "I'm sure there's more."

"We'll find it," Will said.

They set to. Sprawled among the foodstuffs like a couple of Romans, they ate, and kissed, and ate some more, and undressed, and ate some more, juices flowing, mouths full, one appetite growing as the other waned. Mellowed by the wine, they talked freely, Drew unburdening himself of the disappointments of his life over the last decade. He wasn't self-pitying in his account. He simply described in a witty and self-deprecating manner how much he'd fallen shy of his hopes for himself; how, in short, he'd wanted the world and ended up with bankruptcy and a beer belly.

"I don't think queers are very good to one another," he remarked, apropos of nothing in particular, "and we should be. I mean, we're all in this together, aren't we? But fuck, the way you hear people talk in a bar it's *I hate blacks* or *I hate drag-queens* or *I hate muscle-boys* 'cause they're all brainless lunks, and I think: Well fuck, the *whole world* hates us—"

"Not in San Francisco."

"But this is a ghetto. It doesn't count. I go back to Colorado, and my family rags on me day and night about how God wants me to be straight and if I don't mend my ways I'm going straight to hell."

"What do you tell 'em?"

"I say, You may as well tell me to give up breathing, 'cause I'm queer all the way in." He pushed his finger against the middle of his chest. "Heart and soul," he said. "You know what I wish?"

"What?"

"I wish my folks could see us like this right now. Hangin' out, talking, being us. Being happy." He paused, looking at the floor. "Are you happy?"

"Right now?"

"Yeah."

"Sure."

"Because I am. I'm about as happy as I think I've ever been. And I've got a long memory," he laughed. "I can remember seeing you for the very first time."

"No, you can't."

Drew looked up, his expression sweetly defiant. "Oh yes I can," he said. "It was at Lewis's place. He had a brunch, and I came along with Timothy. You remember Timothy?"

"Vaguely."

"He was a big ol' drag queen who'd taken me under his wing. He'd brought me along—little Drew Travis from Buttfuck, Colorado—I guess to show me off. And I was so damn nervous, 'cause there were all these circuit queens there who knew everybody—"

"Or *said* they knew everybody."

"Right. They were dropping names so fast it was like a fucking hailstorm, and once in a while one of them would look at me and check me out like I was a piece of meat. You were late, I remember."

"Oh," said Will. "So you get it from me."

"I got everything from you. Everything I wanted. You lavished attention on me, as if nothing else mattered. Up till then, I wasn't sure I was going to stay. I was thinking: This isn't for me. I don't belong here with these people. I was plotting to get on the next plane home and propose to Melissa Mitchell, who would have married me in a heartbeat and let me do what the fuck I liked behind her back. That was my plan, if being here didn't work out. But you changed my mind."

Gently, Will stroked Drew's face. "No," he said.

"Yes," Drew replied. "You might not remember it that way, but you weren't in my head. That's *exactly* what happened. We didn't even sleep together right away. Timothy got very sniffy and said you weren't good people."

"Did he indeed?"

"He said, oh, I don't know, you were crazy, you were English, you were uptight, you were pretentious."

"I was not uptight. The rest, probably."

"Anyway, you didn't call me, and I was afraid to call you in case Timothy got mad. I was kinda dependent on him. He'd paid for me to fly out, I was living in his apartment. Then you did call."

"And the rest's history."

"Don't knock it. We had some fine times together."

"*Those* I remember."

"And of course by the time we broke up, there was no going back to Colorado for me. I was hooked."

"What happened to Melissa?"

"Ha. You'll like this. She married this guy I used to jerk off with in high school."

"So, she had a thing for fags," Will said, moving behind Drew and letting him lean back against his body.

"I guess maybe she did. I still see her once in a while when I go home. Her kids go to the same school as my brother's kids, so I meet her when I go to pick them up. She still looks pretty good. So," he leaned his head back and kissed Will's chin, "that's the story of my life."

Will hugged him close. "What happened to Timothy?" Will said. "We owe him."

"Oh, he's been dead seven, maybe eight years. I guess his lover walked out on him when he got sick, and he pretty much died without anyone. I heard about it just after Christmas and he'd died on Thanksgiving. He's buried in Monterey. I go down there once in a while. Put some flowers on the grave. Tell him I still think of him."

"That's good. You're a good man, you know that?"

"Is that important?"

"Yeah. I'm beginning to think it is."

They made love then. Not the hectic, no-holds-barred mating of their first romance, eighteen years before, nor the tentative, faintly fearful encounter of a few nights ago. This time they met not as conquests or tricks, but as lovers. They took their sensual time with their detections, passing kisses and touches back and forth with a lazy ease, but by degrees becoming more agitated, each in their way demanding, each in their way conceding. In waves then, they played, pressing steadily toward a destination they had debated and planned. Will had not fucked anyone in four years, and Drew, though he had been a glutton for it earlier in his life, had sworn off the act with so much risk attached. It had never been, even in simpler days, a natural act, despite tales of midwestern farmhands, spit and a little lust. It was a conscious act of desire, especially in the heart of the plague, when the condom and the lubricant had to be at hand, and there had to be, along with the erections, a gentle overcoming of anxiety. Tenderly then, in the nest of pillows, they coupled, to the pleasure of both.

When they finished, Drew went to shower. Mr. Clean, Will called him. This wasn't a new preoccupation; he'd always needed to wash off the sex immediately after he'd come. It was the church boy in him, he explained, to which Will replied, "You just had an Englishman in you. How many people have you got in there?"

Laughing. Drew went into the bathroom and closed the door. Will listened to the muted sound of the shower being turned on— the slap of the water on the tiles, then the change of timbre as the water broke against Drew's back and shoulders and butt. He shouted something, but Will didn't catch it. He stretched in the double luxury of fatigue and satiety, his consciousness drifting. I should shower too, he thought; I'm greasy and sweaty and rank. Drew won't crawl into bed beside me unless I wash. So he held on to consciousness, though it was hard work. Twice he fell into the shallows of sleep. Woke the first time with the shower now turned off, and Drew singing tunelessly as he toweled himself dry. Woke the second time to hear Drew thundering downstairs. "I'm just getting some water," he yelled. "You want anything?"

Woozily, Will sat up. He yawned and gazed down at the felon between his legs. "Busy night?" he said, flipping his cock back and forth. Then he swung his legs over the side of the bed, knocking over one of the candles. "*Fuck,*" he muttered, bending down to right it again, the smell of the extinguished wick sharp in his nostrils. As he stood up, the room pulsed. Thinking he'd risen too quickly, he closed his eyes. White patches throbbed behind his lids. He felt suddenly sick. He stood swaying at the end of the bed for a few moments, waiting for the feeling to pass, but instead it intensified, waves of nausea rising from his belly. He opened his eyes again and started toward the hallway, determined not to end the evening puking in the very room where they'd made such fine love. He got no more than a yard from the bed, then the ache in his belly doubled him up. He dropped to his knees, surrounded by the leavings of their feast, his senses horribly susceptible. He could smell the spoiling of fruit that had been fresh three hours before, of cheese and cream that had been sweet and were now curdling, as though the heat of the room, of the deeds performed in the room, was hastening everything to rot. The stench of it was too much. He began to puke, his belly cramping, the white particles flaring in his head, washing out the room—

And in the midst of the blaze, images from the adventures of the day: a sky, a wall, Bethlynn; Drew clothed, Drew naked; the cat, the flowers, the bridge, all unreeling like a fragment of film tossed into the fire in his head, the throbbing white fire that lay at the end of everything.

God help me, he tried to say, no longer afraid of being found in this state by Drew, only wanting him there to extinguish the blaze—

He raised his head, and squinted through the light toward the door. There was no sign of Drew. He started to crawl toward the landing, knocking over two of the three remaining candles as he did so. The conflagration in his head continued unchecked, the memories still flickering before they were consumed, like moth's wings, fluttering and fluttering—

The waters of the bay, whipped by the wind; the flowers on Bethlynn Reichle's windowsill; Drew's face, sweating in ecstasy—

And then, suddenly, the blaze was gone, extinguished in a heartbeat. He was kneeling three or four yards from the door, the darkness gray, the light gray, the food in which he knelt drained of color, his hands and legs and dick and belly all drained, all gray. It was strangely pleasurable after the assault and the sickness, to be thrown into this cool cell, detached from sensuality. His mind, he assumed, had simply decided enough was enough, and pulled the plug on all but the barest minimum of stimulation. He was no longer overpowered by the stench of rot and curdle, even the glutinous textures of the food around him had been tamed.

The nausea had also receded, but he didn't want to risk any motion until he was certain it had passed completely, so he stayed where he'd found himself when the episode had passed, kneeling by the light of a single candle flame. Drew would come up the stairs very soon, he thought. He'd look at Will and take pity: come to him, soothe him, cradle him. All he had to do was be patient. He knew how to be patient. He could sit in the same position for hours. It wasn't hard. Just breathe evenly and empty the mind of useless thoughts. Sweat them away, then wait.

And look! His waiting was already over. There was a shadow on the wall. Drew was climbing the stairs right now. Thirty seconds and he'd be on the landing, and the moment after he'd be coming to help Will back to sanity. There he was, with a glass of water in his hand, his trousers barely hanging on his hips, his body piebald with the marks Will had left on him. The flesh around his nipples flushed. The teeth marks on his neck and shoulders neat as a tailor's stitch. His face mottled. He raised his head, oh so slowly (in this gray world nothing had urgency), and a puzzled look came over his face as he stared toward the bedroom door. It seemed he couldn't make out Will's face in the murk or, if he could, failed to make sense of what he saw. He smelled the vomit, however, that much was plain. A look of disgust disfigured his face, the ugliness of his expression troubling to Will. He didn't want to see that look on his savior's face. He wanted compassion, tenderness.

Drew had hesitated now and was staring through the open door. His disgust had turned into fearfulness. His breath had quickened, and when he spoke—"Will?" he said—the word was barely audible.

Damn you, Will thought, don't stay out there. Come on in. There's nothing to be afraid of, for God's sake. *Come on in.*

But Drew didn't move. Frustrated now, Will put his hand down into the muck in front of him and raised himself up. He tried to say Drew's name, but for some reason his throat loosed a vile din, more like a bark than a name.

Drew dropped the glass of water. It smashed at his feet.

"Jesus!" he yelled, and started to back away toward the stairs.

What nonsense was this? Will thought. He needed help and the man was moving away?

He lurched toward the bedroom door, trying to call out a second time, but his throat again betrayed him. All he could do was to stagger out onto the landing, into the light, where Drew could see him. His legs were no more reliable than his larynx however. He stumbled at the door and would have fallen amongst the broken glass had he not caught hold of the jamb. He swung around, realizing in this ungainly moment that for some reason his witless dick was hard again, slapping against his stomach as he lurched out onto the landing.

And now, by the light thrown up the stairwell from the hallway below, Drew saw his pursuer.

"*Jesus Christ,*" he said, the fear on his face becoming disbelief. "Will?" he breathed.

This time, Will managed a word. "Yes," he said.

Drew shook his head. "What are you playing at?" he said. "You're freaking me out."

Will's bare feet trod the glass, but he didn't care. He had to stop Drew abandoning him. He caught hold of the banister and started to haul himself along the landing to the top of the stairs. His body felt utterly alien to him, as though his muscles were in the business of reorienting themselves. He wanted to drop back down on his knees to ease their motion; wanted to move sleekly in pursuit of the animal in front of him. He'd been patient, hadn't he? He'd waited in the gray until the quarry showed itself. Now it was time to give chase—

"Stop this, Will," Drew was saying. "For God's sake! I mean it!" Fear had made him shrill. He sounded comical, and Will laughed. Short and sharp. A yelp of a laugh.

The din was too much for Drew. What little courage he'd had broke, and he stumbled backward down the stairs, hollering at Will as he went— something incoherent—and snatching up his jacket at the bottom of the flight. He was barechested and barefoot, but he didn't care. He wanted to be out of the house, whatever the discomfort. Will was at the top of the stairs now and began his descent. The slivers of his glass in his soles were agonizing, however, and after two steps—knowing he was in no condition to catch up with his quarry—he sank down onto one of the stairs and watched Drew while he struggled to unlock the door. Only when it was open, and Drew had sight of the street, did he look back and yell—

"*Fuck you, Will Rabjohns!*"

Then he was gone, out into the night and away.

Will sat on the stairs for several minutes enjoying the cold gusts that came through the open door. His gooseflesh did nothing to dissuade his erection. It ticked on between his legs, reminding him that for many the pleasures of the night were only just beginning. And if for others, why not for him?

XIV

i

There was a club on Folsom called the Penitent. At the height of its notoriety in the midseventies, it had been called the Serpent's Tooth and had been to San Francisco what the Mineshaft had been to New York: A club where nothing was *verboten* if it got you hard. On the wild nights, moving down the streets of the Castro, the serious leather crowd had counted off their pleasuredomes on the knuckles of one well-greased fist and the Tooth had always been one of the five. Chuck and Jean-Pierre, the owners of the club, had long since gone, dying within three weeks of one another in the early years of the plague, and for a time the site had remained untaken, as though in deference to the men who'd played there and passed away. But in 1987 the Sons of Priapus, a group of onanists who'd restored masturbation to the status of a respectable handicraft, had occupied the building for their Monday night circle-jerks. The ghosts of the building had smiled on them, it seemed, because word of the atmosphere there soon swelled the number of the Sons. They organized a second weekly gathering, on Thursdays, and then when that became overcrowded, a third. Almost overnight the building had become a paean to the democracy of the palm. An element of the fetishistic gradually crept into the Thursday and Friday assemblies (Monday remained vanilla) and before long the leaders of the Sons had turned into businessmen; they leased the building and now ran the most successful sex club in San Francisco. Chuck and Jean-Pierre would have been proud. The Penitent had been born.

ii

The club wasn't particularly busy. Tuesdays were usually slow, and tonight was no exception. But for the thirty or so individuals who were wandering the Penitent's bare-brick halls or chatting around the juice-bar (unlike the backroom, this was an alcohol-free party) or idling in the television lounge, watching porno of strictly historical interest, there would be reason to remember tonight.

Just before eleven-thirty, a man appeared in the hallway, whose identity would be described variously by people who later talked about the evening's events. Good-looking, certainly, in a man-who'd-seen-the-world kind of way. Hair slicked back or receding, depending on who was telling you the story. Eyes dark and deep-set, or invisible behind sunglasses, depending, again, on who was recounting the tale. Nobody really remembered what he was wearing in any detail. He wasn't naked, as a few of the more exhibitionist patrons were, that was agreed. Nor was he dressed for casting in any specific scenario. He wasn't a biker or a cowboy or a hardhat or a cop. He didn't carry a paddle or a whip. Hearing this, a certain kind of listener would inevitably ask, "Well what the hell was he *into?*" to which the story-tellers universally replied: *Sex.* Well, not universally. The more pretentious may have said *the pleasures of the flesh,* and the cruder said *meat,* but it amounted to the same thing. This man—who within the space of an hour and a half had created a stir so potent it would become local myth inside a day—was an embodiment of the spirit of the Penitent: a creature of pure sensation, ready to take on any part-ner heated enough to match the fierceness of his desires. In this brave brotherhood, there were only three or four members equal to the challenge, and—not coincidentally—they were the only cele-brants that night who said nothing about the experience afterward. They kept their silence and their fantasies intact, leaving the rest to chatter on what they'd seen and heard. In truth, no more than a half-dozen people remained purely witnesses. As had happened often in the long-ago, but infrequently now, the presence of one unfettered imagination in the crowd had been the signal for general license. Men who had only ever come to the Penitent to watch dared a touch, and more, tonight. Two love affairs began there, and both prospered; four people caught crabs; and one traced his gonorrhea to his loss of control on the stained sofa of the television lounge.

As for the man who'd initiated this orgy, he came several times, and went, leaving the couplings to continue until closing time. Sev-eral people claimed he spoke to them, though he said nothing. One claimed they knew him to be a sometime porn star who'd retired from the business and moved to Oregon. He'd returned to his old hunting grounds, this account went, for sentimental reasons, only to vanish again into the wilderness that always claims the sexual professional.

One part of this was certainly true. The man vanished and did not return, though every one of the thirty patrons that night came back, crabs and gonorrhea notwithstanding, within the next few days (most of them the next night) in the hope of seeing him again. When he did not appear, a few then made it their private mission to discover him in the some other watering hole, but a man seen by the yellowing light of a dim lamp in a secret place is not easily identified elsewhere. The more they thought about him and talked about him, the less clear the memory of him became, so that a week after the event, no two witnesses could have readily agreed on any of his personal details.

And as for the man himself, he could not remember the events of the night clearly, and thanked God for the fact.

iii

Drew had fled home after the encounter on the stairs and, ferreting out the pack of cigarettes he kept for emergencies (though God knows he'd never anticipated an emergency quite like this), he'd sat down and smoked himself giddy while he thought about what he'd just experienced. Tears came, now and then, and a fit of trembling so violent he had to sit with his knees drawn up underneath his chin until it passed. It was no use, he knew, trying to make a sane appraisal of what had happened until tomorrow, for a very good reason: Before setting out for Will's house, he'd dropped what he'd thought was a tab of Ecstasy, just to ease him into a more sensual mood. At the beginning of the evening, before the drug had kicked in, he'd felt slightly guilty about not telling Will what he'd done, but he'd been so careful to present himself as a man whose drug days were behind him that he feared the date would sour if he told the truth. Then the Ecstasy had started to mellow him out, and the guilt had vanished, along with any need to expunge it.

So what had gone wrong? Something venomous in the tablet had turned round and bitten him, no doubt of that. He'd had a bad trip of some kind. But that wasn't the whole answer, at least that's what his instincts told him. He'd had bad trips before, a goodly number. He'd seen walls soften, bugs burst, clothes take flight. This delusion had been qualitatively different in a fashion he presently had no words to describe. Tomorrow maybe, he'd be able to articulate how it had seemed to him Will had been a conspirator with the venom in his system, feeding the madness in Drew's veins with an insanity all of his own. And tomorrow maybe he'd also understand why, when the man he'd just made love to had come out of the bedroom, his head low, his body running with sweat, there had been a moment (no, more than a moment) when Will's face had seemed to smear, his eyes losing all trace of white, his teeth becoming sharp as nails. Why, in short, the man had lost all semblance of humanity and become—for a few heartbeats, something bestial. Too wild to be a dog, too shy to be a wolf; he'd looked, just for a moment, like a fox, yelping with laughter as he came to do mischief.

i

Hugo had never been a sentimentalist. It was one of the bounden duties of a philosopher, he'd always contended, to eschew the mask of cheaply gained emotion and find a purer place, where reality might be studied and assessed without the prejudice of feeling. That was not to say he was not weak, at times. When Eleanor had left him, twelve years ago now, he had found himself susceptible to all manner of claptrap that would have left him untouched at any other time. He'd become acutely aware of how much popular culture promoted *yearning*: songs of love and loss on the radio, tales of tragic mismatches on the soaps he'd catch Adele watching in the afternoon. Even some of his own peers had turned their attentions to such trivialities; men and women of his own age and reputation studying the semiotics of romance. It appalled him to see these phenomena and sickened him that he himself was prone to their blandishments. It had made him doubly harden his heart against his estranged wife. When she'd asked for a reconciliation the following January (she'd left him in July) he had refused it with a loathing that was fueled in no small part by a repugnance at his own frailty. The love songs had left their scars, and he hated himself for it. He would never be that vulnerable again.

But memory still conspired against reason. When every year

toward the end of August the first intimations of autumn appeared—
a chill at twilight and the smoky smell in the air—he would remember
how it had been with Eleanor at the best of times. How proud he'd
been to have her at his side; how happy to see their partnership fruit-
ful: to be a father of sons who would, he'd thought, grow up to idolize
him. They had sat together, he and Eleanor, for evening after evening
in those early years, planning their lives. How he would get a seat at
one of the more prestigious universities and lecture a couple days a
week while he wrote the books by which he would change the course
of Western thought. Meanwhile, she would raise their sons, then—
once the children were independent spirits (which would be quickly,
given that they had such self-willed parents)—she would return to her
own field of interest, which was genealogy. She too would write a
book, very probably, and garner her share of the limelight.

    That had been the dream. Then, of course, Nathaniel had been
killed, and the whole prospectus had become nonsense overnight.
Eleanor's nerves, which had never been good, started to require
higher and higher doses of medication; the books Hugo had planned
to write refused to find their way out of his head and onto the page.
And the move from Manchester—which had seemed an eminently
rational decision at the time—had brought its own crop of troubles.
That first fall had been the nadir, no doubt. Though there had been
plenty of bad times later, it had been the insanities of that October
and November that had scoured him of his former optimism.
Nathaniel, in whom the virtues of the parents (Eleanor's compassion
and physical grace, Hugo's robust pragmatism and cleaving to truth)
had been wed, was gone. Will meanwhile, had become a mischief-
maker, his pranks and his secretiveness only reinforcing Eleanor's
belief that the best had gone from the world, so there was no harm
sedating herself into a stupor.

    Grim memories, all of them. And yet when he thought of
Eleanor (and he often did), the sentimental songs had their way with
him still, and he would feel that old yearning in his throat and belly.
It wasn't that he wanted her back (he'd made new arrangements
since then, and they worked well enough in their unromantic way),
but that the years he'd had with her—good, bad, and indifferent—
had passed into history, and when he conjured her face in his mind's
eye he conjured a golden age when it had still seemed possible to
achieve something important. He yearned then, despite himself. Not
for the woman or for the life he'd lived with her, and certainly not for

the son who'd survived, but for the Hugo who had still been self-possessed enough to believe in his own significance.

Too late now. He would not change the world of thought with a brilliantly argued thesis. He could not even change the expressions on the faces of the students who sat before him at his lectures: slack-faced young dullards whom he could not remotely inspire, and so he no longer tried. He had ceased to read the work of his peers—most of it was masturbatory trash anyway—and the books that had once been his personal bibles, particularly Heidegger and Wittgenstein, languished unstudied. He had exhausted them. Or, more probably, exhausted his interaction with them. It was not that they had nothing left to teach him, but that he had no interest left in learning. Philosophy had not made him one jot happier. Like so much of his life, it was a thing that had seemed to offer value—a repository of meaning and enlightenment—that had proved to be utterly empty.

That was one of the reasons he hadn't moved back to Manchester after Eleanor's departure: He had no interest in rifling the graves of academe for some pitiful nonsense to publish. The other reason was Adele. Her husband, Donald, had died of a creeping cancer two years before Eleanor had left, and in widowhood the woman had become more attentive than ever to the needs of the Rabjohns household. Hugo liked her plain manners, her plain cooking, her plain emotions, and though she was very far from the vintage beauty Eleanor had been, he had no hesitation in seducing her. Perhaps seduction was not quite the word. She had no patience with conniving of any kind, and he'd finally bedded her by telling her outright that he needed the comfort of a woman's company, and suggesting that surely she in her turn missed the company of a man. Now and again, she'd said, she missed having somebody to snuggle up with, especially on cold nights. It had been, the week of this exchange, exceptionally chilly, which fact Hugo had pointed out to her. She'd given him the closest approximation to a sexy smile her dimpled face could manage and they'd retired to bed together. The arrangement had steadily become ritualized. She would sleep at home four nights a week, but on Wednesdays, Fridays, and Saturdays she'd stay with Hugo. When his divorce from Eleanor was finalized, he'd even suggested they marry, but to his surprise she'd told him she was very happy with things just the way they were. She'd had enough of husbands for one lifetime, she told him. This way they weren't bound to one another, and that was for the best.

ii

So life had gone on, in its unremarkable way and, despite his disappointments, Hugo had come to feel more at home in Burnt Yarley than he'd ever thought he would. He was not a great lover of nature (the theory of it was fine, the practice mucky and malodorous), but there was a rhythm to the agricultural year that was comforting, even to an urban soul like his. Fields plowed and seeded and tended and harvested; livestock born and nurtured and slaughtered and eaten. He let the house, which was now far too big for him and run down. He didn't care that the gutters needed mending and the window frames were rotting away. When somebody at the Plow mentioned that the front garden wall had partially collapsed he told them he was glad of the fact: The sheep could get in to clip the lawn.

He was increasingly regarded as an eccentric in the village, he knew; a reputation he did nothing to contradict. He'd once been quite the peacock when it came to suits and accoutrements. Now he simply wore what came to hand, often in faintly outlandish combinations. In crowded places, such as the pub, his deafness (which was slight in his left ear, much worse in his right) made him shout, which only increased the impression of a slightly addled soul. He would sit at the bar drinking brandies for hours on end, opining on any subject that came up; to hear him in shouted debate, nobody would have guessed him a man out of faith with the world. He argued heatedly on politics (he still called himself a Marxist, if pressed), religion (of course, the opiate of the people), race, disarmament, or the French, his debating skills still formidable enough to win two out of every three rounds, even when he was espousing a position he had no belief in, which was to say, most of the time.

The one subject he would not talk about was Will, though of course as Will's reputation had grown, so had people's curiosity. Very occasionally, if Hugo was three or four brandies deep, he'd offer a noncommittal reply to an observation somebody made, but people who knew him well soon came to understand that he was not a proud father. Those with long enough memories knew why. The Rabjohns boy had been a participant in what was surely the grimmest episode in the history of Burnt Yarley. Twenty-nine years on, Delbert Donnelly's daughter still put flowers on her father's grave on the first Sunday of every month, and the reward for information leading to the arrest of his killers (posted by the meat baron in Halifax from whom Delbert had always got his pies and sausage) was still good. At the time of his death, so history told, he'd been playing the Good Samaritan, out in the snow looking for a runaway child, a child who, it was believed by those who still mused on the mystery, had been somehow complicit with the killers. Nothing had ever been proven, of course, but anyone who had followed Will Rabjohns's rise to fame could not help but notice the perversity of his work. Nobody in the village could have used that word, except perhaps Hugo. They would have called it a *mite strange* or *not quite right*, or—if they were in a superstitious mood—*the Devil's business.* It certainly wasn't wholesome or healthy to be going around the world the way he had, finding dying animals to photograph. It was further proof, for those who cared, that Will Rabjohns, man and boy, was a bad lot. So bad, in fact, that his own father would barely admit paternity.

Hugo's silence, however, did not mean Will was not in his thoughts. Though he spoke with his son rarely, and when he did their exchanges were remote, the mysteries of that winter almost three decades before (and of his son's place in those mysteries), vexed him more as the years passed, and for a reason he would never have admitted to anyone. Philosophy had failed him, love had failed him, ambition and ego had failed him: Only the unknown remained to him, as a source of hope. Of course, it was everywhere, the unknown. In the new physics, in disease, in a neighbor's eyes. But his closest brush with it remained the business of that bitter night so many years ago. Had he realized at the time something extraordinary was afoot, he would have paid closer attention: memorized the signs, so that he might later find his way back into its presence. But he had been too busy with the labors of being Hugo to notice. Only now, when those distractions had rotted away, did he see the mystery glinting there, as cold, remote, and constant as a star.

He'd read in *Newsweek* an interview in which his son, when asked what quality he valued most in himself, had replied *patience.* That came from me, Hugo had thought. I know how to wait. That was how he passed the days now, when he wasn't in Manchester. Sitting in his study smoking a French cigarette, waiting. When Adele came in with a cup of tea or a sandwich he would turn his attention to his papers as though he were in profound thought, but as soon as she'd gone he'd be gazing out through the window again, watching cloud shadows pass across the fell that rose behind the house. He didn't know exactly what he was waiting for, but he trusted his wits enough to be certain he'd recognize it when it came.

XVI

The summer had been wet, the rainfall so heavy at the beginning of August that it had stripped and flattened much of the crop, threshing it before its time. Now, a week from September, the fields were still waterlogged, and the hay that had survived the deluge was rotting where it stood.

"It's all right for the likes of you," Ken Middleton, who owned the largest acreage of harvestable land in the valley, had remarked to Hugo in the pub. "You don't have to think about these things like us workin' men."

"Thinkers *are* working men, Kenneth," Hugo had countered. "We just don't sweat doing it."

"It's not just the rain," Matthew Sauls had chimed in. "It's every bloody thing." Sauls was Middleton's drinking comrade, a dour pairing at the best of times. "Even me ol' da says things is just coming apart."

Hugo had been harangued by Matthew's ol' da, Geoffrey, on this very subject earlier in the year when, much against his better judgment, he'd agreed to accompany Adele to the Summer Fayre, where she'd entered her onion pickle in the annual competition. Geoffrey's wife had also entered, and while the two women chatted (with the natural reserve of competitors), Hugo had been left to endure Old Man Sauls. Without the least provocation, the man had launched into a monologue on the subject of murder, the recent killing of a child by another child in Newcastle the particular upon which he hung his grim talk. *It's a different world, these days* he said over and over. What had once been unthinkable was now commonplace. *It's a different world.*

"You know what your ol' da's problem is, Matthew?" Hugo said.

"He's as crazy as a coot," Middleton put in.

"Well, that's undoubtedly true," Hugo replied. "But that's not what I had in mind." He emptied his brandy glass and set it down on the bar. "He's old. And old men like to think everything's coming to an end. It makes it a littler easier to let go."

Matthew didn't reply. He simply stared into his beer. But Middleton said, "Talking from experience, are you?"

Hugo smiled. "I think I've got a few more years in me yet," he said. "Well, gentleman. That was my last for the night. See you, tomorrow, maybe."

It was a lie, of course; he didn't need a few more years to understand ol' da's point of view. He felt it taking shape in himself. There was a certain grim satisfaction to be had in bad news. What man in his right mind, knowing he was not long for the world, would wish it to burgeon and brighten in his absence? Perhaps he would have read the entrails differently if he'd had grandchildren, found reason for optimism in the midst of murder and deluge. But Nathaniel, who would surely have given him fine grandsons and granddaughters, was thirty years dead, and Will an invert. Why should he hope the best for a world that would have nobody he loved in it once he'd gone?

There was pleasure to be taken in playing the prophet of doom, no doubt of that. As he walked home tonight (he always walked even in the dead of winter; he liked his brandy too much to trust himself behind the wheel) there was a spring in his step that would not have been there had the night's debate been more optimistic. Swinging his stick, which he carried more for effect than support, he strode out of the light of the village into the lampless mile of road that took him to his gate. He felt no anxiety, walking in the dark. There were no thugs here; no thieves out to prey on an inebriated gentleman walking alone. It was very seldom he met anyone at all.

Tonight was an exception, however. About a third of a mile outside the bounds of the village he caught sight of two people, a man and a woman, strolling toward him. Though there was no moon, the starlight was bright, and from twenty yards' distance he was able to tell that he didn't know them. Were they tourists perhaps, out enjoying the night air? Fugitives from the city, for whom the spectacle of dark hills and starscape was enrapturing?

The closer he got to them, however, the stronger the impulse became to turn around and head back the way he'd come. He told himself to stop being a silly old fool. All he had to do was wish them a pleasant good evening as they walked past and that would be an end to it. He picked up his pace a little and was about to speak when the man—a striking fellow in the silvery light—said, "Hugo? Is it you?"

"Yes, it's me," Hugo said. "Do I—"

"We went to the house," the woman said, "looking for you, but you weren't there—"

"So we came looking for you," the man went on.

"Do we *know* one another?" Hugo asked.

"It's been a long time," the man said. He looked perhaps thirty-two or thirty-three, but there was something about his poise that made Hugo think this was a trick of the light.

"You weren't a student of mine, were you?"

"No," the man said. "Not remotely."

"Well, then I really can't recall," Hugo said, faintly uncomfortable now.

"We know your son," the woman said. "We know Will."

"Ah," said Hugo. "Well then good luck to you," he said dryly. "Have a good night, won't you?" And with that he started on his way.

"Where is he?" the woman inquired as Hugo passed by.

"I don't know," Hugo replied, not glancing back at her. "He could be anywhere. He flits around, you know. If you're friends of his, you'll know what a *flitter* he is."

"Wait up!" the man said, leaving his lady friend's side to follow Hugo. There was nothing aggressive about his manner, but Hugo took a firmer grip of his stick, just in case he needed to wield it. "If you could just give me a little help here—"

"Help?" Hugo turned to face the man, preferring to stand his ground and send the fellow on his way than have him following.

"To find Will," the man said, his manner all conviviality.

It was an abomination, Hugo thought, the buttonholing manner people had these days. An American import, no doubt. Thirty seconds of conversation and you were bosom buddies. Altogether loathsome. "If you want to get a message to him," Hugo said, "may I suggest his *publishers?*"

"You're his father—"

"That's my burden," Hugo snapped. "But if you're admirers of his—"

"We are," the woman said.

"Then I must warn you he's a terrible disappointment in the flesh."

"We know what he's like," the man said. "We *all* know what he's like, Hugo. You and I particularly."

The inference of kinship here was too much for Hugo. He brandished his stick in front of his face. "We have absolutely *nothing* to say to one another," he said. "Now *leave me alone.*" He started to back away from the man, half expecting him to give chase. But he simply stood with his hands in his pockets, watching Hugo retreat.

"What are you afraid of?" he said.

"Absolutely nothing," Hugo replied.

"That I don't believe," the man said. "You're a philosopher. You know better than that."

"I am not a philosopher," Hugo said, resisting the flattery. "I am a third-rate teacher of third-rate pupils who have no interest whatsoever in anything I impart to them. That is my lot in life and to the extent that I might have done worse, I'm proud of it. My wife lives in Paris with a man half my age, my best beloved son has been dead and buried thirty years, and the other is a self-promoting queer with an opinion of himself out of all proportion to his achievements. There! Are you satisfied? Does that put it plainly enough for you? In short, *may I go?*"

"Oh," said the woman softly. "I'm so sorry."

"What for?"

"You lost a child," she said. "We've lost several, Jacob and I. You never get over it."

"Jacob?" Hugo murmured, and in that instant knew to whom he was speaking. A wave of feeling passed over him that he could not quite identify.

"Yes, it's us," the man said softly, sensing that they'd been recognized.

Relief, Hugo thought. That's what I'm feeling, I'm feeling relief. The waiting's over. The mystery is here, or at least a means of access to it.

"This is Rosa, of course," Steep said. Rosa made a comical little curtsy. "Now, shall we all be friends, Hugo?"

"I . . . don't . . . know."

"Oh, I know what you're thinking. You're thinking about Delbert Donnelly. She was responsible for that and I'm not going to mislead you on the matter. She can be cruel sometimes, dangerous even, when she's roused. But we've paid the penalty for that. We've had thirty years in the wilderness, not knowing where we were going to lay our heads from one night to the next."

"So why did you choose to come back here?" Hugo said.

"We have our reasons," Jacob said.

"Tell him," Rosa prompted. "We came back for Will."

"I can't—"

"Yes, we know," Jacob said, "you don't speak to him and you don't care to."

"That's right."

"Well, let's hope he cares more for you than you do for him."

"What's that supposed to mean?"

"Let's hope he comes running when he hears you're in trouble."

"I hope that's not a threat," Hugo said, "because if it is—"

He didn't see the blow coming. There was no flicker in Steep's eye, no indication, however slight, that his civil chat was now over. One moment he was smiling, all courtesy, the next he struck Hugo such a blow it threw the man five yards.

"Don't do that," said Rosa.

"Shut up," Jacob said, and, going to where Hugo lay sprawled, picked up the stick that the old man had brandished two minutes before. While Hugo moaned at his feet, he examined the stick, moving his hands up and down its length to get its heft. Then he raised it above his head and brought it down on Hugo's body, once, twice, three times. The first blow won a yell of agony. The second a moan. The third, silence.

"You haven't killed him, have you?" Rosa said, coming to Jacob's side.

"No, of course, I haven't killed him," Jacob replied, tossing the stick down beside its owner. "I want him to hang on for a while." He went down on his haunches beside the wounded man. With a solicitousness that would have shamed a doctor, he reached down and lay the back of his fingers against Hugo's cheek. "Are you with me, my friend?" he said. He rubbed his fingers back and forth a little. "Hugo? Can you hear me?" Hugo moaned pitifully. "I'll take that as a *yes*, shall I?" Jacob said. Again, the man moaned. "So here's the plan," Jacob said. "We will be leaving very soon, and if we don't call somebody to come and find you, there's a better than average chance that you'll be dead before dawn. Do you understand what I'm telling you? Nod if you understand." Hugo made a barely perceptible nod. "Good enough. So. It rests with you. Do you want to die here under the stars? Nobody's going to be coming by here tonight, I suspect, so you'll have the place to yourself." Hugo tried to speak. "I didn't understand that, I'm sorry. What did you say?" Hugo made a tiny sob. "Oh now, you're crying. Rosa, he's crying."

"He doesn't want to be left alone," Rosa said. "That's a big thing with you men," she complained. "You're like kiddies half the time."

Jacob returned his attention to Hugo. "Did you hear that?" he said. "She thinks we're kids. She doesn't know the half of it, does she? She doesn't know what we go through. But I'm assuming she's

right. You don't want to be left alone. You want us to find a telephone and have somebody come and find you. Is that right?" Hugo
nodded. "That I will do, my friend," he said. "But here's your side of
the bargain. I don't want you saying a word to Will. Do you understand me? If he comes to see you and you tell him anything about us,
what you're feeling right now—the pain, the panic, the *loneliness*—
will be as nothing beside what we will do to you. Do you hear me? As
nothing. Nod if you understand." Hugo nodded. "That's good. You
needn't agonize about this. He's—what did you call him?—*a self-
promoting queer?* You're not his number one fan, obviously. Whereas
I, I am devoted to him, in my way. Isn't that strange? I haven't seen
him in thirty years, of course, so I may not feel the same . . . " His
voice trailed away. He sighed, and stood up.

"Lie very still," Rosa advised him. "If you've broken your ribs,
you don't want to puncture a lung." Then, to Jacob, "Are you coming?"

"Yes." He looked straight down at Hugo's face. "Enjoy the stars,"
he said.

XVII

i

The morning after the love feast Will woke on the living-room
floor, having apparently slid from the sofa, where he'd made a
nest of the clothes he'd stripped off the night before. He felt like
shit. His entire body ached, even his teeth and tongue. His eyes
burned in their sockets. He got to his feet, somewhat unsteadily, and
made for the bathroom. There he doused his face in cold water, and
then looked at himself in the mirror. The calm and clarity that had
been such a revelation the previous afternoon were gone. The face he
was looking at was just a rag-bag of weary particulars: pallid skin and
red-rimmed eyes and fur-lined mouth. What the hell had he been up
to? He vaguely remembered there being some dispute with Drew, but
he had no idea what it had been about, much less how it had been
resolved, if indeed it had. Clearly he'd been out on the town, and to

judge by the state of his body it had been quite a party. He had scratches on his back and chest, bite-marks on his shoulders. And there was more damning evidence still between his legs: a dick and balls so red-raw they might have been massaged with sandpaper.

"Question one," he said, looking down at his groin, "what the fuck have we been doing? And question two, who the hell do we need to apologize to?"

When he ventured into the bedroom, of course, he was confronted with chaos. The air was rank with rotting food and stale vomit, the floor a garbage heap. He stood in the doorway, surveying the carpet of remnants, while tantalizing flashes of how the celebration here had come to an end entered his head. He'd crawled on all fours through this muck, puking like an overfed Roman in the vomitorium, hadn't he? And out in the hallway, where there was blood and broken glass—he'd cut his foot while he was hauling himself to the top of the stairs.

What had happened after that? His mind refused to confess. Rather than wrack it for answers, he left the fragments of recollection, along with the trash, where they lay and, closing the bedroom door, he went to shower. There was a pattern here, he thought, of sleeping, and waking to visions, and showering, and waking again, as though the cycle of diurnal duties had been turned to the purpose of Lord Fox. A canny trick, this: to use the safest rituals of his domestic life to make him shed his assumptions. Washing himself proved a delicate business—the soap and water found broken skin he hadn't noticed—but he emerged feeling a little better. He was in the process of drying himself when somebody rapped hard on the front door. He wrapped a towel around his middle and headed for the stairs, stepping gingerly past the glass as he went. The rapping came again, and with it Adrianna's voice:

"Hey, Will? *Will?* Are you in there?"

"I'm here," he said, opening the door to her.

"Your phone's not working," she said. "I've been calling for the last hour. Can I come in?" She peered at him as she entered. "Boy did you ever have a late night." He led the way into the kitchen.

"What did you do to your back?" she said, following him. "No, never mind, don't tell me."

"You want some coffee, or—?"

"I'll do it. You should just call England."

"What for?"

"Something's happened to your dad. He's not dead, but there's something wrong. They wouldn't tell me what."

"*Who* wouldn't tell you?"

"Your agents in New York. Apparently somebody was trying to find you, and whoever it was called them, and they tried you, but they couldn't get you, so they tried me, only I couldn't get you—" She kept up the story while Will went into the living room, where he found the phone unplugged. Drew's handiwork, no doubt, so they'd not be disturbed during their night of decadence. Will plugged it back in again.

"Do you know who made the call?"

"Somebody called Adele."

"Adele?"

"Speaking."

"This is Will."

"Oh my God. Oh my God. Will. I've been trying to contact you—"

"Yes, I—"

"He's in a terrible state. Just terrible."

"What happened to him?"

"We don't really know. I mean, somebody tried to kill him, we know that much."

"In Manchester?"

"No, no, here. Half a mile from the house."

"Jesus."

"He was just beaten unmercifully. He's concussed. He's got three broken ribs and a broken arm."

"Do the police know who did it?"

"No, but I think *he* knows, and he's not telling. It's peculiar. And it frightens me, it really does, in case whoever it is," she started to dissolve into tears, "whoever it is . . . comes back . . . I didn't know who else to turn to . . . so . . . I know you and he haven't talked in a long while, but . . . I think you should see him." It was plain enough what she was saying, even if she wasn't putting it in so many words. She was afraid he wasn't going to survive.

"I'll come," he said.

"You will?"

"Of course."

"Oh that's wonderful." She sounded genuinely happy at the prospect. "I know it sounds selfish, but it'd take such a weight off my shoulders."

"It doesn't sound selfish at all," Will said. "I'll make arrangements right now and I'll call you the moment I get into London."

"Shall I tell him?"

"That I'm coming? No, I don't think you should. He may not want to see me for one thing: Better just let it be a surprise."

The conversation ended there. Will gave Adrianna a quick summary of what had happened, and then asked her to see what she could do about arranging a flight: any airline, any time. Leaving her to make the arrangements from the downstairs office, he went up to pack. This meant facing the filth in the bedroom, of course, which wasn't particularly pleasant, but he wrapped up the mess as best he could in the sheets on which the feast had been laid, dumped them all in plastic bags, and left them out on the landing to take downstairs. Then he opened the window to let in some fresh air; hauling his suitcases out of the closet, he set about filling them.

Adrianna secured him a flight out of San Francisco that evening. An overnight flight that would deliver him into Heathrow Airport at around noon the following day.

"If you don't mind," Adrianna said, "I'd like to come in while you're away and look through all those pictures you took down—"

"The consumptives?"

"Yeah. I know you think I'm crazy, but there's a book in those pictures. Or at least an exhibition."

"Help yourself. I don't want to *look* at another photograph right now. They're all yours."

"Isn't that a little extreme?"

"That's how I'm feeling right now. *Extreme.*"

"Any particular reason?"

It was too big a subject to explain even if he'd had the words, which he doubted he did. "Maybe we'll talk about it when I get back," he said.

"Will you stay long?"

Will shrugged. "I don't know. If he's going to die then I'll stay until he does. Isn't that what I'm supposed to do?"

"That's a strange question."

"Yeah. Well, it's a strange relationship. We haven't talked for ten years, remember."

"But you talk *about* him."

"No, I don't."

"Trust me, Will, you talk about him. Offhand remarks, usually, but I've built up a good picture of him."

"You know, that's a damn good idea. I should get a picture of him. Something that'll catch him, for posterity."

"The man who fathered Will Rabjohns."

"Oh no," Will said, heading up to pack his camera, "that wasn't Hugo." And when Adrianna asked him who the hell it was if it wasn't Hugo he refused, of course, to answer.

ii

He went to see both Drew and Patrick before he left for the airport. He had called Drew several times, but nobody picked up, so he caught a cab to the apartment on Cumberland. Through the bars of the security gate he could see Drew's bicycle in the passage, almost certain proof that its owner was in residence, but Will's repeated ringing of the doorbell brought no reply. He'd come prepared for this eventuality, with a scrawled note that he jammed between the gate and the brick; three or four lines simply informing Drew that he had to go to England on short notice, and that he hoped to be in contact again soon. Then he went back to his cab and had it take him up Castro to Patrick's apartment. This time the doorbell was answered, not by Patrick but Rafael. He was sneezing violently, his eyes bloodshot.

"Allergies?" Will said.

"No," Rafael replied. "Pat just came from the hospital. Not good news."

"Is that Will?" Patrick hollered from the living room.

"Go on in," Rafael said softly, and disappeared into the kitchen, still sneezing.

Patrick was sitting in the window—where else?—though the vista of the city was largely obscured by a glacial bank of fog. "Pull up a chair," he told Will, and Will did so. "The view's fucked, but what the hell?"

"Rafael said you were at the hospital."

"I introduced you to my doctor at the party, didn't I? Frank Webster? Tubby little guy, wears too much cologne? I went to see him this morning, and he just told me flat out he'd done all he could. I'm getting weaker and there's nothing more he can do for me." There was a new barrage of sneezes from the kitchen. "Oh jeez, poor Rafael. As soon as he gets upset, he starts sneezing. He'll be like that for hours. I went to his mother's funeral with him and the whole family—he's got three brothers, three sisters—they're all sneezing. I didn't hear a word the priest said." This was sounding more and more like one of Patrick's tales, but what the hell, it was bringing a smile to his face. "Remember that beautiful French guy Lewis used to date? Marius? You had a fling with him."

"No I didn't."

"Then you were the only one. Anyway, he sneezed after he'd come. He sneezed and sneezed and sneezed. He fell downstairs at Lewis's place, sneezing. I swear."

"Terrible."

"You don't believe me."

"Not a word."

Pat glanced at Will, smirking. "So," he said, "to what do I owe the pleasure?"

"You were telling me about Webster."

"It can wait. You've got a purposeful look on your face. What's happening?"

"I have to go to England. I'm catching a flight out tonight."

"This is sudden."

"My father's got a problem. Somebody decided to beat the shit out of him."

"You were here on the night in question," Patrick said. "I'll swear to it."

"I mean badly, Pat."

"How badly?"

"I don't know. I'll find out when I get there. So that's my story. Now back to Webster."

Patrick sighed. "I had a heart to heart with him today. He's been great. We're always in line if somebody comes along with some new medication. But," he shrugged, "I guess we've run out." He looked at Will again. "It's a mess, Will. Getting sick. We've all seen so much of it, and we all know how it goes. Well, it's not going to happen to me." This sounded like Patrick at his defiant best, but there was no resilience in his voice, only defeat. "I had a dream, a couple of nights ago. I was in a forest, a dark forest, and I was naked. Nothing sexual about it. Just naked. And I knew all these things were creeping up on me. Some were coming for my eyes. Some were coming for my skin. They were all going to get a piece of me. When I woke up, I thought: I'm not going to let that happen. I'm not going to sit there and be picked at, piece by piece."

"Have you talked to Bethlynn about any of this?"

"Not about the conversation with Frank. I've got a session with her tomorrow afternoon." He leaned his head back on the headrest, and closed his eyes. "We've talked about you a lot, you'll be pleased to know. And she was always pretty acute about you, before she met you. Now she'll be useless. Like the rest of us, flailing around trying to work out what makes you tick."

"It's no great mystery," Will said.

"One of these days," Patrick said lazily, "I'm going to have a blinding revelation about you, and everything'll suddenly make sense. Why we stayed together. Why we came apart." He opened one eye and squinted at Will. "Were you at the Penitent last night, by the way?"

Will wasn't sure. "Maybe," he said. "Why?"

"A friend of Jack's said he saw you coming out, looking like you'd just done some serious mischief. Of course, I protected your honor. But it *was* you, wasn't it?"

"I don't remember, to be honest."

"My God, that's something I don't hear very often these days. Everybody's too clean and sober. *You don't remember?* You're a throwback, Will. Homo Castro, nineteen seventy-five." Will laughed. "A primitive simian with an oversized libido and a permanently glazed expression."

"There were some wild nights."

"There certainly were," Patrick said with gentle relish. "But I don't want to do it again; do you?"

"Honestly?"

"Honestly. I did it, and it was great. But it's over. At least for me. I'm making a connection with something else now."

"And how does that feel?"

Patrick had again closed his eyes. His voice grew quiet. "It's wonderful," he said. "I feel God here sometimes. Right here with me." He fell silent; the kind of silence that presages something of significance. Will said nothing. Just waited for the something to come. At last, Patrick said, "I've got a plan, Will."

"For what?"

"For when I get very sick." Again, the silence, and Will waiting. "I want you here, Will," Patrick said. "I want to die looking at you, · and you looking at me."

"Then that's what'll happen."

"But it might not," Patrick said. His voice was calm and even, but tears had swelled between his closed lids and ran down his cheeks. "You might be in the middle of the Serengeti. Who knows? You might still be in England."

"I won't—"

"Ssh," Patrick said. "Let me just get all of this said. I don't want somebody telling you what did or didn't happen and you not knowing whether to believe them or not. So I want you to know: I'm planning to die the way I've lived. Comfortably. Sensibly. Jack's with me on it. So's Rafael, of course. And, like I said, I want you here, too." He stopped, wiped the tears off his cheeks with the heels of his hands, and then continued in the same contained manner. "But if you're not, and there's some problem, if Rafael or Jack get into trouble somehow—we're trying to cover all the legal issues to make sure it doesn't happen but there's still a chance—I want to be sure you'll get it sorted out. You're good with that kind of stuff, Will. Nobody pushes you around."

"I'll make sure there's no problem, don't worry."

"Good. That makes me feel a lot happier." Without opening his eyes, he reached out and unerringly took Will's hand. "How am I doing?"

"You're doing fine."

"I don't like weepers."

"You're allowed."

There was another silence, lighter this time, now that the deal had been struck. "You're right," Patrick finally said. "I'm allowed."

Will glanced at his watch. "Time to go," he said.

"Go, baby, go. I won't get up if you don't mind. I'm feeling a little frail."

Will went and hugged him, there in the chair. "I love you," he said.

"And I love you back." He had caught fierce hold of Will's arms and squeezed hard. "You do know that, don't you? I mean, you're not just hearing the words?"

"I know it."

"I wish we'd had longer, Will—"

"Me too," Will said, "I've got a lot of stuff I'd need to tell you about, but I've got to catch this plane."

"No, Will, I mean I wish we'd had longer *together*. I wish we'd taken the time to know one another better."

"There'll be time," Will said.

Pat held on to Will's arms another moment. "Not enough," and then, reluctantly loosening his grip, let Will go.

PART FIVE

He Names
The Mystery

I

i

Home to England, and the summer almost gone. August's stars had fallen, and the leaves would follow very soon. Riot and rot in speedy succession.

You'll find the years pass more quickly as you get older Marcello—the resident wise old queen from Buddies in Boston—had told him an age ago. Will hadn't believed it, of course. It wasn't until he was thirty-one, maybe thirty-two, that he'd realized there was truth in the observation. Time wasn't on his side after all; it was gathering speed, season upon season, year upon year. Thirty-five was upon him in a heartbeat, and forty close on its heels, the marathon he'd thought he was running in his youth mysteriously became a hundred-yard dash. Determined to achieve something of significance before the race was done he'd turned every minute of his life over to the making of pictures, but they were of small comfort. The books were published, the reviews were clipped and filed, and the animals he had witnessed in their final days went into the hands of taxidermists. Life was not a reversible commodity. Things passed away, never to return: species, hopes, years.

And yet he could still blithely wish hours of his life away when he was bored. Sitting in first class on the eleven-hour flight, he wished a hundred times it was over. He'd brought a bagful of books including the volume of poems Lewis had been distributing at Patrick's party, but nothing held his attention for more than a page or two. One of Lewis's short lyrics intrigued him mainly because he wondered who the hell it was about:

> *Now, with our fierce brotherhood annulled,*
> *I see as if by lightning, all*
> *the perfect pains we might have made,*
> *had our love's fiction lived another day.*

It certainly had the authentic ring of Lewis's voice about it. All his favorite subjects—pain, brotherhood, and the impossibility of love—in four lines.

It was noon when he arrived: a muggy, breathless day, its oppressiveness doing nothing for his stupefied state. He claimed his baggage and picked up a rental car without any problem, but once he got onto the highway, he regretted not also hiring a driver. After two nights of less than satisfactory sleep, he was aching and short-tempered; within the first hour of the four-hour trek north, he was several times perilously close to a collision, the fault always his. He stopped to pick up some coffee and some aspirin and to walk the stiffness out of his joints. The weight and heat of the day were beginning to lift; there was rain beyond Birmingham, he heard somebody say, and worse to come. It was fine by him: a good heavy downpour, to cool the day still further.

He got back into the car in an altogether brighter mood, and the next leg of the journey was uneventful. The traffic thinned, the rain came and went, and though the view from the motorway was seldom inspiring, on occasion it achieved a particularly English grace. Placid hills thumbed out of the clay, all velvety with grass or patched with straggling woods; harvesters raised ocher dust as they cut and threshed in the fields. And here and there, grander sights: a ridge of naked, sunstruck rock against the grimy sky; a rainbow, leaping from a water-meadow. He felt a remote reminder of those hours on Spruce Street, wandering two revelatory blocks to Bethlynn's house. There wasn't anything like the same level of distraction here, thank God, but he had the same sense that his gaze was cleansed; that he was seeing these sights, none of which were unfamiliar, more clearly than he had ever before. Would it be the same when he got to Burnt Yarley, he wondered. He certainly hoped so. He wanted to see the place made new, if that were possible; to which end he didn't let himself stew in expectation of what lay ahead, but kept his thoughts in the moment: the road, the sky, the passing landscape.

It became harder to do, however, once he got off the highway and headed into the hills. The clouds broke, and the sunlight moved on the slopes as if commanded, the light beautiful enough to bring him close to tears. It amazed him that having put so many journeys between his heart and the spirit of this place, laboring for more than two decades to discipline his sentiments, its beauty could still steal upon him. And still the clouds divided, and the sun joined up its quilt piece by gilded piece. He was passing through villages he now knew, at least by name. Herricksthwaite, Raddlesmoor, Kemp's Hill. He knew the twists and turns in the road, and where it would bring him to a vantage point from which to admire a stand of sycamores, a stream, the folded hills.

Dusk was imminent, the last of the day's light still warming the hilltops but leaving to the blues and grays of dusk the valleys through which he wound his way. This was the landscape of memory; and this the hour. Nothing was quite certain. Forms blurred, defying definition. Was that a sheep or a boulder? Was that a deserted cottage or a clot of trees?

His only concession to prophecy had been to prepare himself for a shock when he got into Burnt Yarley, but he needn't have concerned himself. The changes wrought upon the village were relatively small. The post office had been remodeled; a few cottages had been tarted up; where the grocer's had once stood there was now a small garage. Otherwise, everything looked quite familiar in the streetlight. He drove on until he reached the bridge, where he halted for a moment or two. The river was high; higher, in fact, then he ever remembered it running. He was sorely tempted to get out of the car and sit for a few minutes before covering the final mile. Maybe even double back three hundred yards and fortify himself with a pint of Guinness before he faced the house itself. But he resisted his own cowardice (for that was what it was) and after a minute or two loitering beside the river, he drove home.

ii

Home? No, never that. Never home. And yet what other word was there for this place he'd fled from? Perhaps that was the very definition of home, at least for men of his inclination: the solid, certain spot from which all roads led.

Adele was opening the door even as he got out of the car. She'd heard him coming, she said, and thank goodness he was here, her prayers were answered. The way she said this (and repeated it) made him think she meant this literally, that she'd been praying for his safe and swift arrival. Now he was here and she had good news. Hugo was no longer on the danger list. He was mending quite nicely, the doctors said, though he'd have to stay in hospital for at least a month.

"He's a tough old bird," Adele said fondly, as she puttered around the kitchen preparing Will a ham sandwich and tea.

"And how are you bearing up?" Will asked her.

"Oh, I've had a few sleepless nights," she admitted almost

guiltily, as though she had no right to sleeplessness. She certainly looked exhausted. She was no longer the formidable no-nonsense Yorkshirewoman of twenty-five years before. Though he guessed her to be still shy of seventy, she looked older, her movements about the kitchen hesitant, her words often halting. She hadn't told Hugo that Will was coming ("Just in case you changed your mind at the last minute," she explained), but she had told his doctor, who had agreed that they could go to the hospital to see him tonight, though it would be well past visiting hours.

"He's been difficult," she said heavily. "Even though he's not fully with us. But he knows how to rub people up the wrong way whether he's sick or well. He takes pleasure in it."

"I'm sorry you've had to deal with this on your own. I know how difficult he can be."

"Well, if he wasn't difficult," she said, with gentle indulgence, "he wouldn't be who he is, and I wouldn't care for him. So, I get on with it. That's all we can really do, isn't it?"

It was simple enough wisdom. There were flaws in any arrangement. But if you cared, you just got on with it.

Adele insisted she drive to the hospital. She knew the way, she said, so it would be quicker. Of course she drove at a snail's pace, and by the time they got there it was almost half past nine. Relatively early by the standards of the outside world of course, but hospitals were discrete kingdoms, with their own time zones, and it might as well have been two in the morning: The corridors were hushed and deserted, the wards in darkness.

The nurse who escorted Will and Adele to Hugo's room was chatty, however, her voice a little to loud for the subdued surroundings.

"He was awake last time I popped my head in, but he may have gone back to sleep. The pain killers are making him a little groggy. Are you his son, then?"

"I am."

"Ah," she said, with an almost coy little smile. "He's been talking about you, on and off. Well, rambling really. But he's obviously been wanting to see you. It's Nathaniel, right?" She didn't wait for confirmation, but whittered on blithely—something about how they moved him to a shared room, and now the man he'd been put in with had been discharged, so he had the room to himself, which was lucky, wasn't it? Will murmured that yes, it was lucky.

"Here we are." The door was ajar. "You want to just go in and surprise him?" the nurse said.

"Not particularly," Will said.

The nurse looked confounded, then decided she'd misheard, and with an asinine smile, breezed off down the corridor.

"I'll wait out here," Adele said. "You should have this moment alone, just the two of you."

Will nodded, and after twenty-one years stepped back into his father's presence.

II

There was a meager lamp burning beside Hugo's bed, its sallow light throwing a monumental shadow of the man upon the wall. He was semirecumbent amid a Himalayan mass of pillows, his eyes closed.

He'd grown a beard and nurtured it to a formidable size. A solid ten-inches long, trimmed and waxed in emulation of the beards of great, dead men: Kant, Nietzsche, Tolstoy. The minds by which Hugo had always judged contemporary thought and art, and found it wanting. The beard was more gray than black, with streams of white running in it from the corners of his mouth, as though he'd dribbled cream into it. His hair, by contrast, had been clipped short and lay flat to his scalp, delineating the Roman dome of his skull. Will watched him for fifteen or twenty seconds, thinking how magisterial he looked. Then Hugo's lips parted, and very quietly he said, "So you came back."

Now his eyes opened and found Will. Though there was a pair of spectacles at the bedside table, he stared at his visitor as though he had Will in perfect focus, his stare as unrelenting as ever, and as judgmental.

"Hello, Dad," Will said.

"Into the light," Hugo said, beckoning for Will to approach the bed. "Let me see you." Will duly stepped into the light of the lamp to be scrutinized. "The years are showing on you," he said. "It's the sun. If you have to tramp the world at least wear a hat."

"I'll remember."

"Where were you lurking this time?"

"I wasn't lurking, Dad. I was—"

"I thought you'd deserted me. Where's Adele? Is she here?" He reached out to pluck his glasses off the nightstand. In his haste he instead knocked them to the ground. "Damn things!"

"They're not broken." Will said, picking them up.

Hugo put them on, one handed. Will knew better than to help. "Where is she?"

"Waiting outside. She wanted us to have a little quality time together."

Now, paradoxically, he didn't look at Will, but studied the folds in the bedcover and his hands, his manner perfectly detached. "Quality time?" he said. "Is that an Americanism?"

"Probably."

"What does it *mean* exactly?"

"Oh,. . . " Will sighed. "Are we reduced to that already?"

"No, I'm just interested," Hugo said. "Quality time." He pursed his lips.

"It's a stupid turn of phrase," Will conceded. "I don't know why I used it."

Stymied, Hugo looked at the ceiling. Then, "Maybe you could just ask Adele to come in. I need a few toiletry items brought—"

"Who did it?"

"Just some toothpaste and some—"

"Dad, who did it?"

The man paused, his mouth working as though he were chewing a piece of gristle. "Why do you assume I know?" he said.

"Why do you have to be so argumentative? This isn't a seminar. I'm not your student. I'm your son."

"Why did you take so long to come back?" Hugo said, his eyes returning to Will. "You knew where to find me."

"Would I have been welcome?"

Hugo's stare didn't waver. "Not by me, particularly," he said with great precision. "But your mother was very hurt by your silence."

"Does Eleanor know that you're in here?"

"I certainly haven't told her. And I doubt Adele has. They hated one another."

"Shouldn't she be told?"

"Why?"

"Because she'll be concerned."

"Then why tell her?" Hugo said neatly. "I don't want her here. There's no love lost between us. She's got her life. I've got mine. The only thing we have in common is you."

"You make that sound like an accusation."

"No. You simply *hear* it that way. Some children are palliatives in a troubled marriage. You weren't. I don't blame you for that."

"So can we get back to the subject?"

"Which was?"

"Who did this?"

Hugo returned his gaze to the ceiling. "I read a piece you wrote in the *Times*, about eighteen months ago—"

"What the hell has—"

"Something about elephants. You did write it?"

"It had my name on it."

"I thought perhaps you'd had some amanuensis write it for you. I daresay you thought you were waxing poetic, but Christ, how could you put your name to that kind of indulgence?"

"I was describing what I felt."

"There you are then," Hugo said, his tone one of weary resignation. "If you feel it then it must be true."

"How I disappoint you," Will said.

"No. No. I never hoped, so how could I be disappointed?" There was such a profundity of bitterness in this, it took Will's breath away. "None of it means a damn thing, anyway. It's all shite in the end."

"Is it?"

"Christ, yes." He looked at Will with feigned surprise. "Isn't that what you've been shrieking about all these years?"

"I don't shriek."

"Put it this way. It's a little shrill for most people's ears. Maybe that's why it's not having any effect. Maybe that's why your beloved Mother Earth—"

"Fuck Mother Earth—"

"No, you first, I insist."

Will raised his hands in surrender. "Okay, you win," he said. "I don't have the appetite for this. So—"

"Oh, come now."

"I'll fetch Adele," he said, turning from the bed.

"*Wait*—"

"What for? I didn't come here to be sniped at. If you don't want a peaceful conversation, then we won't have *any* conversation." He was almost at the door.

"I said *wait*," Hugo demanded.

Will halted, but didn't turn.

"It was him," Hugo said, very softly. Now Will glanced over his shoulder. His father had taken off his spectacles and was staring into middle distance.

"Who?"

"Don't be so dense," Hugo said, his voice a monotone. "You *know* who."

Will heard his heart quicken. "Steep?" he said. Hugo didn't reply. Will turned back to face the bed. "Steep did this to you?"

Silence. And then, very quietly, almost reverentially. "This is your revenge. So enjoy it."

"Why?"

"Because you won't get another like it."

"No, *why* did he do this to you?"

"Oh. To get to you. For some reason that's important to him. He did state his devotion. Make what you will of that."

"Why didn't you tell the police?" Again, Hugo kept his counsel, until Will came back to the bedside. "You should have told them."

"*What* would I tell them? I don't want any part of this . . . connection between you and these creatures."

"There's nothing sexual, if that's what you think."

"Oh, I don't give a damn about your bedroom habits. *Humani nil a me alienum puto.* Terence—"

"I know the quote, Dad," Will said wearily. "*Nothing human is alien to me.* But that doesn't apply here, does it?"

Hugo narrowed his puffy eyes. "This is the moment you've been waiting for, isn't it?" he said, his lip curling. "You feel quite the master of ceremonies. You came in here, pretending you wanted to make peace but what you *really* want is revenge."

Will opened his mouth to deny the charge, then thought better of it, and instead told the truth, "Maybe a little."

"So. You have your moment," Hugo said, staring up at the ceiling. "You're right. Terence does not apply. These . . . creatures are not human. There. I've said it. I've thought a lot about what that means, while I've been lying here."

"And?"

"It doesn't mean very much in the end."

"I think you're wrong."

"Well you would, wouldn't you?"

"There's something extraordinary in all of this. Waiting at the end."

"Speaking as a man who *is* waiting at the end I see nothing here but the same tiresome cruelties and the same stale old pain. Whatever they are, they're not angels. They're not going to show you anything miraculous. They're going to break your bones the way they broke mine."

"Maybe they don't *know* what they really are," Will replied, realizing as he spoke that this was indeed at the heart of what he believed. "Oh, Jesus," he murmured almost to himself. "Yes . . . They don't know what they are any more than we do."

"Is this some kind of revelation?" Hugo said in his driest tone. Will didn't dignify his cynicism with a reply. "*Well?*" he insisted. "Is it? Because if you know something about them I don't, I want to hear it."

"Why should you care, if none of it means anything anyway?"

"Because I have a better chance of surviving another meeting with them if I know what I'm dealing with."

"You won't see them again," Will said.

"You sound very certain of that."

"You said Steep wants me," Will replied. "I'll make it simple for him. I'll go to him."

A look of unfeigned alarm crossed Hugo's face. "He'll kill you."

"It's not that simple for him."

"You don't know what he's like—"

"Yes I do. Believe me. *I do.* We've spent the last thirty years together." He touched his temple. "He's been in my head and I've been in his. Like a couple of Russian dolls."

Hugo looked at him with fresh dismay. "How did I get you?" he said, looking at Will as though he were something venomous.

"I assumed it was fucking, Dad."

"God knows, God *knows* I tried to put you on the right track. But I never stood a chance, I see that now. You were queer and crazy and sick to your sorry little heart from the beginning."

"I was queer in the womb," Will said calmly.

"Don't sound so damn proud of it!"

"Oh, that's the worst, isn't it?" Will countered. "I'm queer and I like it. I'm crazy and it suits me. And I'm sick to my sorry little heart because I'm dying into something new. You don't get that yet, and you probably never will. But that's what's happening."

Hugo stared at him, his mouth so tightly closed it seemed he would never utter another word, certainly not to Will. Nor did he need to, at least for now, because at that moment there was a light tapping at the door. "Can I interrupt?" Adele said, putting her head around the door.

"Come on in," Will said. Then, glaring back at Hugo. "The reunion's pretty much over."

Adele came directly to the bed and kissed Hugo on the cheek. He received the kiss without comment or reciprocation, which didn't seem to bother Adele. How many kisses had she bestowed this way, Will wondered, Hugo taking them as his right? "I brought you your toothpaste," she said, digging in her handbag and depositing the tube on the bedside table. Will saw the glint of fury in his father's eye, to have been seen addle-headed, asking for something he'd already requested. Adele was happily unaware of this. She fairly bubbled in Hugo's presence, Will saw, sweetly content to be coddling him—straightening his sheets, plumping up his pillow—though he gave her no thanks for her efforts.

"I'm going to leave you two to talk," Will said. "I need a cigarette. I'll see you out by the car, Adele."

"Fine," she said, all her focus upon the object of her affections. "I won't be long."

"Good-bye, Dad," Will said. He didn't expect a reply, and he didn't get one. Hugo was staring up at the ceiling again, with the glassy-eyed gaze of a man who has more important things on his mind than a child he would rather had never been born.

III

Leaving the man was like departing a battlefield. The engagement had ended inconclusively, but painful as the conversation had been, it had obliged him to put into words an idea that would have made little or no sense before the events of the last few days: Jacob and Rosa, despite their extraordinary particularities, were strangers to themselves. They did not know what or who they were; the selves to whom their deeds were attributed, fictions. This, he began to believe, was the conundrum at the heart of his agonized relationship with Steep. Jacob was not one man, but many. Not many, but none. He was a creature of Will's invention, as surely as Will, and Lord Fox, were Steep's own creatures, made by a different process, perhaps, but still made. Which thought inevitably begged another conundrum: If there was nobody in this circle who was not somehow dependent upon the volition of another for their existence, could they be said to be divisible entities or were they one troubled spirit: Steep the Father, Will the Son, and Lord Fox the Unholy Ghost? That left the role of Virgin Mother for Rosa, which faintly blasphemous notion brought a smile to his lips.

As he wandered back down the dispiriting corridors to the front of the building he realized that from the very beginning Steep had confessed his ignorance of his own nature. Hadn't he described himself as a man who couldn't remember his own parents? And later, talking of his epiphany, evoked the perfect image of his dissolution: his body lost to the waters of the Neva, Jacob in the wolf, Jacob in the tree, Jacob in the bird?

It was cool outside, the air moist and clean. Will lit a cigarette and plotted as best he could what to do next. Some of what Hugo had said carried weight. Steep was indeed dangerous right now, and Will had to be careful in his dealings. But he *couldn't* believe that Steep simply wanted him dead. They were too tightly bound together; their destinies intertwined. This wasn't wish fulfillment on Will's part: He had it from the fox's own mouth. If the animal was Steep's agent in the curious circle, which he surely was, then he was espousing Jacob's hopes, and what was being expressed when the animal spoke of Will as its liberation, if not the desire that he solve the enigma of Jacob and Rosa's very existence?

He lit a second cigarette, smoked his way through it and immediately lit a third, desperate for the nicotine rush that would help him clarify his thoughts. The only way to solve this puzzle, he knew, was to deal with Steep directly, to go to him, as he'd told Hugo he would, and pray that Steep's desire for self-comprehension overrode the man's appetite for death. He knew how it felt, that appetite; how it had quickened his senses, shedding blood. The very hand that put his cigarette to his lips had been inspired by the knife, hadn't it, exulting in the harm it was capable of doing. He pictured the birds even now, huddling in the cleft of a frozen branch, winking their beady eyes—

"*They see me.*"

"*See them back.*"

"*I do.*"

"*Fix them with your eyes.*"

"*I am.*"

"*Then finish it.*"

He felt a tremor of pleasure down his spine. Even after all these years, all the sights he'd seen that in scale and savagery beggared the little murders he'd performed, he could still taste the forbidden thrill of it. But there were other memories, that in their way held as much power. He brought one of them to mind now and put it between himself and the knife: Thomas Simeon, standing among the blossoms, proffering a single petal.

"*I have the Holy of Holies here—the Ark of the Covenant, the Sangraal, the Great Mystery itself—right here on the tip of my little finger. Look!*"

That was also part of the puzzle, wasn't it? Not just Simeon's metaphysical ideas, but the substance of the simpler exchanges between the two men. Simeon's rejection of Jacob's attempts to coax him back into the company of Rukenau; the promise Steep had made to protect the artist from his patron; the talk of power play between Rukenau and Steep, which had been concluded, Will half-remembered, with some fine, careless words of independence from Steep. What had he said? Something about not knowing who'd made him? There it was again, that same confession. Will's recollection of the conversation between Steep and Simeon was far more patchy than his memory of the knife, but he had the sense that Rukenau had possessed some knowledge of Jacob and Rosa's origins that they themselves did not. Could he have remembered that correctly?

He began to wish he could conjure Lord Fox and quiz him. Not because he believed the creature would have the answers to his inquiries about Rukenau, he would not, but because for all the animal's prickly manner and obscure remarks, he was the closest Will had to a reliable touchstone in this confusion. There was evidence of desperation, Will thought. When a man turns to an imaginary fox for advice, he's in trouble.

"Aren't you cold out here?"

He looked around to see Adele striding across the parking lot toward him. "I'm fine," he told her. "How's Hugo?"

"All settled down for the night," she said, plainly happy to have him comfortably tucked up.

"Time to go home?"

"Time to go home."

He was too distracted to engage Adele in cogent conversation on the way home, but she didn't seem to mind. She chattered on anyway, about how much better Hugo looked today than he had yesterday, and how resilient he'd always been (he seldom caught so much as a cold, she said). And how quickly he would bounce back, she was certain, especially once she got him home where he'd be more comfortable, and she could coddle him. Nobody was ever comfortable in hospital, were they? In fact, a friend of hers, who'd been a nurse, had said to her the very worst place to be ill was a hospital, with all those germs in the air. No, he'd be much better off at home, with his books and his whiskey and a comfortable bed.

The homeward trek took them over Hallard's Back, where for a distance of perhaps two miles the road ran straight across bare moorland. No lights here, no habitations, no trees. Just the pitch-black sweep of moor on either side of the road. While Adele chatted on about Hugo, Will gazed out at the darkness, wondering, with a little chill of guilty pleasure, how close Jacob and Rosa were. Out there in the night right now, perhaps: Rosa hunting hares, Jacob staring at the sealed sky. They didn't need to sleep through the hours of darkness; they weren't prone to the exhaustion of ordinary men and women. They would not wither; nor lose their strange perfection. They belonged to a race or condition that was in some unfathomable fashion beyond the frailties of disease or even death.

That should have made him afraid of them, because it left him defenseless. But he was not afraid. Uneasy, yes, but not afraid. And despite his ruminations in the parking lot, despite all his unanswered questions, there was a corner of his heart that took curious comfort in the fact that this puzzle was so complex. There was little comfort, this voice inside him said, in discovering a mystery at the wellspring of his life so banal his unremarkable mind could readily fathom it. Better, perhaps, to die in doubt, knowing there was some revelation still unfound, than to pursue and possess such a wretched certainty.

IV

i

He slept deeply up in the beamed room that had been his as a boy. There were new curtains on the window and a new rug on the floor, but otherwise the room was virtually unchanged. The same wardrobe, with the mirror on the inside of the door where he had appraised the progress of his adolescence countless times, studied the advance of his body hair, admired the swelling of his dick. The same chest of drawers where he had kept his tiny collection of muscle-boy magazines (filched from newsagents in Halifax). The same bed where he had breathed life into those pictures and dreamed the living bodies there beside him. In short, the site of his sexual coming of age.

There was another piece of that history, albeit small, at work downstairs the following morning. "You remember my boy, Craig," Adele said, bidding the man working under the sink to emerge and say hello.

Of course Will remembered him; he'd conjured up Craig in his coma dream: A sweaty adolescent who for a few hours had roused in the eleven-year-old Will a feeling he could not have named—desire, of course. But what had seemed for a little time attractive in Craig the adolescent—his scowl, his sweat, his lumpen weight—was charmless in the adult. He grunted something unintelligible by way of a greeting.

"Craig does a lot of odd jobs around the village," Adele explained. "He does some plumbing. Some roofing. He's got quite a little business going, haven't you?"

Another grunt from Craig. It was strange to see a grown man (he was fully a foot taller than Adele) standing crab-footed and bashful while his mother listed his accomplishments. Finally, he grunted, "Are you done?" to Adele, and returned to his labors.

"You'll want some breakfast," Adele said. "I'll cook up some eggs and sausage, maybe some kidneys or black pudding?"

"No, really, I'm fine. I'll just have some tea."

"Let me make you a couple of slices of toast, at least. You need feeding up a little bit." Will knew what was coming. "Have you not got a lass to cook for you?"

"I do fine on my own."

"Craig's wife, Mary, is a wonderful cook, isn't she, Craig?" The grunt, by way of reply. "You never thought of getting married? I suppose with your work an' all, it'd be hard having a normal life." She chatted on while she brewed the tea. She'd spoken to the hospital this morning, she said, and Hugo had passed a very comfortable night, the best so far in fact. "I thought we could both go back to see him this evening?"

"That's fine by me."

"What are you planning to do today?"

"Oh, I'll just have a wander down to the village."

"Get reacquainted," Adele said.

"Something like that."

ii

When he left the house a little before ten he was in a quiet turmoil. He knew his destination of course: the Courthouse. Unless he'd missed his guess there he'd find Jacob and Rosa ensconced, waiting for him. The prospect aroused a cluster of contrary feelings. There was inevitably a measure of anxiety, even a little fear. Steep had brutally assaulted Hugo and was perfectly capable of doing the same, or worse, to Will. But his anxiety was countered both by anticipation and curiosity. What would it be like to confront Steep again after all these years? To be a man in his presence, not a boy, to meet him eye to eye?

He'd had a few glimpses of how it might be, in his years of travel: men and women he'd encountered who carried with them some of the power that had attended Jacob and Rosa. A priestess in Ethiopia, who despite the plethora of religious symbols she carried about her neck, some Christian, some not, had spoken in a kind of poetic stream of consciousness that suggested she was deriving her inspiration from no readily named source. A shaman in San Lázan whom Will had watched swaying and singing before an altar heaped with marigolds, and who had given him healthy helpings of sacred mushrooms—*teonanacatl*, the divine flesh—to help him on his own journey. Both extraordinary presences, from whose mouths he might have imagined Steep's grim wisdom coming.

The day was calm and cool, the cloud layer unbroken. He ambled down to the crossroads, from which spot he'd once been able to see the Courthouse. But no longer. Trees that had been svelte thirty years before were now in spreading maturity and blocked the

view with their canopies. He paused just long enough to light up
another cigarette and then headed on his way. He had covered perhaps half the distance when he began to suspect his assumption at
the crossroads had been wrong. Though the trees were indeed fuller
than they'd been, and the hedgerows taller, surely by now he should
have been able to see the roof of the Courthouse? He walked on, the
suspicion becoming certainty the closer he came to the spot. The
Courthouse had been demolished.

He had no need to clamber through a hedgerow to get into the
field that it had dominated. There was now a gate at the spot,
through which, he assumed, the rubble had been removed. The field
had not been returned to agricultural use however; it had been left to
the vagaries of seed and season. He clambered over the gate—which
to judge by its condition had not been opened in many years—and
strode through the tall grass until he came to the foundation, which
was still visible. Grass and wildflowers sprouted between the stones,
but he was able to trace the geography of the building by walking it.
Here was the passage that had led to the courtroom. Here was the
place where he'd found the trapped sheep. Here was the judge's
chair, and here—oh *here*—was the place where Jacob had set his
table—

"Living and dying—"

Oh God help him; God help them both—

"We feed the fire."

It was so long ago, and yet as he stood there, where he'd stood, it
was as if he were a boy again: the languid air darkening around him
as though the survival of the light depended upon the cremation of
moths. Tears came into his eyes: of sorrow, for the act, and for himself, that he was still in his heart unredeemed. The grass and stone
ground dissolved beneath his feet; he knew if he let himself weep
he'd not be able to govern himself.

"Don't do this," he said, pinching the tears from his eyes. He
could not afford to indulge his grief today. Tomorrow, maybe, when
he'd met with Steep and played out whatever grim game lay ahead,
then he could take the time to be weak. But not now, in an open
field, where his frailty might be witnessed.

He looked up and scanned the hills and hedgerows. Perhaps it
was too late. Perhaps Steep was watching him even now, like some
carrion bird, assessing the condition of a wounded animal; waiting, as
Will had waited so many times, for the moment of truth, the

moment when, in tears or desperation, the subject of study revealed its final face. Searching for a title for his second collection, he had made a list of words relating to the business of death and had lived with the alternatives for a month or more, turning them over in his head so often he had them by rote. They were in his head now, coming unbidden.

The Pale Horse and the Totentanz, Cold Meat and Crowbait, A Bed of Clay, A Last Abode, The Long Home—

This last had been a contender for the title: describing the grave to which his subjects were about to be delivered as a place of inevitable return. It was distressing to think of that now, standing as he did within a mile of his father's house. It made him feel like a condemned man.

Enough of this creeping despair, he told himself. He needed relief from it, and quickly. He climbed over the gate, and without a backward glance returned along the road with the determined stride of a man who had no further business in the place behind him. He was out of cigarettes, so he made his way into the village to pick up another pack. The streets were busy, he was pleased to see. There was no little comfort to be had in the sight of people about their ordinary lives: buying vegetables, making small talk, hurrying their children along. In the newsagent's he listened to a leisurely conversation on the subject of the Harvest Festival, the woman behind the counter (plainly the daughter of Mrs. Morris, who'd run the place in Will's youth) opining that it was all very well trying to bring folks in to church with fancy tricks, but she drew a line at services being fun.

"What's the problem with a bit of fun?" her customer wanted to know.

"I just think it's a slippery slope," Miss Morris replied. "We'll have dancing in the aisles next."

"That's better than sleeping in the pews," the woman remarked with a little laugh, and picking up her chocolate bars, made her exit. The exchange had apparently been less jocular than it had seemed, because Miss Morris was quietly fuming about it when she came to serve Will.

"Is this some big controversy?" he asked her. "The Harvest Festival, I mean?"

"Nooo," she said, a little exasperated at herself, "it's just that Frannie always knows how to stir me up."

"Frannie?"

"Yes."

"Frannie Cunningham? I'll be back for the cigarettes—"

And he was out of the shop, looking right and left for the woman who'd just breezed by. She was already on the opposite side of the road, eating her chocolate as she strode on her way.

"*Frannie?*" he yelled, and dodging the traffic raced to intercept her. She'd heard her name being called and was looking back toward him. It was plain from her expression she still didn't recognize him, though now—when he saw her face full on—he knew her. She was somewhat plumper, her hair more gray than auburn. But that look of perpetual attention she'd had was still very much in place, as were her freckles.

"Do we know each other?" she said as he gained the pavement.

"Yes, we do," he grinned. "Frannie, it's me. It's Will."

"Oh my Lord," she breathed. "I didn't ... I mean ... you were—"

"In the shop. Yes. We walked straight past one another."

She opened her arms, and Will went into them, hugging her as fiercely as she hugged him. "Will, Will, Will," she kept saying. "This is so wonderful. Oh, but I'm sorry to hear about your dad."

"You know?"

"Everybody knows," she said. "You can't keep secrets in Burnt Yarley. Well ... I suppose that's not quite true, is it?" She gave him an almost mischievous look. "Besides, your dad's quite a character. Sherwood sees him at the Plow all the time, holding court. How's he doing?"

"Better, thank you."

"That's good."

"And Sherwood?"

"Oh, he had his good times and his bad times. We still have the house together. The one on Samson Street."

"What about your mom and dad?"

"Dad's dead. He died six years ago this coming November. Then last year we had to put mom into a hospice. She's got Alzheimer's. We looked after her at home for a couple of years, but she was deteriorating so fast. It's horrible to watch, and Sherwood was getting in such a depression about it."

"It sounds like you've been in the wars."

"Oh well." Frannie shrugged. "We battle on. Do you want to come back to the house for something to eat? Sherwood'll be so pleased to see you."

"If it's not going to be an inconvenience."

"You've been away too long," Frannie chided him. "This is York-shire. Friends are never an inconvenience. Well," she added, with that mischievous twinkle, "almost never."

V

It was only a fifteen-minute walk back to the Cunningham house, but by the time they arrived at the gate they'd already lost any initial tentativeness and were talking in the easy manner of old friends. Will had given Frannie a quick summary of the events in Balthazar (she'd read about the accident, as she called it, in a magazine article Sherwood had found), and Frannie had prepared him for the reunion with Sherwood by filling in a little of her brother's medical history. He'd been diagnosed with a form of acute depression, she explained, which he'd probably been suffering since childhood. Hence his see-sawing emotions: his sulks, his rages, his inability to concentrate. Though he now had pills to keep it manageable, he was not, nor ever would be, entirely cured. It was a burden he would bear to the end of his life. "It helps to think of it as a test," she said. "God wants us to show Him how tough we are."

"Interesting theory."

"I'm sure He approves of you," she said, not entirely joking. "I mean, if anyone's been through the mill, it's you. All those terrible places you've had to go."

"It's not quite the same if you volunteer though, is it?" Will said. "You and Sherwood haven't had any choice."

"I don't think any of us have got much choice," she said. She dropped her voice. "Especially us. When you think of what happened . . . back then. We were children. We didn't know what we were dealing with."

"Do we now?"

She looked at him with a gaze suddenly shorn of joy. "I used to think—this probably sounds ridiculous to you—but I used to think somehow we'd met the Devil in disguise." She laughed nervously at this. "That *does* sound stupid, doesn't it?" Her laugh disappeared almost immediately, seeing that Will was not laughing with her. "Doesn't it?"

"I don't know what he is," he replied.

"Was," she said quietly.

He shook his head. "Is," he murmured.

They'd reached the gate. "Oh Lord," she said. There was a little quaver in her voice.

"Maybe I shouldn't come in."

"No, you must," she replied. "But we shouldn't talk about this anymore. Not in front of Sherwood. He gets upset."

"I understand."

"I think about it a lot. After all these years, I turn it over in my head. I even did a bit of research a few years ago, trying to get to the bottom of it all."

"And?"

She shook her head. "I gave up," she said. "It was bothering Sherwood, and it was churning everything up all over again. I decided it was better to leave it alone."

She unlatched the gate and started down the path, which was edged on either side by sprays of lavender, toward the front door. "Before we go in," Will said, "can you tell me what happened to the Courthouse?"

"It was demolished."

"That I saw."

"Marjorie Donnelly had it done. Her father was the man—"

"Who was murdered. I remember."

"She had to fight tooth and nail to get it done. There was some Heritage Committee said it was of historical interest. Eventually she hired a dozen slaughterhouse men from Halifax, at least this is what I heard, it might not be true, but I heard they came with sledgehammers in the middle of the night and they did so much damage the place had to be leveled for safety concerns."

"Good for her."

"Don't mention it, please."

"I won't."

"I'm making Sherwood sound worse than he is," she said, digging for her key in her purse. "Most of the time he's fine. Just once in a while something strikes him the wrong way, and he gets so down in the dumps I think he's never going to snap out of it." She'd found the key, and now unlocked the door, calling for Sherwood as she stepped inside. There was no reply. Will followed her in, while she went to look for him upstairs. "He must have gone out walking," she said, coming back downstairs. "He does that a lot."

They talked for the next hour or so over cold chicken, tomatoes, and homemade chutney, the conversation ranging ever more widely as it progressed. Frannie's ebullience and sheer good nature charmed Will thoroughly: She had become an eloquent and deeply compassionate woman. More than ever, as she related her history, he sensed a regret that she'd not been able to move out of this house and find a life for herself, apart from Sherwood and his problems. But that regret was never explicit, and she would have been upset, he guessed, if she'd thought he'd recognized it in her. She was doing her Christian duty caring for Sherwood: no more nor less. If it indeed was a test, as she'd said at the gate, then she was passing it with flying colors.

Not all the talk was of events in Burnt Yarley, however. She ferreted after the details of Will's life and loves with no little gusto, and though he was at first reticent, her sheer persistence won him over. He gave her, in a somewhat bowdlerized version, an account of his emotional adventures, interlaced with a potted history of his career: Drew and Patrick and the Castro, books, bears and Balthazar.

"Do you remember how you were always wanting to run away?" she said to him. "The first day we met, that's what you said you were going to do. And you did."

"It took me a while."

"The point is, you went," she said, eyes shining. "We've all got dreams when we're kids, but most of us give up on them. But you didn't. You went to see the world, the way you said you would."

"Do you get away at all?"

"Not really. Sherwood hates to travel; it makes him nervous. We've been down to Oxford a couple of times, and we pop over to Skipton to see mom in the hospice, but he's much happier when he's here in the village."

"And what about you?"

"I'm happier when he's happiest," she said simply.

"And you never talk about what happened?"

"Very, very seldom. But it's always there, isn't it? I suppose it always will be." She lowered her voice, as though the walls would report the conversation to Sherwood if they heard it. "I still have dreams about the Courthouse," she said. "They're more vivid than any other dream I have. Sometimes I'm there on my own, and I'm looking for his journal. Just going from room to room, knowing he's coming back, and I've got to be *quick.*" The expression on his face must have been the perfect mirror of his thoughts at that moment, because she said, "It is just a dream, isn't it?"

"No," he said softly. "I don't think it is."

She put her hand to her mouth. "Oh Lord," she breathed.

"It isn't your problem," he said. "You two can stay out of it and be perfectly—"

"Is he here?"

"Yes."

"You're sure?"

"Yes."

"How do you know?"

"He's the reason Hugo's in hospital. Steep beat him senseless."

"But why?"

"He wanted to get a message to me. He wanted me back here, to finish what we started."

"He's got his bloody journal," Frannie said. "What more does he want?"

"Separation," Will said.

"From what?"

"From me."

"I don't understand."

"It's hard to explain. We're connected, him and me. I know it sounds ludicrous when we're sitting here talking and drinking tea, but he never quite let go of me." Then more quietly, "And maybe I never quite let go of him."

"Is that why you went to the Courthouse? To find him?"

"Yes."

"Lord, Will. He could kill you."

"I think we're too close for that," he said.

Frannie took a little time to absorb this remark. "Too close?" she said.

"If he touches me, he may end up seeing more than he wants to see."

"There's always Rosa to do the harm for him."

"True," he said. This was an option he hadn't really considered, but of course it was perfectly plausible. Rosa had proved her skills as a murderer a half mile from here; if Steep wanted to keep his distance from Will he could simply set the woman on Will's neck and be done with him that way.

"Rosa made quite an impression on Sherwood, you know," Frannie went on. "He had nightmares about her for years after. I never got him to talk about what happened, but she made her mark."

"And you?" Will said.

"What about me?"

"I've had Steep. Sherwood had Rosa."

"Oh . . . well, I had the journal to obsess over."

"And did you?"

She nodded, looking through him, as though in her mind's eye she was picturing the thing she'd lost. "I never solved it, and that bothered me for years. Did you ever see what it contained?"

"No."

"It was beautiful."

"Really?"

"Oh yes," she said, breathing with admiration. "He'd made all these drawings of animals. Perfect they were. And on the opposite page to the drawing," she was miming the act of opening the book now, staring down at its contents, "there was line after line of writing."

"What did it say?"

"It wasn't in English. It wasn't in any language I've ever been able to find. It wasn't Greek, it wasn't Sanskrit, it wasn't hieroglyphics. I copied a few of the characters down, but I never deciphered any of it."

"Maybe it was nonsense. Something he'd just made up."

"No," she said, "it was a language."

"How do you know?"

"Because I found it in one other place."

"Where?"

"Well, it was strange. About six years ago, just after dad died, I started to take night classes in Halifax, just to get out of the rut I was in. I took courses in French and Italian, of all things. I think because of the journal really; I was still looking for a way to decipher it, deep down. Anyway I met this chap there, and we got on quite well. He was in his fifties, and very *attentive* I suppose you'd say, and we'd talk for hours after the classes. His name was Nicholas. His great passion was the eighteenth century, which I've never really had any interest in, but he invited me to his house, which was extraordinary. Like stepping back in time two hundred and fifty years. Lamps, wallpaper, pictures, everything, was, you know, of the period. I suppose he was a little crazy, but in a very gentle kind of way. He used to say he'd been born in the wrong century." She laughed at the folly of all of this.

"Anyway, I went to his house three or four times and I was browsing in his library—he had a collection of books and pamphlets and magazines, all about the seventeen hundreds—and I found this little book with a picture in it, and there in the picture were some of the hieroglyphics from Steep's journal."

"With an explanation?"

"Not really," she said, the brightness in her voice dulling. "It was frustrating really. He gave me the book as a gift. He'd got it in a job lot from an auction and he didn't care for the pictures very much, so he said to take it."

"Do you still have it?"

"Yes. It's upstairs."

"I'd like to see it."

"I'm warning you, it's very disappointing," she said, getting up from the table. "I pored over it for hours." She headed on into the hall. "But I ended up wishing I'd never seen the bloody thing. I won't be a minute."

She headed up the stairs, leaving Will to wander through to the living room. Unlike the kitchen, which was newly painted, the room might have been left as a shrine to the departed parents. The furniture was plain, eschewing any hint of hedonism; the plant-life (geraniums on the windowsill, potted hyacinths on the table) well tended; the designs of hearth-rug, wallpaper, and curtains a calamity of fuss and mismatched color. On the mantelpiece, to either side of the solid clock, were framed photographs of the whole family, smiling out from a distant summer. Tucked into the frame of one, a yellowed prayer card. On it, two verses:

> *One with the earth below, Lord,*
> *One with the sky above,*
> *One with the seed I sow, Lord,*
> *One with the hearts I love.*
>
> *Make earth of my dust, Lord,*
> *Make air of my breath,*
> *Make love of my lust, Lord,*
> *And life out of my death.*

There was something comforting about the prayer's simplicity; the hope it expressed for unity and transformation. It moved him, in its way.

He was setting the picture back down on the mantelpiece when he heard the front door open, and then quietly close. A moment later an ill-shaven man with pinched and woebegone features, his thinning hair grown to near shoulder length but unkempt, appeared at the living room door, and stared at him through round spectacles.

"Will," he said, with such certainty it was almost as if he'd expected to find Will there.

"My God, you recognized me!"

"Of course," Sherwood replied, proffering his hand as he crossed the room. "I've been following your rise to notoriety." He shook Will's hand, his palm clammy, his fingers bone thin. "Where's Frannie?"

"She's upstairs."

"I've been out walking," Sherwood said, though he had no need to explain himself. "I like to walk." He glanced out of the window. "It's going to rain within the hour." He went to the barometer beside the living room door and tapped it. "Maybe a downpour," he said, peering at the glass over his spectacles. He had the manner of a man twenty or thirty years his senior, Will thought; he'd moved from an adolescent to an old man without a middle-age. "Are you here for long?"

"That's depends on my dad's health."

"How is he?"

"Getting stronger."

"Good. I see him at the pub once in a while. He knows how to start an argument, your dad. He gave me one of his books to read, but I couldn't get through it. I told him, too: I said, It's beyond me, all this philosophy, and he said, Well then there's hope for you yet. Imagine that: There's hope for you yet. I said I'd give him it back but he told me to throw it out. So I did." He grinned. "I told him next time I saw him. I said: I threw out your book. He bought me a drink. Now if I did that they'd call me daft, wouldn't they? Not that they don't anyway. Here comes Daft Cunningham." He chuckled. "Suits me."

"Does it?"

"Oh aye. It's safer that way, isn't it? I mean people let you alone if they think you're three sheets to the wind. Anyhow . . . I'll be seeing you later on, eh? I've got to go soak me feet."

As he turned to go, Frannie appeared behind him. "Isn't this wonderful," she said to Sherwood, "seeing Will again after all this time?"

"Wonderful," Sherwood said, without any great measure of

enthusiasm. "See you again then." A look of bemusement crossed Frannie's face. "Aren't you staying to talk?"

"Well actually I should be on my way," Will said, glancing at his watch. It was indeed time he was off; he'd promised Adele they'd make an early visit to the hospital today.

"Here's the book," Frannie said, passing a slim, dun volume to Will.

Sherwood was meanwhile slipping away up the stairs. "Would you mind letting yourself out, Will?" Frannie said, apparently concerned about her brother's behavior. "I'll give you a ring tomorrow, and maybe you can come back down when Sherwood's feeling a little bit more sociable." With that, she was gone, up the stairs to find out what was amiss.

Will let himself out. The cloud layer had thickened and darkened; rain, as Sherwood had predicted, could not be far off. Will picked up his pace, flipping through the book Frannie had given him as he walked. The pages were as stiff as card, the printing too small to be read on the move. The reproductions were in black and white, and poor. Only the title page was readily legible, and the words upon it brought him to a halt. A *Mystic Tragedy* was the main title. And underneath: *The Life and Work of Thomas Simeon.*

VI

i

He began to study the book as soon as he got back to the house. It was scarcely more than a monograph; a hundred and thirty pages of text, along with ten line reproductions and six plates, which was intended, so the author, one Kathleen Dwyer, stated as: *"a brief introduction to the life and work of an almost entirely neglected artist."*

Born in the first decade of the eighteenth century, Thomas Simeon had been something of a prodigy. Raised in Suffolk, in humble circumstances, his artistic skills had been first noticed by the local vicar, who out of what seemed to be a selfless desire to have a

God-given gift provide joy to as many people as possible, had arranged for the young Simeon's work to be seen in London. Two watercolors from the hand of the fifteen-year-old boy had been purchased by the Earl of Chesterfield, and Thomas Simeon was on his way. Commissions followed: a series of picturesque scenes depicting London theaters had been successful, there had been a few attempts at portraiture (these less well received), and then, when the artist was still a month shy of his eighteenth birthday, there had come the work by which his reputation as a visionary artist was made: a diptych for the altar of St Dominic's in Bath. The paintings were now lost, but by all contemporary reports they had caused quite a stir.

"*Through the letters of John Galloway,*" Dwyer had written, "*we can follow the blossoming of the controversy which attended the unveiling of these paintings. Their subjects were unremarkable: the left hand panel depicting a scene in Eden, the right, the Hill at Golgotha.*

"'*It seemed to everyone who saw them,*' *Galloway reports in a letter to his father dated February 5th, 1721, 'as if Thomas had walked on the perfect earth of Adam's Garden, and set down in paint all he saw; then gone straightaway to the place where Our Lord died, and there made a painting as desolate as the first was filled with the light of God's presence.*'

"*Barely four months later, however, Galloway's tone had changed. He was no longer so certain that Simeon's visions were entirely healthy. 'I have many times thought that God moved in my dear Thom,' Galloway wrote, 'but perhaps that same door which he opened in his breast to give God entrance, he left unattended, for it seems to me sometimes that the Devil came into his soul, too, and there fights night and day with all that is best in Thom, I do not know who will win the war, but I fear for Thomas's presence of mind.*'"

There was more on the subject of Simeon's deterioration around the time of the diptych, but Will skimmed it. He had an hour before Adele had planned their trip to the hospital, and he wanted to have the slim volume read. Moving on to the next chapter, however, he found Dwyer's style thickening as she attempted to make an account of what was clearly a problematic area in her researches. Paring away the filigree and the qualifications, the essence of the matter seemed to be this: Simeon had undergone a crisis of faith in the late autumn of 1722 and may (though documentation was unreliable here) have attempted suicide. He had alienated Galloway, his companion from childhood, and sequestered himself in a squalid studio on the outskirts of Blackheath, where he indulged a growing addiction to opium. So far, predictable enough. But then, in Dwyer's constipated phrasing, came:

"*The figure who would, with his subtle appeals to the painter's now debauched instincts, render the glorious promise of his gilded youth a tarnished spectacle. His name was Gerard Rukenau, variously described by contemporary witnesses as 'transcendalist of surpassing skill and wisdom,' and by no lesser personage than Sir Robert Walpole, 'the very model of what he must become, as this age dies.' To hear him speak was, one witness remarked, 'like listening to the Sermon on the Mount delivered by a satyr; one is moved and repelled in the same moment, as though he arouses one's higher self and one's basest instincts simultaneously.'*

"Here, then," Dwyer theorizes, "*was a man who could understand the contrary impulses that had fractured Simeon's fragile state of mind. A father confessor who would quickly become his sole patron, removing him both from the pit of self-abnegation into which he'd fallen and from the leavening influence his saner friends might have exercised.*"

At this juncture, Will put the book down for a couple of minutes in order to digest what he'd just read. Though he now had a few descriptions of Rukenau to juggle, they essentially canceled one another out, which left him no further advanced. Rukenau was a man of power and influence, that much was clear, and had no doubt powerfully affected Steep. Could *Living and dying we feed the fire* not have been a line from a satyr's sermon? But as to what the source of his power might be, or the nature of his influence, there was little clue.

He returned to the text, sprinting through a few paragraphs that attempted to put Simeon's work in some kind of aesthetic context, in order to pick up the thread of Rukenau's involvement with the painter's life. He didn't have to go far. Rukenau, it seems, had a plan for Simeon's wayward genius, and it soon showed itself. He wanted the painter to make a series of pictures "*evoking,*" according to Dwyer, "*Rukenau's transcendalist vision of humanity's relationship to Creation, in the form of fourteen pictures chronicling the building—by an entity know only as the Nilohic—of the Mundi Domus. Literally, the House of the World. Only one of these pictures is known, and it indeed may be the only one surviving, given that a woman friend of Rukenau, Dolores Cruikshank, who had volunteered to pen an exegesis of his theories, complained in March of 1723 that: 'between Gerard's meticulous concerns for a true reflection of his philosophies, and*

Simeon's aesthetic neuralgia, these pictures have been made in more versions than Mankind itself, each one destroyed for some piffling flaw in conception or execution . . . '"

The one extant painting had been reproduced in the book, albeit poorly. The picture was in black and white, and washed out, but there was enough detail to intrigue Will. It seemed to depict an early portion of the construction process: a naked, sexless figure who appeared to be black-skinned in the reproduction (but could just as easily have been blue or green), was bending toward the ground, in which numerous fine rods had been stuck, as though marking the perimeters of the dwelling. The landscape behind the figure was a wasteland, the dirt infertile, the sky deserted. In three spots fires burned in a crack in the earth, sending up a plane of dark smoke, but that only seemed to emphasize the desolation. As for the hieroglyphics that Frannie had described, they were carved on stones scattered throughout the wilderness, as though they'd been tossed out of the sky as clues for the lone mason.

"What are we to make of this peculiar image?" the text asked. *"Its hermeticisim frustrates us; we long for explanation, and find none."* Not even from Dwyer, it appeared. She flailed around for a couple of paragraphs attempting to make parallels with illustrations to be found in alchemical treatises, but Will sensed that she was out of her depth. He flipped to the next chapter, leaving the rest of Dwyer's amateur occultism unread, and was halfway through the first page when he heard Adele summoning him. He was reluctant to put the book down, and even more reluctant to go and visit Hugo a second time, but the sooner the duty was done, he reasoned, the sooner he'd be back in Thomas Simeon's troubled world. So he set the book on the chair and headed downstairs to join Adele.

ii

Hugo was feeling sluggish. He'd had some pain after lunch, nothing unusual, the nurse reassured Adele, but enough to warrant a dessert of pain killers. They had subdued him considerably and, throughout the three-quarter hour visit, his speech was slow and slurred, his focus far from sharp. Most of the time, in fact, he was barely aware that Will was in the room, which suited Will just fine. Only toward the end of the visit did his gaze flutter in his son's direction.

"And what did you do today?" he asked, as though he were addressing a nine-year-old.

"I saw Frannie and Sherwood."

"Come a little closer," Hugo said, feebly beckoning Will to the bedside. "I'm not going to strike you."

"I didn't imagine you were," Will said.

"I've never struck you, have I? There was a policeman here, said I had."

"There's no policeman, Dad."

"There was. Right here. Rude bugger. Said I beat you. I never beat you." He sounded genuinely distressed at the accusation.

"It's the pills they're giving you, Dad," Will gently explained, "they're making you a little delirious. Nobody's accusing you of anything."

"There was no policeman?"

"No."

"I could have sworn . . . " he said, scanning the room anxiously. "Where's Adele?"

"She's gone to get some fresh water for your flowers."

"Are we alone?"

"Yes."

He leaned up out of the pillow. "Am I . . . making a fool of myself?"

"In what way?"

"Saying things . . . that don't make sense?"

"No, Dad, you're not."

"You'd tell me wouldn't you?" he said. "Yes, you would. You'd tell me because it'd hurt and you'd like that."

"That's not true."

"You like watching people squirm. You get that from me."

Will shrugged. "You can believe what you like, Dad. I'm not going to argue."

"No. Because you know you'd lose." He tapped his skull. "See, I'm not that delirious. I can see your game. You only came back when I'm weak and confused, because you think you'll get the upper hand. Well you won't. I'm your match with half my wits." He settled back into his pillow again. "I don't want you coming here again," he said softly.

"Oh for Christ's sake."

"I mean it," Hugo said, turning his face from Will. "I'll get better without your care and attention, thank you very much." Will was glad his father's eyes were averted. The last thing he wanted at that moment was for Hugo to see what an effect his words were having. Will felt them in his throat and chest and gut.

"All right," Will said. "If that's what you want."

"Yes, it is."

Will watched him a moment longer, with some remote hope that Hugo would say something to undo the hurt. But he'd said all he intended to say.

"I'll get Adele," Will murmured retreating from the bed, "she'll want to say good-bye. Take care of yourself, Dad."

There was no further response from Hugo, whether word or sign. Shaken, Will left him to his silence and headed out in search of Adele. He didn't tell her the substance of his exchange with Hugo; he simply said that he'd wait for her at reception. She told him she'd just been speaking to the doctor and he was very optimistic about Hugo's progress. Another week, she said, and he could probably come home; wasn't that wonderful?

It was raining now. Nothing monsoonal, just a steady drizzle. Will didn't shelter from it. He stood outside with his face turned up to the sky, letting the drops cool his hot eyes and flushed cheeks.

When Adele emerged she was in her usual post-visit flutter. Will volunteered to drive, certain he could shave fifteen minutes off the travel time and be back with the Simeon book before dark. She babbled on happily as they went, mainly about Hugo. "He makes you very happy, doesn't he?" Will said.

"He's a fine man," she said, "and he's been very good to me over the years. I thought when my Donald passed away I'd never have another happy day. I thought the world was at an end. But you know, you get on with it, don't you? It was hard at first because I felt guilty, still living when he was gone. I thought: That's not right. But you get over that after a while. Hugo helped me. We'd sit and talk and he'd tell me to just enjoy the little things. Not try and understand what it was all about, because that was all a waste of time. It was funny that, coming from him. I always thought philosophers were sitting talking about the meaning of life, and there's Hugo saying don't waste your breath."

"And that was good to hear, was it?"

"It helped," she said. "I started to enjoy the little things, the way he said. I was always working so hard when Donald was alive—"

"You still work hard."

"It's different now," she said. "If something doesn't get dusted, I don't fret about it. It's just dust. I'll be dust one of these days."

"Have you got him to go to church?"

"I don't go anymore."

"You used to go twice on a Sunday."

"I don't feel the need."

"Did Hugo talk you into that?"

"I don't get talked into things," Adele said, a little defensively.

"I didn't mean—"

"No, no, I know what you meant. Hugo's a godless man, and he always will be. But I saw the suffering my Donald went through. Terrible it was, terrible, to see him in such a state. And I know people say that's when your faith gets tested. Well, maybe mine did and it wasn't strong enough, because church never meant the same to me after that."

"God let you down?"

"Donald was a good man. Not clever, like Hugo, but good in his heart. He deserved better." She fell silent for a minute or so, then added a coda, "We've got to make the most of what comes along, haven't we? There's nothing certain."

VII

Will spent the rest of the evening with Thomas Simeon, burying himself in this other life as a refuge from his own. It was no use brooding on what had happened at the hospital, with a little distance (and a couple of heart to hearts with Adrianna), he'd be able to put the experiences in a sane perspective. For now, it was best ignored. He rolled a joint, pulled his chair over to the open window, and sat there reading, lulled by the spatter of the rain on the roof and sill.

He'd left off reading with Dwyer moving from occult waters, where she'd plainly been out of her depth, back into the relative comfort of simple biography. Simeon's ever-reliable friend Galloway reappeared at this juncture, having been moved by *"the commands of friendship"* (what had gone on between these two? Will wondered) to separate Simeon from his patron, Rukenau, *"whose baleful influence could be seen in every part of Thomas's appearance and demeanor."* Galloway, it seems, had conspired to save Simeon's soul from Rukenau's clutches; an attempt that, by Dwyer's description, amounted to a physical abduction: *"Aided by two accomplices, Piers Varty and Edmund Maupertius, the latter a disenchanted and much embittered acolyte of Rukenau, Galloway plotted Simeon's 'liberation' as he was later to describe it, with the kind of precision that befitted his military upbringing. It went without incident, apparently. Simeon was discovered in one of the upper rooms of Rukenau's mansion in Ludlow, where, according to Galloway: 'We found him in a piteous state, his once radiant form much wasted. He would not be persuaded to leave, however, saying that the work he and Rukenau were doing together was too important to be left unfinished. I asked him what work this was, and he told us that the age of the Domus Mundi was coming to pass, and that he would be its witness and its chronicler, setting down its glories in paint that popes and kings might know how petty their business was, and putting aside their wars and machinations, make an everlasting peace. How will this be? I asked him. And he told me to look to his painting, for it was there all made plain."*

"Only one of these paintings was to be found, however, and it appears that Galloway took it with him when he and his fellow conspirators left. How they persuaded Simeon to leave with them is not reported, but it is evident that Rukenau made some attempt to get Simeon back and that Galloway made accusations against him that drove him into hiding. Whatever happened, Rukenau now disappears from this story, and Simeon's life—which has less than three years to run—takes one last extraordinary turn."

Will took advantage of the chapter break to go downstairs and raid the fridge, but his mind remained in the strange world from which he'd just stepped. Nothing in the here and now—not the brewing of tea nor the making of a sandwich, not the din of raucous laughter from the television next door, or the shrill delivery of the comedian who was earning it—could distract him from the images circling in his head. It helped that he'd seen Simeon with his own eyes, living and dead. He'd seen the desperate beauty of the man, which had so fixated Galloway that he'd ventured where his rational mind had little grasp, to pluck his friend from perdition. There was something sweetly romantic about the man's devotion to Simeon, who was plainly of another order of mind entirely. Galloway did not understand him, nor ever could, but that didn't matter. The bond between them was nothing to do with intellectual compatibility. Nor, all smutty suspicions aside, was this some unspoken homosexual romance. Galloway was Simeon's friend, and he would not see harm done to one he loved: It was as simple, and as moving, as that.

Will returned to the book with his sustenance, unnoticed by Adele and, settling back beside the window (having first closed it, the night air was chilly), he picked up the tale where he'd left off. He knew, or at least thought he knew, how this story ended, with a body in a wood, pecked and chewed. But how did it arrive there? That was the substance of the thirty remaining pages.

Dwyer had kept the text relatively free of personal judgments so far, preferring to use other voices to comment on Rukenau, for instance, and even then scrupulously quoting both supporters and detractors. But now she showed her hand, and it was no stranger to the Communion rail.

"It is in these last years," she wrote, "recovering from the unholy influence of Gerard Rukenau, that we see the redemptive power of Simeon's vision at work. Chastened by his encounter with madness, he returned to his labors with his ambition curbed, only to discover that with all craving for a grand thaumaturgical scheme sated, his imagination flowered. In his later works, all of which were landscapes, the hand of the artist is in service of a greater Creation. The painting entitled 'The Fertile Acre,' though at first glance a melancholy night pastoral, reveals a pageant of living forms when studied closely—"

Will flipped the page to the reproduction of the painting in question. It was far less strange than the Rukenau piece, at least at first glance: a sloping field, with rows of moon-sculpted sheaves receding from sight. But even in the much-degraded reproduction, Simeon's sly skills were in evidence. He'd secreted animals everywhere: in the sheaves, and the shadow of the sheaves, in the foliage on the oak tree, in the cloak of the harvester sleeping beneath the tree. Even in the speckled sky there were forms hidden, curled up like the sleeping children of the stars.

"Here," Dwyer wrote, "is a mellower Simeon, painting with almost childlike pleasure the secret life of the world; drawing us in to peer at his half-hidden bestiary."

But there was more to the picture, Will sensed, than a visual game. There was an eerie air of expectation about the image, every living thing it contained (except for the exhausted harvester) in hiding, holding its breath as if in terror of some imminent deed.

Will returned to Dwyer's text for a moment, but she had taken her critique off on a hunt for painterly antecedents, and after a few sentences he gave up and returned to the reproduction for further study. What was it about the picture that so intrigued him? It would not have been remotely to his taste if he'd simply happened upon it, knowing nothing of the painter. It was far too coy, with its prettified animals peering out from their bolt-holes in the paint. Coy, and unnaturally neat: the corn in military array, the leaves in spiral bouquets. Nature wasn't like that. The most placid scene, examined by an unsentimental eye, revealed a ragged world of raw forms in bitter and unending conflict. And yet, he felt a kinship with the picture, as though he and its maker were, despite all evidence to the contrary, men of similar vision.

Frustrated that he could not better understand his response to the work, he returned to Dwyer's text, skipping the art critique—which was mercifully short—and moving on to pick up the biographical threads. Whatever she'd claimed about the mellower Simeon, the facts of his life did not suggest a man at peace with himself.

"Between August of 1724 and March of 1725, he moved his lodgings no less than eleven times, the longest period he spent in one place being November and December, which he passed in a monastery at Dungeness. It is not clear whether he went there intending to take vows. If so, it was a passing fancy. By the middle of January he is writing to Dolores Cruikshank—who had been one of Rukenau's cronies three years before but was now, in her own words, quite cured of his influence—and states: 'I am thinking of leaving this wretched country for Europe, where I think I may find souls more sympathetic to my vision than ever I have found in this too rational isle. I have looked everywhere for a tutor who might guide me, but I find only stale minds and staler rhetoric. It seems to me, we must invent religion every moment, as the world invents itself, for the only constant is in inconstancy. Did you ever meet a doctor of divinity who knew this simple truth; or if he knew it, dared speak it out? No. It is a heresy among learned men because to admit it is to unseat themselves from their certainties, and they may no longer lord themselves over us, saying: This is so, and this is not. It seems to me the purpose of religion is to say: All things are so. An invented thing and a thing we call true; a living thing and a thing we call dead; a visible thing and a thing that is yet to be: All Are So. There was one that we both knew who taught this truth, and I was too arrogant to learn it. I regret my foolishness every waking hour. I sit here in this tiny town, and look west to the islands, and pine for him like a lost dog. But I dare not go to him. He would kill me I think, for my ingratitude. Nor could I fault him for that. I was misled by well-meaning friends, but that's no excuse, is it? I should have bitten

off their fingers when they came to take me. I should have choked them with their prayer-books. And now it's too late.

"'I beg you, send me news of him if you have any, so when I look toward the isles I may imagine him, and be soothed.'"

This was powerful stuff, but difficult for Will to sympathize with. He had made his way in the world largely by defying tutelage, so this yearning for a teacher, so passionately phrased that Simeon might have been speaking of physical desire, seemed to him faintly preposterous. To Dwyer also. "It was," she wrote, "*an indication that Simeon was undergoing a profound psychological upheaval. And there was more; a good deal more. In a second letter to Cruikshank, written from Glasgow, less than a week later, Simeon's overripe imaginings are running riot: 'I heard from a certain source that the Man of the Western Isles has finally turned his golden architect to his purpose, and has the foundation of Heaven laid. What source is this, you ask? I will tell you, though you may mock me. The wind, that is my messenger. I have inklings from other sources, it's true, but none I trust as much as the wind, which brought me nightly such reports of all our Certain One has done that I began to sicken for want of sleep, and have retreated to this foul Caledonian town where the wind does not come with such fresh news.*

"'But what use is it to sleep, if I wake in the same state that I lay down my head? I must mend my courage, and go to him. At least that is what I think this hour. The next I may be of another opinion entirely. You see how it is with me? I have contrary thoughts on every matter now, as though I were divided as surely as his architect. That was the trick by which he turned the creature to his purpose, and I wonder if he sowed the same division in my soul, as punishment for my betrayal. I think he would do that. I think he would take pleasure in it, knowing I would come after him at last, and that the closer I came the more set against myself I would become.'

"Here," Dwyer wrote, "*is the first mention of suicidal thoughts. There is no record of any reply from the pen of Mrs. Cruikshank, so we must assume she judged Simeon so far gone he was beyond her help. Once only, in the last of the four letters he wrote to her during his Scottish sojourn does he refer to his art: 'Today I have conceived a plan as to how I may play the prodigal. I will make a portrait of my Certain One upon his island. I have heard it called the Granary, so I will make the painting surrounding him with grain. Then I will take it to him, and pray that my gift assuages his rage. If it does then I will be received into his house and will gladly do his bidding until I die. If it does not, then*

*you may assume I am dead by his hand. Whichever is the case, you will
not hear from me after this.'*

"This pitiful letter," Dwyer here remarked, *"was the last he ever
wrote. It is not the last we hear of him, however. He survives for another
seven months, traveling to Bath, to Lincoln, and to Oxfordshire, relying
on the charity of friends. He even paints pictures, three of which survive. None of them fit the description of the Granary painting he is
planning in his letter to Dolores Cruikshank. Nor is there any record of
his having traveled to the Hebrides in search of Rukenau.*

"It seems most likely that he gave up on the endeavor entirely, and
went south from Glasgow in search of more comfortable lodgings. At
some point in the travels, John Galloway tracks him down, and commissions him to paint the house he and his new wife (he had married in
September of 1725) now occupy. As Galloway reports in a letter, to his
father: 'My good friend Thom Simeon is now at work immortalizing the
house, and I have high hopes that the picture will be splendid. I believe
Thomas has it in him to be a popular artist, if he can just put aside
some of his high-flown notions. I swear if he could he would paint an
angel blessing every leaf and blade of grass, for he tells me he looks
hard to see them, noon and night. I think him a genius, probably; and
probably mad. But it is a sweet madness, which offends Louisa not at
all. Indeed she said to me, when I told her he looks for angels, that she
did not wonder that he failed to see them, for he shed a better brightness than they, and shamed them into hiding.'"

An angel blessing every leaf and blade of grass, there was an
image to conjure with, Will thought. Weary of Dwyer's prose now, of
guesswork and assumptions, he returned to *The Fertile Acre* and studied it afresh. As he did so he realized the connection between this
image and his own pictures. They were before and after scenes, book-
ends to the holocaust text that lay between. And the author of that
text? Jacob Steep, of course. Simeon had painted the moment before
Steep appeared: all life in terror at Jacob's imminence. Will had
caught the moment after: life *in extremis*, the fertile acre become a
field of desolation. They were companion creators, in their way, that
was why his eye came back and back to this picture. It was painted by
a brother, in all but blood.

There was a light tapping at the door, and Adele appeared,
telling him she was off to bed. He glanced at his watch. It was ten-
forty, to his astonishment.

"Goodnight then," he said to her, "sleep well."

"I will," she said. "You do the same." Then she was gone, leaving him to the last three or four pages of Simeon's life. There was little of any consequence in the remaining paragraphs. Dwyer's researchers ran out of steam two months or so before Simeon's passing.

"He died on or about July eighteenth, 1730," she wrote, "having reportedly swallowed enough of his own paints to poison himself. This, at least, is what is widely assumed to be the truth. There are in fact contradictory voices in this matter. An anonymous obituary in The Review, for instance, published four months after Simeon's death, hints darkly that 'the artist had less reason to die than others did to silence him.' And Dolores Cruikshank, writing to Galloway at about the same time remarks that 'I have been trying to locate the physician who examined Thomas's corpse, because I heard a rumor that he'd found curious and subtle dislocations in the body, as though it had been subjected to an assault before death. I thought of the "invisibles" you told me he had been so fearful of when you'd taken him from Rukenau's place. Had they perhaps mounted an attack upon him? But the physician, a Doctor Shaw, has disappeared apparently. Nobody knows where, or why.'

"There was one final oddity. Though John Galloway had made arrangements for his agents to collect the body and have it removed to Cambridge, where he'd arranged for it to be buried with due honors, when they came to do so the remains had already been spirited away. Thomas Simeon's last resting place is therefore unknown, but this writer believes his body was probably taken by land and sea to the Hebrides, where Rukenau had chosen to retreat. It is unlikely, given Rukenau's iconoclastic beliefs, that Simeon was buried in hallowed ground. It's more likely he lies in some anonymous spot. It is only to be hoped that he rests well there, the travails of his life ended before he had truly made any mark upon the art of his time.

"John Galloway was killed in 1724, accidentally shot during a military exercise on Dartmoor. Piers Varty and Edmund Maupertius, who assisted Galloway in the abduction of Simeon from Rukenau's house, both died young: Varty perished of consumption and Maupertius, arrested for smuggling opium in Paris, died of a heart attack in police custody. Only Dolores Cruikshank lived out her biblical span, and more, dying at the age of ninety-one. Much of the correspondence quoted here was in the possession of her heirs.

"As for Gerard Rukenau, despite four years of attempts by this author to uncover the truth behind his legendary existence, little beyond the information contained within these pages could be found. There is no trace of the house in Ludlow from which Galloway suppos-

*edly abducted him, nor are there extant any letters, pamphlets, wills, or
other legal documents bearing his name.*

"*In a sense, none of this matters, Simeon's legacy . . .* "

Will's concentration drifted here, as Dwyer again tried to fit
Simeon's work into an aesthetic context. Simeon the prophetic surre-
alist, Simeon the metaphysical symbolist, Simeon the nature painter.
Then the text just petered out, as though she could not find a personal sentiment that suited her, and had simply let the text come to
a halt.

He put the book down, and looked at his watch. It was a quarter
after one. He didn't feel particularly tired, despite all that the day
had brought. He wandered downstairs, and went to search the
kitchen for something to eat. Finding a bowl of rice pudding, which
had been one of Adele's coups as a cook, he retired to the living room
with bowl and spoon to indulge himself. Her recipe hadn't changed
in the intervening years: The pudding was as rich and creamy as he
remembered it. Patrick would go crazy for this, he thought, and so
thinking picked up the phone and called him. It wasn't Patrick who
answered, but Jack.

"Hey, Will," he said, "how ya doin'?"

"I'm okay."

"You called at the right time. We've got a little meetin' goin' on
here."

"About what?"

"Oh you know . . . stuff. Adrianna's here. Do you want to talk to
her?" He got off the line with curious haste, and put Adrianna on.
She sounded less than her best.

"Are you okay?" he said.

"Sure. We're just having some serious conversations here. How
are you doing? Have you made peace with your dad?"

"Nope. And it's not going to happen. He told me point-blank he
doesn't want me visiting him any more."

"So are you going to come home?"

"Not yet. I'll give you plenty of notice, don't worry, so you can
lay on a big Welcome Home party."

"I think you've partied enough," she said.

"Uh-oh. Who have you been talking to?"

"Guess."

"Drew."

"Yep."

"What's he saying?"

"He thinks you're crazy."

"You defended me, of course."

"You can do that for yourself. Do you want to speak to Pat?"

"Yeah. Is he around?"

"He is, but he's not . . . doing too well right now."

"Sick?"

"No, just a little emotional. We've been having a *heavy* conversation, and he's not in great shape. I mean, I'll get him for you if it's urgent."

"No, no. I'll call back tomorrow. Just send him my love, will you?"

"Do I get some too?"

"Always."

"We miss you."

"Good."

"See you soon."

When he put the phone down, he felt a pang of separation, so sharp it caught his breath. He imagined them now—Patrick and Adrianna, Jack and Rafael, even Drew—going about their business while the fog crept over the hill and ships boomed in the bay. It would be so easy to pack up and creep away, leaving Hugo to heal and Adele to dote. In a day he'd be back amongst his clan, where he was loved.

But there would be no safety there. He might forget the hurt of this place for a few days; he might party himself into a stupor, and put the memories out of his head. But how long could that forgetfulness last? A week? A month? And then he'd be taking a shower or looking at the moth on the window, and the story he had left unfinished would come back to haunt him. He was in thrall to it: That was the unpalatable truth. His intellect and emotions were too thoroughly engaged in this mystery for him to leave. Perhaps at the beginning he'd been merely a conduit, as Jacob had dubbed him, an unwitting sensitive through which Steep's memories had flowed. But he had made himself more than that over the years. He'd become Simeon's echo: a maker of pictures that showed the spoiler's hand at work. There was no escaping that role, no pretending he was just a common man. He had laid claim to vision and with it came responsibility.

If so, so. He would watch, as he had always watched, until the story's end. If he survived, he would bear witness as no one had ever done before: He would a tell a tale of near-extinction from the survivor's side. If not—if he was dispatched into an unnatural grave by the very hand that had made him the witness he was—then he would at least go knowing the nature of his dispatcher, and lie, perhaps, more quietly for the knowledge.

VIII

The pain killers Hugo had been administered denied him easy slumber. He lay as though upon a catafalque in the dimly lit room, while memories came to pay their respects. Some were vague, no more than murmurs and flutterings. But most were crystalline, more real to his heavy-lidded eyes than the idiot nurses who now and then came to check on his state. Happy visitations, most of them: memories of the halcyon years after the war, when his star had been in the ascendant. There had been a period of three or four years following the publication of his first book, *The Fallacy of Thought*, in 1949, when he had been the idol of every iconoclast in English philosophical circles. At the tender age of twenty-four, he had published a book that not only challenged the tenets of logical positivism (all metaphysical investigation is invalid, because it can never be verified), but also existentialism (the chief imperatives of philosophical study are being and freedom). He was later to repudiate much that he'd written in that first book, but that didn't matter now. He forgot his doubts, and remembered only the fine, high times. Debating at the Sorbonne with Sartre (he'd met Eleanor there that spring); making mincemeat of Ayers at a party in Oxford; being told by one of his sometime tutors that he was destined for greatness, that if he kept to his purpose he would change the course of European thought. All perfect nonsense, but he indulged it readily tonight, enjoying the gilded phantoms that glided to his bedside to pay him court. (Sartre was among them, as batrachian as ever, with Simone in tow.) Some of these tribute payers simply smiled and nodded at him, one or two were too drunk to say a word, but many chatted to him in a casual fashion—unimportant opinions, every one. But he listened indulgently, knowing they only sought to impress.

And then, more quietly than even the quietest of the crowd,

came one who did not belong among these blithe memories, and with him, his lady friend, watching Hugo from the bottom of the bed.

"Go away," Hugo said.

The woman—her companion had called her Rosa, hadn't he, out on the dark road?—studied him sympathetically. "You look tired," she said.

"I want the other dreams back," he said. "Damn it, you've frightened them off." It was true. The room had been vacated of all but these two: the smiling beauty and her gaunt and sickly groom. "I told you to *go away,*" Hugo said.

"You're not imagining us," Rosa said. Oh Lord, he thought. "Unless of course, we're *all* illusions. You imagining us imagining you—"

"Don't . . . bother," Hugo said, "I wouldn't let a first-year student get away with that sort of sophistry." Even as he spoke, he regretted his tone. He was supine and light-headed, lying in a bed: This was no time to be condescending. "On the other hand . . . " he began.

"I'm sure you're right," the woman said. She pinched herself. "I feel very real." She smiled, touching her breast now. "You want to feel?"

"No," he said hastily.

"I think you do," she replied, moving along the side of the bed toward him. "Just a touch."

"Your boyfriend's very quiet," Hugo said, hoping to distract her. She glanced back at Steep, who had not moved a muscle since arriving. His gloved hands were clinging to the rail at the bottom of the bed, and he looked so frail in the sickly light Hugo felt less intimidated the more he studied the man. The mesmeric strength he'd displayed on the road seemed to have run out of his heels; though he stared at Hugo hard, it was the fixedness of a man who lacked the will to avert his eyes. Perhaps, Hugo thought, I don't have to be afraid. Perhaps I can talk the truth out of them.

"Does he want to sit down?" Hugo asked.

"Maybe you should, Jacob," Rosa said, to which Steep grunted and retreated to the comfortless chair beside the door.

"Is he sick?" Hugo asked her.

"No, just anxious."

"Any particular reason?"

"Coming back here," the woman replied. "It makes us both a little sensitive. We remember things, and once we start remembering, we can't stop. Back we go, whether we like it or not."

"Back . . . where?" Hugo wondered, putting the question lightly, so as not to seem too interested in the reply.

"We don't exactly know," Rosa said. "Which bothers Jacob a lot more than it bothers me. I think you men need to know these things more than we women do. Isn't that right?"

"I hadn't thought about it," Hugo said.

"Well he frets noon and night about what we were before we were what we are, if you follow me."

"Every inch of the way," Hugo beamed.

"What a man you are," she said.

"Are you mocking me?" Hugo bristled.

"Not at all. I always mean what I say. You ask him."

"Is it true?" Hugo said to Steep.

"It's true," he replied, his voice colorless. "She's everything a man could ever want in a woman."

"And he's everything I ever wanted in a man," Rosa said.

"She's compassionate, she's motherly—"

"He's cruel, he's paternal—"

"She likes to smother—"

"So do you," Rosa pointed out.

Steep smiled. "She's better with blood than I am. And babies. And medicine."

"He's better with poems. And knives. And geography."

"She likes the moon. I prefer sunlight."

"He likes to drum. I like to sing."

She looked at him fondly. "He thinks too much," she said.

"She feels more than she should," he replied, looking back at her.

They fell silent now, their gazes locked. And watching them Hugo felt something very like envy. He'd never known anyone the way these two knew one another, nor opened his heart to be known in his turn. In fact he'd prided himself on how undiscovered he was, how secret, how remote. What a fool he'd been.

"You see how it is?" Rosa said finally. "He's impossible." She feigned exasperation, but she smiled indulgently at her beloved while she did so. "All he ever wants is answers, answers. And I say to him— just go with the flow a little, enjoy the ride a little—but no, he has to get to the truth of things. What are we here for, Rosa? Why were we born?" She glanced at Hugo. "More sophistry, eh?"

"No," Steep said, clucking at her. "I won't have you say that." He pulled himself to his feet, turning his gaze on Hugo. "You may not admit it, but the question runs in your head too, don't tell me it doesn't. It vexes every living thing."

"Now *that* I doubt," Hugo replied.

"You haven't seen the world through our eyes. You haven't heard it with our ears. You don't know how it moans and sobs."

"You should try a night in here," Hugo said. "I've heard enough sobbing to last—"

"Where's Will?" Steep said suddenly.

"What?"

"He wants to know where Will is," Rosa said.

"Gone," Hugo replied.

"He came to see you?"

"Yes, he came. But I couldn't abide his being here, so I told him to go away."

"Why do you hate him so much?" Rosa said.

"I don't hate him," Hugo replied, "I just don't have any interest in him. That's all. I had another son, you know—"

"So you said," Rosa reminded him.

"He was the heart of me. You never saw such a boy. His name was Nathaniel. Did I tell you that?"

"No."

"Well it was."

"So how did Will take it?" Steep said.

Hugo looked faintly annoyed to have been distracted from his reverie. "How did he take *what*?"

"Your sending him away?"

"Oh Christ knows. He's always been secretive. I never knew a thing he was thinking."

"He got that from you," Rosa observed.

"Maybe," Hugo conceded. "Anyway, he won't be coming back."

"He'll come and see you, one more time," Steep said.

"I beg to differ."

"Believe me, he will," Steep replied. "It's his duty." He glanced at Rosa, who now sat gently on the bed beside Hugo. She lay her hand on the patient's chest, lightly.

"What are you doing?" he said.

"Be calm," she told him.

"I am calm. What are you doing?"

"It can be bliss," she said.

Hugo appealed to Steep. "What's she wittering on about?"

"He'll come to pay his respects, Hugo—" Steep replied.

"What is this?"

"And he'll be weak. I need him weak."

Hugo could hear his pulse in his head now, its lazy rhythm soothing. "He's already weak," Hugo said, his voice a little slurred.

"How little you know him," Steep replied. "The things he's witnessed. The things he learned. He's dangerous."

"To you?"

"To my purpose," Steep replied.

Even in his present, dreamy state, Hugo knew they came to the heart of things: *Steep's purpose*. "And . . . what . . . *is* that exactly?" he said.

"To know God," Steep replied. "When I know God, I will know why we were born, she and I. We'll be gathered into eternity, and gone."

"And Will's in your way?"

"He *distracts* me," Steep said. "He puts it about that I'm the Devil—"

"Now, now," Rosa said, as if to soothe him. "You're getting paranoid again."

"He does!" Steep said, with a sudden fury. "What are those damnable books of his if they're not *accusations?* Every picture, every word, like a knife! A knife! Here!" He slammed his fist against his chest. "And I would have loved him! Wouldn't I?"

"You would," said Rosa.

"I would have treasured him, made him my perfect child." Steep rose from his chair now, and approaching the bed, he gazed down at Hugo. "You never saw him. That's the pity of it. For him. For you. You were so blinded by the dead you never knew what lived there, right under your nose. So fine a man, so brave a man, that I have to kill him, before he undoes me, utterly." Steep looked up to Rosa. "Oh be done with it," he said. "He's not worth the breath."

"Be done?" Hugo said.

"Hush," Rosa said. "Clear your mind. It's easier."

"For you maybe," he replied, trying to sit up. But the light pressure she had upon his chest was all she needed to keep him in his place. And the thump of his heart was getting louder, and the weight of his lids heavier.

"Shush," she said, as though to a troubled child, "be still . . . "

She leaned a little closer to him, and her warmth and her breath made him want to curl up in her arms.

"I told you," Steep said softly, "he'll see you one last time. But you won't see him, Hugo."

"Oh . . . God . . . *no* . . . "

"You won't see him."

Again, he tried to rise up out of the bed, and this time she let him come a little way, far enough for her to slip her arm around his body and draw him closer. She had started to sing: a soft and lilting lullaby.

Don't listen to it, he told himself, don't succumb. But it was such a gentle sound—so calm and reassuring—that he wanted to fold himself into the woman's arms and forget the brittleness of his bones, the hardness of his heart, wanted to sigh and suckle—

No! That was death! He had to resist her. There wasn't strength enough in his limbs to free himself. All he could hope to do was put some important thought between his life and the song she was singing, anything to stop him dissolving in her arms.

A book! Yes, he would think of a book he might write when he'd escaped her. Something that would touch and change people. A confessional, perhaps, told with all the vitriol he could muster. Something sharp and bracing, as far from this saccharine song as possible. He'd tell the truth: about Sartre, about Eleanor, about Nathaniel—

No, not Nathaniel, I don't want to think about Nathaniel.

It was too late. The boy's image appeared in his head, and with it the lullaby, full of sweet melancholy. He couldn't fully understand the words, but he got the gist. They were words of reassurance, telling him to close his eyes and sink away, sink away to the place beyond sleep where all the good children of the world went to play.

His eyelids were so heavy now he was looking through slits, but he could see Steep, watching him from the bottom of the bed, waiting, waiting . . .

I will not give you the satisfaction of dying, Hugo thought, and so thinking turned his gaze toward Steep's mistress. He couldn't see her face, but he felt the fullness of her breasts beside his head and dared think there was hope for him yet. He would fuck her in his imagination; yes, that's what he would do: put his erection between himself and death. He would strip her naked in his mind's eye and pin her down, make her sob with his assault till her throat was too raw for lullabies. He started to move his hips against the coverlet.

She stopped singing. "Oh now," she murmured, "what *are* you doing?" She pulled her blouse aside to indulge him, and his undisciplined mouth sought out her nipple, found it, and sucked. Her hand went down under the sheet, under the band of his pajamas, and touched him, tenderly. He shuddered. This wasn't what he'd planned; not at all. He was still a child, despite what she was stroking; still a baby, melting in her embrace like gray butter.

Some other story! Quickly, he had to think of some high and adult thought to speed the beat of his heart, or it would all be over. Ethics? No. Holocausts? No. Democracy, justice, the fall of civilization; no, no, no. Nothing was grim or great enough to save him from the breast, from the stroke, from the ease of lying here and letting sleep take him into darkness.

He heard his heart booming in his head, like syrup on a timpani. He felt the blood in his veins thicken and slow. He could do nothing. Nor, now, did he want to. His eyelids flickered closed, his lips lost their hold upon the nipple, and down he went, down and down, until there was no further left to fall.

IX

Will was awakened by the sound of the telephone ringing, but by the time he cleared the surface of sleep it had stopped. He sat up in bed, fumbling for his watch. It was a little after four: cold, dark, and still. He listened a moment and heard Adele say something, her words, which he failed to grasp, becoming sobs. Turning on the lamp, he found his underwear, pulled it on, and went out onto the landing in time to hear her putting down the phone. He knew what she was going to say before she turned her streaming face up to him. Hugo was dead.

If it was any comfort, the doctor on duty told them when they got to the hospital, he had died peacefully, in his sleep. Very probably heart failure, a man his age, having taken such a beating; but they'd know more tomorrow. Meanwhile, did they want to see him?

"Of course I want to see him," Adele said, clutching Will's hand. Hugo was still in the bed where they'd talked with him twelve hours before, his head propped on the mountainous pillows, his beard laid on his chest like a knitted platter.

"You should say your good-byes first," Adele said, hanging back to let Will approach the bed. He had nothing to say, but he went anyway. There was something faintly artificial about the whole scene—the sheet too perfectly smoothed, the body too symmetrically laid—why should he not also play a part? Bow his head, pretend to be bereft? But standing there looking at the manicured hands and the veins on the eyelids, he could only hear the contempt that had issued from this man over the years, the disparagement and the dismissals. He would never hear that litany again, but nor would he ever earn his way out of it, and there would be pain in that, by and by.

"That's it then," he said softly. Even now, though he knew it was absurd, he half expected his father to open a quizzical eye and call him a fool. But Hugo had gone wherever the sad fathers go and left his son to his confusions. "Goodnight, Dad," Will murmured, and turning from the bed let Adele take his place.

"Do you want me to stay with you?" he asked her.

"I'd rather you didn't, if you don't mind. I'd like to say a few things, just him and me."

He left her to it, wondering what she would say when he'd gone. Would there be tearful professions of love, unleashed now that she didn't fear his censure? Or just a quiet chat, his hand in hers, a gentle admonishment that he'd slipped away so suddenly, a kiss on his cheek with her good-bye. The thought of that moved him far more than the body had. Loyal Adele, who had built her late life around his father, made his comfort her ambition and his affection her touchstone, murmuring in the ruins.

Assuming she would take her time with Hugo he didn't head for the parking lot, which was garishly lit, but took a side door out into the hospital's modest garden. There was enough light shed from the windows for him to be able to see his way to a bench beneath a tree, and there he sat to ponder things awhile. After a few minutes he heard motion in the canopy overhead, then a few tentative trills, as the first birds called up the day. In the east there was a merest silver of cold gray. He watched it like a child watching the minute hand of a clock, determined to detect its motion, but its increments defied him. There was more to see around him, however. Rose bushes and hydrangeas, a wall covered with creeping vine, the murk still too thick to put color on the blooms, but rising by the moment, like a print developing in a tray, the tones dividing. On another day, he might have been enraptured, his eyes greedy for the sight. But now there was no pleasure in either the bloom or the day that was sculpting it.

"What now?"

He looked across the garden, in the direction of the voice. There was a man standing beside the viney wall. No, not a man. Steep.

"He's dead, and you'll never make your peace with him," Steep said. "I know . . . you deserved better. He should have loved you, but he couldn't find it in his heart."

Will didn't move. He sat and watched Steep wander in his direction, some part of him in fear, some part in bliss. This was what he'd come home for, wasn't it? Not the hope of reconciliation: this.

"How long has it been?" Steep said. "Rosa and I were trying to remember."

"Isn't it in your little book?"

"That's for the dead, Will. You're not yet numbered among them."

"Almost thirty years."

"Is it really? Thirty. And you've changed so much, and I haven't. And that's both our tragedies."

"I've just grown up. That's not tragic." He got to his feet now, which motion stopped Steep in his tracks. "Why did you beat my father half to death?"

"He told you."

"Yes."

"Then he also told you why."

"I don't believe you'd be so pretty. You're better than that. He was a defenseless old man."

"If I never touched the defenseless, then I would touch nothing," Steep said. "Surely you remember how quick my little knife can be."

"I remember."

"There isn't a living thing safe from me."

"Now you're exaggerating," said Rosa, drifting out of the shadows behind Steep. "I'm immune."

"I doubt that," Steep replied.

"Listen to him," Rosa said. "Sorry about your father. He needed a little tenderness, that was all—"

"Rosa—" Jacob said.

"So I rocked him for a while. He was so peaceful."

The confession was put so lightly Will didn't understand what was being said at first. Then it came clear. "You murdered him."

"Not murdered," said Rosa. "Murder's cruel and I wasn't cruel with him." She smiled, her face radiant, even in the murk. "You saw how he looked," she said. "How content he was at the end."

"I won't be going so easily," Will said, "if that's what you've got in mind."

Rosa shrugged. "It'll be fine. You'll see."

"Hush," Steep said. "You had your time with the father. The son's mine." Rosa threw him a baleful glance, but kept her silence. "She's right about Hugo," Steep went on. "He didn't suffer. And nor will you. I haven't come here to torment you, though God knows you've tormented me—"

"You began it, not me."

"You held on," Steep said. "Anyone else would have let go. Got himself a wife to love him, children, dogs, *anything*—but you, you held on, haunting me, bleeding me." He was speaking through gritted teeth, his body trembling. "It's got to stop," he said. "Now. Here. It stops here." He unbuttoned his jacket. His knife was at his belt, waiting for his fingers. There was no great surprise in this; Steep was here as an executioner. What surprised Will was how undistressed he was. Yes, Steep was dangerous, but so was he. One touch, flesh to flesh, and he could carry Steep away from this gray morning: back to that wood, perhaps, where Thomas Simeon lay, pecked blind. Where the fox loped; Lord Fox, the beast who had taught him so much. That wisdom was in him now. It made him sly. It made him sleek.

"Touch me then," he said to Steep, reaching out to his enemy, like Simeon showing off his radiant petal. "I dare you. Touch me. We'll see where it takes us." Steep had stopped in his tracks, studying Will sourly.

"You said he'd be weak," Rosa remarked, clearly amused.

"I told you to be quiet," Steep said.

"I've got as much right—"

"*Shut up!*" Steep roared.

"Why don't we just talk this out like reasonable people?" Will said. "I don't want to be haunted any more than you do. I want to let you go. I swear, I want that."

"You can't control it," Steep said. "there's a hole in your head where the world gets in. You probably get it from your crazy mother. A little touch of the psychic. It wouldn't matter if you were dealing with an ordinary man."

"But I'm not."

"No, you're not."

"You're something else. Both of you."

"Yes—"

"But you don't know what, do you?"

"You're more like your father than you think," Steep observed. "Both sniffing after answers, even though your lives hang in the balance."

"Well? Do you know or don't you?"

It was Rosa who answered, not Steep. "Admit it, Jacob," she said. "We don't know."

"Maybe I could help you," Will said.

"No," Steep replied. "You won't persuade me to spare you, so don't waste your breath. I'm not so afraid of my own memories that I can't endure them long enough to slit your throat." He slid the knife from its leather sheath. "The error wasn't yours. I accept that. It was mine. I was alone and I wanted a companion. I chose carelessly. It's as simple as that. If you'd been an ordinary child, you could have had your adventure and gone on your way. But you saw too much. You felt too much." His voice was thick with feeling, not all of it anger, not by far. "You . . . took me . . . to your heart, Will. And I don't belong there."

The light was strong enough, and Steep close enough, that Will could see just how sick with anticipation Steep looked. His face was white and fragile; his beauty—despite the beard and the dome of his brow—become almost feminine, almost lush, while the rest was wasted, his lips, his eyes, the curve of his cheek. He raised the knife, and at the glint of it Will remembered how it felt to have it in his hand. The heft of it, the ease of it. The way it had carried his fingers with it, to do its work. If Steep got within striking distance, there would be no hope of a reprieve. The knife would find Will's life and take it so quickly he'd barely know it was gone.

He glanced to his left, looking for the gate that led out of the garden. It was ten, maybe twelve yards from him. If he moved, Steep would intercept him in three strides at most. His only hope was to stop Steep in his tracks, and the only means he had to do that was a name.

"Tell me about Rukenau," he said.

Steep halted, his face—which in its present state was incapable of concealing his feelings—showing blank astonishment. His mouth opened, but no words emerged. It was Rosa who said, "You know Rukenau?"

By now, Steep had recovered himself enough to say: "Impossible."

"Then how—?"

"It doesn't matter," Steep said, plainly determined not to be distracted from his purpose. "I don't want to hear about him."

"I do," Rosa said, striding toward Steep. "If he knows something, then we should have it out of him." She pushed past Jacob and stood between Will and the knife. It was a little comfort, at least, not to be able to see the blade. "What do you know about Rukenau?"

"This and that," Will said, attempting to keep his manner light.

"See?" said Steep. "He knows nothing."

Will saw a flicker of doubt cross Rosa's face. "You'd better tell me," she said, softly. "Quickly."

"Then he'll kill me," Will said.

"I can persuade him to let you go," she said, her voice dipping close to a whisper. "If you can get a message to Rukenau, tell him I want to be back with him . . . "

Will caught a glimpse of Steep's face over her shoulder. He was tolerating this exchange, but not for much longer. If Will didn't supply further proof of his worth very quickly, the knife would be on him. He took a deep breath, then gave up the only other piece of genuine information he possessed.

"Back in the house, you mean?" he said. "In the Domus Mundi."

Rosa's eyes widened. "*Oh my Lord*," she said. "He *does* know something." She glanced back at Steep. "Did you hear what he said?"

"It's a trick," Steep replied. "It's something he found in my head."

"You never let me see that far," Will countered.

Rosa's eyes were back on Will, blazing. "I want to be back there," she said. "I want to see—"

She didn't have time to finish. Steep caught hold of her arm and pulled her away from Will. Her response was instantaneous. She wrenched her arm from his grip and struck Jacob in the face, almost casually. The blow caught him off-balance. He staggered back, more surprised, Will thought, than hurt. "Don't you *dare* lay a hand on me!" she spat at him, turning back to finish her interrogation of Will. "Tell me quickly what you know," she said. "You help me, I'll help you, I swear it!" She was genuine in this, Will saw. "I told you, I'm not cruel," she went on. "Jacob wanted your father dead, not me. He wanted you weak with grief." Behind her, Steep let out a growling din. She ignored it and kept talking. "We don't have to be enemies. We both want the same thing."

"And what's that?"

"Healing," she said.

And then Steep took hold of her again, more roughly this time, hauling her out of his path. This time she didn't strike him, but turned, loosing a curse at him. What happened next? It was so quick it was hard to tell. Will glimpsed the knife between them, moving as it had in the copse, like lethal lightning. Then it was gone, eclipsed by Rosa as she turned, its blade sinking into her chest. He heard her expel a breath, which turned into a sob, saw her turn her face to Steep, who in that same moment dropped his gaze to the place where the knife had gone. Drawing a second sobbing breath, Rosa pushed her assassin from her. He went, empty-handed, and she teetered for a few seconds, raising her hands to snatch at the blade, which was still buried in her to the hilt.

Her fingers found it and, with a cry that surely woke every patient sleeping in the hospital, pulled it out of her flesh and cast it to the ground. A strange fluid came with it, copiously, spreading down her blouse and into her skirt. She looked down at its progress with a kind of curiosity on her face. Then, lifting her head to fix Steep afresh, she stumbled toward him.

"Oh, Jacob," she sobbed. "What have you done?"

"No, no," he said, shaking his head, tears rolling down his cheeks. "That wasn't my doing—"

"Hold me!" she said, opening her arms and swooning toward him.

It was plain by his expression that he didn't want to touch her, but he had no choice. His body moved to catch her, his arms opening like a mirror of hers, then locking around her, the violence of her fall carrying them both to their knees. He didn't protest his innocence now. He simply lay his sobbing head on her shoulder and said her name, over and over.

Will didn't want to see the end of this. He had a moment to escape, and he took it, giving the pair a wide berth as he crossed to the gate. On his way, his eyes alighted on the murder weapon, lying in the dewy grass where Rosa had dropped it. His instinct was quicker than his doubts. In one motion he stopped and scooped it up, its weight exciting his hand as he went on his way. Only when he'd cleared the gate, and felt safe from pursuit, did he turn to look back at Rosa and Jacob. The pair had not moved. They were still on their knees, Steep clasping the woman to him. Was he sobbing? Will thought so. But the din of birds, rising everywhere to get about the business of the day, was so loud that his grief was drowned out.

X

Over the years, Will had needed to polish his powers of deception until they were virtually flawless—talking his way into places he was not supposed to go to document sights he was not supposed to see. They stood him in good stead in the hours following the confrontation in the rose garden. First in the hospital, minutes after the stabbing, signing the paperwork that allowed his father's body to be tagged and taken away, then in the car with Adele, heading back to the house—through it all he pretended a calm, subdued demeanor and carried it off unchallenged.

He didn't repeat Rosa's confession to Adele, of course. What was the use? Better that she believed her beloved Hugo had died contentedly in his sleep than be troubled with the truth, in all its grotesequerie, especially when that truth brought with it so many questions that Will could not answer. Not yet at least. Enough had been said in the garden for him to dare believe he might yet decode the mystery. Rosa's talk of Rukenau as a living presence (as impervious to the claims of age, it seemed, as she and Steep) and the notion that he was somehow a healer of her pain (had she been foreseeing the wound she was about to sustain?) were both new elements in the story. He had not yet put the pieces together, but he would. What he'd felt in the garden he felt still: Lord Fox remained in him, its spirit effervescent. It would sniff out the truth, however many carcasses it was hidden beneath.

No doubt that would be a dangerous process: Whatever murderous intentions Steep had harbored before dawn were surely multiplied a hundredfold now. Will was no longer simply an error of judgment, a boy with a hole in his head who'd grown into a too-adhesive man. Not only did he possess information (very little, in fact, but Steep didn't know that), he'd also witnessed the wounding of Rosa. As if all of that wasn't enough, Will now had the knife. He felt it tapping against his chest as he drove, secure in the inner pocket of his jacket. If for nothing more, Jacob would come to reclaim it.

Given that fact, Will wanted to separate himself from Adele as soon as possible. Plainly Steep had little compunction about harming people who got between him and his quarry; Adele's life would surely

be forfeit if she was in his path. Luckily, she was already in her pragmatic mode—her tears all dried, at least for now, as she listed all the
things she needed to do. There was the funeral director to contact, and
a coffin to choose, and the vicar at St. Luke's had to be told so that a
service could be arranged. She and Hugo had found a nice plot, she
told Will, near the west wall of the churchyard. Strange, Will thought,
for a man who had scowled at any profession of religious belief, to
eschew the clean ease of cremation in favor of burial among the God-
fearing elders of the village. Perhaps Hugo had done it for Adele's sake,
but even that in its way was remarkable: that he would put his own
feelings aside so as to accommodate her wishes. Especially this decision, this last. Perhaps he had felt more for her than Will had thought.

"He made a will, I do know that," Adele was saying. "It's with a
solicitor in Skipton. A Mr. . . . Mr. . . . Napier. That's it. Napier. I suppose you should be the one to contact him, because you're next of
kin." Will said he'd do that straight away. "First, some breakfast,"
Adele said.

"Why don't you go down to your sister's place for a few hours,"
Will said. "You don't want to be cooking food—"

"That's exactly what I *do* want to be doing," she said firmly. "I've
been happier in this house," they were driving up to the gate as she
spoke, "than any other place I've ever been. And this is where I want
to be right now."

She was plainly not going to be moved on the subject, and Will
remembered her stubbornness well enough to know that further
pressure would only entrench her. Better to eat some breakfast and
assess the situation when he'd filled his belly. He had a few hours of
grace, he suspected, until Steep made another move. There was
Rosa's body for Jacob to deal with, for one thing, that was assuming
she was dead. If she wasn't, he'd presumably be tending to her. She'd
sustained at the very least a grievous wound, delivered by a weapon
that carried more than its share of fatal capacity. But she had out-
lived a human span by many decades (she'd been there on the banks
of the Neva, two hundred and fifty years before), so she was clearly
not as susceptible to death as an ordinary human being. Perhaps she
was even now recovering.

In short, he knew very little, and could predict even less. In such
circumstances, eat. That was Adele's recipe, and by God, it worked.
Both their moods brightened as she cooked and served a breakfast fit
for suicidal kings: bacon, sausage, eggs, kidneys, mushrooms, tomatoes, and fried bread.

"What time did you get to sleep last night?" she asked him as they ate. He told her sometime after one-thirty. "You should lie down for a little while this afternoon," she said. "Two hours is not enough for anyone."

"Maybe I'll find a little time later," he said to her, though he would have to balance out the requirements of fatigue and vigilance to do so.

Fortified by food, tea, and a couple of cigarettes, he made the call to Napier the solicitor, for Adele's peace of mind. Napier expressed his condolences, and confirmed that yes, all the necessary paperwork had been completed two years before, and unless Will intended to contest his father's wishes, all of Hugo's money, and of course the house, would go to Adele Bottrall. Will replied that he had no intention of contesting, and thanking Napier for his efficiency, went to pass the news along to Adele. He found her at the door of Hugo's study.

"I think maybe you should go through his papers rather than me," she said. "Just in case there's, oh, I don't know, things from your mother. Private things."

"We don't have to do it today, Adele," Will said gently.

"No, no, I know. But when the time comes, I'd be more comfortable if you did it."

He told her he would and reported on his conversation with Napier.

"I don't know what I'm going to do with the house," she fretted.

"Don't even think about it right now," Will told her.

"I've never been very good with legal things," she said, her voice softer than he'd ever heard it. "I get confused when solicitors talk."

He took her hand. Her thin fingers were cold, but her skin was creamy soft, despite the years of washing and cleaning. "Adele," he said. "Listen to me. Dad was very organized."

"Yes," she said. "I liked that about him."

"So you needn't worry—"

Suddenly she said, "I loved him, you know." The saying of it seemed to surprise her as much as it did Will; tears came, filling her eyes. "He made me . . . so happy." Will put his arms around her, and she willingly took his comfort, sobbing against him. He didn't insult her grief with platitudes; she had loved this man with all her heart, and now he'd gone, and she was alone. There were no words for that. What little comfort he could offer he offered with his arms, gently rocking her while she cried.

He had seen mourning in a hundred species in his time. Made photographs of elephants at the bodies of their fallen kind, grief in every tiny motion of their mass; and monkeys, maddened by sorrow, shrieking like keening clansmen around their dead; a zebra, nosing at a foal brought down by wild dogs, head bowed by the weight of her loss. It was unkind, this life, for things that felt connection, because connections were always broken, sooner or later. Love might be pliant, but life was brittle. It cracked, it crumbled, while the earth went on about its business, and the sky on its way as though nothing had happened.

At last, Adele drew herself away from him, and mopping up the tears with a much used handkerchief, sniffed and said: "Well, this isn't going to get anything done, is it now?" She drew a sighing breath. "I'm sorry things were the way they were between you and Hugo. I know how he could be, believe me I do. But he could be so wonderful, when he didn't feel as if he had to show off. He didn't have to do that with me, you see. I doted on him and he knew it. And of course he liked to be doted on. I think most men do." She sniffed hard, and for a moment it seemed tears were going to come again, but she got the better of them. "I'm going to call the vicar," she said, tugging her mouth into a wan semblance of a smile. "We'll have to think of some hymns."

When she'd gone, Will opened the study door and peered in. The curtains were partially drawn, a shaft of sunlight falling across the littered desk and onto the threadbare carpet. Will stepped into the room, breathing the scent of books and old cigarette smoke. This had been Hugo's fortress: a room of great men and great thoughts, he'd been fond of saying. The shelves, which covered two full walls from floor to ceiling, were crammed with books. All the usual suspects: Hegel, Kierkegaard, Hume, Wittgenstein, Heidegger, Kant. Will had peered into a couple of these volumes in his youth—a last forlorn attempt to find favor with Hugo—but the contents had been as incomprehensible to him as a page of mathematical equations. On the antique table to the left of the window, the second great collection this room boasted: a dozen or more bottles of malt whiskey, all of them rare, and all savoured when the study door was closed and Hugo was alone. He pictured his father now, sitting in the battered leather chair behind his desk, sipping and thinking. Had the whiskey eased his understanding of the words, he wondered; had his mind slid through the forests of Kant more speedily when slickened by a single malt?

He crossed to the desk, where a third collection was gathered: Hugo's brass paperweights, seven or eight of them, set upon various piles of notes. If any private correspondence with Eleanor survived it would be here in one of the drawers. But he doubted its existence. Even assuming his parents had once been so in love as to exchange passionate *billets-doux*, he could not imagine Hugo preserving them after the separation.

There was a sheaf of papers lying on the blotting pad in the middle of the desk. Will picked them up and flipped though them. They seemed to be notes for a lecture, every other word contested, scribbled, and rewritten, portions of the text so densely annotated it was virtually indecipherable. Opening the curtain a little wider to shed a better light on the desk, he sat down in his father's chair and studied the chaotic sheets, piecing the sense of the text together as best he could.

We deal daily with the squalid facts of our animality, Hugo had written, *putting* (illegible) *a process of self-censorship so engrained we can no longer see it at work. We do not examine the excrement in the bowl or the phlegm in the handkerchief for moral or ethical* (he had first written *spiritual* in place of *ethical,* but struck it out) *indicators.* There followed a paragraph that he had excised completely, crosshatching it in his fervor to erase it. When the text picked up again, it was clearer, but still problematic:

Tears, we may allow, carry a measure of emotional significance. In certain (illegible) *sweat may be . . . (illegible) But as scientific methodologies become increasingly sophisticated their tools charting and (calibrating,* was it, or *calculating*—one of the two) *the nuances of the phenomenal world with an accuracy that would have been unthinkable a decade ago, we are obliged to reconfigure our assumptions. Chemical signifiers—the sap that oozes from our flesh and organs in response to emotional activity—may be found in all our waste products.* Beside this he had scrawled three question marks, as though he was here doubtful of his facts. He plowed on with his thesis nevertheless:

Emotion, in other words, resides in the most despised matter in our local parameters, and it will soon be within the realm of instrument sensitivity that the precise emotional source of these signifiers may be discovered. In short, we will be able to recognize a quality of mucus that carries traces of envy; a sample of sweat containing evidence of our rage; a portion of excrement that may be dubbed loving.

The perverse wit of his father's construction brought a smile to Will's lips; the way that last sentence had been cunningly con-

structed, phrase by phrase, to climax in the inevitable collision of the
sublime and the abject. Had Hugo seriously intended to deliver this
to his students? If so, it would have been quite a sight, Will thought,
seeing the import of what they were being told dawn on them.

There followed two and a half paragraphs that had been
scratched out, and then Hugo had taken up his argument in an even
more unlikely direction, his language growing steadily more ironic.
How are we to read and interpret these glad tidings? he'd written, *this
curious interface between emotions that we hold in high esteem and the
muck that our bodies ooze and expel? In passing these chemical signifiers into the living and sensitive matrix of a world that it pleases us to
characterize as neutral, are we perhaps influencing it in ways neither
our sciences nor our philosophies have hitherto recognized? And further,
in reconsuming the products of this now-tainted reality as food, are we
at some presently indiscernible level continuing a cycle of emotional
consumption: dining, as it were, on a salad dressed with other men's
emotion?*

*At the very least, let us admit the possibility that our bodies are a
kind of marketplace, in which emotion is both the coin and the consum-
able. And if we dare a braver stance, consider that the terrain we have
dubbed our inner lives is, in a fashion we cannot yet analyze or quan-
tify, affecting the so-called outer or exterior world at such a subtle, but
all-pervasive level that the distinction between the two, which depends
upon a clear definition of a nonsentient, material state and us, its
thinking, emoting overlords, becomes problematic. Perhaps the coming
challenge is not, as Yeats had it, that 'the center will not hold,' but that
the boundaries are blurring. All that constituted the jealously defined
expression of our humanity—our private, passionate selves—is in truth
a public spectacle, its sights so universally manifested, and so commonplace, that we can never gain the necessary distance to separate ourselves from the very soup in which we swim.*

Strange stuff, Will thought, as he laid the sheets back on the
blotting pad. Though the word *spiritual* had been very severely
ousted from the text, its presence lingered. Despite the dry humor
and chilly vocabulary of the text, it was the work of a man feeling his
way toward a numinous vision; sensing, perhaps reluctantly, that his
philosophies were out of breath and it was time to let them die.
Either that, or he'd written it dead drunk.

Will had lingered long enough. It was time he got on with the
business of the day, the first portion of which was contacting Frannie
and Sherwood. They needed to be told of events at the hospital, in

case Steep came looking for them. Unlikely, perhaps, but possible. Returning to the living room, Will found Adele busy on the phone, talking, he surmised, to the vicar. While he waited for the conversation to finish, he juggled the relative merits of delivering his message to the Cunninghams by phone or going down to the village to talk with them in person. By the time Adele was done, he'd made his decision. This was not news to be delivered down the telephone line; he'd speak to them face-to-face.

The funeral had been arranged for Friday, Adele told him, four days hence, at two-thirty in the afternoon. Now that she had the date set she could start to organize the flowers, the cars, and the catering. She's already made a list of people to invite. Was there anybody Will wanted to add? He told her he was sure her list was fine and that if she was happy to get on with her arrangements he would take himself down to the village for an hour or so.

"I want you to bolt the front door when I'm not here," he told her.

"Whatever for?"

"I don't want any . . . strangers coming into the house."

"I know everybody," she said blithely. Then, seeing that he wasn't reassured, said, "Why are you so concerned?"

He had anticipated her question and had a meager lie prepared. He'd overheard a couple of nurses talking at the hospital, he told her: There was a man in the area who'd been trying to talk his way into people's homes. He then described Steep, albeit vaguely, so that she didn't become suspicious about the story. He was by no means certain he'd succeeded in this, but no matter: As long as he'd sowed sufficient anxiety to keep her from letting Steep in, he'd done all he could.

XI

i

He didn't go straight to the Cunningham house, but stopped off at the newsagents for a pack of cigarettes. Adele had apparently spoken to others besides the vicar while Will had been in the study, because Miss Morris already knew about Hugo's demise. "He was a

fine man," she said. "When's the funeral?" He told her Friday. "I'll
close up shop," she said. "I want to be there to pay my respects. He'll
be missed, your father."

Frannie was at home, in the midst of housework, apron on, hair
roughly pinned up, duster and polish in hand. She greeted Will with
her usual warmth, inviting him in and offering coffee. He declined.

"I need to talk to you both," he said. "Where's Sherwood?"

"Out," she said. "He disappeared early this morning, while I was
still getting up."

"Is that unusual?"

"No, not when he's feeling unwell. He goes up into the hills,
sometimes stays out all day, just walking. Why, what's happened?"

"A great deal, I'm afraid. Do you want to sit down?"

"That bad?"

"I don't know if it's bad or good right now," he said.

Frannie untied her apron and they sat in the armchairs either
side of the cold hearth. "I'll keep this as short as I can," he said, and
gave her a five-minute summary of events at the hospital. She
offered a few words of condolence regarding Hugo, but then kept her
silence until he reported on the effect the name Rukenau had had
upon Rosa and Jacob.

"I remember that name," she said. "It's in the book, isn't it?
Rukenau was the man who hired Thomas Simeon. But how does that
all fit with the happy couple?"

"They're not a happy couple anymore," Will said, and went on
to tell her the rest. Her expression grew more astonished by the
moment.

"He killed her?" she said.

"I don't know if she's dead. But if she isn't, it's a miracle."

"Oh, my Lord. So what happens now?"

"Eventually Steep's going to want to finish what he started. He
may wait until dark, he may—"

"Just come knocking."

Will nodded. "You should pack up a few things and get ready to
leave as soon as Sherwood comes home."

"You think Steep'll come here?"

"He may. He's been here before."

Frannie glanced toward the front door. "Oh, yes," she said softly.
"I still dream about it. Dad in the kitchen, Sher on the stairs, me
with the book in my hand, not wanting to give it to him." She had
visibly paled in the last few moments. "I have a horrible feeling, Will.

About Sherwood." She got to her feet, wringing her hands. "What if he's with them?"

"Why are you even thinking that?"

"Because he never quite let go of Rosa. In fact he thought about her all the time, I'm pretty sure. He only admitted to it once or twice, but she was never far from his mind."

"All the more reason you should pack and be ready to go," Will said, getting to his feet. "I want us out of here the moment Sherwood comes back."

She headed out into the hall, talking as she went. Will followed. "You said earlier you weren't sure whether the news was good or bad," she remarked. "Seems to me, it's all bad."

"Not for me it isn't," Will said, "I've been living in Steep's shadow for thirty years, and now I'm going to be free of him."

"If he doesn't kill you," Frannie said.

"I'll still be free."

She stared at him. "It's as desperate as that?" she said.

"It is what it is," he replied, with a little shrug. "You know, I don't regret knowing him: He made me who I am, and how can I regret being me?"

"I'm sure a lot of people do. Being who they are, I mean."

"Well, I'm not one of 'em," he said. "I've got a lot more out of my life than I ever thought I would."

"And now?"

"Now I've got to move on. And I can feel it happening. Things moving in me."

"I want you to tell me."

"I don't think I've got the words," he said. He smiled. Then, seeing the quizzical look on her face, he said, "I'm . . . excited. I know that sounds weird, but I am. I was afraid there wouldn't be closure to all of this. Now I'm going to have it, one way or another."

She broke her gaze and hurried upstairs, calling back down to him as she reached the landing. "Have you got any way of defending yourself against him?"

"Yes I have."

"Are you going to tell me what?"

"Just something," he said, reaching inside his jacket and touching the knife, which he had not done since picking it up. He felt the thrill of its history in his fingers, and knew he should let it go. But his flesh refused. His fingers tightened around the gummy hilt, instantly addicted to the rush it supplied. Oh, the harm this knife could do—

It would not be hard to kill Steep, to slide the blade deep into his unhappy flesh and stop his heart. And if he had no heart to stop, then the knife would just go on cutting holes in him, until he was a thing of scraps, with the life pouring out everywhere.

"Will?"

Frannie was calling from upstairs.

"Yes?"

"Didn't you hear me? I've been yelling."

Lost in the blade's brutalities, he hadn't heard a word. "Is there a problem?" he called back, opening his jacket as he did so. His hand was still clamped to the hilt of the knife, his knuckles white.

"I'd just like a cup of tea!" Frannie yelled back.

It was such an absurd contrast—the knife in his hand, filthy with Rosa's juices, and Frannie's thirst for tea—that it snapped him from his reverie completely. He pulled his knife-hand free, and closed his jacket as though he were slamming Pandora's Box.

"I'll brew some," he said, and went through to the kitchen, his body aching as he moved. He could not at first understand why. It was only as he washed his hand clean under the cold tap that he realized it was the scars left by the bear that were troubling him, as though his system was punishing him for denying it the pleasure of the blade by awakening old pains. He would have to be careful, he realized. The knife was not to be treated lightly. If and when he wielded it, there could be consequences.

His hand cleansed, he busied himself about the kitchen preparing the tea, hearing Frannie thumping about above. He had brought the threat of calamity into her life, but her sanguine manner suggested she had vaguely expected it. Like him, she had been marked; so had Sherwood. Not as profoundly, perhaps, but then who was to say? If Sherwood had not fallen prey to Rosa, perhaps his mental state would have improved over the years, and Frannie would have been freed of her responsibilities to him. Courted, perhaps; married, perhaps. Lived a fuller, happier life than had been her lot.

He was filling the enamel teapot with boiling water when he heard the front door open and close, and Frannie calling from above, "Is that you, Sherwood?"

Instead of declaring himself, Will hung back. Frannie was coming downstairs now. "I was getting worried about you," she said. Sherwood mumbled something Will couldn't hear. "You look terrible," Frannie said. "What on earth's happened?"

"Nothing—"

"Sherwood?"

"I'm just not feeling very well," he said, "I'm going up to bed."

"You can't. We have to leave."

"I'm not going anywhere."

"Sherwood, we have to. Steep's come back."

"He won't touch us. It's Will—" He stopped in mid-sentence, and looked toward the kitchen door, where Will had stepped into view.

"Is Rosa still alive?" Will said.

"I don't know what you're talking about," Sherwood said. "Frannie, what's he talking about? We don't have to leave. Will's just here to cause trouble as always."

"Who told you that?" Frannie said.

"It's obvious," Sherwood replied, staring at the floor rather than his sister's face. "That's what he's always done."

"Where is she, Sherwood?" Will said. "Did he bury her?"

"*No!*" Sherwood shouted. "She's my lady and she's alive!"

"Where?"

"I'm not telling *you!* You'll hurt her."

"No I won't," Will said, stepping out of the kitchen. The move alarmed Sherwood. He turned suddenly and bolted for the front door.

"It's all right!" Frannie yelled, but he wasn't about to be persuaded. He was out of the door at a dash, with Will on his heels. Down the path to the gate, which was open, through it and off to the left, and left again, cannily avoiding the street, where traffic might slow him, to make for the open ground behind the house. Will pursued him up the dirt track, yelling vainly for him to stop, but Sherwood was too quick. If he made it out to the open field, Will knew, the chase was lost. Frannie had outmaneuvered him however. Out of the back of the house she came, and ran straight at Sherwood to intercept him, catching such firm hold of him he couldn't wrest himself free fast enough to be out of her grip before Will caught up.

"Calm down, calm down," she said to him.

He ignored her, and turned his ire on Will. "Why did you have to come back?" he yelled. "You spoiled everything! Everything!"

"Now you hush yourself!" Frannie snapped. "I want you to take a deep breath and calm down before you hurt somebody. Now ... I suggest we all go back into the house and talk like civilized people."

"First he has to take his hands off me," Sherwood demanded.

"You're not going to run, are you?" Frannie said.

"No," Sherwood replied sourly.

"Promise?"

"I'm not a kid, Frannie! I said I wouldn't run, and I won't."

Will unhanded him, and Frannie did the same. He didn't move. "Satisfied?" he sulked, and slouched back into the house.

ii

Once inside, Will left Frannie to ask the questions. Plainly he was the enemy as far as Sherwood was concerned, and there would be no answers forthcoming if he was doing the inquiring. She began by reciting a shortened version of what Will had told her. Sherwood was silent throughout, staring at the floor, but when she told him Hugo had been murdered by Steep and McGee—which fact she cleverly kept back (at first simply saying Hugo was dead) until almost the end of her monologue—Sherwood could not conceal the fact that he was shaken. He'd been fond of Hugo, according to his last conversation with Will, and became fidgety and then tearful as Frannie described Rosa's part in it.

At last he said, "I only wanted to save her from Steep. She can't help herself."

He looked up at his sister now, blisters of tears in his eyes. "Why would he hurt her if she wasn't trying to free herself? That's what she wants to do."

"Maybe we can help her," Will said. "Where is she?"

Sherwood hung his head again.

"At least tell us what happened," Frannie said gently.

"I met her a few days ago on the fells when I was out walking. She said she'd been looking for me; she needed my help. She asked me if I could find her somewhere to sleep, now that the Courthouse was gone. I knew I should be afraid of her, but I wasn't. I'd imagined seeing her again so often. Dreamed about meeting her just the way I did, up there in the sun. She looked so lonely. She hadn't changed at all. And she told me how happy she was to see me again. I was like an old friend, she said, and she hoped I thought of her the same way. I told her I did. I said I'd get her rooms at the hotel in Skipton, but she said no, Steep refused to stay in a hotel, in case somebody locked the doors while he was asleep. I don't understand why, but that's what she said. She hadn't even mentioned Steep until then, and I was disappointed. I thought maybe she'd come back on her own. But the way she begged me to help her, I saw she was afraid of him. So I said I knew a place they could go. And I took her there."

"Did you see Steep?" Frannie asked him.

"Later I did."

"He didn't threaten you?"

"No. He was quiet, and he looked sick. I almost felt sorry for him. I only saw him once."

"What about this morning?" Will said.

"I didn't see him this morning."

"But you saw Rosa?"

"I heard her, but I didn't see her. She was lying in the dark; she told me to go away."

"How did she sound?"

"Weak. But she didn't sound as if she was dying. She would have asked me to help her if she'd been dying. Wouldn't she?"

"Not if she thought it was too late," Will said.

"Don't say that," Sherwood snapped. "You said we could help her two minutes ago."

"How can I be sure of anything until I *see* her?" Will replied.

"Where is she, Sher?" Frannie said. Sherwood was looking at the floor again. "*Come on*, for God's sake. We're not going to hurt her. What's the problem?"

"I just don't want to *share* her," Sherwood said softly. "She was my little secret. I liked it that way."

"So she dies," Will said, exasperated. "But at least you haven't shared her. Is that what you want?"

Sherwood shook his head. "No," he murmured. Then, even more quietly, "I'll take you to her."

XII

Happiness had always sharpened Jacob's appetite for its contraries. Blithe from some successful slaughter he would invariably make straightaway for a cultured city where he could seek out a tragic play, better still an opera, even a great painting, that would stir up the rich mud of feelings he kept settled most of the time. Then he would indulge his passions like a reformed drunkard left among the brandy barrels, imbibing until he sickened on the stuff.

Unlike happiness, however, despair only wanted its like. When he was in its thrall, as he was now, his nature drove him to discover more of the very feelings that pained him. Others sought out palliatives for their wounds. He looked only for a harsher grade of salt.

Until now, he'd always had a cure for this sickness. When the despair became too much for him to bear, Rosa would be there to coax him from the brink of total collapse and restore his equilibrium. Sex had more often than not been her means; a little hide the sausage, as she'd been fond of calling it in her more bumptious moods. Today, however, Rosa was the cause of his despair, not its cure. Today she was dying, by his hand, her hurt too deep to be mended. He had laid her down in the murk of their shuttered house and, at her instruction, left her there.

"I don't want you anywhere near me," she'd said. "Just get out of my sight."

So he'd gone. Out of the village and up the slope of the fell, looking for a place where his despair might be amplified. His feet knew where to take him: to the wood where the damnable child had shown him visions. He would find plenty of fuel for his wretchedness there, he knew. There was nowhere on the planet he regretted setting foot more than that arbor. In hindsight he'd made his first error offering the knife to Will. His second? Not killing the boy as soon as he'd realized he was a conduit. What strange sympathy had been upon him that night, that he'd let the brat go, knowing that Will's mind was filled with filched memories?

Even that stupidity might not have cost him so dearly if the boy had not grown up queer. But he had. And undisturbed by the call to fecundity he'd become a far more powerful enemy—no, not enemy; something more elaborate—than he would have been if he'd married and fathered children. Steep had never been comfortable in the company of queers, but he'd felt, almost against his will, a kind of empathy with their condition. Like him, they were obliged to be self-invented; like him, they looked in at the rest of the tribe from its perimeters. But he would have gladly visited a holocaust on the entire clan if it would have kept this one, this Will, from crossing his path.

Fifty yards from the wood, he halted and, looking up from his boots, surveyed the panorama. Autumn was close; he could smell its bruising touch in the air. It was a time of the year he'd often set out walking, taking a week or two off from his labors to explore the backwaters of England. Despite the calamities of commerce, the country still possessed its sacred places if a traveler looked hard and carefully enough. Communing with the ghosts of heretics and poets he had strode the country from end to end over the years: walked the straight roads where the Behemists had gone and heard them call the very earth the face of God; idled in the Malvern Hills, where Langland had dreamed of Piers Plowman; strode the flanks of barrows where pagan lords lay in beds of dirt and bronze. Not all these sites had noble histories. Some were lamentable places, fields and copses where believers had died for their Christ. At Aldham Common, where Rowland Taylor, the good rector of Hadleigh, had been burned at the stake, his fire fueled from the hedgerows that still grew green about the spot; and Colchester, where a dozen souls or more had been cremated in a single fire for a sin of prayer. Then to more obscure spots still, places he'd found only because he listened like a fly at a dying man's mouth. Places where unhallowed men and women had perished for love or faith or both. He envied the dead, very often. Standing in a plowed field some September, crows cawing in the fleshless trees, he thought of the simplicity of those whose dust was churned in the dirt on his boots, and wished he had been born with a plainer heart.

He would not visit these places again, not this autumn, nor ever. His life, which had been in its curious way a model of stability, was changing: by the day, by the hour. Though he would certainly silence Rabjohns, the deed would not repair the damage that had been done. Rosa would still die, and he would be left alone in his despair, spiraling down and down. Given that there would be nobody to check his descent, he would keep going until he could fall no further. Then he would perish, most likely by his own hand, and his vision of a naked earth would be left in other, less honorable, hands.

No matter, he thought, as he resumed his trek toward the wood. There were plenty of men who were in unwitting service of the same ideal. He'd had the questionable pleasure of meeting a brace of them in his time: crazed military men, in a few cases, many of these psychotics; a few who knew precisely the name of their evil, and simply pleasure in it; but most—these the most interesting to speak with— men who were not personally inhumane, but who sat in their offices like bland accountants, orchestrating pogroms and ethnic cleansing for fiscal and political reasons. Whatever their natures, they were his allies to a man, as likely to wipe out a species as he, in their pursuit of ambition. Some did so in the name of profit, some in the name of freedom, some simply because they could. The reasons didn't really matter to him. What mattered was the consequences. He wanted to see Creation dwindle, family by family, tribe by tribe, from the vast to the infinitesimal, and he'd always needed the autocrats and the technocrats to help him achieve his goal. But whereas they were indiscriminate and crude, often unaware of the damage they'd done, he had always plotted against life with the greatest precision— researching his victims like an assassin, so as to be familiar with their habits and their hideaways. Once marked for death, few had escaped him. He knew of no finer feeling than to sit with one of the dead and record its details in his journal, knowing that when corruption had claimed the corpse he and only he possessed a record of how and when this line had passed into history.

This will not come again. Nor this. Nor this . . .

He had reached the border of the wood now. A gust of wind moved through the trees, overturning the coins of sun on the ground. He stepped among them, gingerly, while the wind came again, shaking down a few early leaves. He went directly to the place where the birds had sat that distant winter. A spring nest sat in the fork of the branches, forsaken now that it had served its function as a nursery, but still intact. Standing at the spot where the birds had fallen, he remembered the vision Rabjohns had made him endure with vile ease—

Simeon in the sunlight, a day from death, refusing the call of his patron, eloquent, even in his despair. And then the same scene, a day and a moment later. Simeon dead, under the trees, his body already carrion—

Steep let out a little moan, working the heels of his hands against his eyes to press the sight from his head. But it wouldn't go. It pulsed behind his lids, as though he were seeing it now for the first time in all its cruel particulars: the claw marks upon Thomas's cheek and brow, where the birds had skipped as they pecked out his eyes; the dung spattered on his thigh, where some animal had voided itself while sniffing around; the curl of hair at his groin, miraculously untouched though the manhood that had nestled there had been ripped away and left the place all blood, but for this golden tuft.

He did not imagine that killing the conduit would heal his deepening anguish. He was in its thrall now, and would be swallowed utterly. But when he finally succumbed to it, he would do so with his wits his own. There would be no trespasser among his thoughts, treading where his griefs lay tenderest. He would die alone, in the belly of his despair, and nobody would know what last thoughts visited him there.

It was time to go. He had put off the moment long enough, fearful of his own weakness. He would have liked to have his knife in his hands as he strode down the hill—it knew the business of slaughter more intimately than even he. But no matter. Murder was an old art; older than the beating of blades. He would find some means by which to do the deed before the moment was upon him: a rope, a hammer, a pillow. And if all else failed, he had his hands. Yes, perhaps that was best, to do it with his hands. It was honest, and simple, and like the error that would be connected with the deed, the work of flesh and flesh. The neatness of this pleased him and, in his present state a little pleasure, however it was won, was not to be despised.

XIII

There had been no butcher's shop in Burnt Yarley since the passing of Delbert Donnelly, and since the demolition of the Courthouse, no Donnellys either. Donnelly's daughter, Marjorie, and her family had gone to live in Easdale, and his widow had departed for the high life in Lytham St. Annes. The shop had passed though several hands—it had been a hairdresser's, a thrift shop, a greengrocer's, and was now once again a hairdresser's. The Donnellys's residence, however, had never been sold. There was no suspicious reason for this—Delbert was not reported to walk its bare boards, chomping on pork pies—it was simply an ugly, charmless house that had been overpriced for the market. For a buyer interested in privacy it was an ideal purchase, however, surrounded as it was by a seven-foot privet hedge that had once been Delbert's pride and joy. Had he paid as much attention to his personal appearance as he had to his hedge, some had observed, he would have been the smartest man in Yorkshire. Well, Delbert was probably more unkempt than ever, under St. Luke's sod, and his hedge had run riot. These days the Donnelly house could barely be seen from the road.

"Whatever made you think of bringing Rosa here?" Frannie asked Sherwood as he pushed open the gate.

He gave her a guilty look. "I've been coming here on and off as long as it's been empty," he said.

"Why?"

"Dunno," he said. "So I could be on my own."

"So all those times I thought you were out walking the hills you were here?"

"Not always. But a lot of the time." He picked up his pace to get a little ahead of Frannie and Will, then turning said, "I have to go in without you. I don't want you frightening her."

"Frannie should stay out here by all means," Will said. "But you're not going in alone. Steep may be in there."

"Then the three of us go in," Frannie said. "No ifs, ands, or buts." And so saying she strode on up the gravel path to the front door, leaving the men to catch up. The front door was open, the interior relatively bright. The source of illumination was not electric light but two gaping holes, the larger six foot wide, in the roof, courtesy of the storms that had raged the previous February. Ninety-mile gusts had stripped off the slates and icy rains had pummeled the boards to tinder. Now the day shone in.

"Where is she?" Will whispered to Sherwood.

"In the dining room," he replied, nodding down the hall. There were three doors to choose from, but Will didn't have to guess. From the furthest of them came Rosa's voice. It was weak, but there was no doubting its sentiments.

"Don't come near me. I don't want anyone near me."

"It's not Jacob," Will said, going to the door and pushing it open. There were shutters at the window, and they were almost closed, leaving the room murky. But he found her readily enough, lying against the wall to the right of the chimneybreast, her bags around her. She sat up when he entered, though with much effort.

"Sherwood?" she said.

"No. It's Will."

"I used to be able to hear so clearly," Rosa said. "So he hasn't found you yet?"

"Not yet. But I'm ready when he does."

"Don't deceive yourself," she said. "He'll kill you."

"I'm ready for that, too."

"Stupid," she murmured, shaking her head. "I heard a woman's voice—"

"It's Frannie. Sherwood's sister."

"Bring her here," Rosa said. "I need tending to."

"I can do it."

"*You will not*," she said. "I want a woman to do it. Go on," she said.

Will returned to the hallway. Sherwood was closer to the door, eager to be inside. But Will told him: "She wants Frannie."

"But I—"

"That's what she wants," Will replied. Then to Frannie, "She says she needs tending to. I don't think she'll let us take her to a doctor. But try to persuade her."

Frannie looked more than a little doubtful, but after a moment's hesitation she slid past Sherwood and Will, and entered.

"Is she going to die?" Sherwood said, very softly.

"I don't know," Will told him. "She's lived a very long life. Maybe it's time."

"I won't let her," Sherwood said.

Frannie was back at the door. "I need some gauze and some bandages," she said. "Go back to the house, Sherwood, and bring whatever you can find. Is there still running water in the house?"

"Yes," said Sherwood.

"You can't persuade her to let us take her to a doctor?"

"She won't go. And I don't think they'd be able to do much for her anyway."

"It's that bad?"

"It's not just that it's bad. It's *strange*. It's not like any wound I ever saw before," she shuddered. "I don't know if I can bring myself to touch her again." She glanced at Sherwood. "Will you *go*?" she said.

He was like a dog being sent from the kitchen, glancing over his shoulder as he went to be certain he wasn't missing a scrap. At last, he made it to the front door and slipped away.

"What do we do once she's bandaged up?" Frannie wanted to know.

"Let me speak to her," Will said.

"She said she didn't want either of you in there."

"She's going to have to put up with it," Will said. "Excuse me."

Frannie stood aside and Will stepped back into the room. It was darker than it had been a few minutes before, and warmer, both changes, he guessed, brought about by Rosa's presence. He couldn't even see her at first, the shadows around the mantelpiece had become so dense. While he was trying to work out where in the darkness she was standing, she said, "Go away."

Her voice gave him her whereabouts. She had moved four or five yards to the corner of the room farthest from the door. The shutters, which were to her left, remained open a little way, but the daylight fluttered at the sill, stopped from entering by the miasma she was giving off.

"We need to talk," Will said.

"About what?"

"What you need from me," he said, attempting his most conciliatory tone.

"I killed your father," she said softly. "And you want to help me? You'll forgive me if I'm suspicious."

"You were under Steep's influence," Will said, taking a tentative step toward her. Even that stride was enough to thicken the atmosphere around him. Though he stared hard into the corner where she stood the murk resembled a picture taken in too low a light level, a patch of granular gray.

"Under Steep's influence? Me?" She laughed in the darkness. "Listen to you! He needs me a lot more than I need him."

"Really?"

"Yes, really. He's going to go crazy without me. If he hasn't already. I was the one who kept his feet on the ground."

Will had perhaps halved the distance between the door and the corner of the room while she spoke, but he was no closer to seeing Rosa. "I wouldn't come any nearer if I were you," she warned.

"Why not?"

"I'm coming apart," she said. "I'm *unknitting*. It's a dangerous place for you to be right now."

"And Frannie?"

"She's fine. Women are a lot less susceptible. If she can seal me up, I may survive a day or two."

"But you won't heal?"

"I don't want to heal!" she replied. "I want to find my way back to Rukenau, and I'll be happy . . . " She drew a deep, ragged breath. "You asked me what I needed from you," she said.

"Yes—"

"Take me to him."

"Do you know where he is?"

"On the island."

"Which island?"

"I don't think I ever knew. But you know where he is—"

"No, I don't."

"But in the garden."

"I was bluffing."

There was a sound of motion from the corner of the room, and a wave of heat came against Will's face. He felt slightly sickened and was sorely tempted to retreat to the door. But he held his ground, while the murk in front of him coalesced, and he began to see Rosa. She was like a phantom of her former self, her once luxurious hair falling straight to either side of her hollow-eyed face. She had her hands clamped to the wound, but she could not entirely conceal its strangeness. There were motes of pale matter, some glinting like gold, skittering over her fingers. Some trailed up her body, clinging to her breasts. Others flew like sparks from a bonfire and, exhausting themselves in their flight, were extinguished.

"So you can't deliver me to Rukenau?" she said.

"I can't take you straight to him, no," Will confessed. "But that doesn't mean—"

"Just another liar—"

"I had no choice."

"You're all the same."

"He was going to kill me."

"It wouldn't have been any great loss," she said sourly. "One liar more or less. Just go away!"

"Hear me out—"

"I've heard all I want to hear," she said, starting to turn from him.

Without thinking, he moved toward her, intending another appeal. She caught the motion from the corner of her eye and, thinking perhaps that he meant her some harm, she reeled around. In that instant the fragments of brightness on her hands found purpose. They grew frenetic, and in a heartbeat fused, flying from her body in a bright thread. It came at Will too fast for him to avoid it, grazing his shoulder as it snaked toward the ceiling. A fleeting contact, but enough to throw him off balance. He reeled for a moment, his legs so weak they refused to bear him up. Then he sank down to his knees while a kind of euphoria ran through him, its source the place where the thread had grazed his flesh. He felt, or imagined he felt, its energy spreading through his body, sinew, nerve, and marrow illuminated by its passage, blood brightening, senses shining—

He saw the thread on the ceiling now, dividing again, like a string of tiny pearls dropped in defiance of gravity and snapping. They rolled away in every direction, the weaker ones going out on the instant, the stronger striking the walls before they ran out of light.

Will watched them as he might have watched a meteor shower, head back, mouth wide. Only when every one had been extinguished did he look back at their source. Rosa had retreated to her corner, but Will's eyes had been lent an uncanny strength by the luminescence and in the moments before it died in him, he saw her as he had never seen before. There was a creature of burnished shadow in her, dark and sleek and protean. A creature held in check by all that she'd become over the years, like a painting so degraded by accruals of grime and varnish and the hands of inept restorers that its glory was now no longer visible. And just as surely as his revelatory gaze saw through to the core of her, so she in her turn saw something miraculous in him.

"So tell me," she said, her voice low, "when did you become a fox?"

"Me?" he said.

"It moves in you," she replied, staring at him, "I can see it there, plainly."

He looked down at his body, half expecting the power that had emanated from her to have worked some physical change in him. Absurd, of course, it was still pale, sweaty flesh he was looking down at. More disappointing still, the last of the light was going out in him. He could feel its gift passing away and was already mourning it.

"Steep was right about you," she said. "You're quite a creature. To have a spirit move in you that way and not be driven crazy."

"Who says I haven't been driven crazy?" he said, thinking of the troubled path that had brought him to his possession. "You know that I see something in you, don't you?"

"If you do then look away," she said.

"I don't want to. It's beautiful." The burnished creature was still visible, but only just, its alien elegance receding into Rosa's wounded substance. "Oh Lord," he murmured. "I've just realized, I've seen this before. This body inside you."

She didn't speak for a moment, as though she couldn't make up her mind whether to be drawn into this inquiry or not. But she could not resist. "Where?" she said.

"In a painting," he said. "By Thomas Simeon. He called it the Nilotic."

She shuddered at the syllables. "Nilotic?" she said. "What is that?"

"Somebody who lives on the Nile."

"I was never," she shook her head; began again, "I remember an island," she said, "but not a river. Not that river, as least. The Amazon, yes. I went with Steep to the Amazon to kill butterflies. But never the Nile . . . " her voice was fading as she spoke, and the last of her other self disappeared from sight. "Yet . . . there's truth in what you say. Something moves in me as the fox moves in you."

"And you want to know what it is."

"Only Rukenau knows that," she said. "Will you take me to Rukenau? You're a fox. You can sniff him out."

"And you think he'll explain it."

"I think if he can't, then nobody can."

He found Frannie sitting at the bottom of the stairs, reading a yellow and well-trodden newspaper she'd found in one of the rooms. "How's she doing?" she asked.

He clung to the door frame, his limbs still weak. "She wants to find Rukenau. That's about the only thing in her mind right now."

"And where's he?"

"If he's anywhere, he's up in the Hebrides, where the book said he went. She doesn't know what island."

"Do you want us to take her?"

"Not us. Me. If you can bandage her up, I'll take over from there."

Frannie closed the newspaper and tossed it to the dusty boards. "And what do you think's on this island?"

"Worst case scenario, a lot of birds. Best case? Rukenau, and the Domus Mundi, whatever the hell that is."

"So you're suggesting I should stay here while you go off and see?" Frannie said with a tight little smile. "No, Will. This is my moment too. I was there at the beginning. And I'm going to be there at the end."

Before Will could respond the front door was pushed open, and Sherwood came in, nursing a bag of medications. "I've brought every bandage I could find," he said, dumping the bag in Frannie's arms.

"All right," said Will. "Here's the plan. I'm going to go back to my Dad's house and tell Adele I've got to leave—"

"Where are you going?" Sherwood wanted to know.

"Frannie'll explain," Will said, coaxing his still nervous limbs into motion. He lurched past Sherwood to the front door.

"Please be quick," Frannie said, "I don't want to be here when—"

"Don't even say it," Will told her. "I'll be quick as I can, I promise."

Then he was out of the door at a stumble, down the path, and out into the street. He wanted to run barefoot, or naked, the way he'd once imagined himself walking to Jacob in the Courthouse, the fire in him turning snow to steam. But he kept the desires of boy and fox hidden as he made his way home. They'd have their moment. But not yet.

XIV

i

Adele wasn't alone. There was a meticulously polished car parked outside the house and inside, its owner, a sprightly, even gleeful fellow by the name of Maurice Shilling, the undertaker. Will took Adele aside and explained that he was going to have to leave for a day or two. She of course wanted to know where he was going. He lied as little as possible. A woman friend of his was sick, he told her, and he was going to drive up to Scotland to do what he could to comfort her.

"You will be back for the funeral?" she said.

He promised he would. "I feel bad leaving you on your own right now."

"If it's a mission of mercy," Adele said, "then you should go. I've got everything under control."

He let her return to Mr. Shilling and went upstairs to fetch some more robust attire. Sitting on the bed lacing up his boots he chanced to glance out of the window just as the sun broke the clouds and lay a patch of gold on the hillside. The laces went untied as he watched, his spirit suspended in a moment of grace. This isn't a dream of life, he thought, nor a theory, nor a photograph. This is life itself. And whatever happens now we've had our moment, the sun and me. Then the clouds closed again, and the gold vanished, and heading back to the business of threading and tying he found his eyes wet with gratitude for the epiphanies he'd been granted. The visions in

Berkeley, the visitations of the fox, the touch of Rosa's thread: Each
had been a kind of awakening, as though he'd stirred from his coma
with a hunger for sentience that would not be sated by a single transformation. How many times would he have to waken, until he was as
conscious as a man could be? A dozen? A hundred? Or did it go on
forever, this rousing of the spirit, the skins of his slumbers stripped
away only to uncover another dream, and another?

Downstairs, Mr. Shilling was still talking about flowers, coffins,
and prices. Will didn't interrupt the negotiations—Adele was perfectly
capable of driving a hard bargain on her own—but slipped quietly into
his father's study to look for an atlas. All the oversized books were collected on one shelf, so he didn't have to search far. It was the same battered edition he remembered from his childhood, furnished whenever
he had geography homework. Much of it was out of date by now, of
course. Borders had shifted, cities been renamed or destroyed. But the
Western Isles were constants, surely. If wars had ever been fought over
them, the peace treaties had been signed centuries ago. They were
inconsequential, a scattering of colored dots on a paper sea.

Happy with his prize, he slipped out of the study and, collecting
his leather jacket from the hook by the door, left the house, while Mr.
Shilling waxed lyrical about the comfort of a well-pillowed coffin.

ii

"There's nothing to be afraid of," Frannie had been told by Rosa
when she went back in with the bandages. Her instincts had told her
otherwise. The cloying heat, the prickly air, the way the sound of
Rosa's pain drummed upon the boards: They conspired to give the
impression that an invisible thunderhead hung about the woman,
and no words from Rosa were going to reassure Frannie that she was
safe in its proximity. Fear made her swift. Instructing Rosa to clamp
her fingers around the wound to close it, she pressed a wad of gauze
against it as though it were a perfectly natural wound, and then
taped the gauze down with a half-dozen foot-long pieces of tape. To
finish the job off she wrapped a length of bandage around the
woman's body, though this was, she knew even as she was doing it,
absurdly overzealous. As she was finishing the work, however, Rosa
lay her hand on Frannie's shoulder and murmured the one word
Frannie had feared hearing, "Steep."

"Oh Lord," Frannie said, looking up at her patient. "Where?"

Rosa had her eyes closed, her gaze roving behind her lids. "He's
not here," she said. "Not yet. But he's coming back. I can feel it."

"Then we should get going."

"Don't be afraid of him," Rosa said, her eyes flickering open. "Why give him the pleasure?"

"Because I *am* afraid," Frannie said. Her mouth was suddenly arid, her heart noisy.

"But he's such a pathetic thing," Rosa said. "He always was. There were times when he was gallant, you know, and honorable. Even loving, sometimes. But mostly he was petty and dull."

Despite her newfound urgency, Frannie could not help but ask the begged question, "Why did you stay with him so long if he was such a waste of time?"

"Because it hurts me to be separated from him," Rosa said. "It's always been less painful to stay than to go."

Not such a strange answer, Frannie thought; she'd heard it from a lot of women over the years. "Well this time you go," she said. "We go. And to hell with him."

"He'll follow," Rosa replied.

"If he follows, he follows," Frannie said, crossing to the door. "I just don't want to face him right now."

"You want Will here."

"Yes, I—"

"You think he can save you?"

"Maybe."

"He can't. Believe me. He can't. He's closer to Jacob than he realizes."

Frannie turned from the door. "What do you mean?"

"I mean they're a part of one another. He can't save you from Jacob, because he can't save himself."

This was too big a notion for Frannie to chew on right now, but it was certainly something to be filed away for later consumption. "I'm not going to abandon Will, if that's what you're suggesting."

"Just don't depend on him," Rosa said. "That's all."

"I won't."

She opened the door and looked for Sherwood. He was sitting on the front step, stripping bark off a twig. Rather than call to him— who knew how near Steep was?—she went to the step to rouse him from his thoughts. When she reached him she saw that his eyes were red-rimmed. "Whatever's wrong?" she said.

"Rosa's dying, isn't she?" he said, wiping snot from his nose with the back of his hand.

"She'll be fine," Frannie replied.

"No, she won't," Sherwood said. "I feel it in my stomach. I'm going to lose her."

"Now stop that," Frannie gently chided him. She took the stripped stick out of his hands and tossed it away, then caught his arm and pulled him to his feet. "Rosa thinks Steep's in the vicinity."

"Oh, Lord." He glanced out toward the street. Frannie had already looked that way. It was empty, as yet.

"Maybe we should go out the back," Sherwood suggested. "There's a garden and a gate that takes us out onto Capper's Lane."

"That's not a bad idea," Frannie said, and together they made their way back down the hall to where Rosa was standing. "We're going out the—"

"I heard you," Rosa said.

Sherwood had already made his way through the kitchen to the back door and was now attempting to haul it open. It was stuck. He cursed it ripely, kicked it, and tried again. Either the kicks or the curses did the trick. With the hinges objecting noisily and the rotted wood around the handle threatening to splinter, it opened up. What lay beyond was a wall of green, the bushes, plants, and trees that had once been the Donnelly's little Eden now a jungle. Frannie didn't hesitate. She plunged into the thicket and plowed through it, raising lazy swarms of seeds as she went. Rosa plunged after her, stumbling a little, her breath raw.

"I see the gate!" Frannie called back to Sherwood and was within half a dozen strides of it when Rosa said, "My bags! I left my bags."

"Forget them!" Frannie said.

"I can't," Rosa said, turning around to head back to the house. "My life's in there."

"I'll fetch them!" Sherwood said, sweetly delighted to be of service, and darted back toward the house, with Frannie telling him to be quick about it.

There was a time of curious calm when he'd gone. The two women standing in the bower, dwarfed by sunflowers and banks of hydrangeas, bees in the rampant roses, and blackbirds in the sycamore. It was, for a moment, a haven, and they felt quite safe from harm.

"I wonder . . . " Rosa said.

Frannie looked round at her. She was staring at the sun, unblinking. "What?"

"If it wouldn't be better to just lie down here and die." There was a smile on her face. "Better not to know, better not to ask even . . ." Her hands had gone to the bandages, and were pulling at them. "Better to flow . . ." she said.

"Don't!" Frannie said. "For goodness' sake!" She pulled Rosa's hands away from the bandaging. "You mustn't do that."

Rosa kept staring at the sun. "No?" she said.

"No," Frannie replied.

Rosa shrugged, as though the notion had merely been a passing fancy, and let the bandaging alone.

"Promise me you won't do that again," Frannie said.

Rosa nodded, the directness of her stare almost childlike. Lord, but she was a strange creature, Frannie thought. One moment something to be feared, wrapped in thunder, then a bitter woman talking of the brotherhood of Jacob and Will, now this wide-eyed innocent, gently compliant when chastised. All of these were true Rosas, she suspected, in their way: All part of who the woman had been down the years, though perhaps the truest self lay under the bandages, aching to flow—

Only now, with this minor crisis managed, did Frannie's thoughts return to Sherwood. What the hell was he doing in there? Telling Rosa to stay put she went back into the house, calling for Sherwood as she went. There was no reply. She crossed the kitchen and stepped into the hallway. The front door was still open. There was no sound from either above or below.

And then he was there, in front of her, reeling out of Rosa's room with his eyes wide and his mouth wide, a low moan escaping him. And right behind him came Steep, his hand clasped to the nape of Sherwood's neck. They appeared so quickly Frannie stumbled backward in shock.

"Let him go!" she screamed at Steep.

At the shrill din she uttered, Jacob's glacial expression broke and, much to her astonishment, he did as she'd demanded. Sherwood's moan stopped and he fell forward, unable to bear himself up. She couldn't support him either. Down he went, sprawling, carrying her down to her knees beside him.

Only now did Steep speak. "This isn't him," he said quietly.

Frannie looked up at him, guiltily thinking—even in the terror and confusion of this moment—that she'd misremembered him. He wasn't the forbidding fiend she'd pictured whenever she recalled handing over the journal. He was beautiful.

"Who *are* you?" he said, staring down at brother and sister.

"Will isn't here," Frannie said. "He's gone."

"Oh, Jesus," Steep murmured, retreating down the hall. He'd got maybe three yards when Rosa said, "Another mistake?"

Frannie didn't look around. She turned her attention to Sherwood, who was still gasping on the ground. Sliding her hand beneath his head, she lifted him up a little way. "How are you doing?" she said.

He stared up at her, his mouth working to make a reply, but failing. He licked his lips, over and over, then tried again; still no sound emerged.

"It's all right," she said. "You're going to be all right. We'll get you out into the fresh air."

Even now she assumed he'd been saved by her intervention. There was no blood on him; no sign of assault. He simply needed to be taken out of this awful place, out among the sunflowers and the roses. Steep wouldn't stop them. He'd made an error in the shadowy room, thinking he'd caught Will. Now he'd realized his mistake, he'd let them go.

"Come on," she told Sherwood, "let's get you up."

She unknitted her hand from her brother's and put both her hands beneath him to help hoist him into a sitting position. But he just lay there, staring up at her face, licking his lips, licking his lips.

"*Sherwood*," she said, trying again.

This time she felt a tremor pass through his body, nothing significant. But at the same moment he simply stopped breathing.

"*Sherwood*," she began to shake him. "Don't do this." She pulled her hands out from under his body and head and opened his mouth to apply the kiss of life. Rosa was saying something behind her, but she didn't hear what and didn't care right now. She breathed into his mouth. Inflated his lungs. Put pressure on his chest to expel the air, then breathed into him again. Repeated the procedure; and again; and again. But there was no sign of life. Not even a flicker. His poor body had simply ceased.

"This can't be happening," she said, raising her head. Her eyes were stinging but her tears weren't coming yet. She could see Sherwood's killer perfectly clearly, standing in the hall on the spot to which he had retreated. If she'd had a gun in her hand she would have shot him through the heart right there and then. "You bastard," she said, her voice coming out like a growl. "You killed him. You killed him."

Steep didn't respond. He simply stared at her, blank-eyed, which only enraged her more. She started to step over Sherwood's body toward him, but before she could do so Rosa caught hold of her arm.

"*Don't,*" she said, pulling her back toward the kitchen.

"He killed him—"

"And he'll kill you," Rosa said. "Then you'll both be dead, and what will that prove?"

Frannie didn't want to hear reason right now. She tried to wrench herself free of Rosa's grip, but despite the woman's wound she remained strong, and would not let Frannie go. There was a moment of uncanny silence when nobody moved. Then came the sound of footsteps on the gravel path, and a moment later Will was at the doorstep. Steep looked round at him, his motion lazy.

"Stay away," Frannie yelled to Will. "He's," she could hardly get the words out, "killed Sherwood."

Will's gaze went from Steep's face down to Sherwood's body, then back up to Steep again. As he did so he reached into his jacket and pulled the knife into view.

"We're leaving," Rosa said to Frannie, very quietly. "We can't do anything here. Let's just . . . leave it to the boys, shall we?"

Frannie didn't want to leave. Not with Sherwood lying there on the dusty ground, glassy-eyed. She wanted to close his lids and put him somewhere comfortable, at very least cover him up. But she knew in her gut Rosa was right: She had no place in what was unfolding down the hall. Will had already made it plain to her how private his business with Steep was, even if it was fatal business. Reluctantly, she allowed Rosa to take her arm and coax her to the back door and out into the lush green.

Of course the bees were still droning in the overgrown flower beds. Of course the blackbirds were still raising a sweet chorus in the sycamore. And of course nothing was as it had been three minutes before, nor could ever be again.

XV

It was very simple. Sherwood, poor Sherwood, was dead, sprawled there on the floor, and his murderer was standing here right in front of Will, and there was a knife in Will's hand, trembling to be put to its purpose. It didn't care that Steep had once been its owner; it only wanted to be used. *Now, quickly!* Never mind that the flesh it would be butchering belonged to the man who'd treated it like a holy relic. All that mattered was to glint and glitter in the deed, to rise and fall and rise again red.

"Have you come to give that back to me?" Steep said.

Will could barely mumble a reply, his mind was so filled with the knife's advertisements for its skills. How it would lop off Steep's ears and nose, reduce his beauty to a wound. He sees you still? Scoop out his eyes! His screams distress you? Cut out his tongue!

They were terrible thoughts, sickening thoughts. Will didn't want them. But they kept coming.

Steep on his back now, naked. And the knife opening his chest— one, two!—exposing his beating heart. You want his nipples for souvenirs? Here! Here! Something more intimate perhaps? Meat for the fox—

And before Will knew what he was doing, his hand was up, the knife exalting. It would have opened Steep's face to the bone a moment later had Steep not reached up and caught the blade in his fist. Oh, it stung him, even him. His perfect lips curled in pain and a hiss came between his perfect teeth, a soft hiss that died into a sigh, as he expelled every vestige of air.

Will attempted to pull the knife out of his grip. Surely it would slice the sheath of Steep's palm and free itself; its edges were too keen to be contained. But it didn't move. He tugged again, harder. Still it didn't move. And again he pulled, but still Steep held it fast.

Will's eyes flickered from the knife to his enemy's face. Steep had not drawn breath since he'd exhaled his sigh; he was staring at Will, his mouth open a little way, as though he were about to speak.

Then, of course, he inhaled. It was no common breath, no simple summoning of air. It was Steep's reprise of what had happened on the hill, thirty years before, except that this time he was the one commanding the moment, unknitting the world around them. It flickered out on the instant, the floor seeming to fall away beneath their feet, so that Will and Steep seemed to hang above a velvet immensity, connected only by the blade.

"I want you to share this with me," Steep said softly, as though he had found a fine wine and was inviting Will to drink from the same cup. The darkness was solidifying beneath their feet: a roiling dust, ebbing, and flowing. But all around them otherwise, darkness. And above, darkness. No clouds, nor stars, nor moon.

"Where are we?" Will breathed, looking back at Steep. Jacob's face was not as solid as it had been. The once smooth skin of his brow and cheek had become grainy, and the murk behind him seemed to be leaking though his eye. "Can you hear me?" Will wanted to know. But the face before him continued to lose coherence. And now, though Will knew this was just a vision, panic began to grow in him. Suppose Steep deserted him here, in this emptiness?

"Stay," he found himself saying, like a child afraid to be left alone in the dark. "Please stay—"

"What are you frightened of?" Steep said. The darkness had almost claimed his face entirely. "You can tell me."

"I don't want to get lost," Will replied.

"There's no help for that," Steep said. "Not unless we know our way to God. And that's hard in this confusion. This *sickening* confusion." Though his image had almost disappeared completely now, his voice remained, soft and solicitous. "Listen to that din—"

"Don't go."

"*Listen*," Steep told him.

Will could hear the noise Steep was referring to. It wasn't a single sound, it was a thousand, a thousand thousands, coming at him from every direction at once. It wasn't strident, nor was it sweet or musical. It was simply insistent. And its source? That was coming too, from all directions. Tidal multitudes of pale, indistinguishable forms, crawling toward him. No, not crawling: *being born*. Creatures spreading their limbs and purging themselves of infants that, even in the moment of their birth, were ungluing their legs to be fertilized and, before their partners had rolled off them, were spreading their limbs to expel another generation. And on and on, in sickening multitudes, their mingled mewlings and sighings and sobs the din that Steep had said drowned out God.

It wasn't hard for Will to fathom what he was witnessing. This was what Steep saw when he looked at living things. Not their beauty, not their particularity, just their smothering, deafening fecundity. Flesh begetting flesh, din begetting din. It wasn't hard to fathom, because he'd thought it himself, in his darkest times. Seen the human tide advancing on species he'd loved—beasts too wild or too wise to compromise with the invader—and wished for a plague to wither every human womb. Heard the din and longed for a gentle death to silence every throat. Sometimes not even gentle. He understood. Oh Lord, he understood.

"Are you still there?" he said to Steep.

"Still here," the man replied.

"Make it go away."

"That's what I've been trying to do all these years," Steep replied.

The rising tide of life was almost upon them, forms being born and being born, spilling around Will's feet.

"Enough," Will said.

"You understand my point of view?"

"Yes—"

"Louder."

"*Yes!* I understand. Perfectly."

The admission was enough to banish the horror. The tide retreated and a moment later was gone entirely, leaving Will hanging in the darkness again.

"Isn't this a finer place?" Steep said. "In a hush like this we might have a hope of knowing who we are. There's no error here. No imperfection. Nothing to distract us from God."

"This is the way you want the world?" Will murmured. "Empty?"

"Not empty. Cleansed."

"Ready to begin again?"

"Oh no."

"But it will, Steep. You might drive things into hiding for a while, but there'll always be some mudflat you missed, some rock you didn't lift. And life *will* come back. Maybe not human life. Maybe something better. But *life*, Jacob. You can't kill the world."

"I'll reduce it to a petal," Jacob replied, lightly. Will could hear the smile in the man's voice as he spoke. "And God'll be there. Plain. I'll see him, plain. And I'll understand why I was made." His face was starting to congeal again. There was the wide, pale brow, sheltering that deep, troubled gaze, the fine nose, the finer mouth.

"Suppose you're wrong," Will said. "Suppose God wanted the world to be filled? Ten thousand kinds of buttercup? A million kinds of beetle? No two of anything alike. Just suppose. Suppose you're the enemy of God, Jacob. Suppose . . . you're the Devil and you don't know it?"

"I'd know. Though I can't see Him yet, God moves in me."

"Well," said Will, "he moves in me too." And the words, though he'd never thought he'd hear them from his own tongue, were true. God *was* in him now. Always had been. Steep had the rage of some Judgmental Father in his eye, but the divinity Will had in him was no less a Lord, though He talked through the mouth of a fox and loved life more than Will had supposed life could he loved. A Lord who'd come before him in innumerable shapes over the years. Some pitiful, to be sure, some triumphant. A blind polar bear on a garbage heap; two children in painted masks; Patrick sleeping, Patrick smiling, Patrick speaking love. Camellias on a windowsill and the skies of Africa. His Lord was there, everywhere, inviting him to see the soul of things.

Sensing the certainty moving in Will, Steep countered in the only way he knew how.

"I put the hunger for death in you," he said. "That makes you mine. We might both regret it, but it's the truth."

How could Will deny it, while that knife was still in his hand? Taking his gaze from Steep's face, he sought the weapon out, following the form of the man's shoulder, along his arm to the fist that was still gripping the blade, and down, down to his own hand, which still grasped the hilt.

Then, seeing it, he let it go. It was so simple to do. The sum of the blade's harms would not be swelled by his wielding of it, not by a single wound.

The consequence of his letting go was instantaneous. The darkness was instantly extinguished, and the solid world sprang up around him: the hall, the body, the staircase that led up to the open roof, through which straight beams of sun were coming.

And in front of him, Steep, staring at him with a curious look on his face. Then he shuddered, and his fingers opened just enough to allow the blade to slide from his grip. It had opened his palm, deeply, and the wound was seeping. It wasn't blood that came, however. It was the same stuff that had seeped from Rosa's body, finer threads from a smaller wound, but the same bright liquor. Fragments of it curled lazily around his fingers and, without thinking what he was doing, Will reached out to touch it. The threads sensed him and came to meet his hand. He heard Steep tell him no, but it was too late. Contact had been made. Once again, he felt the matter pass into him and through him. This time, however, he was prepared to watch for its revelations, and he wasn't disappointed. The face before him unveiled itself, its flesh confessing the mystery that lay beneath. He knew it already. The same strange beauty he'd seen lurking in Rosa was here in Steep too: the form of the Nilotic, like something carved from the eternal.

"What did Rukenau do to you two?" Will said softly.

The flesh inside Steep's flesh stared out at him like a prisoner, despairing of release. "Tell me," Will pressed. Still it said nothing. Yet it wanted to speak; Will could see the desire to do so in its eyes; how it wanted to tell its story. He leaned a little closer to it. "Try," he said.

It inclined its head toward him, until their mouths were only three or four inches apart. No sound escaped it, nor could, Will suspected. The prisoner had been mute too long to find its voice again so quickly. But while they were so close, gaze meeting gaze, he could not waste its proximity. He leaned another inch toward it, and the Nilotic, knowing what was coming, smiled. Then Will kissed it, lightly, reverently, on the lips.

The creature returned his kiss, pressing its cool mouth against his.

The next moment, as had happened with Rosa, the thread of light burned itself out in him, and was gone. The veil fell instantly, obscuring what lay beneath, and the face Will was kissing was Steep's face.

Jacob pushed him away with a shout of disgust, as though he'd momentarily shared Will's trance and only now realized what the power inside him had sanctioned. Then he fell back against the wall, clenching his wounded hand tightly closed to be certain no more of this traitorous fluid escaped, and with the back of his other hand, wiped his lips clean. He scoured every trace of gentility from his face as he did so. All perplexity, all doubt, were gone. Fixing Will with a rabid gaze, he reached down and picked up the knife that lay between them. There was no room for further exchange, Will knew. Steep wasn't going to be talking about God or forgiveness any longer. All he wanted to do was kill the man who'd just kissed him.

Even though he knew there was no hope of peace now, Will took his time as he retreated to the door, studying Steep. When next they met, it would be death for one of them; this would most likely be his last opportunity to look at the man whose brotherhood he had so passionately wanted to share. A kiss such as they'd exchanged was nothing to a man who was certain of himself. But Steep was not certain, never had been. Like so many of the men Will had watched and wanted in his life, he lived in fear of his manhood being seen for what it was, a murderous figment, a trick of spit and swagger that concealed a far stranger spirit.

He could watch no longer, another five seconds and the knife would be at his throat. He turned and took himself off across the threshold, down the path and out into the street. Steep didn't follow.

He would brood a while, Will guessed, putting his thoughts in murderous order before he began his final pursuit.

And pursue he would. Will had kissed the spirit in him and that was a crime the figment would never forgive. It would come, knife in hand. Nothing was more certain.

PART SIX

He Enters The
House Of The World

I

Will emerged from the Donnelly house in a daze and remained that way for the next hour or so. He was aware of getting into Frannie's car, Rosa half-lying across the seat behind him, and their taking off out of the village as though they had a horde of fallen angels on their heels, but he was monosyllabic in his responses to Frannie's inquiries, resenting her attempts to snap him out of his fugue. Was he hurt? she wanted to know. He told her no. And Steep, what about Steep? Alive, he told her. Hurt? she asked. Yes, he told her. Badly enough to kill him? she asked. He told her no. Pity, she said.

A little while later, they stopped at a garage and Frannie got out to use the pay phone. He didn't care why. But she told him anyway when she got back into the driver's seat. She'd called the police, to tell them where to find Sherwood's body. She was stupid not to have done it earlier, she said. Maybe they would have caught Steep.

"Never," he said.

They drove on again in silence. Rain began to spatter the windshield, fat drops slapping hard against the glass. He wound the window halfway down, and the rain came in against his face, and the smell of the rain too, tangy, metallic. Slowly, the chill began to rouse him from his trance. The numbness in his knife hand started to recede, and his fingers and palm began instead to ache. As the minutes past he began to pay some attention to the journey he was on, though there was nothing of any great significance to be noted. The roads they were traveling were neither jammed nor deserted, the weather neither foul nor fine; sometimes the clouds would unleash a little rain, sometimes they would show the sliver of blue. It was all reassuringly mundane, and he took refuge from his memories of Steep's vision by making himself its witness. There to his left was a car carrying two nuns and a child; there was a woman putting on lipstick as she drove; there was a bridge being demolished and a train running parallel to the motorway for a little distance, with men and women rocking in its windows, staring out, glassy-eyed. There was a sign, pointing north to Glasgow: one hundred eighty miles.

And then without warning, Frannie said, "I'm sorry. We have to stop," and bringing the vehicle over to the side of the highway, got out. It was all Will could do to stir himself from his seat, but at length he did so. The rain was coming on again; his scalp ached where the drops struck.

"Are you sick?" he asked her. It was the first time he'd put a sentence together since they'd left the village, and it took effort.

"No," Frannie said, wiping rain from her eyes.

"Then what's wrong?"

"I have to go back," she said. "I can't . . . " She shook her head, plainly enraged at herself. "I shouldn't have left him. What was I thinking? He's my own brother."

"He's dead," Will said. "You can't help him."

She covered her mouth with her hand, still shaking her head. There were tears mingling with the rain, running down her face.

"If you want to go back," Will said, "we'll go back."

Frannie's hand slid from her face. "I don't know what I want," she said.

"Then what would *Sherwood* have wanted?"

Frannie gazed forlornly at the bundled figure in the back of the car. "He would have done his damnedest to make Rosa happy. Lord knows why, but that's what he would have done." She looked at Will now, her expression close to utter despair. "You know, I've spent most of my adult life doing things to accommodate him?" she said. "I suppose I may as well do this one last thing." She sighed. "But this *is* the last, damn it."

Will took over the wheel for the next stage of the journey.

"Where are we headed?" he wanted to know.

"To Oban," Frannie told him.

"What's in Oban?"

"It's where you catch the ferries for the islands."

"How do you know?"

"Because I almost went, five or six years ago, with a group from the church. To see Iona. But I canceled at the last minute."

"Sherwood?"

"Of course. He didn't want to be left alone. So I didn't go."

"We still don't know which island we're heading for," Will said. "I got an old atlas from the house. Do you want to run through the names with Rosa, to see if any of them ring a bell?" He glanced over his shoulder. "Are you awake?"

"Always," Rosa said. Her voice was weak.

"How are you feeling?"

"Tired," she said.

"How's the bandage holding up?" Frannie asked her.

"It's intact," Rosa said. "I'm not going to die on you, don't worry. I'll hold on till I see Rukenau."

"Where's the atlas?" Frannie wanted to know.

"On the floor behind you," Will told her. She reached round and picked it up. "Have you considered that Rukenau may be dead?" Will said to Rosa.

"He had no plans to die," Rosa replied.

"He might have done it anyway."

"Then I'll find his grave and lie down with him," she said. "And maybe his dust will forgive mine."

Frannie had found the Western Isles in the atlas, and now began to recite their names, starting with the Outer Hebrides. "Lewis, Harris, North Uist, South Uist, Barra, Benbecula, and Arran." Then on to the Inner, "Mull, Coll, Tiree, Islay, Skye . . . " Rosa knew none of them. There were some, Frannie pointed out, that were too small to be named in the atlas; maybe it was one of them. When they reached Oban they'd get a more detailed map, and try again. Rosa wasn't very optimistic. She'd never been very good remembering names, she said. That had always been Steep's forte. She'd been good with faces, however, whereas he—

"Let's not talk about him." Frannie said, and Rosa fell silent.

So on they went. Through the Lake District to the Scottish border, and on, as the afternoon dwindled, past the shipyards of Clydesbank, alongside Loch Lomond and on through Luss and Crianlarich up to Tyndrum. There was for Will an almost sublime moment a few miles short of Oban when the wind brought the smell of the sea his way. Forty some years on the planet, and the chill scent of sharp salt still moved him, bringing back childhood dreams of the faraway. He had long ago made these dreams a reality, of course, seen more of the world than most. But the promise of sea and horizon still caught at his heart, and tonight, with the last of the light sinking west, he knew why. They were the masks of something far more profound, those dreams of perfect islands where perfect love might be found. Was it any wonder his spirits rose as the road brought them down through the steep town to the harbor? Here, for the first time, he felt as if the physical world was in step with its deeper significance, the forms of his yearning made concrete. Here was the busy quayside from which they would depart, here was the Sound of Mull, its unwelcoming waters leading the eye out toward the sea. What lay across those waters, far from the comfort of this little harbor, was not just an island; it was the possibility that his spirit's voyage would find completion, where he would come to know, perhaps, why God had seeded him with yearning.

II

He had expected Oban to be just a bland little ferry port, but it surprised him. Though night had fallen by the time they found their way down to the quay, both town and harbor were still abuzz: the last of the summer's tourists window-shopping or out to drink or dine; a gang of youths playing football on the Esplanade; a small flotilla of fishing boats heading out on the night tide.

There was a ferry leaving as they arrived at the dock, all alive with lights. Will parked the car beside the ticket office, which was in the process of closing up for the night. A somewhat severe looking woman told Will that the next sailing would be at seven the following morning, and that no, he didn't need to book passage.

"You can get aboard at six," the woman said.

"With the car?"

"Aye, you can take your vehicle. But the morning boat's only for the Inner islands. Which were you headin' for?"

Will told her he hadn't yet made up his mind. She gave him a small booklet of timetables and fares, and along with it a glossy brochure describing the various islands the Caledonian MacBrayne ferries visited. Then she said again that the first sailing was at seven sharp the following morning and pulled the ticket window shutter down.

Will returned to the car with the brochures and the information, only to find the vehicle empty. Frannie he discovered sitting on the harbor wall, watching the departing fishing boats. Rosa, she informed him, had taken herself off walking, refusing Frannie's offer of accompaniment.

"Where did she go?" Will asked.

Frannie pointed to the distant harbor wall, which jutted out into the sound.

"I suppose it's stupid to worry about her," Will said. "I mean, I'm sure she can look after herself. Still . . . ." He returned his gaze to Frannie, who was staring down into the dark waters lapping against the wall seven or eight feet below. "You look deep in thought," he remarked.

"Not really," she said, almost coyly, as though she were a little embarrassed to admit the fact.

"Tell me."

"Well, I was just thinking about a sermon, of all things."

"A sermon?"

"Yes. We had a visiting vicar at St. Luke's three Sundays ago. He was pretty good, actually. He talked about—what was the phrase he had?—doing holy work in a secular world." She glanced up at Will. "That's what this trip feels like, at least to me. It's as though we were on a pilgrimage. Does that sound daft?"

"You've sounded dafter."

She smiled, still looking at the water. "I don't mind," she said. "I've been sensible for far too long." She looked at him again, her meditative mood passed. "You know what?" she said. "I'm *starved.*"

"Should we try and check into a hotel?"

"No," she said. "I vote we just eat and then sleep in the car. What time does the ferry depart?"

"Seven o'clock sharp," Will said. Then, with a fatalistic shrug, "Of course we're not sure if it's even going where we need it to go."

"I say we go anyway," Frannie said. "Go and never come back."

"Don't pilgrims usually return home again?"

"Only if there's something to go home *for.*"

They walked along the esplanade looking for somewhere to eat, and as they walked Frannie said, "Rosa doesn't think you can be trusted."

"Why the hell not?"

"Because all you care about is Steep. Or you and Steep."

"When did she say this?"

"When I was bandaging her up."

"She doesn't know what's she's talking about," Will said.

They walked in a silence for a little distance, past a couple of lovers who were leaning against the harbor wall, whispering and kissing.

"Are you going to tell me what happened in the house?" Frannie finally said.

"Isn't it pretty obvious? I tried to kill him."

"But you didn't do it?"

"As I said, I tried. Then he grabbed hold of the knife, and . . . and I got a little glimpse of what I think he was before he became Jacob Steep."

"And what's that?"

"It's what Simeon painted. The thing that built the Domus Mundi for Rukenau. A Nilotic."

"Do you think Rosa's one as well?"

"Who knows? I'm just trying to put the pieces together. What do we know? Well, we know Rukenau was some kind of mystic. And I'm assuming he found these creatures—"

"On the Nile?"

"That's all the word means, as far as I know. It doesn't have any mystical significance."

"Then what? You think they literally built a house?"

"Don't you?"

"Not necessarily," Frannie said. "A church can be stones and a spire, but it can also be the middle of a field, or the bank of a river. Any place people gather to worship God."

It was plain she'd given the matter considerable thought, and Will liked her observations. "So the Domus Mundi could be," he struggled for the words to catch the idea, "a place where the world gathers?"

"It doesn't make much sense when you put it like that."

"If nothing else," Will said, "it reminds me not to be so damn *literal*. What's all this about? It's not about walls and roofs. It's about . . . " Again, he struggled for the words. But this time he had them, from Bethlynn, of all people. "Working change and inducing visions."

"And you think that's what Steep's trying to do?"

"In his screwed up way, yes, I think it is."

"Do you feel sorry for him?"

"Is that what Rosa told you?"

"No, I'm just trying to understand what's gone on between you."

"He murdered Sherwood. That makes him my enemy. But if I

had a knife in my hand now, and he was standing in front of me, I couldn't kill him. Not anymore."

"That's pretty much what I thought you'd say," Frannie said. She had come to a halt and now pointed across the road. "I spy a fish and chip shop."

"Before we get to the fish and chips, I want us to finish this conversation. It's important you feel you can trust me."

"I do. I think. I suppose I'd prefer if you were ready to kill him on sight after what he did. But that wouldn't be very Christian of me. The thing is, we're just ordinary people—"

"No, we're not."

"I am."

"You wouldn't be here—"

"*I am*," she insisted. "Really, Will. I'm an ordinary person. When I think about what I'm doing here it puts the fear of God into me. I'm not ready for this, not even a little. I go to church every Sunday, and I listen to the sermon, and do my best to be a good Christian woman for the next six days. That's the limit of my religious experience."

"But that's what this is," Will said. "You know that, don't you?"

She looked past him. "Yes. I know that's what this is," she said. "I just don't know if I'm ready for that."

"If we were ready it wouldn't be happening to us," Will said. "I think we have to be afraid. At least a little. We have to feel like we're out of our depth."

"Oh Lord," she said, expelling the words on a sigh. "Well, we are that."

"I was hungry when we started this conversation," Will said. "Now I'm ravenous."

"So we can eat?"

"We can eat."

There were delicious decisions to be made in the fish and chip shop. Fresh haddock or fresh scaithe? A glutton's portion of chips, or one size larger? Bread and butter with that? And salt and vinegar? And, perhaps the most significant choice of them all: Whether to eat it on the premises (there was a row of plastic-topped tables along one wall, beneath a mirror decorated with painted fish) or to have it wrapped in yesterday's *Scottish Times* and devour it al fresco, sitting on the harbor wall? They decided on the former, for practicality's sake. It would be easier to study the brochures Will had been given if they were sitting at a table. But the brochures were neglected for the next fifteen minutes while they ate. It wasn't until Will had subdued the ache in his belly that he started to flip through the *Guide to the Islands*. It wasn't very illuminating, just a predictably fulsome description of the glories of the Western Isles: their unspoiled beaches, their peerless fishing, their breathtaking scenery. There were thumbnail sketches of each of the islands, accompanied in several cases by a photograph. Skye was "the island famed in song and legend," Bute boasted, "the most spectacular Victorian mansion house in Britain," Tiree, "whose name means the granary of the islands, is a birdwatcher's paradise."

"Anything interesting?" Frannie asked him.

"Just the usual patter," Will said.

"You've got ketchup round your mouth."

Will wiped it off, his gaze returning to the brochure as he did so. What was it about the island of Tiree that kept drawing his attention? *Tiree is the most fertile of the Inner Hebrides*, the brochure said, *the granary of the islands*.

"I'm so full," Frannie said.

"Look at this," Will said, turning the brochure in Frannie's direction and pushing across the littered table.

"Which part?" he said.

"The piece about Tiree." She scanned it quickly. "Does it mean anything to you?"

She shook her head. "No, I don't believe so. Birdwatching . . . white, sandy beaches. It all sounds very nice, but—"

"Granary of the islands!" Will said suddenly, snatching the brochure up. "That's it! *Granary!*" He got up.

"Where are we going?"

"Back to the car. We need your book about Simeon!"

The streets had emptied in the time they'd been dining; the window-shoppers returned to their hotels for a nightcap, the lovers to their bed. Rosa had returned too. She was sitting on the pavement with her back to the harbor wall.

"Does the Island of Tiree mean anything to you?" Will asked her. She shook her head.

Frannie had the book out of the car and was flipping through it. "I remember a lot of references to Rukenau's island," she said, "but there weren't any specifics." She passed it over to Will.

He took it over to the harbor wall, and sat down.

"You smell satisfied," Rosa remarked. "Did you eat?"

"Yes," he said. "Should we have brought you something?"

She shook her head. "I'm fasting," she replied. "Though I was tempted by some of the fish they were hauling in off the jetty."

"Raw?" Frannie said.

"It's best that way," Rosa replied. "Steep was always good catching fish. He'd step into a river and tickle them into a stupor—"

"Got it!" Will said, waving the book. "Here it is!" He paraphrased the passage for Frannie's benefit. Hoping to rediscover a place in Rukenau's affections, Simeon had planned a symbolic painting, one that showed his sometime patron standing among piles of grain, "as befits his island." "That's the connection, right there!" he said. "Rukenau's island is Tiree. Look! It's a granary, just the way Simeon was going to paint it."

"That's pretty flimsy evidence," Frannie observed.

Will refused to be deflated. "It's the place. I *know* it's the place," he said. He tossed Dwyer's book over to Frannie and dug the timetable out of his pocket to consult it. "Tomorrow morning's sailing is to Coll and Tiree, via Tobermory." He grinned. "Finally," he said. "We got lucky."

"Do I take it from all this yelping that you know where we're going?" Rosa said.

"I think so," Will said. He went down on his haunches beside her. "Will you get back into the car now? You're not doing yourself any favors sitting down there."

"I'll have you know some Good Samaritan tried to give me money for a bed," she said to him.

"And you took it," Will said.

"You know me so well," Rosa replied wryly, and opened her fist to show him the coinage.

With a little more persuasion Rosa finally consented to be returned to the car, and there the three of them passed what remained of the night. Will slept better than he expected to, doubled up in the driver's seat. He woke only once, his bladder full, and as quietly as he could he got out of the car to relieve himself. It was four-fifteen, and the ferry that would take them out to the islands in the morning, the *Claymore*, had docked. There were already men at work on deck, and on the quay, loading cargo and preparing for the early sailing. Otherwise, the town was still, the esplanade deserted. He pissed lavishly in the gutter, scrutinized only by three or four gulls who were idling the night away on the harbor wall. The fishing boats would be coming in soon, he guessed, and they'd have fish scraps to breakfast on. Before returning to the car he lit a cigarette and, begging the pardon of the gulls, sat on the wall gazing out into the dark water that lay beyond the harbor lights. He felt curiously content with his lot. The cold smell of the water, the hot sharp smoke in his lungs, the sailors preparing the *Claymore* for her little voyage: All were pieces of his happiness. So too was the presence he felt in him as he sat watching the water—the fox spirit whose senses sharpened his, and who was wordlessly advising him: *Take pleasure, my man. Enjoy the smoke and the silence and the silken water. Take pleasure not because it's fleeting, but because it exists at all.*

He finished his cigarette and went back to the car, slipping back into his seat without waking Frannie, whose face was lolling against the window in sleep, her breath rhythmically misting the cold glass. Rosa also appeared to be asleep, but he was not so certain she wasn't pretending, a suspicion he had confirmed when he himself had started to doze again and heard her whispering at the very limit of audibility behind him. He could not grasp what she was saying and was too weary to think about it, but just as sleep took him, in one of those flashes of lucidity that come at such times, he deciphered the syllables she was speaking. She was reciting a list of names. And something about the fond way she spoke them, interspersing the list with a sigh here, or oh my sweet there, made him think these were not people she'd met along the way. They were her children. This then was the thought that carried him into sleep: Rosa was remembering her dead children as she waited for the day and was reciting their names in the dark, like a prayer that had no text, just a list of the divinities to whom it was directed.

III

It had always been Steep's preference, when he was about the business of slaughtering mating couples, to kill the male first. If he was dealing with the last of a species, of course—which was his great and glorious labor—the dispatch of both genders was academic. All he needed to do was kill one to insure that the line was ended. But he liked to be able to kill both, for neatness' sake, starting with the male. He had a number of practical reasons for this. In most species the male was the more aggressive of the sexes, and for his own protection it made sense to incapacitate the husband before the wife. He'd also observed that females were more likely to demonstrate grief at the demise of their mates, in the throes of which they could be readily killed. The male, by contrast, became vengeful. All but two of the serious injuries he'd sustained over the years had come from males that hc had unwisely left to kill after the female and which had thrown themselves upon him with suicidal abandon. A century and a half since the extinction of the great auk on the cliffs of St. Kilda, he still bore the scar on his forearm where the male had opened him up. And in cold weather there was still an ache in his thigh where a blaubok had kicked him, seeing its lady bleeding to death before its eyes.

Both were painful lessons. But more painful than either the scars or the ill-knit bones was the memory of those males who had, through some failing of his, outmaneuvered him and escaped. It had happened seldom, but when it had he had mounted heroic searches for the escape, driving Rosa to distraction with his doggedness. Let the brute go, she'd tell him, ever the pragmatist, just let him die of loneliness.

Oh, but that was what haunted him. The thought of a rogue animal out in the wild, circling its territory, looking for something that was its like and coming back at last to the place where its mate had perished, seeking a vestige of her being—a scent, a feather, a shard of bone—was almost unbearable. He had caught fugitives several times under such circumstances, waiting for them to return to that fatal place, and murdering them on the spot where they mourned. But there were some animals that escaped him completely, whose final hours were not his to have dominion over, and these were a source of great distress to him. He dreamed and imagined them for months after. Saw them wandering in his mind's eye; growing ragged, growing rogue. And then, when a season or two had passed, and they had not encountered any of their own species, losing the will to live; fleabitten and bony-shanked, becoming phantoms of veldt or forest or ice floe, until they finally gave up all hope and died.

He would always know when this finally happened, or such was his conviction. He would feel the animal's passing in his gut, as though a physical procedure as real as digestion had come to its inevitable end. Another dinning thing had gone into memory (and into his journal) never to be known again.

This will not come again. Nor this. Nor this . . .

It was no accident that his thoughts turned to these rogues as he traveled north. He felt like one of their pitiful number now. Like a creature without hope, returning to its ancestral ground. In his case, of course, he was not looking for signs of his lady wife. Rosa was still alive (it was her trail he was following, after all), and he would certainly not mope over her remains when she passed away. Yet for all his eagerness to be rid of her, the prospect left him lonely.

The night had not gone well for him. The car he'd stolen in Burnt Yarley had broken down a few miles outside Glasgow, and he had abandoned it, planning to steal a more reliable vehicle at the next service station. It turned out to be quite a trek, two hours walking beside the highway, while a cold drizzle fell. He'd make sure he stole a Japanese car next time, he thought. He liked the Japanese, an enthusiasm he'd shared with Rosa. She'd liked their delicacy and their artifice; he liked their cars and their cruelty. They had a nice indifference to the censure of hypocrites, which he admired. They needed shark fins for their soup? They took them, and dumped the rest of the carcasses back in the sea. They wanted whale oil for the lamps? Damn it, they'd hunt the whales, and tell the bleeding hearts to go sob on someone else's doorstep.

He found a shining new Mitsubishi at the next service station and, well pleased with his acquisition, went on his way through the night. But his melancholy thoughts would not be banished; they returned again to memories of murder. There was a simple reason he kept his mind circling on these grim images; it kept an even grimmer memory at bay. But that memory refused to be dispatched to the bay of his skull. Though he filled his head with blood and despair, the thought returned and returned—

Will had kissed him. Oh God in Heaven, *the queer had kissed him* and lived to boast about it. How was that possible? *How?* And why, though he'd wiped his hand back and forth across his mouth until his lips were raw, did they only remember the touch better with each assault? Was there some shameful part of him that had taken pleasure in the violation?

No, no, there was no such part. In others maybe, in weaker men, but not in him. He had simply been taken by surprise, expecting a blow and getting filth instead. A lesser man might have spat the kiss in his violator's face. But for a man as pure as he, unmoved by doubt or ambiguity, the kiss had been worse than any blow. Was it any wonder he felt it still? And would continue to feel it, no doubt, until he had the silvers of his enemy's lips between his fingers, pared from his face.

By six in the morning he had reached Dumbarton, and the sky was brightening in the east. Another day beginning, another round of trivialities for the human herd. He saw the morning rituals underway in the street through which he drove. Drapes drawn back to waken the children, milk collected off the doorsteps for the morning tea, a few early commuters trudging to the bus stop or the train station, still half in dreams. They had no idea what their world was coming to, nor, if they'd been told, would they have cared or understood. They just wanted to get through their day and have the bus or the train deliver them home again, safe and sound.

His mood lightened watching them. They were such clowns. How could he not be amused? On through Helensburgh and Garelochhead he drove, the narrow road becoming heavily trafficked as the day proceeded, until at length he reached the town he'd long ago realized was his destination: Oban. It was seven forty-five. The ferry, he was told, had sailed on time.

IV

Will, Frannie, and Rosa had boarded the *Claymore* at six-thirty. Though the morning air was on the nippy side of bracing, they were happy to be out of the car, which had become a little ripe toward the end of the night, and into the open air. And Lord, was the day fine, the sun rising in a cloudless sky.

"Ye canna ask for a nicer day to be sailing," the sailor who'd stowed their car had observed. "It'll be as calm as a lily pond all the way out tae the islands."

Frannie and Will made for the ship's bathrooms, to wash the sleep out of their eyes. The facilities were modest at best, but they both emerged looking a little more presentable, and went back on deck to discover Rosa seated at the bows of the *Claymore*. Of the three, she looked the least travelworn. There was a freshness to her pallor and a brightness in her eyes that utterly belied her wounded state.

"I'll be fine just sitting here," she said, like an old lady who wanted to be as little bother as possible to her companions. "Why don't you two go off and have some breakfast?"

Will offered to bring her something, but she told him no, she was quite happy as she was. They left her to her solitude and, with a short detour to the stern to watch the harbor receding behind them, the town picture-perfect in the warming sun, they went below to the dining room, and sat down to a breakfast of porridge, toast, and tea.

"They won't recognize me if I ever get back to San Francisco," Will said. "Cream, butter, porridge . . . I can feel my arteries clogging up just looking at it."

"So what do people do for fun in San Francisco?"

"Don't ask."

"No. I want to know, for when I come over and see you."

"Oh, you're going to come see me?"

"If you'll have me. Maybe at Christmas," she replied. "Is it warm at Christmas?"

"Warmer than here. It rains, of course. And it's foggy."

"But you like the city?"

"I used to think it was Paradise," he said. "Of course, it's a different place from when I first arrived."

"Tell me," she said.

The prospect defeated him. "I wouldn't know where to begin."

"Tell me about your friends. Your . . . lovers?" She ventured this tentatively, as though she wasn't sure she had her vocabulary right. "It's so different from anything I've ever experienced."

So he gave a guided tour of life in Boy's Town, over the tea and toast. A quick verbal gazeteer to begin with, then a little about the house on Sanchez Street, and on to the people in his circle. Adrianna, of course (with a footnote on Cornelius), Patrick and Rafael, Drew, Jack Fisher, even a quick jaunt across the bay for a snapshot of Bethlynn. "You said at the beginning it had all changed," Frannie reminded him.

"It has. A lot of people I knew when I first lived there are dead.

Men my age, some younger. There are a lot of funerals. A lot of men in mourning. It changes the way you look at your life. You start to think: Maybe none of it's worth a damn."

"You don't believe that," Frannie said.

"I don't know what I believe," he told her. "I don't have the same faith you have."

"It must be hard when you're in the middle of so much death. It's like an extinction."

"We're not going anywhere," Will said with unshakable conviction, "because we don't come from anywhere. We're spontaneous events. We just appear in the middle of families. And we'll keep appearing. Even if the plague killed every homosexual on the planet, it wouldn't be extinction, because there's queer babies being born every minute. It's like magic." He grinned at the notion. "You know, that's exactly what it is. It's magic."

"I'm afraid you've lost me."

"I'm just playing." He laughed.

"What's so funny?"

"This," he said, slowly spreading his arms to take in the table, then Frannie, then the rest of the dining room. "Us sitting talking like this. Queer politics over the porridge. Rosa sitting up there, hiding her secret self. Me down here talking about mine." He leaned forward. "Doesn't it strike you as a little funny?" She stared at him blankly. "No, I'm sorry. I'm getting out of hand."

The conversation was here interrupted by the waiter, a ruddy-faced man with an accent Will found initially unintelligible, asking them if they were finished. They were. Leaving him to clear the table, they headed up on deck. The wind had strengthened considerably in the hour or so they'd been breakfasting, and the gray-blue waters of the sound, though far from choppy, were flecked with spume. To the left of them, the hills of the Island of Mull, purple with heather, to the right the slopes of the Scottish mainland, more heavily wooded, with here and there signs of human habitation—most humble, some grand—set on the higher elevations. An aerial wake of herring gulls followed the ship, diving to pluck pieces of food, courtesy of the galley, out of the water. When the birds were sated, they settled on the ship, their clamor silenced, and beadily watched their fellow passengers from the railings and the lifeboats.

"They've got an easy life," Frannie observed as another well-fed gull came to perch amongst its brethren. "Catch the morning ferry, have breakfast, then catch the next one home."

"They're practical buggers, gulls," Will said. "They'll feed on anything. Look at that one! What's he eating?"

"Coagulated porridge."

"Is it? Oh hell, it is! Straight down!"

Frannie wasn't watching the gull, she was watching Will. "The look on your face—" she said.

"What?"

"I'd have thought you'd be tired of watching animals by now."

"Not a chance."

"Were you always like this? I don't think you were."

"No. I owe it to Steep. Of course he had ulterior motives. First you see it, then you kill it."

"Then you put it in your scrapbook," Frannie added. "All neat and tidy."

"And quiet," Will said.

"Was quiet important?"

"Oh yes. He thinks we'll hear God better that way."

Frannie mused on this a moment. "Do you think he was born crazy?" she finally said.

There was another silence. Then Will said, "I don't think he was born."

The ferry was coming into Tobermory, its first and last stop before they slipped from the sound and out into the open sea. They watched the approach from the bow, where Rosa was still seated. Tobermory was a small town, barely extending beyond the quayside, and the ship was at the dock no more than twenty minutes (long enough to unload three cars and a dozen passengers) before it was on its way. The swell became noticeably heavier once they cleared the northern tip of Mull, the waves bristling with white surf.

"I hope it doesn't get any worse than this," Frannie remarked, "or I'm going to get seasick."

"We're in treacherous waters," Rosa remarked, these the first words she'd uttered since Frannie and Will had joined her. "The straits between Coll and Tiree are notorious."

"How do you know?"

"I got chatting with young Hamish over there," she said, nodding toward a sailor who was lounging against the railing ten yards from where Rosa sat.

"He's barely old enough to shave," Will replied.

"Are you jealous then?" Rosa chuckled. "Don't worry, I'm not going to do the dirty with him. Not in my present state. Though Lord knows he's a pretty thing, don't you think?"

"He's a little young for me."

"Oh there's no such thing as too young," Rosa said. "If he can get hard he's old enough. That's always been my theory."

Frannie's face reddened with fury and embarrassment. "You're disgusting, you know that?" she said, and stalked off down the deck.

Will went after her, to calm her down, but she could not be calmed.

"That's how she got her claws into Sherwood," she said. "I've always suspected it. And there she is, crowing about it."

"She didn't mention Sherwood."

"She didn't have to. God, she's sickening. Sitting there lusting after some fifteen-year-old. I won't have anything more to do with her, Will."

"Just put up with it for a few more hours," Will said. "We're stuck with her till we find Rukenau."

"She doesn't know where she's going any more than we do," Frannie said.

Will didn't say so, but he was tempted to agree. He'd hoped that by now Rosa would be in a more focused frame of mind, that the voyage would have somehow aroused buried memories in her, something to prepare them for whatever lay ahead. But if she felt anything, she was concealing it very effectively. "Maybe it's time I had a heart-to-heart with her," Will said.

"She hasn't got a heart," Frannie said. "She's just a dirty-minded old . . . whatever she is." She glanced up at him. "Go talk to her. You won't get any answers. Just keep her away from me." With that she headed off toward the bow. Will almost went after her to try to placate her further, but what was the use? She had every right to her disgust. For himself, however, he found it impossible to feel any great horror at who or what Rosa was, despite the fact that she'd taken Hugo's life. He puzzled over this as he returned to the bow. Was there some flaw in his nature that kept him from feeling the revulsion Frannie felt?

He was stopped in his tracks by two gulls that came swooping down in front of him to squabble over a crust of waterlogged bread one of them had dropped in flight. It was a vicious and raucous set-to, beaks stabbing, wings thrashing and, as he watched it played out, he had his question answered. He watched Rosa the way he watched the gulls. The way, in fact, he'd watched thousands of animals over the years. He made no moral judgments about her because they weren't applicable. There was no use judging her by human standards. She was no more human than the gulls squabbling in front of him. Perhaps that was her tragedy, or perhaps, like the gulls, it was her glory.

"It was just a little joke," Rosa said when he came back to sit beside her. "That woman's got no sense of humor." The *Claymore* was swinging around, and a low-lying island was coming into view. "Hamish tells me this is Coll," Rosa said, getting up and leaning against the railing.

The island was in stark contrast to the lush wooded slopes of Mull, flat and undistinguished.

"I don't suppose you recognize any of this?" Will asked her.

"No," she said. "But this isn't where we're getting off. This is the sister island. Tiree's much more fertile. The Land of Corn, they used to call it."

"Did you get all this from Hamish?" Rosa nodded. "Useful lad," Will said.

"Men have their uses," she said. "But you know what." She gave Will a shy little glance. "You live in San Francisco, yes?"

"Yes."

"I love that city. There used to be a drag bar on Castro Street I'd always frequent when we were in the city. I forget its name now, but it was owned by a lovely old queen called Lenny something or other. This amuses you?"

"Somewhat. The idea of you and Steep in a drag bar."

"Oh, Steep was never with me. It would have sickened him. But I always enjoyed the company of men who like to play the woman. My sweet *viados* in Milan, oh my, some of them were so beautiful."

If the conversation over breakfast had been strange, this was a damn sight stranger, Will thought. Just about the last thing he'd expected to do on this voyage was to listen to Rosa extol the virtues of cross-dressing.

"I've never understood what was so interesting about it," Will said.

"I've always loved things that weren't what they seemed," Rosa replied. "And for a man to deny his own sex, and corset himself and paint himself, and be something that he isn't because it touches a

place in his heart . . . that has a kind of poetry about it, to my mind."
She smiled. "And I learned a lot from some of those men, about how
to pretend."

"Pretend to be a woman, you mean?"

Rosa nodded. "I'm a confection too, you see," she said, with
more than a trace of self-deprecation. "My name isn't even Rosa
McGee. I heard the name in a street in Newcastle, somebody calling
for *Rosa, Rosa McGee,* and I thought: That's the name for me. Steep
got his name from a sign he saw. A spice importer was the original
Steep. Jacob liked the sound of it so he took it. I think he murdered
the man later."

"Murdered him for his name?"

"Perhaps more for the fun of it. He was vicious when he was
young. He thought it was his duty to his sex to be cruel. Pick up a
newspaper, and it's plain what men are like."

"Not every man kills things for the pleasure of it."

"Oh, that's not what he learned," Rosa said, with a look of weary
frustration at Will's stupidity. "I took as much pleasure in killing as
he did. No, what he learned was to pretend there was purpose in it."

"How young were you when he was learning? Were you children?"

"Oh no. We were never children. At least not that I remember."

"So before you chose to be Rosa, who were you?"

"I don't know. We were with Rukenau. I don't think we needed
names. We were his instruments."

"Building the Domus Mundi?" She shook her head. "So do you
not remember being with him?"

"Why should I? Do you remember what you were before you
were Will Rabjohns?"

"I remember being a baby, very vaguely. At least I think I do."

"It may be the same for me, once I get to Tiree."

The *Claymore* was now perhaps fifteen yards from the jetty at
Coll and, with the ease of one who'd performed the duty countless
times, the skipper brought the vessel alongside. There was a flurry of
activity below, as cars were driven off and passengers disembarked.
Will paid little attention. He had more questions to ask Rosa and
was determined to voice them all while she was in a voluble mood.

"You said something about Jacob learning to be a man—"

"Did I?" she said, feigning distraction.

"But he was already a man. You said so."

"I said he wasn't a child. That's not the same thing. He had to learn the way men are in the world, as I had to learn the ways of women. None of it came naturally to us. Well . . . perhaps some of it. I do remember thinking one day how I loved to hold babies in my arms, how I loved softness and lullabies. And Steep didn't."

"What did Steep love?"

"Me," she said, with a sly smile. "At least," the smile went, "I imagined he did, and that was enough. It is sometimes. Women understand that; men don't. Men need things certain. All certain and fixed. Lists and maps and history. All so that they know where they are, where they belong. Women are different. We need less. I could have been quite happy to have children with Steep. Watch them grow, and if they died, have more. But they always perished, almost as soon as they were born. He'd take them away, to save me the pain of seeing them, which showed he felt something for me, didn't it?"

"I suppose so."

"I named them all, even though they only lived for a few minutes—"

"And you remember all the names?"

"Oh yes," she said, turning her face from him to hide her feeling, "every one."

By now the *Claymore* was ready for departure. The mooring ropes were cast off, the engines took on a livelier rhythm, and the last stage of the voyage was underway. Only when they were some distance from the island did Rosa finally look around at Will, who was sitting down, lighting up a cigarette, to say, "I want you to understand something about Jacob. He wasn't barbaric all his life. At the beginning, yes, he was a fiend, he really was. But what did he have for inspiration? You ask most men what it is that makes them men and it won't be a very pretty list. But I mellowed him over the years—"

"He drove entire species out of existence, Rosa—"

"They were only animals. What did it matter? He had such fine thoughts in his head, such godly thoughts. Anyway, it's there in the Bible. We've got dominion over the birds of the air—"

"And the beasts of the field. Yeah, I know. So he had all these fine thoughts."

"And he loved to give me pleasure. He had his troubled times, of course, but there was always room for music and dancing. And the circus. I loved the circus. But he lost his sense of humor, after a time. He lost his courtesies. And then he began to lose me. We were still traveling together, and there'd be times when things were almost like the old days, but the feelings between us were slipping away. In fact the night we met you we were planning to go our separate ways. That's why he went looking for company. And found you. If he hadn't done that we wouldn't be where we are now, any of us. It's all connected in the end, isn't it? You think it's not, but it is."

She returned her gaze to the water.

"I'd better go and find Frannie," Will said. "We'll be arriving soon."

Rosa didn't reply. Leaving her at the railing, Will wandered the length of the deck and found Frannie sitting on the starboard side, sipping a cup of coffee and smoking a cigarette.

"I didn't know you smoked."

"I don't," she said. "But I needed it. Want some coffee? The wind's chilly." He took the plastic cup and drank. "I tried to buy a map," she said, "but the ship store's closed."

"We'll get one on the island," Will said. "Speaking of which, . . . " He got to his feet and went to the railing. Their destination was in view. A line of land as unpromising as Coll, the waves breaking against its rocky shores. Frannie rose to stand beside him and together they watched as the island approached, the *Claymore*'s engines slowing so that the vessel might be safely navigated through the shallow waters.

"It doesn't look very hospitable, does it?" Frannie remarked.

It was certainly spartan at this distance, the sea surging around dark spits of rock that rose to bleak headlands. But then the wind veered and carried the scent of flowers off the land, their honey fragrance mingled with the sharp scents of salt and kelp, and Frannie murmured, "Oh Lord," in appreciation.

The *Claymore*'s approach had become a tentative crawl now, as the vessel made its cautious way to the jetty. And as it did so the charms of the island steadily became more apparent. The waters through which the vessel plowed were no longer dark and deep, but as turquoise as any Caribbean bay, and swooned upon beaches of silver-white sand. There were a few cattle at the tide's edge, apparently grazing on seaweed, but the beaches were otherwise deserted. So too were the grassy dunes that rose from them, rolling away to meet the lush meadows of the island's interior. This was where the scent of vetch and sea-thrift and crimson clover originated: expanses of fertile pasture dotted here and there with modest houses, whitewashed and brightly roofed.

"I take it all back," Frannie said. "It's beautiful."

The village of Scarinish, which was little more than a couple rows of houses, was now in view. There was more activity on its pier than there'd been at Coll: fully twenty people waiting for the *Claymore* to dock, along with a lorry loaded with goods and a tractor with a cattle pen in tow.

"I should probably go and fetch Rosa," Will said.

"Give me the car keys," Frannie said. "I'll meet you downstairs."

Will headed back to the bow, where he found Rosa at the railing still, studying the scene ahead.

"Do you recognize anything?" he asked her.

"Not with my eyes," she said. "But . . . I know this place."

There was a gentle bump and creak as the *Claymore* nudged the pier, then the sound of welcoming shouts from both land and ship.

"Time to go," Will said, and escorted Rosa down into the hold, where Frannie was already in the car. Will got into the passenger seat beside her, and Rosa slipped into the back. There was an uncomfortable silence while they waited for the ferry's door to be opened. They didn't have to wait long. After a couple of minutes, sunlight flooded the hold and one of the crew played at traffic control, signaling the half-dozen vehicles alighting here out one by one. There was a second, longer delay on the pier itself, while the laden lorry moved out of the way of the exiting cars, this maneuver performed with great hullabaloo, but no sense of urgency. Finally, the congestion was cleared, and Frannie drove them down the pier into the village itself. It was no longer than it had appeared from the seaward side: just a few rows of small but well-kept houses with even smaller, well-kept walled gardens, all facing the water, and a scattering of older buildings, some in disrepair, several in ruin. There were also a few shops, among them a post office and a small supermarket, its windows bannered with news of this week's bargains, their silent advertisements still too loud for the hush of the place.

"Do you want to go and get us a map?" Frannie suggested to Will, bringing the car to a halt outside the supermarket. "And maybe some chocolate?" she called after him, "and something to drink?"

He emerged a couple of minutes later with two bags of purchases, "For the road," as he put it: biscuits, chocolate, bread, cheese, two large bottles of water, and a small bottle of whisky.

"What about the map?" Frannie said, as he loaded the bags onto the back seat beside Rosa.

"*Voilá*," he said, pulling a small folded map from his pocket, and along with it a twelve-page tourists' guide to the island, written by the local schoolmaster and crudely illustrated by the schoolmaster's wife. He passed the booklet back over his shoulder to Rosa, telling her to flip through it for any names or places that rang a bell. The map he opened on his lap. There wasn't much to study. The island was twelve miles long and at its broadest three miles wide. It had a trio of hills: Beinn Hough, Beinn Bheag Bhaile-mhuilinn, and Ben Hynish, the summit of the latter being the highest point on the island. It had several small lochs and a handful of villages (described as townships on the map) around its coast. What few roads the island boasted simply joined these townships—the largest of which consisted of nine houses—by the most direct route, which, given the flatness of the terrain, was usually something approaching a straight line.

"Where the hell do we start?" Will wondered aloud. "I can't even pronounce half these names."

There was a glorious poetry in the words, however: Balephuil and Balephetrish, Baile-Mheadhonach and Cornaigmore, Vaul and Gott and Kenavara. And they lost little of their power in translation: Balephuil was the Town of the Marsh, Heylipout, the Holy Town, Bail-Udhaig, the Town of Wolf Bay.

"If nobody's got any better ideas," Will said, "I suggest we start here." He pointed to Baile-Mheadhonach.

"Any particular reason?" Frannie wanted to know.

"Well, it's almost in the middle of the island, for one thing." In fact that was its unglamorous translation: Middle Town. "And it's got its own cemetery, look." There was a cross to the south of the village and beside it the words *Cnoc a' Chlaidh*, translated as Christian burial ground. "If Simeon was buried here, we may as well start out by looking for his grave." He glanced over his shoulder at Rosa. She'd put down the booklet and was staring out of the window, the fixedness of her expression such that Will looked away immediately so as not to disturb her meditations. "Let's just go," he said to Frannie. "We can follow the coast road west as far as Crossapol. Then we make a left inland."

Frannie eased the car out into what would have been the flow of traffic, if there'd been any traffic, and within perhaps a minute they had passed the outskirts of Scarinish, and were on the open road, a road so straight and empty she could have driven blindfolded and more than likely brought them to Crossapol.

V

There were among the Western Isles places of great historical and mythological significance, where battles had been fought and princes hidden, and stories made that haunted listeners still. Tiree was not among them. The island had not passed an entirely uneventful life, but it had been at best a footnote to events that flowered in their full splendor in other places.

There was no more obvious example of this than the exploits of St. Columba, who had in his time carried the Gospel throughout the Hebrides, founding seats of devotion and learning on a number of islands. Tiree was not thus blessed, however. The good man had lingered on the island only long enough to curse a rock in Gott's Bay for the sin of letting his boat's mooring rope slip. It would be henceforth barren, he declared. The rock was dubbed *Mallachdaig*, or Little Cursed One, and no seaweed had grown on it since. Columba's associate, St. Brendan, had been in a more benign mood during his fleeting visit and had blessed a hill, but if the blessing conferred some inspirational power on the place nobody had noticed: There had been no revelations or spontaneous healings on the spot. The third of these visiting mystics, St. Kenneth, had caused a chapel to be built in the dunes near the township of Kilkenneth, which had been so named in the hope of persuading him to linger. The ruse had failed. Kenneth had gone on to greater things, and the dunes—more persuaded by wind than metaphysics—had subsequently buried the chapel.

There were a handful of stories through which St. Columba and his gang did not wander, all of which remained part of the anecdotal landscape, but most of them were dispiritingly domestic in scale: a well on the side of Beinn Hough, for instance, called *Tobar nan naoi beo*, the Well of the Nine Living, because it had miraculously supplied a widow and her eight homeless children with a lifetime's supply of shellfish; a pool close to the shore at Vaul, where the ghost of a girl who had drowned in its depths could be seen on moonless nights, singing a lonely lullaby to lure living souls into the water with her. In short, nothing out of the ordinary; islands half the size of Tiree boasted legends far more ambitious.

But there was a numinosity here none of the rest of the isles possessed and at its heart was a phenomenon that would have turned St. Columba from a gentle meditative into a wild-eyed prophet had he witnessed it. In fact, this wonderment had not yet come to pass when the saint had hopscotched through the islands, but even if it had he would most likely have been denied sight of it, for those few islanders who had glimpsed the miracle (and, presently living, they numbered eight) never mentioned the subject, not even to those they loved. This was the great secret of their lives, a thing unseen, yet more certain than the sun, and they were not about to dilute its enchantment by speaking of it. In fact, many of them limited their own contemplation of what they'd sensed, for fear of exhausting its power to enrapture them. Some, it was true, returned to the place where they'd been touched in the hope of a second revelation, and though none of them saw anything on their return visits, many were granted a certainty that kept them content for the rest of their lives: They left the place with the conviction that what they had failed to see had *seen them*. They were no longer frail mortals, who would live their lives and pass away. The power on the hill at Kenavara had witnessed them and, in that witnessing, had drawn them into an immortal dance.

For it lived in the island's very being, this power; it moved in sand and pasture and sea and wind, and the souls it saw became part of these eternals, imperishable. Once witnessed, what did a man or woman have to fear? Nothing, except perhaps the discomforts that attended death. Once their corporeal selves were shed, however, they moved where the power moved and witnessed as it witnessed, glory on glory. When on summer nights the Borealis drooped its color on the stratosphere, they would be there. When the whales came to breach in exaltation, they would rise, too. They would be with the kittiwakes and the hares and with every star that trembled on Loch an Eilein. It was in all things, this power. In the sandy pastures adjoining the dunes (or the *machair* as it was called in Gaelic), and in the richer, damper fields of the island's midst, where the grass was lush and the cattle grazed themselves creamy.

It did not much concern itself with the griefs and travails of those men and women who never saw it, but it kept a tally of their comings and goings. It knew who was buried in the churchyards at Kirkapol and Vaul; it knew how many babies were born each year. It even watched the visitors, in a casual fashion, not because they were as interesting as whales or kittiwakes, they weren't, but because there might be among them some soul who would do it harm. This was not beyond the bounds of possibility. It had been witnessing long enough to have seen stars disappear from the heavens. It was not more permanent than they.

Rosa said, "Stop the car."

Frannie did as she was instructed.

"What is it?" Will asked, turning round to look at Rosa.

Her eyes were welling with tears as he watched, while a smile befitting a painted Virgin rose on her lips. She reached out and fumbled with the door handle, but in her present distracted state she couldn't get it to open. Will was out of the car in a heartbeat and opening the door for her. They were on an empty stretch of road, with unfenced pasture off to the right, grazed by a few sheep, and to their left a band of flower-studded grass that became a gently sloping beach. Overhead, terns wheeled and darted. And much, much higher, a jet on its way west, reflecting earth-light off its silver underbelly. He saw all this in a moment or two, his senses quickened by something in the air. The fox moved in him, turning its snout to the sky and sensing whatever Rosa had sensed.

He didn't ask her what it was. He simply waited while she scanned the horizon. Finally she said, "Rukenau's here."

"Alive?"

"Oh yes, alive. Oh my Lord, alive." Her smile darkened. "But I wonder what he's become after all these years."

"Do you know where we can find him?"

She held her breath for a moment. Frannie had gotten out of the car and started to speak. Will put his finger to his lips. Rosa, meanwhile, had started to walk away from the car, into the pasture. There was so much sky here; a vast, empty blue, widening before Will as his eyes grew ambitious to take it in. What have I been doing all these years, he thought, putting boxes around little corners of the world? It was such a lie to do that, to stand under skies as wide as this and record instead some mote of suffering. Enough of that.

"What's wrong?" he heard Frannie say.

"Nothing," he said. "Why?" Before she could reply he realized that like Rosa, his eyes had filled with tears. That he was smiling and weeping in the same strange moment. "It's okay," he said.

"Are you all right?"

"Never better," he said, brushing his tears away.

Rosa had finished her contemplations, it seemed, for now she turned round and walked back toward the car. As she approached she pointed off toward the southwest of the island.

"It's waiting for us," she said.

VI

With the map in front of him and Rosa, like a living compass, on the seat behind him, it quickly became apparent to Will where they were headed. To Ceann a' Bharra, or Kenavara, a headland at the southwestern tip of the island, described in the overwrought language of the guidebook as *"a precipice that rises out of the ocean sheer on either flank, and sheerer still at the headland itself, from the heights of which the Skerryvore Lighthouse may be spied, marking the last sign of a human presence before the mighty Atlantic rolls away to the empty horizon."* It was, the booklet warned, *"the only spot on our glorious island that has been a scene of tragedy. The great profusion of birdlife on Kenavara's crags and ledges has drawn the attention of ornithologists for many years, but regrettably the crags are dangerous to even the most expert of climbers, and a number of visitors have been killed in falls from the cliffs while attempting to reach inaccessible nests. The beauty of Kenavara's best appreciated from the safety of the beaches that flank it. Venturing on the headland itself, even in broad daylight and fine weather, carries with it risk of serious injury or worse."*

It certainly wasn't the easiest of places to reach. The road carried them through a tiny cluster of houses, maybe ten in all, which were marked on the map as the village of Barrapol, and then on down toward the western shore of the island, where it divided, about four hundred yards shy of the beach, the good road making a right turn toward Saundaig, while the lefthand fork became a track over the bumpy grass. According to the map even this disappeared after a few hundred yards, but they took it as far as they could, as it ran parallel to the shore. Their destination was less than a half-mile ahead: an undulating peninsula, its flanks scored and gullied, so that it looked not to be one continuous spot of land, but three or four hillocks, with fissures of naked rock between, falling away into the sea.

The track had now petered out altogether, but Frannie drove on toward the headland, cautiously negotiating the increasingly uneven turf. Hares bounded ahead of the car, making preposterous leaps in their alarm; a sheep, grazing on the *machair* far from the flock, dashed away, bug-eyed with panic.

The ground was getting progressively sandier, the wheels turning up fans of earth behind the car.

"I don't think we're going to be able to drive much further," Frannie said.

"Then we'll go by foot," Will said. "Are you all right with that, Rosa?"

She murmured that yes, she'd be fine, but once she got out of the car it was clear that her physical state had deteriorated in the last quarter hour. Her skin had lost all its gleam, the whites of her eyes become faintly jaundiced. Her hands were trembling.

"Are you sick?" Will said.

"I'll get over it," she said. "It's just . . . coming here again," she let her gaze stray towards Kenavara, reluctantly, Will thought. The bright, smiling woman who'd strode back toward the car on the Crossapol road had been cowed; he didn't exactly know why. Nor was Rosa going to tell him. Despite her sudden frailty she set off toward the cliffs, striding ahead of Will and Frannie.

"Let her lead," Will whispered.

So they wove their way through the *machair* toward Kenavara, the reason for the headland's fatal reputation becoming more apparent as they approached. The waves were beating hard against the shore to their right, but their violence was nothing compared to the fury with which they came against the cliffs. And rising out of the spume as though born from the waves and given wings, tens of hundreds of birds, their din a raucous counterpoint to the boom of the water.

Not all of them claimed the cliffs as their home. A solitary tern appeared overhead, sniping in a bitter voice at these intruders and, when they didn't retreat, swooped down as though to peck at them, veering off a few inches short of their scalps. Frannie sniped back, waving her arms to shoo the tern away.

"Bloody bird!" she yelled up at it. "Leave us alone!"

"It's just protecting its territory," Will said.

"Well I'm protecting my scalp!" Frannie snapped. "*Go on!* Bugger off! Damn thing!"

It continued its attacks for another five minutes, until they were almost at the slope of the headland itself. Rosa was still leading the way, not even glancing behind to confirm that Will and Frannie were still following.

"I wonder where she's going," Frannie said.

There was no sign of any human presence on the headland whatsoever—not a fence, not a cairn, not even a sign to warn people from straying where they could come to harm. And yet Will didn't doubt that this was Rukenau's home (and, most likely, Thomas Simeon's resting place). He didn't need Rosa to confirm it; he could feel it in his own body. His skin was tingling, his teeth and tongue and eyeballs ached, his blood thumped in his ears, its rhythms audible through the din of sea and birds.

Now that they'd emerged from the protective troughs of the *machair* the wind came at them off the ocean, gusting so strongly that all three were staggering, heads down.

"You want to hang on to me?" Will yelled to Frannie over the bluster. She shook her head. "Just be careful," he shouted. "The ground's not very safe."

That was an understatement. The whole headland was a mass of traps, the lush, springy turf suddenly dropping away, sheer, into a darkness filled with the booming of the sea. The grass itself was slick with the mist that rose from these gullies, squeaking beneath their heels as they went in pursuit of Rosa. She seemed to move more surefootedly than her companions, for all her frailty, the gap between the two parties steadily widening as they proceeded. Sometimes Will and Frannie lost sight of her altogether, when the route brought either they or she to a dip in the ground. The sides of some were extremely steep, and Frannie preferred to negotiate them on her butt, clinging to fistfuls of slippery grass for purchase. All the while, the birds wheeled overhead. Gulls and guillemots, fulmar petrals and kittiwakes, even a hoodie-crow, up to see what the hoopla was all about. None of them made any attempt to attack, as the tern had done. This was so assuredly their terrain, what did they have to fear? These pitiful people clinging white-knuckled to rock and clod were no threat to their sovereignty.

At last Frannie caught hold of Will's arms and, pulling him close enough that she could be heard over the din of the birds, said, "Where the hell's Rosa gone? We haven't lost her, have we?"

Will scanned the land ahead. There was indeed no sign of Rosa. They were no more than five hundred yards from the end of the headland, but there were still dozens of places she could have disappeared, spots where the ground sloped away into marshy hollows, rocky outcrops marking fissures and crevices.

"Stay here a moment," Will said to Frannie, and retraced their steps to the highest vantage point in the vicinity: a lichen-covered boulder fully ten feet high. He proceeded to scale it. He was no great climber at the best of times, he was too gangly, and by now a succession of sleep-deprived nights was taking its toll on both his strength and his coordination. In short, it was a laborious attempt, and by the time he reached the top he was panting and sweaty. He studied the vista before him as logically as his giddy head would allow, looking for some sign of Rosa, but could see none and was about to scramble down again when he caught sight of something pale, half-hidden in the dark rocks a hundred yards ahead.

"I see her!" he yelled to Frannie, and slithering down from his perch with even less dignity than he'd had climbing it, led Frannie to the place. His eyes had not been playing tricks. Rosa was lying on the ground, her face completely ashen, her teeth chattering. The yellowish color in her eyes had become almost golden. When she raised her eyes to him her gaze was no longer entirely human, and some profound repugnance in him—an animal fear of something that was not natural—kept him from going too close to her.

"What happened?" he said.

"I slipped, is all," she said. Was her voice subtly changed too? He thought so. Or was it the fact that she seemed to be speaking close to his ear, in a whisper, when she was lying three yards away? "Get me up," she demanded.

"Is he here?" Will said.

"Is *who* here?"

"Rukenau."

"Just *get me up.*"

"I want an answer first." Will said.

"It's none of your business," Rosa replied.

"Look. You wouldn't even *be* here—" Will began.

She gave him a look that, had she not so plainly been in a severely weakened state, would have shaken him to his core, a salutary reminder that though he'd seen a half-dozen Rosa McGees in the last two days, some of them almost gentle, they were all fabrications. The true thing she was—the thing with aureate gaze and a voice that spoke in the bones of his head—that thing didn't care how it had come here or what civilities it might owe those who'd brought it. All it wanted now was to be in the House of the World, and it was too weak to waste its time with a show of courtesy.

"*Get me up,*" she said again, reaching out toward Will.

He didn't move to help her. He simply studied her face, waiting for her impatience to betray her. And so it did. She could not help but look past him to the place she wanted to be, demanding again to be helped up.

Will followed the line of her gaze, past the rocks that lay between them and the sward at the crown of the cliffs, to a spot that seemed from this distance quite unremarkable, just a patch of marshy ground. She caught his trick instantly and began to harangue him afresh.

"You don't *dare* go there without me!"

"Don't I?" he said.

She turned her fury on Frannie. "Tell him, woman! He dare not enter that house without me!"

"Maybe you should stay with her?" Will said to Frannie. She put up no argument. By the expression on her face it was apparent the atmosphere of the place had unsettled her deeply. "I promise I won't step inside without you."

"You'd better not," Frannie said.

"If she tries anything tricky, *yell*."

"Oh you'll hear me, don't worry," Frannie said.

Will glanced back at Rosa. She'd given up her protests now and was lying back against the rock, staring up at the sky. It seemed her eyes were mirrors at that moment, waves of sun and shadow moving across them. He looked away, distressed, and said to Frannie, "Don't go near her." Then he was off, toward the place between the rocks.

VII

He was happy not to be following in Rosa's footsteps and happy to be alone. No, never alone. The fox was with him as he went, like a second self. It was more agile than he, and several times he felt its energies urging him to walk where his lumpen body didn't dare go. It was also more cautious. His eyes darted about looking for signs of threat; his nose was uncommonly sensitive to the scents in the wind. But there was no evidence of danger. Nor, though he was now fifteen yards from the rocks, was there any sign of a house or the ruins of a house.

He glanced back toward Frannie and Rosa, but the ground had dipped so steeply he could no longer see them. To his right, no more than a yard from his uncertain feet, the ground fell away into a cleft of black rock a little wider than a man's body. One slip, he knew, and he was gone. And wouldn't that be a pitiful end for a journey that had taken so many years and covered so many miles, from a hill and a runaway hare, from a flame and a handful of moths, from the wastes of Balthazar and a bloody bear, coming to take him in her arms? A few more yards, a few more seconds, and he'd be there at the doorstep and that journey would be ended. There'd be understanding, there'd be revelation, there'd be an end to the ache in him.

Ahead of him was a patch of bright green turf, sparkling with moisture and starred with yellow vetch. Beyond it, a small rocky outcrop, which the birds apparently used to crack their catch upon, because it was littered with broken crab shells and spattered with white shit. Beyond that, the boulders between which Rosa had been staring so intently.

It wasn't a particularly tricky maneuver to get from where he stood to his destination, but he took his time, his body trembling with a mixture of fatigue and exhilaration. He crossed the patch of grass without incident, though it was as slick as ice beneath his boots, then he proceeded to clamber up the outcrop, the gully at his back. The first couple of handholds were simple enough, but the higher he climbed the more his body's betrayal escalated. His eyes began to flicker wildly, turning the rock in front of him to a blur. His hands and feet had become numb. There was a good deal more than exhaustion at work, he realized. His body was responding to an outside influence, some energy in the air or earth that was tempting his system to treason. The blurring of his sight was sickening; he felt nausea rising in him. To ward it off he closed his eyes, tight, trusting to what little feeling he had left in his hands to guide him up the rest of the way. It was a dangerous business, given that the gully was right behind him to swallow him if he fell, but the risk paid off. Three more handholds and he was up onto the top of the rock, brushing shards of crab shells off his palms.

He opened his eyes. Their motion had quieted a little in the murk behind his lids, but as soon as the light hit them they began to spasm again. He reached out to grab hold of the boulders on either side of him, focusing as best he could on the patch of green that lay between them. Then, keeping his numbed hands pressed against the stones, he started to fumble his way into the windless passage.

It was not just his sight and sense of touch that had gone awry. His ears had joined the rebellion. The chorus of wheeling birds and the boom of surf had decayed into a general noise that sloshed around in his skull like mud. All he could hear with any clarity was his own raw breath, drawn and delivered. He would not be able to get much further in this state, he knew. Another three, four steps and his dead legs would fold up under him or something in his head would snap. The house had put up its defenses, and they were successfully repelling him.

He forced his barely functioning limbs to take another step, clinging to the boulders as best he could to keep from trusting his full weight to his legs. How far was he from the grassy space that had once been his destination? He no longer knew. It was academic anyway. He would never make it. And yet, the idiot ghost of that ambition remained, haunting his failing sinews.

Maybe another step, another two steps, just to see if he could make it to the open space.

"*Come on*," he muttered to himself, the syllables as raw as his breath. "*Move . . .*"

His growls worked. His reluctant legs carried him another step and another after that. Suddenly the wind was on his face again. He had reached the end of the passage and was out into the open air.

Having no other choice, he let go of the boulders, and sank down to his knees. The ground was sodden beneath him, cold water spattered up against his groin and belly. He teetered for a few minutes and then pitched forward onto his hands. The scene was an incoherent blur before him: a haze of green for the earth, a haze of gray above it for the sky. He was about to close his eyes against the sight when he glimpsed, in the middle of this muddied field of vision, a silver of clarity. It was thin, but *sharp*, as though his eyes, for all their cavorting, had here resolved their confusions. He could see every blade of grass in crystalline detail, and the sun-gilded fringes of the clouds, as they slid past the aperture.

It's open, he thought. The door's open, just a fraction, and I'm looking through it, peering into the house the Nilotic built. His legs would not carry him to the place, but he'd damn well get there on his hands and knees. As he started to crawl he remembered the solemn promise he'd made to Frannie and felt a spasm of guilt that he was breaking it. But he wasn't so mortified that it slowed his crawl. He wanted to be there more than anything right now. More than promises, certainly. More than life probably, and sanity, too.

Keeping his eyes fixed on the silver of the open door, he crawled through the muck to the place where it stood, and forsaking all he hoped, believed, and understood, entered the House of the World.

VIII

The last Frannie saw of Will he was attempting to scale the rocky outcrop at the head of the gully. Then her attention had been claimed by Rosa, who'd started to moan piteously, tearing at her bandages. When Frannie looked back in Will's direction, he'd gone. She assumed at first he'd scaled the rocks and was now through the passage and onto the slope beyond, but though she watched for him, she saw no sign. Slowly, a grim possibility took shape: that in the minute or so that she'd been trying to stop Rosa reopening her wound, Will had lost his balance and toppled back into the gully. The longer she stared and failed to see him the more probable this came to seem. She hadn't heard him cry out, but with the birds so loud was that any great surprise?

Fearing what she would see, she ventured from Rosa's side and followed Will's route along the edge of the gully, yelling to him as she went.

"Where are you? For God's sake answer me! Will?"

There was no reply. Nor was there any sign of his having fallen. No blood on the rocks, no place where the grass had been uprooted. But these absences were little comforts. She knew perfectly well he could have slipped down into the gully without leaving a trace: a straight fall between the rocks, down into the impenetrable darkness.

She had almost reached the head of the gully by now, the spot where she'd last seen Will. Should she climb up and see if he was simply squatting on the far side of the rocks? Of course she should. But something drew her eyes back to the gully, and she stared into its abyss, afraid now to call his name, afraid he'd answer out of the darkness.

And then she saw him—or thought she did—lying in the depths of the gully maybe twenty feet down. Her heart beating feverishly, she got down on her knees and went to the very edge of the gully to verify what she was seeing. There was no doubt. There was no doubt. There was a man lying on the rocks at the bottom of the gully. It could only be Will. She tried yelling to him, but he didn't move a muscle. Perhaps he was already dead, perhaps he was merely stunned. Certainly she couldn't waste time going for help: a half hour back to the car, another ten, twenty minutes to find a phone, how much longer before rescuers appeared? She had to do something herself, find a way down into the gully and help him. It was a grim prospect. She'd never been agile, even as a girl, and though the relative slightness of her build would make it physically feasible for her to clamber down into the darkness, if she herself slipped she'd end up broken-bodied beside Will and that would effectively be the end of both of them. Two more fatalities to add to the headland's grim reputation.

But she had no other choice. She plainly couldn't leave Will to die. She simply had to put her fears aside and get to work. Her first task was to find the safest route of descent. She walked back along the gully in the seaward direction until she found a spot where the walls of the crevice were relatively close together, so that she might descend using both sides for hand- and footholds. It wasn't perfect— perfect was a ladder with a large cushion at its base—but it was the best she was going to get. She sat down on the tuft of grass beside the spot and dangled her feet over the edge. Then, without giving herself time to doubt the wisdom of what she was doing, she slipped her bottom off the grass and, after a few heart-quickening moments with her feet in midair and her body sliding off the tuft, her toes found a ledge on the opposite wall, against which she now braced herself. There followed a minute of clumsy maneuvering while she turned herself around so that she was facing the grass off which she'd slid. There were probably ten easier ways to do what she was doing, she thought, but right now her brain wasn't quick enough to think them through.

She glanced down before she made her next move, which was an error. Her muscles seized up for several seconds, and she could feel the sweat oozing out of her palms and armpits, its smell sour with fear.

"Take hold of yourself, Frannie," she chided herself. "You can do this."

Then, taking a deep breath, she renewed her descent, hold by hesitant hold, only this time she didn't make the mistake of looking down—at least not all the way down—but limited her gaze to the rock, studying it for nicks and cracks where she might find purchase.

Only once, when she thought she heard somebody calling to her, did she look up, hesitating for a moment to listen for the cry again. It came, but it was not a human voice, it was just one of the birds whose call had an almost human timbre. She returned to the labor of descent determined not to look up at the sky again, whether she heard cries or no. It was upsetting, seeing the light bounded by two walls of rock, getting narrower as she descended. From now on she would look no further than her hands and feet, until she was down beside Will and planning their ascent.

Rosa had long ago ceased to care what Frannie thought or did, but she was intrigued, albeit remotely, to see the woman disappearing from sight into the crevice. Had she got too close to the Domus Mundi and had her wits burned up? If so, it surely hadn't been much of a fire. Well, never mind. She was gone now, and wouldn't be coming back, which left Rosa alone. She let her head drop back against the shit-splattered rock and stared up at the sky. The clouds had covered the sun completely now, at least to human eyes. But she could see it still, or imagined she could: a bright ball flaming in the glorious nowhere of space.

Was that where she belonged, she found herself wondering. When she was no longer Rosa, which would be soon, very, when her wounded body gave up the last of its life, would she ascend like smoke, and be gone toward the sun? Or into the dark between the stars, perhaps. Yes, that would be better. To be lost in the dark utterly and forever, a nameless thing that had endured too may lifetimes, and lost its appetite for life and light.

But before she went, perhaps she still had it in her to reach Rukenau's step, to knock and ask him: *What was it for? Why did I live?*

If she was going to do so then she was going to have to do it soon, what little strength she had left was quickly departing her body. She had thought it would give her one last burst of vitality if she opened her wound, like a whip applied to her own back. But she'd simply traumatized her body further, and there was precious little power left in her.

She took her eyes from the sun and pushed herself into a sitting position. As she did so her instincts provided some information she'd been expecting to receive: Steep had set foot on the island. She didn't doubt the report. She and Steep had traced each other over vast distances in their time; she knew what his proximity felt like. He was on

his way. When he arrived he would do murderous harm, and she had
little or no defense against it. All she could do was to press her body
to her purpose and hope to reach the door before he did. Perhaps
Rukenau would play judge and jury, perhaps he would find fault with
Steep and stop him in his tracks. Or perhaps the house was empty,
and they would come into its chambers like thieves into a looted
palace, expecting glory and finding nothing. The notion gave her a
thrill of perverse pleasure: After this desperate pursuit they might
both end up empty-handed. And she could die and go to the darkness
between the stars. And he would live, and live, because the man he'd
become was afraid of death, and that would be his punishment for
being death's agent, that he could never be delivered from existence,
but would go on and on.

IX

It had entertained Jacob mightily to go among the stoic fisherman
of Oban as though the harbor were the shores of Galilee, and he
looking for disciples. He found one after a little search; a man in his
late sixties by the name of Hugh who had been pleased to take a passenger over to Tiree for a modest sum. The fee was quickly agreed
upon and they left a little after eight-fifteen, following the route of
the *Claymore* up the sound. The ship was of course a great deal more
powerful than Hugh's little boat, but unlike the *Claymore* they did
not have any ports of call to delay them along the way, so that they
came into the little harbor at Scarinish no more than two hours after
the ferry.

The voyage had refreshed and replenished Jacob. He had not
slept, but he had fallen into a meditative mood as he watched the
sea. He had never understood why it was so often thought to be a
feminine element. Yes, there were tides in a woman's body that were
not to be found in a man, and yes, it was the place of genesis. But it
was also ambitious and dispassionate, slow in its workings against the
land, but inevitable. Surely then it was the earth that was woman's
lot, the nurturing place, warm and fertile. The deeps belonged to
men.

So he mused as they sailed. And by the time he stepped off the boat onto the pier his mind was pleasantly lulled, as though he had just finished writing in his journal and was ready to turn a fresh page.

He decided against stealing a vehicle to finish his journey. The island was small and, though he doubted it was well policed, this was not the time to risk being delayed by an officer of the law. He went into the post office and asked the affable girl behind the counter if maybe she knew of a taxi service. The girl said that indeed she did; the island's only taxi was owned and driven by her brother-in-law Angus, and she would be happy to phone him. She did so and told Jacob the car would be outside within a quarter of an hour. It took rather longer than that, but finally the aforementioned Angus drove up in his twenty-year-old Volkswagen, and asked Steep where he wanted to go.

"Kenavara," Jacob told him.

"Now d'you mean Barrapol?"

"No. I mean the cliffs," Jacob said.

"Well. I can't drop you there," Angus replied. "There's no road."

"Just get me as close as you can."

"That'll be Barrapol," Angus said.

"That's fine. Barrapol's fine."

What would have happened to him, he wondered as they drove, if he'd never left the islands? Never taken a human name, never pretended to be something other than he was and in that process mislaid the truth of his nature; if he'd gone to live instead far from inquiring eyes on Uist or Harris or a piece of sea-girdled rock that was, like him, nameless? Would he have found the silence he needed, and found God in it? He doubted it. Even here, in this spartan place, there was too much life, too much distraction. Sooner or later, the passion for absence that had driven him would have risen into his thoughts.

His driver was, of course, chatty. Where had Jacob come from, he wanted to know, and where was he staying? Did he know Archie Anderson, of Barrapol? Jacob answered the questions as best he could, all the while thinking about God and namelessness, as though he were two people. One, the human being he'd been playing for so long, the man making small-talk with the driver; the other the being who moved behind that pretense, the being who had left this island with murder on his mind, the being who was going home. It was in sight now, that home. The long headland of Ceann a' Bharra, where Rukenau had laid the foundations of his empire. Despite the conversation they'd had as they left Scarinish, Angus wanted to know if he couldn't drop his passenger off at some particular house. He knew everyone in Barrapol, he said (it wasn't difficult, there were less than a dozen houses), Iain Findlay and his wife, Jean, the McKinnons, Hector Cameron.

"Just take me to the end of the road," Jacob said, "and I'll make my own way from there."

"Are you sure now?"

"I'm sure."

"Well, you're the man who's payin'."

Where the road withered to a track, Jacob got out and paid Angus twice what he'd charged. Very happy with this minor windfall, Angus thanked him and offered a card with his number in case Jacob needed a taxi for the return journey. He was so plainly proud to have a card with his name printed on it (he'd had them made up in Oban, he said) that Jacob accepted it graciously and, thanking him, began the trek through the *machair* to Kenavara. The look of unalloyed pleasure on the man's face when he'd produced the card remained in Steep's mind long after the car had disappeared and left him among the leaping hares. Oh, to have once known a simple pride like that, he thought, just once.

He pocketed the card, but of course he would never have need of it. There would be no return journey, not from the House of the World.

X

The polished grass had gone from beneath Will's feet. The clouded sky had vanished overhead. He had entered a large room, the walls of which looked to be made of caked earth, which glistened faintly as though still damp. Apparently his theorizing with Frannie about the abstract or metaphysical nature of the Domus Mundi had been wide of the mark. It was a tangible reality, at least as far as his now-calmed senses could tell: the walls, the darkness, the warm stagnant air, which filled his head with a stew of fetid scents. Things were rotting here, some of them going to a sickening sweetness, some of them to a bitter smell that stung his sinuses. He didn't have to look far for the source of at least some portion of this stench. All manner of detritus had been dumped around the chamber, some of it in a drift against the wall to his left that was fully seven or eight feet tall. He wandered over to inspect the trash a little more closely, wondering as he did so where the light in the room was coming from. There were no windows, but there were, he saw, hairline cracks in the walls from which the luminescence was seeping. It was not, he thought, daylight. It was warmer, yet not quite so warm as fire or candlelight.

Examining the contents of the rubbish heaped against the wall, another mystery: Though most of the drift was simply a clotted mass of incoherent forms, like the scourings of an enormous drain, there were several tree branches amongst the garbled mass. Was this stuff that had been washed up against the cliff, he wondered, which Rukenau had for some reason hauled up into the house? They certainly weren't native species; the island had no trees. Nor were these small branches. The largest of the boughs was as thick as Will's thigh.

Turning his back on the filth he made his way across the room to an archway that led to an adjacent chamber. The scene here was just as dispiriting. The same dirt walls and floor; a ceiling too high to be properly made out, but surely raised of the same charmless stuff. If indeed this house was built to hold up a mirror to the world's condition, Will thought, then the planet was in a foul state indeed.

That idea ignited a suspicion in him. Suppose the substance of his conversation with Frannie had after all been correct, and this stinking place was a mirror the Domus Mundi was holding up to his own psyche? If he'd learned anything in the weeks since emerging from his coma it was that his mind and the reality it perceived were not in a fixed relationship. They were like volatile lovers in a heated affair, each constantly reassessing the state of their passion in the light of what they believed the other was feeling. So here he was in a place so canny it could render itself invisible to the casual eye. It took no great leap of faith to believe that such a place could have even more sophisticated ways to defend itself, and what more certain way to traumatize trespassers than to confront them with the murk of their own minds?

He pondered how best to put this thesis to the test; how to pierce the buttery rot that surrounded him and find the force that lay beyond it, if indeed there was a force to be found. While he plotted, he surveyed more closely the contents of the room in which he was standing. There were, he saw, a few pieces of domestic junk among the incoherent filth. Over in one corner was the remnants of a chair and close to it an overturned table, in the center of which a fire had been made. He wandered over to it, curious as to what clues it might offer up. A meal had been had here. There was a partially eaten fish lying in the ashes and beside it a scattering of fruit: a couple of apples, an orange, and a still succulent mango, which had been roughly torn apart and partially devoured. Assuming this was all his mind's invention, were these perverse mementos of Drew's love feast?

He went down on his haunches to examine the evidence, picking up the largest portion of the mango and sniffing it. The juice was sticky, the smell sweetly fragrant. If it was an illusion, then it was a damn good one. He tossed the fruit back among the ashes and stood up, surveying the room for other objects to scrutinize. He realized he was overlooking the obvious: the walls themselves. He strode across the room and examined the dirt. It was, as he'd suspected, moist in places, almost as though it were suppurating. He touched one of the wetter places and his fingers came away dirty. He touched it again, pressing his fingers into the muck. They slid in maybe half an inch, and might have gone in deeper, but his hand was suddenly arrested by a tingling sensation that passed up through his wrist and into his forearm. He withdrew his hand, aware instantly where he'd felt this before: It was the same order of sensation that had coursed through his sinews when he'd been with Rosa in Donnelly's house, and later, when he'd confronted Steep. This bright matter was the essential stuff of all three: Rosa, Jacob, and Domus Mundi.

Once again, he longed to luxuriate in the feeling, but he had no time for such indulgences. He had to keep to his purpose. He stepped away from the wall and perused it. Where his fingers had pierced the dirt a tempting luminescence was spilling out. This isn't something my mind's inventing, he thought to himself, his certainty as sudden as it was absolute. The dirt and the light it concealed, the fish and the fruit lying on the ashes, all of it was real. Charged with new confidence, he crossed to the nearest door (the room had three) and entered a narrow but immensely tall passage, which was so clogged with rubbish in one direction that it was impassable. He headed in the other direction for maybe twenty yards, thinking as he went that either the house occupied the entire summit of Kenavara to the limit of the cliffs, or else it was somehow constructed in defiance of physical laws and contained an immensity belied by its perimeters. He was about to turn into another chamber when he heard the sound of somebody sobbing further down the passage. Following the sound, he passed through a small antechamber into the largest room he had yet discovered, and the most littered. There were heaps of rubbish everywhere, much of it, as before, unrecognizable. But there was also evidence of somebody having tried to make some order of the chaos. A table with a chair set close by, a pitiful nest of twigs and leaves made in one of the corners, with what looked to be a garment rolled up for a pillow.

He didn't have to look very far to find the man whose dwelling this was, the fellow was kneeling across the room from the door through which Will had entered. There was an elaborate arrangement of garbage on the ground in front of him, which he was studying as he sobbed, his hands to his face.

Will got halfway across the room before the man looked up. As soon as he did he was on his feet, his hands dropping from his face, which was filthy, but for the places where his tears had run. It was hard to judge his age when he was in such a pitiful condition, but Will guessed him to be less than thirty. His bespectacled features were gaunt, his clogged beard and mustache in severe need of trimming, his greasy hair the same. His clothes were in as beleaguered a state as the rest of him, his threadbare shirt and jeans glued to his malnourished body with filth. He looked at Will with a mingling of fear and disbelief.

"Where did you come from?" he said. Judging by his accent, there was a well-educated Englishman under all the dirt.

"I came from . . . out there," Will told him.

"When?"

"Just a few minutes ago."

The man got to his feet, and approached Will. "Which way did you come?" he said. Then, lowering his voice, "Could you find your way back?"

"Yes, of course," Will replied.

"Oh God, oh God," the man started to say, his breathing getting faster, "this isn't some trick, is it?"

"Why would I trick you?"

"To make me leave her." He narrowed his eyes, studying Will with some suspicion. "You want to have her for yourself?"

"Who?"

"Diane! My wife!" His suspicion was plainly deepening into certainty. "Oh that's it, isn't it? This is Rukenau's idea of a bloody *joke*, trying to tempt me away. Why's he so cruel? I've done everything he asked me, haven't I? *Everything.* Why can't he just let us go?" His pleas hardened into assertions. "I'm not going *anywhere* without her, do you hear me? I refuse! I'll rot here if I have to. She's my wife, and I'm not leaving—"

"I get the picture," Will said.

"I mean it—"

"I told you: I understand."

"And if he wants to make me—"

"Will you *shut up a minute?*"

The man stopped his protests and blinked at Will from behind his spectacles, his head cocked a little, like a bird.

"I just wandered in here three minutes ago. I swear. Now, can we talk sensibly?"

The man looked a little embarrassed at his outburst. "So the place caught you too," he said softly.

"No," Will said. "I wasn't *caught.* I came in of my own free will."

"Why would you do that?"

"To find Rukenau."

"You came looking for Rukenau?" the man replied, as though this were tantamount to insanity.

"Yes. Do you know where he is?"

"Maybe," the man said testily.

Will approached him. "What's your name?"

"Theodore."

"Do folks call you Theodore?"

"No. They call me Ted."

"Can I call you Ted, too? Is that all right?"

"Yes. I suppose so."

"That's a good start. I'm Will. Or Bill. Or Billy. Anything but William. I hate William."

"I hate Theodore."

"I'm glad we've cleared that up. Now, Ted, I need you to trust me. In fact, we have to trust one another, because we're both in the same mess, aren't we?" Ted nodded. "So. Why don't you just tell me about," he was going to say Rukenau, but he changed his mind at the last minute and instead said, "your wife."

"Diane?"

"Yes, Diane. She's here somewhere, you said?" Again, the downcast eyes and the nervous nod. "But you don't know where."

"I know . . . vaguely," he said.

Will lowered his voice. "Has Rukenau got her?"

"No."

"Well, help me out here," Will pleaded. "Where is she?"

Ted's mouth grew tight and his eyes narrowed behind his smudged spectacles. Again, that birdlike glance up at Will. Then he seemed to decide that he would speak, and out it all came. "We didn't mean to come in here. We were just walking, you know, on the cliffs. I liked to birdwatch before I got married and I persuaded Diane to come along with me. We weren't doing anything we shouldn't. We were just walking, watching the birds."

"You don't live on the island."

"No, we were on holiday, going from island to island. A sort of second honeymoon."

"How long have you been in here?"

"I'm not exactly sure. I think we came in on the twenty-first."

"Of October?"

"No. *June.*"

"And you haven't stepped outside since?"

"One time I found the door, purely by chance. But how could I leave, with Diane still here? I couldn't do that."

"So is there anybody else here?"

His voice dropped to a whisper. "Oh yes. There's *him*—"

"Rukenau?"

"And there's others too. People who came in like Diane and me, that he's never let out. I hear them, now and then. One of them sings hymns. I've been trying to make a map," he said, casting a glance down at the arrangement of garbage on the ground. The twigs and pebbles and little heaps of dirt were apparently his attempt to re-create the house in miniature.

"Tell me what's where," Will said, going down on his haunches beside the map. He felt like a convict plotting an escape with a crazed felon, an impression that was only strengthened by the gleam of pride on Ted's face as he crouched on the other side of the model and proceeded to explain it.

"We're here," he said, pointing to a spot in the maze. "I've made this my base of operations. This little white stone way over here is the man who sings the hymns. As I said, I've never seen him, because he just runs away when I go near."

"And what's this?" Will asked, directing Ted's attention to a large space which was criss-crossed with lengths of thread.

"That's Rukenau's room."

"So we're not that far?" Will said, looking round at the door that he guessed would lead him to Rukenau.

"You don't want to go there," Ted said to him. "I swear."

Will got to his feet. "You don't have to come with me," he said.

"But I need you to help me find Diane."

"If you know where she is, why haven't you fetched her your-self?"

"Because the place she's gone . . . it's too much for me," he looked embarrassed to be admitting this. "I get . . . overwhelmed."

"By what?"

"The feelings. The light. The things that come into my head. Even Rukenau can't stand it."

Now Will was curious. If he was understanding Ted's ramblings correctly, there was still a part of this house that delivered on the description that he'd heard Jacob make of it all those years ago. *It's glorious*, he'd said to Simeon. *If we were together, we could go deep, deep inside. We could see the seed of the seed, I swear."*

That was where Ted's wife was, presumably. *Deep, deep inside,* where the weak-hearted couldn't go without paying the price of tres-pass.

"Let me speak to Rukenau first," Will said. "Then we'll go find her. That's a promise."

Ted's eyes suddenly flooded with tears, and he came as close to a spontaneous expression of thanks as a sober Englishman ever gets: he grasped Will's hand and shook it. "I should give you a weapon," he said. "I don't have much—just a few sharpened sticks—but they're better than nothing."

"What do we need weapons for?"

"There's plenty of animals in this place. You'll hear them through the walls."

"I'll take my chances."

"Are you sure?"

"Absolutely sure. Thank you."

"As you like," Ted said. He went to the little cache of sticks that lay beside his bed. "I'll bring two, for when you change your mind," he said. Then he led the way out of his little sanctum. The adjacent room was substantially darker, and it took Will a moment to orient himself.

"Slow down," he told Ted, who had already negotiated his way across the murky ground to the archway on the far side. In his effort to catch up with the man, he stumbled against something underfoot and fell forward in the darkness. The trash he landed on was barbed; it raked his face and flank, tearing his pants and piercing his leg. He let out a cry of pain, which turned into a stream of curses as he flailed about. Ted came to his aid and was in the process of disentangling him when a deep grinding sound brought his efforts to a halt.

"Oh Lord, no," the man breathed.

Will looked up. Light was now spilling into the room, warmer than the luminescence from the walls, its source a doorway that was opening across the chamber. It was twice the height of a man, and a foot or more thick, its immensity moved by a system of ropes and weights. There was a fire burning in the room beyond, perhaps several, and forms moving in the air, wreathed in smoke. And from the heart of the smoke, a languid inquiry, "Do you have something for me, Theodore?"

It was plain by the expression on Ted's face that he wanted to flee. But it was equally plain that he was too cowed or traumatized to do so.

"Come to me," the speaker said. "Both of you. And put your sticks down, Theodore."

Ted shook his head in despair, and tossing down the weapons he was carrying, made his way toward the door with the reluctance of a dog in fear of a beating.

Will got to his feet and quickly assessed the damage he'd done himself. There was nothing significant, just a few scrapes. Ted was already at the door, his head bowed. Will wasn't so reverent. Head raised, eyes eager, he made his way across the antechamber and, bypassing Ted at the threshold, made his way into the presence of Gerard Rukenau.

XI

Though in principle Frannie's descent should have become easier as the distance she had to fall decreased, the further from the sunlight she ventured the slimier the rocks became and the rarer the handholds. More than once she was within a hair's-breadth of falling and would have done so had she not twisted around to wedge herself across the gully as she slipped. If she survived this, she thought, she'd have plenty of bruises as souvenirs.

There was another problem: It was much darker down here than she'd expected it to be. She had only to look up—which against her better judgment she did—to see why. The clouds had been steadily thickening as she descended, and the sliver of sky still visible to her was iron gray. There'd be rain soon, she guessed, which would make the ascent even more problematic. Well, it was too late for regrets. She'd made it down without serious injury; maybe she'd find a simpler route by which to ascend, she hoped, with Will.

She didn't let go of the gully wall until she was certain she had her feet on solid ground. Once she did so she looked back up the crevice to locate Will, but the overhang blocked her view. She started toward him, calling to him as she went, reassuring him that she was on her way. There was no reply, and she feared the worst: He'd cracked his skull open, broken his neck; she'd find him lying there, as lifeless as the rock he was sprawled upon. Steeling herself for the sight, she ducked under the overhang, and there, a few yards ahead of her, was the body that had seduced her down into this wretched crack. It wasn't Will. Lord God Almighty, it wasn't Will! It was a human body surely enough, but a very old one. It was virtually a mummy in fact, wrapped up in bandages and cloth. She was relieved, of course, but almost angry at herself for the wasted time and effort making the descent. Steeling herself against the sight, she examined the cadaver a little more closely. Several of its wrappings had rotted away, revealing flesh the color of tobacco. Its head was particularly upsetting to look at, the skin dried tight over the bones of the skull, the lips pulled back from its pearly teeth. Was this Rukenau, she wondered? Had he perished and been buried, or at least hidden away, here in the gully, either by his acolytes or perhaps by fearful islanders unwilling to lay his bones in hallowed ground? She studied the body for some clue, walking around it as she did so. And there in the rotted remains of the casket she found the evidence she needed to identify him: a collection of a half-dozen paintbrushes, bound together with cord and what looked like sealing wax. She loosed a little moan of satisfaction at solving the puzzle. This wasn't Rukenau: It was the corpse of Thomas Simeon. She remembered only vaguely what the book had said on the subject. The body had been stolen, she recalled, and hadn't somebody, perhaps Dwyer, theorized that it had been taken north and buried on Rukenau's island? So it had. A strange and in its way pitiful end to a strange and pitiful life: to be preserved in whatever they'd used for embalming fluids back then, wrapped up in finery, and hidden away like a secret treasure.

Well, that was one question answered. But it begged another. If Will wasn't down here, then where the hell was he? He'd failed to answer her when she'd called to him, so it was still perfectly possible that he was in trouble; the question was *where?*

The rain had begun to fall, and to judge by the force of water running down the sides of the crevice it was heavy. Attempting to clamber back up at the spot where she'd descended would be folly: She'd have to find another method. It was a long trek down to the sea, so she decided first to make her way up to the head of the gully in search of an easier escape route. If she failed to find one, then she'd try the other end, though the way the waves had been beating against the headland it would be difficult to find a means of egress there without risk of being washed away. All in all, not a very appetizing menu of alternatives, but, damn it, she'd got herself into this mess and she would get herself out.

So thinking, she started on her way up to the head of the gully. It got a little brighter a few yards on, the walls far enough apart that the rain came directly down upon her. It was cold, but she was sweaty after her exertions, and she put her face up to the downpour to be cooled. As she did so, she heard Steep say:

"Look at the state of you."

Despite her extreme frailty, Rosa hadn't remained on the rocks where Frannie had left her, but had crawled, with painful sloth, to the rocks at the end of the gully. There she had collapsed, unable to move her limbs another inch. And there Steep had found her. He kept his distance from her, stepping close for a moment only in order to pull her hand away from her face, then stepping back again as though Rosa's weakness was contagious.

"Take me inside," she murmured to him.

"Why should I do that?"

"Because I'm dying, and I want to be there . . . I want to see Rukenau for myself one last time."

"He won't want to see you in this state," Jacob said. "Wounded and gasping."

"Please, Jacob," she said. "I can't get there on my own."

"So I see."

"Help me."

Jacob thought about this for a moment. Then he said, "I think not. Really, it's better I go to him on my own."

"How can you be so cruel?"

"Because you betrayed me, love, going with Will. Making me follow you like some lost dog."

"I had no choice," Rosa protested. "You weren't going to bring me here."

"True," Steep said.

"Though Lord knows, after all we've suffered together, the grief . . . " She looked away from Steep now, the tremors in her body escalating. "I've thought so often . . . if we'd had healthy children, perhaps we'd have grown kinder over the years instead of more cruel."

"Oh *Christ*, Rosa," Steep said, his voice oozing contempt. "Surely you don't still believe that nonsense? We *had* healthy children."

She didn't move her head, but her eyes slid back in Steep's direction. "No," she murmured. "They were—"

"Healthy, bright little babies—"

"Brainless, you said—"

"Perfect, every one of them."

"*No* . . . "

"I fertilized you to keep you happy; then I killed them so they wouldn't get underfoot. And you truly never realized?" She said nothing. "Stupid, stupid woman."

Now she spoke. "My children . . . " she murmured, so softly he didn't catch her words.

"What did you say?" he asked her, leaning a little closer to her.

Instead of speaking, she screamed, *"My children!"*—the sound she emitted shaking the rock on which she lay. Jacob tried to retreat, but she had the force of grief in her sinews, and she reached for him before he could escape. Her scream wasn't her only weapon in this assault. Even as she caught hold of him with her left hand her right tore at the bandages that bound her wound and the braided brightness went from her as though it wanted to devour him—

In the gully below, Frannie had barely clamped her hands over her ears to stop out the scream when she felt a hail of pebbles and wet dirt come down upon her head. She had crept closer to the end of the gully in order to hear the conversation better. Now she regretted her curiosity. The din that issued from Rosa made her sick to her stomach, despite her attempts to block it out. She reeled round, her body responding more to instinct than instruction, and staggered away down the gully, her feet slipping on the slimy stones. She'd got maybe six or seven yards when some portion of the ground—shaken by the din—capitulated, and the fall of clods of dirt and stone became calamitous.

Seeing the brightness escaping Rosa's abdomen, Steep had lifted his hands to protect his face, fearing it intended to blind him. But it was not his face it flew toward, nor was it his heart, nor even his groin. It was his hand the light sought, or rather the wound upon the palm of that hand, which his own blade had opened up.

It was he who had cried out, then, his alarm melding with Rosa's rage in such a powerful combination that the very ground was shaken into collapse.

Overhead, birds ceased their wheeling and swooped toward the safety of their nests. In the surf, seals dove deep so as not to hear the tumult. Amid the dunes, hares bolted for their burrows, and cattle in the meadow shat themselves in terror. And in the houses and bars of Barrapol and Crossapol and Balephuil, and on the open roads between, men and women about their daily labors ceased them on the instant. If they were in company they exchanged troubled looks, and if they were alone went straightaway into company.

And then, just as suddenly as it had begun, it was gone.

The avalanche in the gully had its own momentum, however. The falling stones grew larger in size as the ground gave way, filling the air with so much dirt and debris that Frannie could see nothing. She had retreated almost as far as Thomas Simeon's resting place, and there waited while the crevice shook from end to end.

At last, the rockfall subsided, and the dust-thickened air began to clear. She kept her distance for a little while, however, fearing either a fresh din from above or some further collapse. There was neither, however, and after a minute or two she started back up the gully to see how the land now lay. There was far more light than there had been previously, despite the grimy air. The ground that surrounded the end of the gully had entirely fallen away, she saw, delivering a great tonnage of fractured stone, earth, and grass into the crevice,

where it had formed a chaotic slope. She had her means of ascent
here, at least, if she was willing to dare such a perilous route. She
studied the rim of the hole, looking for some sign of life, but she saw
none. Apart from the occasional drizzle of dirt from the raw edges of
the hole, the scene was motionless.

At the bottom of the incline, she paused to roughly plan her
route, and then began to climb. It was easier than her descent, but
it was by no means simple. The rocks had barely settled, and with
every step she feared for their solidity; meanwhile the rain was
pouring down, turning the dirt to mud. A third of the way up she
elected to finish the climb on all fours, which meant that in no
time she was virtually muddied from head to foot. No matter, there
was less chance of her toppling backward that way, and when one of
her foot- or handholds proved treacherous, she had three others for
fail safes.

As she came within a couple of yards of the top of the slope,
however, she felt something touching her leg. She looked down and
to her horror saw Rosa lying partially buried in the churned dirt, her
outstretched hand clutching blindly at Frannie's ankle. The expression she wore resembled nothing Frannie had seen on a human face
before, her mouth grotesquely wide, like that of a landed fish, her
golden eyes, despite the rain's assault, unblinking.

"Steep?" she gasped.

"No. It's me. It's Frannie."

"Did Steep fall?"

"I don't know. I didn't see—"

"Lift me up," Rosa demanded. To judge by the splaying of her
limbs, she'd broken a number of bones, but she was plainly indifferent to the fact. "Lift me up," she said again. "We're going into the
house, you and me."

Frannie doubted she had the strength to haul the woman further
than the top of the incline. But even if she could do that little service
it would surely be the last she provided for Rosa. The woman's death
was imminent, to judge by her quickening gasps and by the violence
of the tremors passing through her body. Redistributing her weight on
the rocks, Frannie bent to clear the debris off Rosa's body. The bandages had been torn from her wound, Frannie saw, and though it was
partially clogged with mud, the same uncanny iridescence she'd first
seen in Donnelly's house flickered in its depths.

"Did Steep do this to you?" she asked.

Rosa stared sightlessly at the sky. "He cheated me of my children," she said.

"I heard."

"He cheated me of my life. And I'm going to make him suffer for it."

"You're too weak."

"My wound's my strength now," Rosa said. "He's afraid of what's broken in me," she shaped a terrible smile, as though she had become Death itself, "because it's found what's broken in him . . . "

Frannie didn't try to make sense of this. She simply bent to the task of cleaning the body, and then, once that labor was done, of attempting to raise Rosa into a position that allowed her to be lifted. Once she had her arms beneath the woman, she found to her astonishment that a curious strength passed between them. Her body became capable of what it could never have achieved a minute before: She lifted Rosa out of the dirt and carried her—not without effort, but with some measure of confidence—up the remainder of the incline to secure ground. The scene looked like a battlefield. Fresh fissures had opened in the earth, running in all directions from the place where Rosa and Jacob had clashed.

"Now to your left—" Rosa said.

"Yes?"

"Do you see a piece of open ground?"

"Yes."

"Carry me to it. The house is there."

"I don't see anything."

"That's because it has ways to fold itself out of your sight. But it's there. Trust me, it's there. And it wants us inside."

XII

The sound of the avalanche was audible in the Domus Mundi, but Will took little notice of it, distracted as he was by the scale of the spectacle before him, or, more precisely, *above* him. For it was there that Gerard Rukenau, the satyric sermonizer himself, had cho-

sen to make his home. The considerable expanse of the chamber
was criss-crossed with a complex network of ropes and platforms,
the lowest of them hanging a little above head height, while the
highest were virtually lost in the shadows of the vaulted ceiling. In
places, the knotted ropes were so densely intertwined, and so
encrusted with detritus, that they formed almost solid partitions,
and in one spot a kind of chimney that rose to the ceiling. To add
further to the sum of these strangenesses, there were scattered
throughout the structure items of antique furniture collected, perhaps, out of that mysterious house in Ludlow from which Galloway
had liberated his friend Simeon. Among this collection were several
chairs, suspended at various heights, and two or three small tables.
There was even a platform heaped with pillows and bedclothes,
where, presumably, Rukenau laid his head at night. Though the
cords and branches from which all of this was constructed were
filthy, and the furniture, despite its quality, much the worse for wear,
the obsessive elaboration of knots and partitions and platforms was
beautiful in the flickering luminescence that rose from the bowls of
pale flame that were set around the web, like stars in a strange fir-
mament.

And then, from a location perhaps forty feet above Will's head,
at the top of the woven chimney, Rukenau's voice came floating
down.

"So now, Theodore," he said. "Who have you brought to see
me?" His voice was more musical than it had sounded when he'd
been summoning them. He sounded genuinely curious as to who this
stranger in their midst might be.

"His name's Will," Ted said.

"I heard that much," Rukenau replied, "and he hates William,
which is sensible. But I also heard you came looking for me, Will,
and that's far more intriguing to me. How is it you've come looking
for a man who's been removed from human sight for so long?"

"There's still a few people talking about you," Will said, looking
up into the murky heights.

"You mustn't do that," Ted whispered to him. "Keep your head
bowed."

Will ignored the advice and continued to stare up at the mesh.
His defiance was rewarded. There was Rukenau, descending through
the myriad layers of his suspended world, stepping from one precarious perch to another like a tightrope walker. And as he made his

descent, he talked on, "Tell me, Will, do you know the man and woman making such a ruckus outside?" he asked.

"There's a man?" Will said.

"Oh yes, there's a man."

It could only be one, Will knew, and he hoped to God that Frannie had got out of his path. "Yes, I know them," he told Rukenau, "but I think you know them better."

"Perhaps so," the man above him replied, "though it's been a very long time since I drove them out of here."

"Do you want to tell me why you did that?"

"Because the male did not bring my Thomas back to me."

"Thomas Simeon?"

Rukenau halted in his descent. "Oh Jesu," he said. "You really do know something about me, don't you?"

"I'd still like to know more."

"Thomas came back to me, at last. Did you know that?"

"Once he was dead," Will said. This piece of the story was a guess on his part, fueled by Dwyer's theorizing, but the more he persuaded Rukenau he knew, the more he hoped the man would confess. And Dwyer had been right in her deductions it seemed, for Rukenau sighed and said: "Indeed, he came back to me a corpse. And I think a little of my own life went out of me when he was laid in the rocks. He had a greater supply of God's grace in his little finger than I have in my entire being. Or ever had."

Now after a little pause to mull this admission over, he continued to descend, and by degrees Will got a better sense of him. He was dressed in what had once been fine clothes, but which now, like almost everything in the house, were besmirched and encrusted. Only his face and hands were pale, uncannily pale, so that he resembled a bloodless doll. There was nothing brittle about his motion however; he moved with a kind of sinuous grace, so that despite his excremental garb and the blandness of his features, Will could not take his gaze from the man.

"Tell me," Rukenau said, as he continued his descent, "how is it you know these people at the threshold?"

"You call them Nilotics, is that right?"

"Almost, but not quite," Rukenau said. Once again he paused. He was now perhaps ten feet above Will's head and perched upon a platform of bound boughs. He went down on his haunches and studied Will through the mesh as a fisherman might, to study his catch.

"I think despite your acuity you haven't quite comprehended their natures yet. Is that not so?"

"You're right," Will said. "I haven't. That's why I came here, to find out."

Rukenau leaned forward a little further and pulled aside a portion of encrusted rope in order to see his subject better, which in turn gave Will a clearer view of Rukenau. It wasn't simply his sinuous motion that carried an echo of the serpentine. There was a gloss to his flesh which put Will in mind of a snake, as did his total absence of hair. He had no eyebrows, nor lashes, nor any sight of hair on his cheek or chin. If this was some dermatological disease, he didn't seem to be suffering any other effects. In fact he fairly radiated good health—his eyes gleamed, and his teeth shone, uncommonly white.

"You came here out of *curiosity?*" he said.

"I suppose that's part of it."

"What else?"

"Rosa . . . is dying."

"I doubt that."

"She is. I swear."

"And the male? Jacob? Is he sickening too?"

"Not the way Rosa is, but yes . . . he's sickening."

"Then," Rukenau chewed on this a moment, "I think we should continue this conversation without young Theodore. Why don't you go fetch me some sustenance, my boy?"

"Yes, sir—" Ted replied, thoroughly cowed.

"Wait—" Will said, catching hold of Ted's arm before he could leave. "Ted had something to ask you for."

"Yes, yes, his wife," Rukenau said, wearily. "I hear you sobbing over her, Theodore, night and day. But I can do nothing for you, I'm afraid. She doesn't care to see you any longer. That's the long and short of it. Don't take it too personally. She's just become enthralled with this damnable place."

"You don't like it here?" Will said.

"*Like it?*" Rukenau replied, his mask of pleasantry evaporating in a heartbeat. "This is my *prison*, Will. Do you understand me? My purgatory. Nay, I would say, my *Hell.*" He leaned down a little and studied Will's face. "But I wonder, when I look at you, if perhaps some gracious angel hasn't sent you to set me free."

"It can't be that difficult to get out of here, surely," Will said. "Ted told me he found his way back to the front door without—"

Rukenau interrupted, his voice all exasperation. "What do you suppose would happen to me if I stepped outside these walls?" he said. "I've shed a lot of skins in this house, Will, and I've cheated the Reaper doing so. But the moment I step beyond the limits of this abominable place my immortality is forfeit. I would have thought that would have been plain enough to a man of your wisdom. Tell me, by the way, what do they call we magi in your age? Necromancer always sounded theatrical to my ear; and Doctor of Philosophy entirely too dusty. The fact is, I don't think there ever was a word that suited us. We're part metaphysicians; part demagogues."

"I'm none of those things," Will said.

"Oh, but there's a spirit moves in you," Rukenau said. "An animal of some kind, is it?"

"Why don't you come down and see for yourself?"

"I could never do that."

"Why not?"

"I've told you. The house is an atrocity. I have sworn I will not set foot on it. Ever again."

"But you're the one who had it built."

"How is it you know so much?" Rukenau said. "Did you get all this from Jacob? Because let me tell you, if you did, he knows less than he thinks."

"I'll tell you everything I know, and where I learned it," Will said. "But first—"

Rukenau looked lazily at Ted. "Yes, yes, his wretched wife. Look at me, Theodore. That's better. Are you sure you want to leave my employ? I mean, is it such a burden to fetch me a little fruit or a little fish?"

"I thought you told me you never left the house?" Will said to Ted.

"Oh he doesn't go *out* to get it," Rukenau said. "He goes *in*, don't you, Theodore? He goes where his wife has gone, or as close as he dares."

Will was confounded by this, but he did his best to keep the bewilderment from his face. "If you really want to leave," Rukenau went on, "I will make no objection. But I'm warning you, Theodore, your wife may feel otherwise. She went into the soul of the house, and she was enamored of what she found. I have no power over that kind of stupidity."

"But if I could somehow get her back?" Ted said.

"Then if your new champion here will stay in your place, I would not prevent your leaving. How's that? Will? Is that a fair bargain?"

"No," Will said, "but I'll accept it."

Ted was beaming. "Thank you," he said to Will. "Thank you. Thank you. Thank you." Then to Rukenau, "Does that mean I can go?"

"By all means. Find her. If she'll come to you, that is, which I frankly doubt . . ."

This talk didn't wipe the smile from Ted's face. He was gone in a moment, darting off across the chamber. Before he'd even reached the door he'd started calling his wife's name.

"She won't come to him," Rukenau said, when Ted had exited the chamber. "The Domus Mundi has her. What does he have to offer her by way of seduction?"

"His love?" Will said.

"The world doesn't care for love, Will. It goes on its way, indifferent to our feelings. You know that."

"But perhaps—"

"Perhaps what? Go on, tell me what's on your mind."

"Perhaps we haven't shown it enough love ourselves."

"Oh would that make the world kind?" Rukenau said. "Would that make the sea bear me up if I was drowning? Would a plague rat elect not to bite me, because I professed my love? Will, don't be so childish. The world doesn't care what Theodore feels for his wife, and his wife is too entranced with the glamor of this miserable place to look twice at him. That is the bitter truth."

"I don't see what's so enchanting about this place."

"Of course you don't. That's because I've worked against its seductions over the years. I've had them sealed from my sight with mud and excrement. Much of it my own, by the way. A man passes a lot of shit in two hundred and seventy years."

"So it was you that covered the walls?"

"At the beginning it was my personal handiwork, yes. Later, when people made the mistake of wandering in, I turned their hands to the task. Many of them died doing it, I'm afraid—" He interrupted himself, rising to his feet on his perch. "Oh now," he said. "It begins."

"What's happening?"

"Jacob Steep has just entered." There was a barely perceptible tremor in Rukenau's voice.

"Then you'd better tell me what you know about him," Will replied. "And do it quickly."

XIII

Now that he was in the House, Steep saw the perfection of the route that had brought him here. Perhaps, after all, he had not returned into the Domus Mundi to perish, as least not yet. Perhaps he had come into this place to do his ambition greater service. Rosa had been right when she accused him of loving the slaughter; he always had, always would. It was one of his appetites as a man—to love the hunt, the blood-letting and the kill came as naturally as voiding his bladder. And now, back in this house, he would have the opportunity to feed that appetite as never before. Once Will and Rosa were dead, and Rukenau too, he would sit at the heart of the Domus Mundi, and oh *what he would do.* He would show the merchants who raped the world from their boardrooms, and the popes who sanctioned harvests of hungry children, and the potentates who salved their loneliness with shows of destruction, sights that would astonish them. He would be chillier than an accountant's ledger, crueler than a general on the night of a coup d'état.

Why hadn't he seen the ease of this before? Stupidity, was it? Or cowardice, more like, afraid to return into the presence of the man who'd wielded such power over him. Well, he wasn't afraid any longer. He would not waste any more time with knives hereafter (except for Rukenau, perhaps; Rukenau he would stab). In his dealings with the rest of the world, he would be far cleverer. He would poison the tree while it was still a seed, and let all who ate from it perish. He would warp the fetus in the womb and blight the harvest before it even showed itself. Nothing would survive this holocaust, nothing: It would, in time, be the end of everything, except for God and himself.

All his life had been, he realized, a preparation for this return, and the conspiracies mounted against him by the woman and the queer, even that kiss, that vile kiss, had been ways to bring him, all unknowing, to this threshold.

He was astonished when he stepped inside, to see how changed the place was. He went down on his haunches and scraped at the ground: It was covered with a layer of excrement, animal and human mingled. The walls were the same, and the ceiling. The whole house, which had been so transcendent at its creation, so light, had been concealed behind layers of dirt. Rukenau's doing, no doubt. Steep wasn't surprised. For all his metaphysical pretensions, Rukenau had at heart been a foolish and frightened man. Hadn't he dispatched Jacob to bring Thomas home to the island, because he'd needed an artist's vision to understand what he'd wrought? In lieu of that comprehension, what had he done? Covered the glories of the Domus Mundi with clay and shit.

Poor Rukenau, Jacob thought, poor, human Rukenau. And then the thought became a shout, which echoed off the walls as he strode in search of his sometime master. "*Poor Rukenau! Oh, poor, poor Rukenau!*"

"He's calling my name—"

"Ignore him," Will said. "I need to know what he is."

"You already know," Rukenau replied. "You used the very word yourself. He's a Nilotic."

"That's a location, not a description. I need to know details."

"I know the legends. I know the prayers. But I don't know anything that could pass for the truth."

"Just spit it out, whatever it is!"

Rukenau looked at him balefully, and for a moment it seemed he would say nothing; then the words came, and once begun there was no stopping them. No time for questions or clarifications. Just an unburdening.

"I am the bastard son of a man who built churches," he said. "Great places of worship my father made, in his time. And when I was old enough, though I'd not been brought up in the bosom of his family, I sought him out and said: I think I have just a little of your genius in me. Let me walk in your footsteps; I'll be your apprentice. Of course, he'd have none of it. I was a bastard. I couldn't be there, in public view, embarrassing him in the eyes of his patrons. He drove me away. And when I went from his house I said: So be it. I'll find my own way in the world, and I'll make a place where God wants so much to come that He'll leave all my father's fine churches empty.

"I learned magic; I became quite a learned fellow. And quite admired, I fancy. I didn't care much. I'd had all the admiration I needed in a year or two. Then I went off around the world, in search of the secret geometries that make holy places holy. I went to Greece to look at the temples, and to India to see what the Hindu had done.

And on my way home, to Egypt, to see the pyramids. There I heard tell of a creature who had, according to legend, made temples from the altars of which a priest might see the Creator's labors at a single glance.

"It sounded preposterous, of course, but I journeyed up the Nile in search of this nameless angel, prepared to use whatever magical makings I possessed to bring it to my purpose. And in a cave near Luxor, I found the creature, which I dubbed a Nilotic. I brought it back here, and with Simeon's help I laid plans for the masterpiece it would build. A place so holy that all my father's churches would fall into ruin, and his memory be despised." He made a sour laugh at his own folly. "But of course it was too much for us all. Simeon fled and lost his mind. The Nilotic grew impatient, and left me, even though I had confounded its memories of itself and, without my help, it would remain in ignorance. And I . . . stayed here, determined to master what I'd made." He shook his head. "But there's no mastering the world, is there?"

He was interrupted here by another shout from Steep.

"I think he'd disagree with you," Will said.

"Why am I afraid?" Rukenau said. "I've no desire to live." He looked at Will with distressing rabidity in his eyes. "Oh but Jesu, *keep it from me.*"

"You controlled it before," Will pointed out. "Do the same again."

"How can I do to it what's already done?" Rukenau spat. "You have to find persuasions of your own."

With that he started to scramble back up the ropes, his panic making him nimble. He'd only got a few yards however, when Will heard Steep's footfall across the chamber and looked round to see the man lurching into view. He looked far worse than he had in Donnelly's home. He was rain-sodden, and spattered with mud from brow to boots, the orbits of his eyes pressing brightly at his flesh, his body shaking. He looked like a man who would die very soon.

Even his voice, which at its most monotonal had still been persuasive, was scoured of charm. "Has he told you the story of our lives, Will?" he said.

"Some of it."

"But you'd like to know still more. And apparently you're willing to perish for the privilege." He shook his head. "You should have left me alone, both of you. Lived and died in ignorance."

"You wanted to be touched," Will said.

"Did I?" Steep replied, as though he was now quite ready to be persuaded on the subject. "Maybe I did."

There was a motion on the web overhead and, with almost theatrical slowness, Steep looked up. Rukenau had by now retreated to the heights.

"You can't hide up there," Steep said to him. "You're not a child. Don't make yourself ridiculous. Come down." He took the knife out of his jacket. "Don't make me crawl up there."

"Let him be," Will said.

"Please," Jacob replied, a little pained. "This isn't your business. Why don't you go and look at the pretty lights? Go on. Take a look, while you still can. I'll join you in a little while." He spoke to Will as though to a child. "*Go on!*" he yelled suddenly, reaching up to catch hold of the net. "*Rukenau! Come down!*" He shook the net with astonishing violence. Clots and scabs of filth rained down on both his head and Will's; the ropes creaked and in several places snapped; a chair was shaken free and fell, smashing on the ground.

Plainly no words of Will's were going to calm him, which left Will with only one option. He strode toward Jacob and caught hold of the man, laying his palm against the man's neck.

There was no intake of breath this time, no earth-moving tremor. There was only a sudden blinding dust, a bitter red, in which Will glimpsed, all in the same moment, a thousand geometrics, vast as cathedrals, moving, opening, some of them, like rigorous flowers, while brightening glyphs—the language of Simeon's paintings and of Steep's journal—blazed from them. These weren't Jacob's memories, Will realized. They were the Nilotic's thoughts or some portion thereof: an array of mathematical possibilities far more overwhelming than the wood or the fox or the palace on the Neva.

Gasping, he let Jacob go and stumbled away from him. The assault of forms didn't leave his head immediately, however: They continued to move in his mind's eye for several seconds, blinding him. If Jacob had chosen to strike him down in that moment Will would have been as vulnerable as a sheep in a pen, but Steep had more pressing business. By the time Will had recovered his sight Jacob had given up shaking the web and was climbing it. And as he climbed, he yelled to Rukenau, "Don't be afraid. It has to happen to us all. *Living and dying, we feed the fire.*"

XIV

Of all the bizarreries that Frannie had experienced on this journey none was quite as shocking to her as stepping over the threshold of the Domus Mundi with Rosa. To be standing in daylight one moment surrounded—as far as her naïve senses were concerned—with grass and sky, and the next to be in a dark, poisonous place with the sun and the sea gone: It was terrifying. She was glad she had Rosa with her or she'd certainly have panicked, and this would not be, she thought, a good place to lose your self-control.

Rosa demanded to be set down once they were in the house and went with a few stumbling steps to the nearest wall. There she passed her hands over the surface, leaning a little closer to sniff at it. "Shit," she said. "He's covered the wall in shit." She called to Frannie, "is it all like this?"

"As far as I can see."

"Ceiling the same?"

Frannie looked up. "Yes." Rosa laughed. "Is it different from the way you remember it?"

"I don't much trust my memories, but I don't think it was a sewer when I was last here. Rukenau must have done this."

She started to probe the wall with her fingers, pulling away cobs of filth once she had her fingers deep enough. There was a source of light beneath the excrement, Frannie saw, a luminescence that seemed to ripple as Rosa worked, as though it sensed that somebody was laboring to unveil it. This was no illusion. The larger the hole Rosa tore in the wall became, the more apparent the muscular motion in the light. And there were colors in the brightness, brilliant darts of turquoise and tangerine. The caked dirt was no match for this energy, now that it sniffed its liberation. What had first been a rain of small cobs of filth rapidly escalated, as Rosa's labors inspired the light to shake itself lose. Cracks spread up and out from the place where Rosa had begun, the caked dirt losing its grip as word of revolution spread.

Frannie watched astonished as the process unfolded before her and, not for the first time on this journey, wished Sherwood could have been at her side to share the sight. Particularly this: His Rosa, the woman he'd idolized, turning her hands to such transformative labor. Frannie felt blessed to witness it.

And as more and more of the mystery that Rukenau had concealed came into view, Frannie began to make some fledging sense of its nature. The colors that gleamed and shone in the wall were hints of living things. Nothing whole yet, but intimations: a flicker of stripes on a pulsing flank, the glitter of hungry eyes, a spreading canopy of wings. Nor were these presences going to be readily restrained, that much was already apparent. They were too vital, too eager. The more ambitious of them were spreading into the room, spilling the echoes of their forms into the grateful air, like sparks flying from an uncontainable fire.

"Help me up," Rosa demanded, and Frannie duly went to her aid, though she did so without looking at Rosa, she was so enraptured by the spectacle of burgeoning forms.

"We have to go and find Rukenau," Rosa said, her thin fingers digging into Frannie's shoulder. She reached up and touched Frannie's face. "Are you looking at the world?" she said.

"Is that what this is?"

"This is the Domus Mundi," Rosa reminded her. "And whatever you're seeing now, there's far finer to see. Now come on, I need your strength a little while longer."

She didn't need to be carried any more; she had clearly gained some measure of vigor from being in the house. But her sight was not restored, and she needed Frannie to lead her, which Frannie was happy to do. By the time they had crossed the first chamber into the room beside it, the message of rebellion had overtaken them. A dry rain of dirt particles started to fall upon them as cracks opened in the vaulted ceiling, and the room was already brighter than the space they'd left, the blaze flickering from fissures on every side. There were sounds rising to accompany the spectacle, though, like the first hints of sight, they were at present undifferentiated, a murmur from which now and then a more specific noise would come. An elephant trumpeting, perhaps, a whale making song, a monkey howling in a churning tree—

But Rosa heard something closer to her heart.

"That was Steep," she said.

There was indeed a human voice, afloat in the brimming sea of

422   CLIVE BARKER

sounds. Rosa picked up her pace, the same word coming with every breath:

"Jacob. Jacob. Jacob. Jacob."

Will couldn't see what was happening between Rukenau and Steep—they were too far from him, their struggle obscured by the ropes—but he saw the consequences. The structure, for all its complexity, had not been built to withstand the struggle now going on inside it. Ropes were being pulled from their roots in the wall, bringing clods of dead dirt with them. Light and motion were coming in their stead, illuminating the spreading collapse. Places where the burden of furniture was the heaviest were the first to go. A table came crashing down, claiming two of the more substantial platforms as it fell, delivering them all in splinters to the shaking ground. There were fissures here too, and shafts of roiling brightness coming to swell the sum of light. More than light, life. That was what Will saw in the swaths of unfurling color: the throb and shimmer of living things.

As the ropes and platforms continued to fall, he had sight of Jacob and Rukenau. They looked, he thought, like something Thomas Simeon might have painted: two spirits engaged in a life-and-death struggle on the shaking heights. Rukenau was by no means accepting his fate. He was using his ease among his perches to keep his body out of Steep's way. But Jacob wasn't going to be denied his quarry. Without warning he dropped to his knees and caught hold of the precarious lace of rope on which they swayed and shook it so hard that Rukenau pitched forward. Will saw Jacob's knife hand rise up to meet the other man's chest and, though he couldn't see the weapon, Will knew by the shriek escaping Rukenau's lips that the blade had found its home. Rukenau started to topple, but as he did so caught hold of his executioner, so that they both fell, locked together, dividing the mesh with their combined weight as they hurtled to the ground.

The house shook. Rosa stopped in her tracks and uttered a little sob. "Oh now," she breathed. "What have you done?"

"What's happened?" Frannie said.

She got no answer, but she no longer needed Rosa to locate Steep, because she heard him for herself, his voice unmistakable.

"Done now, are you?" he was saying. "Are you done?"

Rosa was stumbling ahead of Frannie, who followed her through a narrow door into a trash-filled passage. Several times Rosa fell as she scrambled toward her destination, but she was up the instant after and out of the passage, with Frannie on her heels, into Rukenau's chaotic chamber.

Will caught a motion out of the corner of his eye and was vaguely aware that somebody had entered, but he could not unglue his gaze from the sight on the ground long enough to see who it was.

Jacob had got to his feet and was tearing at the ropes that had caught about him as he fell. Rukenau had no hope of rising ever again, however. Though he was still alive, his body twitching, Jacob's knife was buried in the man's body and blood was coming from the wound in copious amounts. His filthy shirt and waistcoat were already completely soaked, and the blood was now pooling around him.

Will was still outside Jacob's field of vision, but he knew he would not remain so for very long. Once the Nilotic looked his way, it would come and finish its threatened work. Though it was hard to look away, he turned his back and slipped off, choosing as his means of exit the door though which Ted had disappeared in pursuit of his wife. Only when he reached it did he think to look back across the chamber at those who'd lately entered, and there saw both Frannie and Rosa. Neither had eyes for him. Both were looking at Rukenau's cavorting body.

Jacob had finally tired of that same sight, however, and looking up, turned his eyes on Will. Very slowly, he shook his head as if to say: Did you think you could escape me? Will didn't wait for the creature to start in pursuit of him. He ran.

The same process of revolution was underway in every room as had begun in Rukenau's chamber, the walls stripped of the concealing filth, the life beneath spilling into view. But there was something more startling still, Will realized. The walls, for all that they contained, were not solid. He could see to the left and right of him into rooms he'd never visited, rooms where the same message of liberation had come, and the house making its glories known. No wonder Jacob had trembled with remembrance in Eropkin's ice palace; this was what he'd dimly recalled in that frigid bedroom. A site of exquisite lucidity, of which the palace, for all its glory, was but a remote echo.

Ahead of him now, the place to which Rukenau had superstitiously referred when speaking of how Ted's wife had been lost. Seeing it in front of him, the source, the heart, he felt as he had on Spruce Street to the hundredth power. News of the world coming to him in all its abundance, like a blaze of light between dividing clouds, climbing in fierceness as the vapors melted away. Soon, he would be blinded, surely. But so be it. He would look until his eyes gave out; listen till his ears could take no more.

From somewhere behind him he heard the Nilotic calling for him. "Why are you running?" Jacob said to him. "There's nowhere you can hide."

It was true. Any chance of escaping detection was denied him now. But that was an insignificant price to pay for the bliss of moving though this marvelous place. He glanced behind him to find that Steep was no more than twenty yards away. It seemed to Will he could see the Nilotic's form moving in the man, as though Steep's addled flesh had caught the fever of revolution and was resigning its concealments.

His own body was doing the same thing, he thought; he could feel the fox in him, *vulpes vulpes*, rising as the hunt quickened—a last, primal transformation as he fled into the fire. And why not? The world made miracles like this every moment of every day: egg into chick, seed into flower, maggot into fly. Now man into fox? Was that possible?

Oh yes, said the House of the World. *Yes, and yes, and always yes*—

Rosa had halted a little way from Rukenau and waited until his thrashing subsided. Now it had. Now he lay still, except for his gasping chest, and his eyes, which went to the woman and fixed on her as well as they were able.

"Stay . . . away . . . from . . . me," he said.

Rosa took his demand as her cue to approach, halting a yard from him. It seemed he was afraid that she intended him harm, because he used what little strength he had to haul his hand up to shield his face. She didn't try to touch him however. "Such a very long time," she said, "since I was here. But it doesn't seem more than a year or two. Is that because we're at the end of things? I think maybe it is. We're at the end, and nothing that went before seems of any consequence."

Her words seemed to find an echo in Rukenau, because as she spoke, tears came. "What did I do to you?" he said. "Oh Lord." He closed his eyes, and the tears ran.

"I don't know what you did," Rosa said. "I only want an end to it."

"Then go to him," Rukenau said. "Go to Jacob and heal yourself."

"What are you saying?"

Rukenau opened his eyes again. "That you're two halves of the same soul," he said. She shook her head, not comprehending. "You trusted me, you see; you said I was better company than you'd had in two hundred years." He looked away from her and stared at the bright air above his head. "And once I had your trust I put you to sleep, and I spoke my liturgies and undid the sweet syzygy of your being. Oh I was proud of myself, playing God that way. *Male and female madeth He.*"

Rosa let out a low moan. "Jacob's a part of me?" she said.

"And you of him," Rukenau murmured. "Go to him, and heal both of your spirits before he does more harm than even he can calculate."

There was a man squatting in the passage ahead of Will, his hands clamped over his eyes so as to shut out the vision rising around him. It was Ted, of course.

"What the hell are you doing down there?" Will and the fox said to him.

He didn't dare unstop his eyes, at least until Will demanded he do so. "There's nothing to be afraid of, Ted," he said.

"Are you joking?" the man replied, uncovering his eyes long enough to confirm that he was talking to Will. "The place is coming down on our heads, for God's sake."

"Then you'd better find Diane pretty damn quick," Will said. "And you're not going to do it sitting on your ass. Get up and get moving, for God's sake." Shamed into action, Ted got to his feet, but kept his eyes half closed. Even so, he couldn't help but flinch at the sights that were surging from the walls.

"What *is* all this?" he sobbed.

"No talking!" Will said, knowing Steep was closing on them, stride for stride. "Just get moving."

Even if they'd had the time to debate the visions brimming about them, Will doubted there was any explanation for them that fell within their frame of knowledge. The Nilotic had built a house of numinosities, that was all Will knew. The means by which it had done so was beyond his grasp, nor finally, was it important to know. It was the work of a sublime being, that was all that mattered—a holy mason whose labor had created a temple such as no priest had ever consecrated. If Will's eyes ever distinguished the patterns moving around him, he knew what he would see: the glory of creation. The tiger and the dung beetle, the gnat's wing and the waterfall. It was perhaps, not the house that smeared their particularities, but his brain, which would have perished from the sheer excess of all that these swelling clouds of life contained, had he seen them precisely.

"This . . . is such . . . a glorious . . . *madness*," he gasped as he moved on with Ted, toward the source. And from that insanity a figure now emerged, a woman with a branch in one hand, heavy with figs, and in the other, clutched tightly, a fat salmon thrashing and glistening as though it had moments before been snatched from a river.

"Diane?" Ted said.

It was she. And seeing her ragged, tear-stained husband the woman dropped her bounty and went to him, opening her arms. "Ted?" she said, as though she didn't quite believe what she was seeing. "Is it you?"

She might in other circumstances have been quite a plain woman. But the light loved her. It clung to her weight as her sodden clothes clung; it ran over her full breasts; it played around her groin and lips and eyes. No wonder she'd been seduced by the place, Will thought. It had made her radiant, glorifying her substance without cavil or complaint. She was impermanent, of course, no less than the fish or the figs. But in the space between birth and dissolution, this life called Diane, she was made marvelous.

Ted was a little afraid to put his arms around her. He held back, puzzling out what he was seeing.

"Are you my wife?" he said.

"Yes, I'm your wife," she said, plainly amused.

"Will you come with me, out of here?" he asked her.

She glanced back the way she'd come. "Are you leaving?" she said.

"We all are," Ted replied.

She nodded. "I suppose . . . yes, I'll come with you," she said, "if you want me to."

"Oh." He caught hold of her hand. "Oh God, Diane." Now he embraced her. "Thank you. Thank you—"

We'd better move, the fox murmured in Will's head, *Steep's not far behind.*

"I have to go," he said to Ted, slapping him on the back as he moved on past the couple.

"Don't go any further," Diane said to him. "You'll get lost."

"I don't mind," Will told her.

"But it'll be too much," she replied. "I swear, it'll be too much."

"Thanks for the warning," he said to her and, giving Ted a grin as he passed, walked on toward the heart of the house.

XV

i

Frannie had not gone with Rosa in pursuit of Steep. She'd stayed in Rukenau's chamber, watching in astonishment as the walls shed their covering. It was not the safest place to be by any means, not with the dirt and rope and furniture overhead in steady collapse. But she had no intention of taking shelter, not when she had risked so much to be here. She would watch the process to the end, however heavy the downpour became.

Her presence did not go unnoticed. A minute or so after Rosa's departure, Rukenau turned his head in Frannie's direction and, focusing what was left of his sight upon her, asked her if Rosa had found Jacob yet. Not yet, she told him. She could see the object of his inquiries making her way through the unfurling walls in pursuit of Jacob; she could see Jacob too, moving in the brightness. The figure that truly caught her attention, however, was Will, who was furthest from her, but who by some trick of place or sight, was in sharper focus than either Rosa or Jacob, his form perfectly delineated as he walked the brightening air.

I'm losing him, Frannie thought. He's going away from me and I'll never see him again.

The man on the ground in front of her said, "Won't you come a little closer? What's your name?"

"Frannie."

"Frannie. Well then, Frannie, could you raise me a little? I want to see my Nilotic."

How could she refuse him? He was beyond doing her any harm. She knelt down beside him and put her arm under his body. He was heavy, and wet with blood, but she felt strong and she'd never been squeamish, so it wasn't a difficult task to lift him up as he'd requested, until he had a view through the veils of the house.

"Do you see them?" she asked him.

He managed a blood-red smile.

"I see them," he said. "And that third? Is it Ted or Will?"

"That's Will," she said.

"Somebody should warn him. He doesn't know what he's risking, going so deep."

In the cool furnace of the world, Will heard Steep call his name. Once upon a time, he would have turned eagerly at the sound of that voice, hungry for the face that owned it. But there were finer sights to see all around him; the creatures whose designs had been abstractions until now were finally parading their forms before him. A flock of parrotfish broke against his face, a wave of flamingoes ruddied the sky; he waded ankle-deep through a lush field of otters and rattlesnakes.

"Will," Steep said again.

Still he didn't turn. If the creature strikes me down from behind, he thought, so be it; I'll die with my head full of life. A boulder split before him, and spilled a bounty of chicks and apes; a tree grew around him, as though he were its rising sap and, spreading overhead, blossomed with striped cats and carrion crows.

And as he saw them, he felt Steep's hand on his shoulder, felt Steep's breath at his neck. One last time, the man said his name. He waited for the coup de grâce, while the tree grew still taller and shedding its fine fruit, blossomed a second time.

The fatal blow didn't come. Instead, Steep's hand slid from his shoulder, and Will heard the fox say: *Oh, I think maybe you should take a look at this.*

He wouldn't have attended to any other voice but that. Ungluing his eyes from the spectacle a moment, he glanced back toward Steep. The man was no longer looking at Will. He had himself turned round and was staring at the figure who had pursued him through the house to this spot. It was Rosa, but only just. To Will's eyes she seemed to have become a wonderful patchwork. The woman she'd once been was still visible, of course—her exquisite features, the ripeness of her body—but the brightness that had seeped from her in Donnelly's house was in greater evidence than ever, flowing copiously from her wound, and as it came it inspired the form inside her form to show itself more plainly.

Will heard Steep say: *Stay away from me,* but there was no weight in his words, nor belief that his order would be obeyed. She kept coming toward him, slowly, lovingly; her arms lifted from her sides a little way, palms out, as though to show him the innocence of her intent. And perhaps it was indeed innocence. Or perhaps this was her last, and slyest, deceit—to play the pliant bride, folded in veils of light, delivering herself to his mercy. If so, it worked. Instead of defending himself against her, he let the brightness wash around him, and he was engulfed.

Will thought he saw a shudder pass through Steep's form, as though Jacob was suddenly aware that he was caught and was trying to shake himself free. But it was too late. The man he'd been was lost already, his exhausted form flayed away by light, uncovering the mirror image of the face that was even now supplanting the last of Rosa. Will saw her human features make a smile as they were dissolved, then the Nilotic was there in all its burnished perfection, moving through the circling confluence of light to marry its form with the form in Steep. This was the final conundrum, solved. Jacob and Rosa weren't separate creatures; they were each a part of the Nilotic, divided and grown forgetful of who they were. Living in the world with stolen names, learning the cruel assumptions of their gender from what they saw about them, unable to live apart, though it was a torment to be so close to the other, yet never close enough.

Oh, now look what you've done . . . Will heard the fox say in his head.

"What's that?"

You've set me free.

"Don't go yet."

Oh Lord, Will. I want to be gone.

"Just a little while. Stay with me. Please."

He heard the fox sigh. *Well,* the beast said, *maybe just a little while . . .*

* * *

Rukenau shuddered in Frannie's embrace. "Are they whole?" he said. "I can't see them clearly."

Frannie was dumb with disbelief. Hearing Rukenau speak of dividing the Nilotic was one thing, seeing that process reversed another entirely.

"Did you hear me?" Rukenau said. "Are they whole?"

"Yes . . . " she murmured.

Rukenau sank back against her arm. "Oh God in Heaven, the crimes I committed against that creature," he said. "Will you forgive me?"

"Me?" Frannie said. "You don't need forgiveness from me."

"I'll take it wherever I can find it," Rukenau replied. "Please."

He was clearly in extremis, his voice so frail Frannie had difficulty catching his words, his clownish face slackening. It was, she knew, the last service he would require of her. And if it gave him comfort, why not? She leaned a little closer to him, so that she could be certain he heard her.

"I forgive you," she said.

He made a tiny nod and for a moment his eyes focused upon her. Then the sight went out of them, and his life stopped.

The braids of light in which the Nilotic had been wed to itself were dispersing now, and as they did so the creature turned and looked at Will. Simeon had not done too badly with the portrait he'd painted, Will thought. He'd caught the grace of the creature well enough. What he'd failed to capture was the alien cadence of its proportions; its subtle otherness, which made Will a little fearful it would do him harm.

But when it spoke, his fears fled.

"*We have come such a distance together,*" it said, its voice mellifluous. "*What will you do now?*""

"I want to go a little further," Will replied, glancing back over his shoulder.

"*I'm sure you do,*" the Nilotic said. "*But believe me when I tell you it wouldn't be wise. Every step we take we go deeper into the living heart of the world. It will take you from yourself, and at last, you will be lost.*"

"I don't care."

"*But those who love you will care. They'll mourn you, more than you know. I would not wish to be responsible for another moment's suffering.*"

"I just want to see a little more," Will said.

"*How much is a little?*"

"I'll let you be the judge of that," Will said. "I'll walk with you a while, and we'll turn back when you tell me it's time."

"*I won't be coming back,*" the Nilotic said. "*I intend to unmake the house and must unmake it from its heart.*"

"Then where will you go?"

"*Away. From men and women.*"

"Is there anywhere like that left?"

"*You'd be surprised,*" the Nilotic said, and so saying, moved past Will and proceeded on into the mystery.

It had not explicitly forbidden Will to follow it, which was all the invitation he needed. He went in cautious pursuit of it, like a spawning fish climbing waters that would have dashed him to death without the Nilotic ahead of him to breast the flow. Even so, he quickly understood the truth in its warnings. The deeper they ventured the more it seemed he was treading not among the echoes of the world, but in the world itself, his soul a thread of bliss passing into its mysteries.

He lay with a pack of panting dogs on a hill overlooking plains where antelope grazed. He marched with ants, and labored in the rigors of the nest, filing eggs. He danced the mating dance of the bower bird, and slept on a warm rock with his lizard kin. He was a cloud. He was the shadow of a cloud. He was the moon that cast the shadow of a cloud. He was a blind fish; he was a shoal; he was a whale, he was the sea. He was the lord of all he surveyed. He was a worm in the dung of a kite. He did not grieve, knowing his life was a day long, or an hour. He did not wonder who made him. He did not wish to be other. He did not pray. He did not hope. He only was, and was, and was, and that was the joy of it.

Somewhere along the way, perhaps among the clouds, perhaps among the fish, he lost sight of his guide. The creature that had been, in its human incarnations, both his maker and his tormentor, slipped away and was gone out of his life forever. He was vaguely aware of its departure and knew that its going to be a signal that he should stop and turn round. It had trusted him with his destiny; it was his responsibility not to abuse the gift. Not for his sake, but for those who would mourn him if he was lost to them.

He shaped all these thoughts quite clearly. But he was too besotted to act upon them. How could he turn his back on these glories, with so much more to see?

On he went then, where only souls who had learned the home-ward paths by heart dared to go.

ii

I'm a witness, Frannie thought. That's what I'm meant to do right now: Watch these events as they unravel and keep them clear in my head, so that I can be the one who tells everything, when all these wonderful sights have passed away.

And pass they would. That was becoming more evident by the moment. The first sign she had that the house was beginning to unknit was a spatter of cold rain on her head. She looked up. The ceiling of Rukenau's chamber was now dissolving, the living forms that had spilled from it disappearing. They didn't melt, they were just lost to her sight as a more familiar scene reestablished itself. Indeed she was tempted to believe that they remained around her, but simply became unavailable to her senses. She was not altogether unhappy at this. Though the sight of gray clouds shedding gray rain was less inspiring than the glories passing from her view, they had the virtue of familiarity. She was not obliged to gorge on them, afraid she'd miss some choice glory.

The walls were also receding from her, just as the ceiling had, layer upon layer of flickering lucidity subsumed. That roiling wall, alive with silver life, was tamed into a simple sea; that other, green and glistening, the crown of Kenavara. Here were the birds now—the kittiwakes, the cormorants, the hoodie-crow—while underfoot her eyes caught a glimpse of the lives that lay below her in the earth— the seeds, the worms—before that vision was also dimmed, and she was staring at the excremental mud that the rain was making from the sheddings of the house.

Remember how this is, she told herself, while she kneeled in the mud. This presence of all things, seen and unseen, around and about; remember. There will be days in your life when you'll need to have this feeling again, to know that all that's gone from the world hasn't really gone at all; it's just not in sight.

There were more people than she'd expected sharing the clifftop with her; all, she assumed, released from the maze of the Domus Mundi. There was an old man standing up in the downpour some twenty yards from her shouting hallelujahs at the sky; there was a woman a few years her senior who was already wandering back toward the body of the island, as if in fear that she would be claimed again if she didn't escape the cliff. There was a young couple, shamelessly hugging and kissing with a passion the icy rain could not chasten.

And there was Will. He hadn't gone wherever the creature who'd made the house had gone. He was here still, standing gazing out toward the sea, glassy-eyed. She got to her feet to go to him, glancing down at Rukenau as she did so. She was astonished at what she saw. His flesh, now that it was no longer rocked in the cradle of the house, had succumbed to the claim of his true age. His skin had split in a dozen places and was being driven off his withered muscle by the pelting rain. His blood had already been sluiced from the corpse, so that it looked like something a child might have made from papier-mâché and paint, and now, having grown bored with the game, abandoned in the mud. Even as she watched, its chest caved in, its contents gone to mush and jelly. She took her eyes off it, knowing when she looked again it would have been received into the sodden earth. There were worse ways to disappear, she thought, and went to Will.

He was not staring at the sea, as she'd initially thought. Though his eyes were wide open, and when she said his name he made a guttural sound that she took to be a response, his thoughts were not with her, but about some business that was claiming most of his attention.

"I think we should go," she said to him.

This time he didn't even murmur a response, but when she took his arm, as now she did, he went with her, neither seeing nor blind, back over through the mud and rain toward the *machair*.

By the time they reached the car, the rainstorm had passed over the island and was headed for America. Night was on its way; there were lights in the cluster of houses at Barrapol, and stars coming out between the ragged clouds. She got Will into the passenger seat without any problem (it was almost as though he were in a trance, capable of responding to simple instructions, but in every other way absent); then she backed the car up until she reached the road and drove through the rapidly descending twilight to Scarinish. There'd be a ferry tomorrow; they'd be back on the mainland by evening, and—if she drove through the night—home by the following morning. That was as far as she was presently willing to project her thoughts: as far as the kitchen and the teapot and the comfort of her bed. Only when she was safely back in her own house would she think about what she'd seen and felt and suffered since the man at her side had come back into her life.

XVI

The following day went pretty much as she'd anticipated. They passed an uncomfortable night in the car, parked just outside Scarinish, and at noon or thereabouts boarded the ferry for the return journey to Oban. Her only problem on the drive south was her own exhaustion, which she kept at bay with copious amounts of coffee. But it still crept up on her, so that by the time she finally got home, at four in the morning, she was barely able to keep her thoughts in order. For his part, Will remained in the same trancelike condition that had possessed him since the destruction of the house. It was plain to her he knew she was there beside him, because he could answer questions as long as they were simple (do you want a sandwich, do you want a cup of coffee?), but he wasn't seeing the same world that she was seeing. He had to fumble to find the coffee cup and, even when he did, deposited half the contents over him as he drank from it. The food she plied him with was eaten mechanically, as though his body was going through the motion without the assistance of his conscious mind.

She knew where his thoughts resided. He was still enraptured by the house, or by his memories of it. She did her best not to resent him for his detachment, but it was hard when the problems of the here and now were so demanding. She felt abandoned; there was no other word for it. He was inviolate in his trance, while she was exhausted, confused, and frightened. There would be questions to answer when people realized she was back from her travels, difficult questions. She wanted Will there to help her formulate some answers to them. But nothing she said to him roused him from his fugue. He stared on into middle distance and dreamed his dreams of the Domus Mundi.

There was a worse betrayal to come. When she woke the following morning, having passed four grateful hours in her own bed, she discovered he'd vacated the couch where she'd put him to rest, and wandered out of the house, leaving the front door wide open. She was infuriated. Yes, he'd witnessed a great deal in the House, but so had she, and she hadn't gone wandering off in the middle of the night, damn it.

She called the police after breakfast and made her presence known. They were at the house three quarters of an hour later, plying her with questions about all that had happened in the Donnelly house. Plainly they viewed her departure from the scene of Sherwood's demise as strange, perhaps even evidence of mental imbalance, but not an indication of guilt. They already had their suspects: The two itinerants who had been seen in the vicinity of the Donnelly house for two or three days prior to the murder. She was happy to name them and to offer detailed descriptions; and yes, she was certain they were the same pair who had tormented Will, her brother, and herself all those years ago. What, they wanted to know, was the connection between Sherwood and these two, that he'd been there in the Donnelly house in the first place? She told them she didn't know. She had followed her brother there, she said, intending to bring him home, and had discovered Steep in mid-assault. Then she'd given chase. Yes, it had been a stupid thing to do, of course. But she'd been witless with shock and anger, surely they understood that. All that she had been able to think about was finding and confronting the man who'd murdered her brother.

How far had she tracked him, the detectives wanted to know. Here she told her direct lie. Only as far as the Lake District, she'd said; then she'd lost them.

Finally, the oldest of the detectives, a man by the name of Faraday, came to the question she'd been waiting to hear.

"How the hell does Will Rabjohns fit into the picture?"

"He came along with me," she said simply.

"And why did he do that?" the man said, watching her intently. "For old times' sake?"

She said she didn't know what he was talking about, to which the detective replied that unlike his two companions, he was very familiar with what had happened here all those years ago; he'd been the man who'd tried to get the truth out of Will. He'd failed, he admitted. But a good policeman—and he counted himself a good policeman—never closed a file while there were questions unanswered. And there were more unanswered questions in this file than any other on his shelves. So again, he said, what had been going on

that she and Will had been together in this? She pretended innocence, sensing that Faraday, for all his doggedness, was no closer to
understanding the mystery here than he'd been thirty years before.
Perhaps he had some suspicions, but if they were anywhere close to
the mark they were unlikely to be the kind he could have voiced in
front of his colleagues. The truth lay very far from the usual realm of
investigation, where a man like Faraday probably only ventured in his
most private ruminations. Though he pressed his suit, she returned
only the blandest answers, and he finally gave up on the business,
defeated by his own reluctance to put the pieces in their true order.
Of course he wanted to know where Will was now, to which Frannie
truthfully answered that she didn't know. He'd disappeared from the
house this morning, and could be anywhere.

Stymied in his inquiries, Faraday warned that this interview
would not be the end of the matter. There would be identifications to
be made if and when the culprits were apprehended. She wished him
luck in finding them, and he departed, with his colleagues in tow.

The interview had taken up almost all of the day, but with what
was left of it she set about the melancholy business of planning
Sherwood's funeral. She would go over to the hospice in Skipton
tomorrow and find out from the doctors if they thought she
should tell her mother the sad news. Meanwhile, she had a lot of
organizing to do.

In the early evening, she answered the door to find Helen Morris, of all people, come to offer her condolences. Helen had never
been a particularly close friend, and Frannie harbored the suspicion
that the woman had come calling to garner some gossip, but she was
glad of the company anyway. And it was comforting, in its petty way,
to know that Helen, who was one of the most conservative women in
the village, saw fit to spend a few hours with her. Whatever people
were surmising about events in the Donnelly house, they would not
find Frannie culpable. It made her think that perhaps she owed
Helen and the rest of the folks puzzling over this mystery a helping
hand. That maybe in a month or two, when she was feeling a little
more confident, she'd stand up between the hymns at the Sunday
service and tell the whole sad and wonderful truth. Maybe nobody
would ever speak to her again if she did so; maybe she'd become the
Madwoman of Burnt Yarley. And maybe that would be a price worth
paying.

XVII

Out on the hills, Will just kept moving, his body trekking the cold slopes while his spirit wandered in far stranger places. He plunged deep into ocean trenches and swam with forms that had not yet been found or named. He was carried as a motey insect over peaks so remote the tribes in the valley below believed divinities lived upon them. But he knew better now. The creators of the world had not retreated to the heights. They were everywhere. They were stones, they were trees, they were shafts of light and burgeoning seeds. They were broken things, they were dying things, and they were all that sprang up from things dying and broken. And where they were, he was too. Fox and God and the creature between.

He wasn't hungry, nor was he sleepy, though in his passage he encountered beasts that were both. He seemed sometimes to travel in the dreams of sleeping animals: in dreams of the hunt, in dreams of coupling. He seemed sometimes to be a dream himself: a dream of the human, being experienced by an animal. Perhaps dogs barked in their sleep, sensing his proximity; perhaps the chick grew restless in the egg when he brought it news of the light. And perhaps he was nothing but a figment in his own haunted thoughts, inventing this journey, so as not to go back, not ever go back, to the city of Rab-johns and the house of Will.

Every now and then, he'd cross the path of the fox, and he'd move on before the animal could make its formal farewells and depart. But somewhere along the way—who knew how many days has passed?—he chanced upon the creature in the back yard of a house he vaguely knew. It had its head in the garbage, and was rifling through the muck with no little enthusiasm. Will had better places to linger than here and was about to depart for those places, but the fox turned its besmirched face his way and said, "Do you remember this yard?"

Will didn't answer. He hadn't spoken to anybody in a long time and didn't particularly want to start talking now. But the fox was ready with an answer anyhow. "This is Lewis's house," the creature said. "Lewis? The poet?" he prompted. Will remembered. "This is where you saw a raccoon, so rumor tells, doing much as I'm doing now."

Will broke his silence, finally. "I did?" he said.

"You did. But that's not why you're here."

"No . . ." Will said, now sensing the significance of his presence.

"You know why, don't you?"

"Yes. I'm afraid I do."

So saying, he left the yard, and went out into the street. It was early evening, the sky still warm with light toward the west. He walked along Cumberland to Noe; then on to Nineteenth and so to Castro Street. The sidewalks were already crowded, so he assumed it was either Friday or Saturday, a night when people were casting off the restraints of the working week and were out on the town.

He didn't know what form he had traveling here, but he soon found out. He was nobody; he was nothing. Not a single gaze came his way as he climbed Castro, not even to despise him. He walked among the beauties and the watchers of beauties (and who here wasn't one or the other?) unnoticed, past the tourists out to see how homosexual heaven might look, and the hustlers, checking their pants and their reflections, and the high queens, pronouncing on every other sight they saw, and the sad, sick men who were out because they feared they'd not see another party night. He passed through this throng like the ghost he'd perhaps become, his trek bringing him at last to the house at the summit where Patrick lived.

I've come to see him die, he realized. He looked around him for some sign of the fox, but the scurrilous animal, having brought him here, was now hiding its head. He was alone in this business; already slipping up the steps and through the door into the hall. Here he halted for a moment, to gather his wits. This was the first place of human habitation he'd visited in a little while, and it felt like a tomb to him: the silent walls, the roof keeping out the sky. He wanted to turn and leave, to get back out into the open air. But as he started up the stairs to the apartment door, the memories began to come. He'd undressed Patrick climbing these stairs, so eager to have him naked he couldn't wait until the key was in the lock; stumbled over the threshold, hauling his lover's shirt from his pants, fumbling with his belt, telling Patrick how fine he was, how perfect in every particular: chest and nipples and belly and prick. No man in Castro had been more beautiful, nor any wanted him more in return.

He was at the apartment door now, and through it, and moving toward the bedroom. Somebody was crying there, pitifully. He hesitated before entering, afraid of what he would discover on the other side. Then he heard Patrick speak.

"Please stop that," he said, gently, "it's very depressing."

I'm not too late, Will thought, and slipped through the door into the bedroom.

Rafael was standing at the window, obediently stifling his tears. Adrianna was sitting on the bed, watching her patient, who had before him a bowl of vanilla pudding. His condition had deteriorated considerably in the days since Will had departed for England. He'd lost weight and his pallor was sickly, his eyes sunk in bruisy shadow. Plainly he needed to sleep; his eyelids were heavy, his features slack with exhaustion. But Adrianna was gently insisting he first finish his food, which he did, conscientiously scraping the bowl to be sure he'd eaten it all.

"I'm done," he said eventually. His voice was a little slurred, his head nodding, as though he might fall asleep with the spoon still in his hand.

"Here," Adrianna said. "Let me take those from you."

She took the bowl and spoon from him and set them on the bedside table, where there sat a small squad of pill bottles. Several of them had been left with their tops unscrewed, Will saw. All of them were empty.

A sickening suspicion rose in Will. He looked at Adrianna, who, despite her stoical expression, was plainly having difficulty holding back tears of her own. This wasn't just any dinner she'd been telling Patrick to finish up. There'd been more than pudding in the bowl.

"How do you feel?" she asked him.

"Okay," Patrick said. "A little light-headed, but . . . okay. It wasn't the best pudding I ever tasted, but I've had worse." His voice was thin and strained, but he was doing his best to put some music into it.

"This is wrong—" Rafael said.

"Don't start again," Adrianna told him sternly.

"It's what I want," Patrick said firmly. "You don't have to be here if it bothers you."

Rafael looked back at him, his face knotted up with contrary feelings. "How long . . . does it take?" he murmured.

"It's different from person to person," Adrianna said to him. "That's what I heard."

"You've got time to get a brandy," Patrick said, his eyes closing for a time, then opening again as though he was waking from a five-second doze. He looked at Adrianna. "It's going to be strange . . . " he said dreamily.

"What's going to be strange?"

"Not having me," he replied, with a dazed smile. His hand, which had been rhythmically smoothing a wrinkle in the sheet, now slid over the coverlet and caught hold of her hand. "We've talked a lot over the years, haven't we . . . about what happens next?"

"We have," she said.

"And I'm going to find out . . . before you—"

"I'm jealous," she said.

"Bet you are," he replied, his voice steadily failing him.

"I can't bear this," Rafael said, coming to the bottom of the bed. "I can't listen to this."

"It's okay, baby," Patrick said, as though to comfort him. "It's okay. You've done so much for me. More than anyone. You just go have a cigarette. It'll be all right. Really it will." He was interrupted by the sound of the doorbell. "Now who the *fuck* is that?" he said, a spark of the old Patrick momentarily ignited.

"Don't answer it," Rafael said. "It could be cops."

"And it could be Jack," Adrianna said, rising from the bed. The doorbell was being rung again, more urgently. "Whoever it is," she said, "they're not going to go away."

"Why don't you go, babe?" Patrick said to Rafael. "Whoever it is send them away. Tell them I'm dictating my memoirs." He chuckled at his own joke. "Go on," he said, as the bell was rung a third time.

Rafael went to the door, glancing back at the man in the bed as he went. "What if it is the cops?" he said.

"Then they'll probably kick the door in if you don't answer it," Patrick said. "So go. Give 'em hell."

At this, Rafael made his departure, leaving Patrick to sink back down among the pillows. "Poor kid," he said, his eyes fluttering closed. "You'll take care of him, won't you?"

"You know I will," Adrianna reassured him.

"He's not equipped for this," Patrick said.

"Are any of us?" she replied.

He squeezed her hand. "You're doing fine."

"How about you?"

He opened his weighted eyes. "I've been trying to think . . . of something to say when it's time. I wanted to have something . . . pithy, you know? Something quotable."

He was slipping away, Will could see, his words becoming steadily more slurred, his gaze, when he once again opened his eyes, unfocused. But he wasn't so far gone he failed to hear the voices from the front door: "Who is that?" he asked her. "Is it Jack?"

"No . . . it sounds like Lewis."

"I don't want to see him," Patrick said.

Rafael was having trouble keeping Lewis out, however. He was doing his best to insist Lewis leave, but he clearly wasn't being attended to.

"Maybe you should just go lend a hand," Patrick suggested. Adrianna didn't move. "Go on," he insisted, though all the force had left him. "I'm not going anywhere yet. Just don't . . . take *too* long."

Adrianna got to her feet and hurried to the door, clearly caught between the need to stay with Patrick and the need to keep Lewis from disturbing her patient's peace of mind. "I won't be a minute," she promised, and disappeared into the hall, leaving the door a little ajar. Will heard her calling ahead as she went, telling Lewis this wasn't the time to come calling unannounced for God's sake, so would he *please* leave?

Then, very quietly, Patrick said: "Where . . . the hell did you come from?"

Will looked back at him and saw to his astonishment Patrick's hazy, puzzled gaze was fixed on him as best it could be fixed, and there was a small smile on his face. Will went to the end of the bed and looked at him. "You can see me?" he said.

"Yes, of course . . . I can see you," Patrick replied. "Did you come with Lewis?"

"No."

"Come a little closer. You're a bit fuzzy around the edges."

"That's not your eyes, that's me."

Patrick smiled. "My poor, fuzzy Will." He swallowed, with some difficulty. "Thank you for being here," he said. "Nobody said you were coming . . . I would have waited . . . if I'd known. So we could talk."

"I didn't know I was coming myself."

"You don't think I'm being a coward, do you?" Patrick said. "I . . . just couldn't bear the . . . the idea of withering away."

"No, you're not being a coward," Will replied.

"Good," Patrick said. "That's what I thought." He drew a long, soft breath. "It's been such a busy day," he said, "and I'm tired . . . " His lids were closing, slowly. "Will you stay with me a while?"

"All the time you want," Will said.

"Then . . . always," Patrick said, and died.

It was that simple. One moment Patrick was there, in all his sweetness. The next he was gone, and there was only the husk of him, its miracle departed.

Barely able to breathe with grief, Will went to Patrick's side and stroked his face. "I loved you, my man," he said. "More than anyone in my life." Then, in a whisper, "Even more than I loved Jacob . . . "

The exchange out in the hall had come to an end now, and Will could hear Adrianna coming back toward the bedroom, talking to Patrick as she approached. All was well, she told him. Lewis had gone off home to write a sonnet. Then she opened the door, and for a moment, as she looked into the room, it seemed she saw Will standing beside the bed; she even began to say his name. But her powers of reason persuaded her senses they were wrong—Will couldn't be here, could he?—and she left the word unfinished. Her gaze went instead to Patrick, and she let out a soft sigh that was as much relief as sorrow. Then she closed her eyes, silently instructing herself to be calm, Will guessed, to be, as she had always been, the rock in times of emotional turmoil.

Rafael was in the hallway just outside the bedroom door, calling her name.

"You'd better come in and see him," she said. There was no reply from Rafael. "It's all right," she said. "It's over. It's all over." Then she went to the bed, and sat down beside Patrick and stroked his face.

For the first time since departing into the Domus Mundi, Will longed to be back in his own body, wished he was there beside Adrianna, offering what comfort he could. Lingering unseen this way was uncomfortable; he felt like a voyeur. Maybe it would be better just to go, he thought; leave the living to their grief, and the dead to their ease. He belonged in neither tribe, it seemed, and that unfixedness, which had been a pleasure to him as he went through the world, was now no pleasure at all. It only made him lonely.

Out into the hallway he went, past Rafael, who was standing a yard from the bedroom door, as yet unable to enter, through the apartment to the door, down the stairs, and out into the street. Adrianna would serve Patrick well, he knew. She'd always been tender and pragmatic in equal measure. She'd rock Rafael, if he wanted to be rocked; she'd make sure the body was presentable for the medics when they arrived; she'd scrupulously remove all the evidence of the suicide, and if anybody questioned what had happened tell such barefaced lies nobody would dare challenge her.

But for Will, there were no such distractions. There was only the terrible emptiness of a street that had always been the way to Patrick's house, indeed would always be the way to Patrick's house, but that now no longer led anywhere important.

What now? he wondered. He wanted to be away from this city, back into the painless river from which he'd been hauled, that torrent where loss could not touch him, and he could swim inviolate. But how did he get there? Perhaps he should go back to Lewis's house, he thought; perhaps the fox, who had plotted to bring him on this sad trek, was still sorting through the garbage and could be persuaded to reverse the process, unmake his memories and return him to the flow of things.

Yes, that's what he'd do; go back to Cumberland.

The streets were busier than ever, and at the intersection of Castro and Nineteenth, where the foot traffic was particularly heavy, Will caught sight of a face he recognized. It was Drew, moving through the crowd on his own, doing his best to present a contented face to the world, but not doing a very good job of it. He came to the corner and could not seem to make up his mind which way he wanted to go. People pushed on past him, on their way to this bar or that, a few glanced his way, but, getting no reciprocal smile from him, looked elsewhere. He didn't seem to care much. He simply stood in the flow, while party-goers moved on about the business of the evening.

Will started in his direction, though it was not his intended route, moving easily through the crowd. When he was perhaps twenty yards from the corner, Drew apparently decided he wasn't ready for a night of revelry, because he turned and headed back the way he'd come. Will followed him, not certain why he was doing so (he could offer neither solace nor apologies in his present state), but unwilling simply to let Drew go. The crowd thickened in front of him and, though in his present state he was able to pass through them without resistance, he had not yet got the confidence of his condition. He proceeded with more caution than was strictly necessary and almost lost sight of Drew. He pressed his spirit forward, however; on through the throng of men and women (and a few who were in transit), calling after Drew, though he knew had no hope of being heard. *Wait*, he yelled; *Drew, please wait!*

And as he ran, and the figures turned to a blur around him, he remembered another such chase, pursuing a fox through the flickering wood, while the light of wakefulness waited for him at the finishing line. This time he didn't attempt to slow himself as he had that first time, didn't try to look over his shoulder at the street and the crowd, fearful he would not see it again. Drew had emerged from the knot of bodies at the intersection and was now no more than ten yards ahead of Will, staring at the sidewalk as he trudged back home.

As the distance between them closed, however, Drew seemed to hear something and, raising his head, glanced back toward Will, the third and last soul to whom he was momentarily visible tonight. Will saw him scan the crowd, his expression sweetly expectant. Then his face grew brighter, and brighter still, and Castro, and the crowd, and the night that contained them both, went away into the west, and he woke.

XVIII

He was in the wood, his head laid in the very spot where the birds had fallen. Though it was still night in California, here in England day had come; a crisp, late-autumn day. He unknitted his aching joints and sat up, the turmoil he'd felt leaving Patrick's side soothed somewhat by the quiet ease of his waking state. There was quite a litter around him. Some half-eaten fruit, a couple of discarded slices of bread, much of it on its way to rot. If these were, as he guessed, the remains of meals he'd had up here, then he'd been resident a goodly span. He put his hand to his chin, and found what was probably a week's growth of beard. Then he cleared the gum of sleep from his eyes and got to his feet. His left leg was numb, and it took a little while to shake it back into life. While he did so, he looked up through the bare branches at the sky.

There were birds up there already, circling over the fells. He knew how fine it felt to have wings. He'd been in the heads of eagles, lately, and in hummingbirds as they siphoned the blossom. The time for such bliss was past, however. He had taken the journey—or rather his spirit had—and now he was returned into himself to be in the world as a man. There was sorrow here, of course. Patrick was gone; so was Sherwood. But there was also the work the fox had called him to; sacred work.

He put his full weight on his leg to test its reliability and, finding it strong enough to bear him up, hobbled away from his littered nest under the tree and out to the edge of the wood. There had been a light frost the night before, and though the sun was showing itself between the clouds, it had too little warmth to melt the glaze; it glistened on the slopes and fields, roads and roofs. The scene before him, both above and below, looked like a picture made by a miniaturist of such genius that every part of it may be scrutinized, down to the smallest spiral of a fern or the flimsiest nuance of a cloud, and would be found to be perfectly delineated, just waiting for the eye and soul to see it.

How long did he linger at the edge of the wood, drinking all this down? Long enough to watch a dozen little ceremonies below: cows brought to a trough; washing hung on a line; the postman on his early rounds. And then, after a time, the four black cars winding in slow procession from Samson Street toward St Luke's.

"Sherwood . . . " Will murmured, and limping still, started the slope, leaving a track of sharper green in the frosted grass. The church bell had begun to toll, and its echo came off the fells, filling the valley with its news: A man is dead. Take notice that a good soul has gone on his way; and we're the poorer for it.

He was only halfway down the hillside by the time the funeral convoy reached the gates of the church, which was on the far side of the valley. It would take him another half hour at least, given his limp and his fatigue, to reach the place, and even if it did he suspected he would not be welcome there in his present condition. Perhaps Frannie would be happy to see him, though he couldn't be certain. For the rest of the mourners, however, his filthy figure stumbling to the graveside would only be a distraction from the business of the hour, which was to pay their respects to the dead. Later, when the coffin was in the ground, he'd find a quiet time to visit the churchyard and say good-bye. For now, he would pay better service to Sherwood's memory by keeping his distance.

The coffin had been lifted from the back of the hearse and was now being carried into the church, the mourners filing in behind. The first figure to come after it was, he assumed, Frannie, though he could not make out her face at this distance. He watched while the congregation entered the church, and disappeared, leaving the drivers to lounge against the church wall and chat among themselves.

Only now did he continue on down the slope. He would go back to Hugo's house, he decided: There he could bathe, shave, and change his clothes, so that by the time Adele came back from the funeral (where she'd surely be) he'd be looking more presentable.

But as he got to the bottom of the hill, he was waylaid by the sight of the village streets, which were as far as he could see completely deserted. He could afford to put off going back to the house for a few minutes, he thought, and took himself over the bridge.

The bell had long since ceased tolling; the valley was hushed from end to end. But as he wandered down the street, enraptured by the stillness of the scene, he heard the sound of something behind him. He looked back. There on the bridge stood a fox, ears pricked, tail flicking, watching him. There was nothing about its appearance that made him think that this was Lord Fox, or even one of his innumerable descendants, except for the fact of its presence here, defying him to question it. He'd seen better kempt creatures, to be sure, but then the fox could have made the same observation in reply. They'd both had wild lives of late, both lost some of their early glory; grown ragged, grown a little crazed. But they still had their wiles, they had their appetites. They were alive, and ready for another day.

"Where are you off to?" he asked the fox.

The sound of his voice breaking the quiet of the street was enough to startle the animal, and on the instant it turned and briskly departed back over the bridge and up the pale slope, gathering speed as it ascended, though it had no reason to run except for pleasure's sake. He watched it until it gained the ridge of the fell. There it trotted for a little way, then disappeared from sight.

The question he'd asked it was here answered. *Where am I off to? Why, I'm away, somewhere I can be close to the sky.*

Will watched the hillside and the track upon it for a little while longer, hearing in his head what Lord Fox had demanded when the animal had first appeared at his bedside. *Wake up*, it had said. *Do it for the dogs, if you must. But wake up.*

Well, he had, finally. The season of visions was at an end, at least for now, and its inciter had departed, leaving Will to take his wisdom back to the tribe. To tell what he'd seen and felt in the heart of the Domus Mundi. To celebrate what he knew, and turn it to its healing purpose.

He looked off toward his father's house, picturing as he did so the empty study, where that last undelivered lecture lay yellowing on the desk; then he let his eyes wander to the church, and to the bleak churchyard where Sherwood's remains would presently be laid; finally returning his gaze to the village streets.

It would be in him always, the spirit of this place. Wherever his pilgrimage took him he would carry these sights, along with the sorrows and the ambitions that had moved in him here. But for all their significance, he would not let them keep him from his ministry another moment. Just as the fox had taken its way off where it could be true to its nature, so would he.

Turning from the deserted village, and from the church and the house, he walked down to the river and, following the track that wound beside it, began his journey back to his only true and certain home, the world.